Janet,
There are...
thanks on hands clapping
to offer you. Many, many
thanks! xxoo

POISON
GIRLS

CHERYL L. REED

DIVERSIONBOOKS

Diversion Books
A Division of Diversion Publishing Corp.
443 Park Avenue South, Suite 1008
New York, New York 10016
www.DiversionBooks.com

For more information, email info@diversionbooks.com

First Diversion Books edition September 2017.
Print ISBN: 978-1-68230-826-4
eBook ISBN: 978-1-68230-825-7

LSIDB/1708

In memory of
Michelle

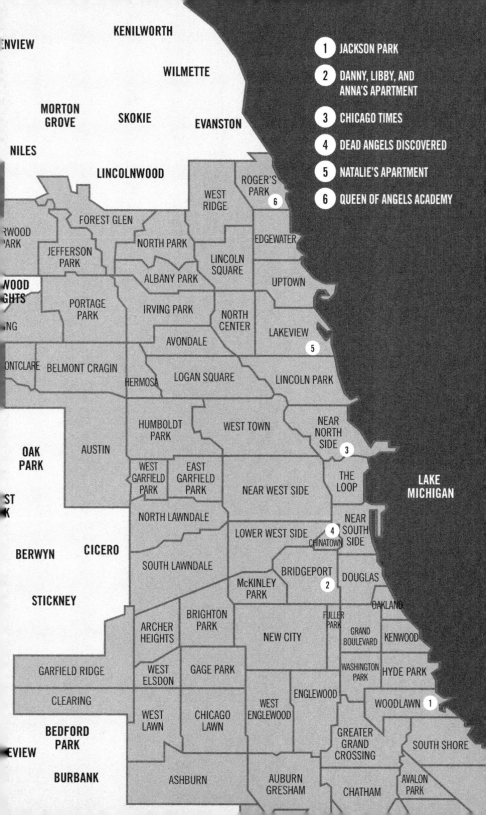

CHAPTER ONE

June 13, 2008

POISON HEROIN TAKES THREE

GIRLS' BODIES FOUND IN CHINATOWN

Chicago Times

Before we knew their names, we dubbed them the Dead Angels. They were high school juniors from the Queen of Angels Academy, and when the cops found them, they had rosaries in their purses and Sweet Jesus in their veins. That's what the street folks called the deadly heroin that sent more than two hundred and fifty people to the morgue that summer. Several were white teenage girls—just like the Dead Angels. The poisoned heroin probably caused many more deaths, but no one noticed until the body of Rosie Green, a distant cousin to the Mayor, turned up in a Bridgeport neighborhood alleyway two blocks from the family's home.

Once the mayoral connection surfaced, my editors at the *Chicago Times* became obsessed with discovering how young white girls were being lured to their deaths. Heroin overdoses typically involved hardcore junkies—prostitutes, homeless veterans, hustlers, and a few suburban boys pumped with enough testosterone to think they could conquer anything. But the white girls who were ending up in the morgue were private school students taking Advanced Placement Calculus and studying for their SATs: they didn't fit the profile, which made their deaths novel—and news.

The coroner couldn't find collapsed veins or track marks on

the white girls, so they likely weren't addicts. There was no short-age of theories, though. Some believed white kids were targeted to make a statement about race in the most racially divided city in the country. A few suggested the teenagers were collateral damage in a war between gangs and cops. The conspiracy theorists thought it was an attempt to sway white voters from backing Chicago's black presidential candidate. My sources offered the most chilling theory: The girls were thrill-seekers, daring one another in esca-lating contests to become "vampirettes"—girls who survived the most potent form of heroin, conquered death, and returned with a mysterious power.

Theirs was a story I was aching to tell. I was the only female crime reporter at the paper. Usually I was sent to hold the hands of victims' families. Choice assignments like the Dead Angels were normally fielded by senior reporters, mostly middle-aged guys who smelled like nervous sweat and whose desks displayed a smattering of photos: smiling kids and devoted stay-at-home wives—remind-ers that they were the *breadwinners*, that their jobs *mattered*. My editors would never say so because it would be outright chauvin-ism, but they thought covering crime was too dangerous for a *girl*. They saw themselves as gentlemanly and paternal by assigning me *safer* crime stories: interviewing mothers of young kids shot by stray gunfire, rape victims, parents of molested children.

Admittedly, crime reporting was a gruesome business, but what drove me was unraveling the Why. What compels a man to shoot a stranger for his iPhone? Why does a man crush a woman's skull with a baseball bat for a few dollars? What motivates a man to spike drugs with poison that kills his buyers? You only get *that* when you talk to The Man. And The Criminal was almost always A Man.

If it were up to my editors, I'd be handing out tissues to crying parents until they laid me off, like dozens of other reporters who'd been let go from my newspaper and our tabloid competitor, the *Chicago Sentinel*. Newspapers were dying. No one wanted to pay for news when they could get it off the Internet for free. Besides, I didn't have any of those smiling kid photos on my desk. I was The Single Girl With A Cat. And everyone knows, those are the ones who end up getting canned.

The poisoned heroin story, though, had the power to change all that. No one could find The Man—or Men—selling the spiked heroin. And his victims were as much a mystery, mostly because they seemed complicit in their own deaths.

So I went looking for girls who survived—if there were any. I thought they just might talk to a female reporter. They just might tell her *who* sold them the drugs and *why* they inhaled, injected, or smoked an unknown drug from an unknown dealer in an unknown part of town.

• • •

They found the Angels' bodies on Friday the thirteenth, a detail the competing tabloid screamed in its headlines. That morning, someone had called Streets & Sans complaining about rats near an abandoned Chinatown building. After the street crew discovered the girls' remains, a sanitation worker got on the city scanner and started babbling about dead bodies and ghosts. I arrived before the TV trucks but after the squad cars. An ambulance, its lights blaring, raced away immediately. We were told everyone inside the house was dead. An hour later, though, we were still standing outside, the sun glaring down at us unforgivingly as we leaned over the sticky yellow police tape. Normally detectives would have offered us ghoulish jokes—"she wants a refund" or "guess she won't be doing early acceptance at Harvard"—but that day they wouldn't even look in our direction, knowing that with three white victims anything they said could make headlines.

I needed a detail, an interview no one else had, anything that would propel the story forward and keep my name off the layoff list. But the Chinatown crime scene seemed all too familiar: a treeless side street with rows of squat, two-story houses squished behind miniature front yards and uneven sidewalks.

It was there, as I stood on the fault lines of the sidewalk, sweat dripping into my eyes, the stench of sewer filling my nose, that I first noticed *her* amid the gawkers. She was taller than the stooped Chinese ladies and the old leather-faced men who had nothing better to do than congregate in the middle of a workday. In the haze of the heat, she seemed like an apparition, her body shimmering as if the sunlight radiated through her, making her speckled copper skin glow and her rust-colored hair flicker as if it were on fire. Not until she turned her luminous green eyes on me did I realize why she seemed so familiar: she had my face from when I was a teenager.

My freckles had paled with age, my red hair wasn't as vibrant, but even at thirty-three, I could have passed as the girl's older sister. She giggled as she posed for a photo with an officer who couldn't help but grin as she nestled into the crook of his shoulder. She seemed so self-assured, yet ethereal, the sunlight enveloping her in a golden halo. Was I witnessing a wrinkle in time, a window in the universe opening to reveal a younger version of myself? I wonder now if my life would have turned out differently if I'd let the feeling pass, that déjà vu sense of connection with someone I'd never met.

With a loud *thwack!* the crime scene sergeant stepped out of the two-flat's front door. As if in a dream, I moved slowly through the pack of reporters who were firing off questions, hearing them but not caring about what they were saying. I felt my feet against the pavement before I realized what I was doing. I had never left a crime scene review—even a cluster fuck like this one—but my instincts told me to catch up with the girl.

"Hey!" I yelled after her, my voice dull and hollow, my stride picking up.

She was with another girl. The two kept walking. I continued shouting as I ran after them. When I was within arm's reach, they turned around. They wore matching pink flip-flops, halter tops, and tight jean cutoffs with fringes, all wrapped up with an attitude, as if they expected every guy to stare as they passed.

"What do you want?" the redhead asked, her hand perched on her slim hip.

Up close, I could see she'd already experienced a harsher side of life than I had at her age. Her front tooth was chipped, a gap exposed when she removed a cigarette from her mouth. (At her age, I was still wearing braces with freakish headgear, an experience that inspired a lifelong habit of noticing other people's teeth.) Her eyelids were coated in a neon shade of jade, accented by clumps of mascara. Though it was past two o'clock in the afternoon, she looked as if she'd just gotten out of bed, her hair slightly matted on one side, her eyes red and squinty.

"You got a minute?" I tapped the plastic press credentials hanging around my neck.

"You a reporter?" the other girl asked. It sounded like an accusation. She was about five inches shorter than the redhead. Her pale skin and jet black hair suggested Goth, but around her neck hung a tiny confirmation cross.

I dug out a business card with my cell phone number scrawled on the back.

The dark-haired girl read my name aloud to see if the redhead recognized it.

"Nat-a-lie De-la-ney?"

The redhead shrugged.

"So what?" said the dark-haired girl, chomping on her gum.

I held up my reporter's notebook. "What're your names?"

"You going to put us in the paper?" the redhead asked.

"Depends on what you know."

"Not sure I want to tell you anything," the shorter one said. Her thin lips mashed against her teeny nose, as if she smelled something foul. Her diminutive features made her seem fragile.

I waited for them to fill the silence.

"I'm Anna," the redhead finally said. She had a pretty voice, like someone who practiced her diction, who tried to sound sweet and mannered. "This is my cousin, Libby."

"You have any last names or are you just one-word girls, like Madonna and Pink?"

Anna rolled her eyes and sighed loudly. "Reid," she said, then pointed at her cousin. "Reilly."

"Reid and Reilly? You're shitting me, right? Alliterated last names? That's original."

Anna grinned maliciously. Her freckles looked like flecks of rust splattered across her nose. Her lips were smudged with pink gloss, slipping onto her skin as if she couldn't color within the lines of her face.

"You live in this neighborhood?" I asked.

They exchanged glances. "Not far," Anna said.

"What are you doing over here?"

Anna stuck her tongue through the gap in her teeth. "A girl's gotta do what a girl's got to do. Too much fun last night and well, here I am with a hole in my head." It sounded like lyrics to a crude rap song.

"She chipped her tooth," Libby translated. Her river-colored eyes were a duller version of her cousin's. She nervously twisted her cross, twirling it over and over until the chain was so tight it nearly choked her. "We're going to the dentist. Daddy says they're cheaper in Chinatown."

"We live in Bridgeport," Anna added a little too eagerly.

Bridgeport, the neighborhood just south of Chinatown, was where the Mayor, until recently, had lived in the house inherited from his famous father, who also was once mayor. Irish, Polish, and Mexican immigrants had lived in the neighborhood for decades. Its cheap rents and boarding houses drew the city's newcomers.

While it's true that you can learn much about a person from their address, it is especially true in Chicago. The city is a collection of seventy-seven distinct communities, almost city-states, each retaining unique characteristics. Any native Chicagoan could tell you young strivers lived in Lakeview on the North Side because of its access to the beach and the bars, while established wealth preferred nearby Lincoln Park. No one would confuse Englewood, the city's poorest neighborhood on the South Side, where singer Jennifer Hudson grew up, with neighboring Back of the Yards, once home of the stockyards. A true Chicagoan would be able to tell you that Kenwood, with its historic mansions, was where famous murderers Leopold and Loeb had lived. And, despite being called the Hyde Park Senator, Chicago's presidential candidate actually lived in Kenwood. Hyde Park had its own distinction: there were more Nobel laureates there per square mile than anywhere else in the world.

If the girls lived in Bridgeport, my guess was Libby's father was working-class poor and not a native Chicagoan. Based on her twangy accent, she was probably from Indiana. As soon as her father could afford it, they would move to a neighborhood that offered better housing and schools.

"You girls know anything about *that house?*" I pointed toward the dull, yellow two-flat. It seemed unlikely the girls had just happened to pass by a crime scene where girls their own age had died. They knew something or someone involved. Maybe girls from their school had tried H, maybe they were hoping to try it, too.

They stared at me, their eyes questioning what was in it for them. I dug out a pack of cigarettes and held it out. Libby shook her head. Anna gawked at the red carton lined with gold foil.

"What are these?" She pulled a brown cigarette from the pack and rolled it between her fingers.

"Clove," I said, as I flicked my lighter. "They taste sweet."

She sucked in a long drag and blew out a string of smoke, then licked her lips as if she were trying to identify the spices on her tongue. I watched, recognizing her mannerisms—the way she cocked her head and jutted out her chin; how her eyes seemed to televise her inner emotions, amber when she seemed annoyed and deep green when she appeared content. She was taller and thinner than I was at her age, but we shared the same features, the same inquisitive gaze, the same enthusiasm to try new things. Studying this doppelgänger, this younger version of myself, I wondered if this was how mothers felt when they watched their daughters behave with the same inherited quirks.

There was one big difference between Anna and my teenage self, and I couldn't stop staring at it.

"It's a snake," she said, following my gaze to the tattoo on her calf. Her red fingernails traced the animal's body, etched in light green, its tail faded at her anklebone. The only finished part was the snake's head, its large skull and pin-like eyes animated in red ink. "It's rare and only comes out at night." She winked.

I'd heard people call heroin users "snake eyes," and wondered if that applied to Anna, who struck me as an odd sort of girl to be roaming the streets, hanging out near heroin houses, and seeking out black-market dentists. I again pointed at the house surrounded by cops and reporters.

"Did you see anyone go in there?"

Libby looked down at the chipped polish on her toenails. She always seemed to be waiting for Anna to speak first.

"Don't know," Anna said. "Lots of people went there. You know, it was a place…where you could *smoke* with other people."

"Did you guys ever go *smoke* in there?"

"Why do you want to know so much?" Anna asked.

"I'm working on a story about why girls are winding up dead. You know, girls like you. *White girls.*"

Anna tossed back her flaming hair. "It's because they buy their stuff from people they don't know."

Libby shot Anna a warning look.

Anna ignored her. "You gotta know who's giving you a ride, you know?"

"Do you guys ever go for *a ride*?"

Libby shifted from foot to foot. Though her black outfit screamed city girl, the choppy cadence of her voice, her awkwardness, and her shy gaze convinced me she was from rural Indiana.

Anna let out a nervous giggle: "A girl's gotta try everything. You only live once."

I was surprised at her casual indifference to the girls whose bodies still lay in the yellow house. Something about her party girl image didn't strike me as genuine. It was as if she had dressed for the part: her distressed jeans were bleached in all the right places, her exposed bra straps were black, not white like her cousin's, and her eyes had a stylish flick of black at the corners that was all the rage in the fashion magazines but had yet to hit Chicago. And then there was that amateurish tattoo that looked like it had come from a stick-on kit. The result was an odd mix of grit and glamour—not exactly street urchin, not strictly suburban teen. She'd adopted sophisticated affectations: a raised eyebrow, a dismissive shrug, a glare down her bony nose, a curt tone. I wondered which adults in her life she was mimicking.

"So what do your parents say about all this?"

"My dad works nights," Libby erupted. "My mom lives in the 'burbs. They don't say shit."

"My dad's in prison. And my mom doesn't care about anyone but my stepdad," Anna said. "I'm living with Libby and Uncle Danny."

"You guys know anyone who died of this stuff? Friends from school?"

"Shit, we got better things to do than school," Anna said and groaned.

"Like what?"

"You know—*adventures*." Anna raised her eyebrows and cocked her head coyly.

"You mean riding around with neighborhood boys and stealing beer?"

Anna spat, barely missing my shoes. "Jesus, we're fifteen, not twelve, lady."

"Oh, I see." I clicked my tongue, not bothering to hide my doubt. "So what *adventures* do fifteen-year-old girls have?"

"You got a car?" Anna asked, looking around.

I pointed to my red convertible. The exposed leather seats were baking in the sun, and I realized how stupid I'd been to leave the top down.

"Cool," Libby said, her face lighting up for the first time.

"Maybe you could give us a ride downtown?" Anna asked.

"Maybe. Sometime." Was she trying to rope me into one of their adventures? I closed the cardboard cover of my reporter's notebook, slid it into my purse, and lit a cigarette. "Off the record—what counts as fun these days?"

They looked at each other, their eyes seeking permission.

"You're not gonna write this down?" Libby asked.

I shook my head and exhaled a long string of smoke, pretending I was one of the cool girls from my high school.

"When my dad goes to work, we go out," Libby said. Her voice was proud, yet confessional quiet. "We go downtown, see bands and stuff. You know...we meet people. We go to these parties in warehouses where people...dress up."

"One time we got this guy to take us to Six Flags. He paid for everything," Anna bragged. "And last night we met up with these guys in the park—"

Libby swatted her cousin. The two looked at me with strained smiles.

One thing I'd learned as a reporter was that people wore their stories like skin. If you paid attention, you could tell which narratives mattered. There was a certain vibe, an energy that came through when people talked about their lives. While some stories dropped like stones in water, others formed huge ripples, stirring everything in their wake. Talking to Anna and Libby, I could sense a growing undertow.

"Aren't you afraid you're going to wind up like the girls in that house?" They followed my eyes to the coroner's men carrying out the first black body bag.

Libby pulled at her cousin's shirt. "C'mon, Anna. Let's go. We gotta go."

Anna jerked free of her cousin's grasp and stood within inches of my face, sucking on her bottom lip as if she were debating whether to tell me something.

"So you really want to know what girls are into, huh?" Her

cheeks were flushed and a flicker in her eyes made me feel as if she were teasing me, as if she knew something about me I didn't. "Maybe we can hang out sometime, give you a little show, if you're not too *scared*."

Libby shook her head and protested, "No way! She's too *old*."

I stepped toward Anna, my nose nearly touching her chin. "I'm game, *girlfriend*. Bring it on."

Libby grabbed Anna by the arm and pulled her. Anna walked sideways, looked back at me, and grinned, as if she realized the value of the secret she possessed. Then the two girls reached the corner and disappeared.

CHAPTER TWO

June 13, 2008

POISON HEROIN HURTS PRESIDENTIAL CAMPAIGN

HYDE PARK SENATOR VOWS TO FIGHT DRUGS

Chicago Sentinel

Two hours later, I was still thinking of Anna. It was what she didn't say that nagged at me. I wondered if it was all a ploy, whether she really knew anything about white girls doing heroin, whether she'd really follow through on her vague invitation. Most likely it was just talk. But something, call it street intuition, told me we'd meet again. Her kind—the clever, gaming sort—always showed up, often when I least expected it.

I parked in the bowels of Michigan Avenue's lower level, the cavernous highway that runs beneath the city's downtown streets. I stepped around manhole covers that reeked of waste then climbed the stairs to the crowds above on the glittery Magnificent Mile. Pushing through the rotating doors, I emerged into the coolness of the *Times*'s stone lobby. Chiseled in the walls were pithy quotes from famous white men, with the exception of Flannery O'Connor. Hers, etched over an elevator, was my favorite: "The truth does not change according to our ability to stomach it."

When the elevator doors opened to the newsroom on the fourth floor—symbolizing the Fourth Estate—an air of expectation greeted me. A hum of anxiety hung over the sweep of cubicles where reporters wore headsets and looked like telemarketers, their eyes fixed on their computer terminals, their fingers *tap-tap-tapping* at plastic keyboards. Any moment one of us might be asked to write an obituary or race out to O'Hare to cover a plane crash. The unpredictability interspersed with the routine made us a little edgy, the rhythm of our daily lives beating to the metronome of a looming deadline.

Lately a new kind of stress had infiltrated the newsroom, whispers of bankruptcy and more layoffs. The real estate under our feet was worth more than what we produced; all we had to do was look out our windows at Donald Trump's shimmering turquoise skyscraper rising from the foundation of another newspaper that leased space in a hotel to save money. Meanwhile, the *Times*'s gothic tower, with its beady-eyed gargoyles and its façade embedded with stones collected by its reporters all over the world—the Great Wall of China, the Taj Mahal, the Great Pyramid—resembled a medieval fortress, outdated and antiquated, a historic artifact amid the city's burgeoning skyline of sleek blue metal and glass. That summer it was well-known in the newsroom that the *Times*'s publisher was considering an offer to turn our ornamental tower into luxury condos with an Olympic-size swimming pool amid its flying buttresses.

The newsroom was relatively quiet that Friday afternoon. Many reporters had taken off early. Others were hurriedly filing stories so they could slip out for happy hour. As I walked down the cluttered aisles, only a few heads turned. Reporters rarely talked to one another, preferring instead to send emails.

Passing the editor-in-chief's glass office, I could hear Odis grilling some assistant editor. They both looked up as I walked by, the assistant's eyes pleading me to interrupt. Odis's gaze rose only to my breasts before he went back to questioning the junior editor. I knew well how it felt to be under his intense scrutiny, curt words firing off his tongue, his spit showering his victims with invectives.

Across the room Amy Jarvis, the metro editor, yelled: "Delaney!"

Amy's looks had once turned heads. But her sagging backside and drooping double chin made her look like a melted wax version of her former self. That didn't stop her from flirting as if she were still a perky young blonde. The paper tolerated Amy's behavior in the same way it tolerated guys who made sexist jokes. If you could write or edit a great story, no one cared if you bathed or beat your wife. Amy's advantage was that she was the only woman among the paper's top white male editors; she provided the appearance of diversity.

I cleared newspapers off a chair in her office and heard her door latch behind me.

"I want to show you something," she whispered in a conspiratorial tone. She flicked off the top of a silvery department store box, ruffled through its stiff tissue paper and raised a black lacy bodice with dangling garters. "This is what I bought over lunch. What do you think?" Her face beamed.

I could feel my cheeks burning, and I had to swallow a tickle in my mouth. "Well…"

"It's okay to look, Delaney. It's just *underwear*." She held the lingerie to her chest and twisted from side to side, admiring her image reflected from a glass frame on the wall. "I try not to show it at work, but sometimes you can't hide a *Playboy* body. Lingerie makes me feel so—powerful." Her eyes danced with narcotic ecstasy.

I looked down at the carpet and coughed. "Hey, I met a couple of girls today near the Chinatown homicides. I think they know something."

"Hmm…" Amy continued to prance before the makeshift mirror. "What do you think *he'd* do if I just showed up in his office wearing this under a raincoat?"

"Your husband?"

She gave me an annoyed look. Though it was widely rumored that Amy and Odis were having an affair, I preferred not to imagine the two together.

"Amy…I think these girls could be into heroin."

Her face darkened. "So find out."

I got up to leave. Amy pulled on my arm.

"Stay objective this time, Nat, okay? Don't get attached. Remember: you're a reporter, not a social worker."

We both knew what she was referring to—my failed attempts at intervening in the lives of people I'd met on the street. The latest was a homeless woman who claimed her identity had been stolen and she had lost her house in the process. I'd spent weeks trying to line her up with temporary housing, pleading with various non-profits to give her a job, only to find out after my stories hit the paper that she was a schizophrenic who had multiple identities. There'd been a string of others, but none as public or as embarrassing. Odis called them "lapses in judgment." Amy just said I had a girly heart.

I smiled and patted Amy's arm. Her black lace bodice lay crumpled in her lap.

"Go for it." Hearing Anna's voice in my head, I parroted her mantra: "A girl's gotta try everything. You only live once."

• • •

At my desk, I buried my forehead into my palms, trying to think of a lead that would land my story on Page One. The smell of leather-wood piqued my nose, and I looked up into strange, black eyes. He was leaning over my cubicle, his face hovering near my own, his trendy narrow glasses magnifying his intensity. His ink black hair was swept back from his face, accentuating contrasting features: ecru skin, charcoal eyebrows, and a speckled goatee. He looked vaguely Italian, but his suspicious demeanor suggested something Eastern European, setting him apart in a newsroom of mostly pale Irish. Julian was the paper's enigmatic business editor, known for his acerbic remarks. He had worked at the *Wall Street Journal* and the *New York Times*, and reporters admired and feared him. He was not one to make small talk, and his dismissive nature hadn't earned him friends among the editor ranks.

"Busy?" He offered a strained smile.

"You could say that. On deadline." I banged at my keyboard.

"I'll make it quick. We got an anonymous tip back in business that one of the big Olympic donor's kids was arrested a few days ago. Then the cops dropped the charges."

"Yeah? I'm not on the *celebrity beat.*"

He ignored my sarcasm. "The cops searched his car and found prescription drugs and *syringes.*"

I sat up straighter. "I'm listening."

"Think you could ask your cop buddies to slip you the arrest report?" He pumped his eyebrows.

"Why are you asking me and not those guys?" I glanced at the row of senior crime reporters, yakking as they leaned back in their chairs, tossing a football back and forth, clearly *not* on deadline.

Julian narrowed his eyes at the men. "You know why. You have the best police sources. Don't know how you do it—"

"Are you intimating that I *sleep* with my sources?"

"That's not what I meant. You're...*dogged.* That's all. Those guys," he nodded toward my male counterparts, "might get to it next week, if at all."

I took out my reporter's notebook and a pen. "Your Daddy Warbucks kid got a name?"

Julian leaned away from my cubicle. "The story's kind of *sensitive.*"

"Forget it then. I'm not a fucking gofer." I swiveled around to face my computer. It didn't matter that his good looks made me jittery. I'd learned the hard way not to do grunt work for guys who grinned and paid me back in compliments.

Julian cleared his throat, leaned over my terminal, and whispered near my ear. "It's like this: we heard he's a *Kennan.*" His lips twitched as he stifled a grin.

While most people associated the political Kennan clan with Boston, a spur of the family had for decades owned and run the Merchandise Mart, the monolithic art deco building that took up two city blocks.

"Be pretty ironic to have a Kennan peddling drugs, don't you think?" His black-pea eyes widened at the suggestion of scandal.

"If the arrest angle has legs, I want in."

"*That's* why I'm talking to you." He slapped his palm against the top of the cubicle, signaling the end of our conversation.

As I watched Julian walk away, I wondered how it was that *he* got the tip and not me. A sharp whistle rose above the keyboard clacking and the hum of computers. I turned around to see Ben, a columnist who shared a cubicle wall with me, shaking his head.

"He *sure* is a beauty," he said, fluttering his eyes.

"Ben, he has kids and lives in the suburbs. *Not* your type."

"Oh *honey*, I wasn't talking about for me." He clasped a hand on each side of his face in mock surprise. "I meant for *you*. A real looker, that one. From what I hear, he's not *attached*."

Ben was an eccentric little man who'd started working at the paper when the newsroom was filled with white men in suits who wrote their stories on typewriters and smoked at their desks. From his photos, he'd once had a head of dark hair. Now he wore expensive fedoras to hide his wispy white comb over. I guessed Ben was in his sixties, but it was hard to tell with the unlined boyish face and high forehead reminiscent of Truman Capote. Ben agonized over his columns, his half-moon glasses riding low on his nose as he chewed on the end of a pen. He wrote everything longhand on yellow legal pads before scrupulously typing his columns at the computer with his index fingers.

Ben had taken a liking to me when I arrived at the *Times*. Dazed and awestruck at our first meeting, I'd told him that I'd grown up reading his stories, studying them to understand the writing craft. He rarely fielded genuine compliments about his *bons mots* and greedily lapped up my praise. When a cubicle opened up next to his, Ben advised me to claim it. He'd been giving me advice, personal and professional, ever since.

"He's married," I protested a little too quickly.

"Not so. I heard the ex is an attorney. I think the term is *amicable* divorce. He's one of those every-other weekend daddies. That leaves two weekends a month for someone *very special*." He winked.

"C'mon, Ben. You know I don't have time for a boyfriend."

"Oh honey. You're getting a little *too mature* to be dating men just for their *aesthetics.*" He licked his lips. "You need a real man. One who is going to provide you a future and sire you some children. You don't want to end up having to work at my age in a dump like this. If it weren't for my sick desire to get a paycheck, I'd be living the high life, eating tuna from a can and watching soap operas on a television with bunny ears. But *you,* you have your whole life ahead of you. You don't have to spend it chasing thugs. Though I know you love those bad boys with their tattoos and their big biceps and their *guns.*"

I tried to hold back a smile. Ben was a keen observer. More times than I could count, he'd correctly predicted a suspect's character. He was like my own personal criminal profiler.

"The only things I'm chasing are dead bodies and a phantom drug dealer."

Ben moved toward our shared partition, decorated with tchotchkes he'd scavenged from colleagues' desks after they were unceremoniously escorted from the building. Marching across our ledge was a dinosaur, a black Corvette, a red caboose, the Michelin man, a Democratic donkey, a *Star Wars* storm trooper, and a family of trolls with bright purple synthetic hair. Ben liked to think that hanging on to these worthless knickknacks somehow preserved the memory of their former owners. He poked his nose between the purple-haired trolls and spoke in an eerie whisper, as if we were sharing ghost stories over a campfire.

"Your killer is someone who has a love-hate relationship with rich girls. You watch. It'll be some guy who never really fit in, someone with a grudge acting out some private rage. *I think* he's targeting these girls."

• • •

I spent the rest of the afternoon on the phone, cobbling together details: the Dead Angels were all on the honor roll; one was class president, another had her daddy's gold Amex card in her wallet. Apparently, the killer wasn't motivated by money.

I dialed Detective Mobley's pager. Michael Mobley—Mo, for short—was a homicide detective I had cultivated as a source, although he didn't like that word. He preferred to see himself as a government censor trying to make sure I got my stories straight. Mo claimed he liked me because I "didn't take shit" and my articles were "mostly okay"—a ringing endorsement from a third-generation cop and decorated Marine from the Iraq War.

Mo and I usually met at Sullivan's, a touristy downtown steakhouse with an upstairs cigar lounge. Mo had expensive tastes in cigars, and he liked to smoke on my tab. Occasionally he asked about the men in my life, but he never made a pass. Maybe he'd heard the rumor floating around the police station that I was a lesbian. Cops always assume tough women are gay.

Mo's cover story, in case we were ever caught together, was that we were lovers. Mo might get a few *attaboys* for sleeping with a reporter—but he'd definitely get fired for providing information to one. Institutional racism weighed in our favor too, since few would automatically link a white reporter with a black cop. We were careful, and no one suspected—or so we thought.

The red light lit up on my phone. The number was blocked. I suspected it was Mo.

"Yeah?" I answered.

"*National Inquirer*, please."

"Sure, if you give me Internal Affairs. There's this crooked cop…"

"Ha, ha," he trilled like a girl.

"I need some advice."

"Don't marry him."

CHAPTER THREE

June 13, 2008

DEAD ANGELS WERE CELEBRATING START OF SUMMER

FRIENDS SAY GIRLS WERE NOT DRUG USERS

Chicago Times

Sullivan's was packed. The wait-list ran two pages long. I squeezed between women in slippery, low-cut dresses and slid behind men in suits, steeped in peppery cologne. Then I climbed the back stairs to the cigar lounge. A few men were seated at the bar, others were scattered among leather couches. Most were puffing on cigars and staring at overhead televisions. There was no sign of the short, burly man whose uniform consisted of dark blazers and tan pants with buffed wingtips.

I settled on a couch, its cool leather sticking to my skin. A waitress passed, and I yelled my order: a dirty martini with bleu cheese-stuffed olives. "Please," I added with a smile. She and I were the only women in the room. The men clustered together, laughing in low tones. The cigar smoke made the air smell like tobacco and baked cherries. I rummaged through my big black bag that carried my life—cell phone, reporter's notebooks, tape recorder, wallet, makeup, metal flask, and wet wipes—looking for my cloves. I felt the waxed paper that contained the fifty-five-dollar Arturo Fuente Opux X BBMF cigar I'd bought earlier. The brand was Mo's favorite, probably because the initials officially stood for "Big

Bad Mother Fucker." Eventually I found my own smokes. I lit one, closed my eyes, and inhaled the sweetness.

I wished Friday nights meant fancy restaurants, steak and martinis with a boyfriend, followed by dancing, a walk along the river, and falling into bed after midnight, tipsy and adventurous. I had just put down my martini when two callused hands covered my eyes. A smoker's voice whispered in my ear, drawing out each syllable like a horror film villain: "Does Your Honey Know You're All Alone?"

I twisted from his grip. "Hey, you! Sit down and have a drink."

Mo sank into a chair, waved over the waitress, and ordered a single-malt whiskey with a twist of lemon. He looked more like a Marine sergeant than a cop. Most Chicago cops looked like they'd eaten too many paczkis, the Polish doughnuts Chicagoans were crazy about. Thanks to pickup basketball, Mo managed to keep his weight down. He was compact with the muscular arms and beefy chest of a much younger man. His short hair had started to gray at the temples, setting off his tawny skin. Mo wore no jewelry. He preferred to blend in, to be as nondescript as possible. He used prejudice in his favor, hoping that people overlooked him as a black man. For the most part he succeeded. If you were to see Mo from a side angle or the back, you might not give him a second look. But if you ever looked Mo in the face, you would never forget him. He had the most remarkable blue eyes. I called them lake water eyes. They were bright and beguiling and reminded me of the cerulean blue waters of Lake Michigan.

I pulled out the Arturo Fuente. Mo cocked his head and eyed me suspiciously but took the cigar. His hands shook as he lit the cigar, but he didn't take his eyes off me. I imagined he was negotiating internally about what he would tell me.

"You workin' the heroin deaths, huh?" he asked in his South Side voice that reminded me of Hambone Blues on the radio. "Any leads?"

I forced a laugh. "You must be desperate if you're asking me.

What was it today? Was that the same dealer who knocked off the girls from Lakeview last week? Or is this a copycat?"

Mo's eyes widened. "You know about that theory, huh?"

"Why's he picking young girls from nice families? How do they hook up with him? Is this a lone dealer or a gang that's dishing bad drugs?"

Mo shook his head. "Not sure. At first we thought it was just a bad batch of drugs being moved by the Gangster Disciples or the Mickey Cobras or even the New Breeds. Everything keeps gentrifying south of the Loop, so all the known drug corners have been forced to move. Then we thought one of the gangs was trying to sell some potent shit to attract new business. But every time we bust them, their baggies ain't pure enough for a match. Most of the black folks who've died of hotshots have been junkies, but these girls were *drug virgins*." He liked that word—virgin—anything to conjure up the image of sex without saying sex.

"The thing is," he continued with barely a breath, "it could be anybody, and maybe half a dozen dealers are all competing for H-heads who *want* to tempt fate. Every time one of them dies, it's like an advertisement and another hundred H-heads go looking for that killer dust. We showed up to one entire heroin house full of bodies."

"Jesus." I imagined the corpses fanned out like some Jim Jones Kool-Aid fest.

"Now we're thinking it might be a lone guy. The superintendent—you know he's former FBI—made us send our stuff to Quantico. You know what those geniuses came up with? 'The dealer works alone; he's someone with a superiority complex. He may be a racist, someone who really hates white girls.' Here's my profile: He's some bitter brother who just wants attention, and he's smart enough to know knocking off some rich girls from Lincoln Park or the 'burbs is the best way to do that. Or maybe he's just a fucking idiot who doesn't know how to cut heroin. Whaddaya think? I would be a supremo G-man, huh?"

Mo's order arrived, and he gulped the drink, holding his finger for the waitress to stand by. Then he ordered another with a beer chaser. Normally, Mo sipped his scotch.

"Heavy day, huh?"

He clinked his whiskey glass against my martini stem and stared at me longer than usual.

"How is it these kids ended up on the South Side?" I asked. "How did they know where to get the heroin?"

Most heroin in Chicago was sold on the West Side, along the Eisenhower Expressway, known as Heroin Highway. But the poisoned heroin seemed to be concentrated on the South Side, which made the deaths all the more suspicious and significantly narrowed the number of suspected dealers.

Mo shrugged and drew on his cigar.

"How are the murders connected, Maxwell Smart?" Mo liked it when I made references to famous detective characters.

He ran his palm across his head and forced a smile that exposed slender, tobacco-stained teeth.

"Not sure, Agent 99." He started on his second whiskey. "The superintendent is pressuring us to make this case. He says the Mayor thinks this could hurt our chances for the Olympics. Even our illustrious Hyde Park Senator is pissed. It's hurting his image as a presidential candidate. Chicago is officially the murder capital of the country. Congratufuckinglations! But what are we supposed to do? We're not magicians here, and we're not psychiatrists. How are we supposed to find some nut job, some Ted Kaczynski *nigga* selling killer dust? We got no juice on this. We just keep rounding up every guy on the South Side with a record of possession. It's a long list."

"Anyone pop out?"

His face broke into a vicious smile. "How 'bout I just give you the goddamn list and maybe you could investigate and get back to us?"

"Come on, you gotta give me something. So far this is all stuff I've already heard."

He rubbed his chin. "Okay, but only a couple of people know this…" He stopped short, shook his head. "Nah! It'd get me fired."

We sat for several minutes, feigning interest in the Cubs and Sox games on the overhead plasma screens. Finally, Mo relented. "Don't you fuck me on this."

Cops, like reporters, can't keep secrets. What's the point of knowing something if no one knows you know? Cops spend most of their time analyzing suspects, analyzing themselves, turning details over again and again, trying to make sense of the irrational acts of criminals. Being a cop means access. It means walking in unauthorized territory, carrying guarded reports and photos, and hearing confessions. The only way they can differentiate themselves is to talk about what they know, overhear, or suspect. And, despite the television image of the stoic guys in blue, cops are compact vessels, their emotions tightly wound around their internal organs, knotted until something bursts. That's when they spew.

I nodded to the terms; this was way off the record.

"The drugs—they're cut with fentanyl. It's a drug more potent than morphine. It's not the heroin that's killing them. It's the fentanyl. They call it 'Poison' on the street. Those fucking H-heads ask for it by name. Its brand is a skull and crossbones."

I leaned forward, urging him on.

"And the drugs today? They're the same," he continued. "The same cut. The same batch. It's synthetic fentanyl. It's the same bastard today as the other deaths. At least that's what the preliminary tests show."

"If it's a lone guy, what's his motive?"

"I think he's got a God complex. He wants to decide who should live and who should die. Maybe somebody he *loved* died of a heroin overdose and nobody cared. *Boo-hoo.* Now he's going to make people care." He scrunched up his face in a mock sob. Then he bent toward me in a conspiratorial posture and lowered his voice. "I think he moves in a lot of circles. Those North Side girls probably ended up with the wrong dealer who saw their ivory skin and knew offing them wouldn't be destroying his client base. He knew they were one-time buyers—vampire girls."

"So only white girls are in danger?"

"Nah." He slapped the air between us. "I think this guy could change his MO. He's smart. He's been incarcerated. He knows the system, and he's clever enough to throw us off."

Mo sank back into his chair, looking exhausted.

We drank quietly, mulling over his theories. Then I remembered Julian's tip.

"Hey, what can you tell me about a Kennan kid getting arrested for illegal possession of prescription drugs? Apparently you guys dropped the charges."

Mo bunched up his lips. "Wouldn't be the first time."

"I hear he had *syringes* in his car."

"Where'd you hear that?"

"Can't say. Is it true?"

"I'll get back to you. Got any other bombs you wanna drop?"

My phone vibrated in my bag, and I pulled it out. The text read: "Jackson Park. One hour."

"Something you want to tell me?" He leaned forward as if he could read my phone upside down.

I looked away. "I may have something, but you have to promise you're not going to follow me or send any of your snitches after me."

Mo put down his beer and nodded.

"I met some white girls today near the house with the Dead Angels. They might be into H—or know girls who are."

"So?"

"You never know." I shrugged. "I might hang out with them sometime. If you know a name of a suspect, you need to tell me. That way I'll know if I'm in danger."

I didn't expect Mo to approve of my befriending girls doing heroin. Cops are always leery of competition, and reporters are always dismissive of police warnings. I'd heard Mo's ominous words of caution over the years. I thought appealing to his chivalrous nature might goad him into giving me the identity of the heroin killer—if he knew it.

Mo played with his watch, then turned to me with a fierceness in his eyes.

"I don't got a name. Nat, we just don't know who it is. I'm telling you the truth. So don't go meeting druggies. You got a gun in that bag? 'Cause that's what it's going to take to protect yourself."

I stood up to leave. "I'll call you if I run into trouble."

Mo stood too. Even in the dim bar light I could see his lips quivering. "Goddamn it, Natalie. You're way out of your league on this one."

"If you know something, tell me *now*. Otherwise…Well, it's on your conscience."

He grabbed my elbow. "Don't be a cowboy. They don't live too long."

I shook loose of his grip. "Would you say that if I were a male reporter?"

He laughed. "If you were a guy, we wouldn't even be drinking together."

I headed toward the stairs, looking back to see Mo watching me. I knew he was debating whether he should follow.

CHAPTER FOUR

June 13, 2008

MAYOR ORDERS POLICE TO FIGHT HEROIN
DESK COPS ASSIGNED TO STREETS
Chicago Monthly

The sun dipped behind skyscrapers, reflecting a golden glow in my rearview mirror. I drove through the South Loop, past its former tenements recently revamped into trendy condos, then hit the dead zone of the upper South Side, a vast hole in the skyline where Chicago's high-rise housing projects once stood. For as far as you could see, there were clusters of 18-story projects, dozens of them, with names like Stateway Gardens and Robert Taylor Homes. Mo had grown up here along with thousands of other blacks. Now long stretches of gravelly, empty fields marked where the buildings had been ripped out of the ground.

I was surprised Anna had called so soon. Most times I didn't hear from people I met on the street until they were in trouble—often in jail or needing money. Whatever Anna's reasons, I was certain her motives weren't pure. Still, her invitation was the break I needed to enter that shadow world of girls shooting smack. Nothing—not Mo's dire warnings or the prickly sensation radiating across my scalp—was going to stop me.

A few blocks farther, brick townhouse developments rose next to crumbling Greystones. The houses continued to get bigger and bigger until they became the mansions of Kenwood, beautiful

Georgian homes with stately porches and long driveways that led to coach houses. Eventually these grand structures gave way to the more modest Victorians and row houses of Hyde Park, my childhood neighborhood.

I turned off Lake Shore Drive at the Museum of Science and Industry, its white wedding cake façade overlooking the glassy pond of Jackson Park, and pulled into the rear lot. Lou Gramm's haunting voice on the stereo filled the car—"*And it feels like the first time, like it never did before.*"

Being back in Hyde Park made me think of Jake and how many times we'd made out in this very spot after his baseball games. I rested my head against the steering wheel, remembering how he'd smelled of cut grass and talcum powder, how he had dirt in the crevices of his elbows and in the creases under his eyes, how his sweat smelled sweet, the faint musk of cologne lingering on his skin. I could say Jake was my first boyfriend, but that wouldn't really be accurate. Jake was more like a cicada, turning up every three or four years without warning, making a lot of noise and then disappearing. Until one day he never reappeared.

Anna couldn't have known how much this park meant to me, how many painful memories it resurrected. She couldn't have known that my interest in her and the Poison Girls derived from a dark time in my life, a time when I'd loved a young man who was in love with heroin.

A car door slammed nearby. A family was packing up a grill and cooler. One of the kids was fussing; his screams jolted me back to reality. I left the car and started along the path around the pond, choosing a bench near the creek where I watched ducks swim by under a darkening sky. In the distance, a man walked his pit bull. He wore a red basketball jersey, shorts that drooped to his knees, and a Sox ball cap turned backwards. As he neared, I guessed he was about twenty-four. He had big hands and a chest twice as big as his waist. He didn't so much walk as twist from side to side—a gangster swagger. His gray eyes fixed on mine.

"Some mean motherfuckers hang out here," he said, sitting down next to me.

"Oh? You one of them?"

He snorted. "You're one of those brave white women, huh?"

For the most part, I didn't have a reason to be afraid. As soon as people learned I was a journalist, they wanted to tell me their story. Talking to a reporter meant they *mattered*. And even though I told them I was from the *Chicago Times*, they *always, always* asked when they would see themselves on TV, as if I could film them with my eyeballs.

It continually amazed me what complete strangers would confess to a reporter. My editors said I had a sympathetic face. Others called it a gift, the ability to make strangers trust me and reveal their secrets. And then there were the professional jealousies, the innuendos that I got people to talk because I smiled and batted my eyelashes. Whenever I'd come back with a good story from a reluctant source, my male counterparts made snide comments: "Guess you have to wear a skirt to get an interview like that..." Not that they ever saw me in a skirt.

I looked down at the man's pit bull sniffing my leg and wondered how many of the male reporters I knew would sit next to this gangbanger and his dog.

He pulled on the steel leash. "Heel, Rascal." Then he flashed a mouth full of glitter—a grill that sparkled with what looked like diamonds but were surely rhinestones. He had a thick jaw and wore a gold chain bearing a charm of a clenched fist. I memorized his features, in case I ever had to pick him out of a lineup. Despite his high cheekbones and fat, girlish lips, he had the hardened body of a man who had lifted weights in prison.

"It's okay," he said. "You're just a potential human. White people haven't evolved yet."

I stood to walk away.

He grabbed my arm.

"Don't go." He smiled that mouth full of silver. "I was just kidding. You white folks are too damn serious." He let go of my arm and held out his hand. "I'm Lester." He pronounced it Lest-*ah*.

I nodded, refusing his outstretched palm. "Keep your hands to yourself. Got it, Lest-*ah*?"

"Okay, Snow White." He laughed, a guttural *hey-hey-hey* that sounded dirty.

"What are you doing here?"

"So now you up in my business?"

"You sat down in mine."

He raised his eyebrows. "I got some girls to meet. That okay with you?"

"Hmm. And what are you going to do with *some girls,* Lest-*ah*?" He was such a player. It was a small pond. I figured we were both there to meet the same girls.

"What? You a fuckin' social worker?"

I pulled out the credentials tucked inside my shirt. My press card, after all, was my protection—at least it offered that illusion. He bent over and touched the various laminated photos stamped with official emblems as if he could spot a fake. I smelled alcohol on his breath and pungent aftershave on his neck.

"And just what are you reportin' on down here?"

"The heroin deaths."

He sucked in air and sat back against the bench. Rascal whined at his feet, his eyes tracking the ducks.

"The *Chicago Times.* That's that Jew paper, right?"

"What?"

"Jews control the media. Everybody knows that."

"Our CEO is Jewish, but what has that got to do with anything?"

"Snow White, don't you know all of us is under Israel's control?"

I shook my head. He looked like a rapper and talked like a zealot. "What are you saying?"

"It don't matter. What you put in that paper, people read. And people believe it. Right?"

"Some people."

"I mean the police read your stories, right? The politicians, the aldermen? All those folks believing what a Jew paper say?"

"It's not a *Jewish* newspaper."

"So if I tell you something and you put it in that paper, everybody gonna read it, right?"

"That's a lot of ifs."

"I can show you the real story, Snow White. But you can't use my name. Got it?"

I nodded.

He licked his lips and rolled his shoulders. "I gotta protect myself. There's lots goin' on down here. People think they know stuff, but they don't know shit. And the po-lice, they don't know the shit they don't know. But Lest-*ah* knows." He nodded as if all that knowledge were ready to tumble out in front of me.

"Why would you want to tell me anything?"

"I ain't gonna tell ya *everything*. I could be one of those secret people—like in the movies." His face brightened with the thought.

"You mean a confidential source?"

We heard giggling coming from just beyond the curve in the path. Anna and Libby came into sight, playfully shoving each other. Lester dropped Rascal's leash and the dog ran up to the girls, happy-barking and wagging his tail. The girls stooped and petted Rascal, cooing at the sloppy grin on his face. Either Rascal was a shitty guard dog or this wasn't the first time he'd met the girls.

Anna looked up and saw me, then screamed and ran toward us. "You came!" Libby sulked behind her.

In the twilight, the girls looked older. They'd changed into tight T-shirts and jeans, their eyes heavily outlined as if with a butcher's grease pencil. Anna's lips were slick with sparkly gloss, and her hair was thick and wavy, the auburn tendrils cascading down her back. Libby's hair was twisted in pixie braids.

"You know her?" Lester pointed at me.

"We met today in Chinatown. She's just going to hang out

with us. Okay?" Anna's voice was testy, but she backed away from him as if she were afraid.

Lester looked like he was going to deck her; instead, he grabbed the back of her neck and pulled her face toward his. He smothered her lips with his own, then pushed her away, catching her wrist and twisting it in his big hand.

"You shoulda fuckin' asked me first."

Anna squirmed and pulled back her arm, rubbing the red fingerprints he'd left on her wrist.

Lester motioned for us to follow him toward a distant line of trees, their upper branches blowing like ceremonial flags.

I should have paid more attention to the hair on my skin rising, the ducks clacking and flying away, the wind picking up and the leaves whipping off the ground, as if Nature were issuing a warning. But I didn't. I just mindlessly trailed Lester.

"What's happening?" I whispered to Anna.

"We're gonna try some H."

I stopped. Lou Gramm's chimerical words about the *first time* echoed in my head.

Anna was nearly at the tree line. "Come on," she pleaded, motioning with her arm.

I had to decide whether I was going to cover the story or I wasn't. Watching adults smoke crack and shoot up heroin for a story was one thing, but witnessing teenage girls experiment with drugs suddenly struck me as callous, as if I were condoning their ruin. Many reporters would have walked away. And not before delivering a stern warning. But how else could I get the truth about why girls were trying heroin—and dying for it? I could hear Amy's voice in my head: *Stay objective. You're not a social worker.* We were only supposed to report the news, not change it, not get involved. But that didn't stop me from being human, and right then I felt like a piece of shit for being there.

I caught up to Anna and tugged at her shirt. "Do you really want to do this?"

Her eyes radiated excitement. "You only live once."

I followed as she continued under the trees, a familiar dread bubbling up my throat. Libby and Lester were already huddled over something smoldering in Lester's hand. As we got closer, I could see it was a piece of tinfoil with a brown lump in the middle. "This ain't no ordinary hit, ladies. This be *brown shugah.*" Lester beamed proudly.

He continued to heat the foil with a cigarette lighter. We watched as the lump melted. Then Libby cupped her mouth to a cardboard toilet paper roll and held it over the foil, breathing in the smoke. She seemed to know what to do without Lester coaching her. It made me wonder if the Dead Angels had known what they were doing when they injected Poison. Or had someone been there to coach them?

Libby made a harsh sucking noise, her face engulfed in the heroin cloud. Strands of braids fell across her face, but she kept inhaling. At first her breaths were smooth and regular, then labored and high-pitched. When she reached her highest octave, Libby straightened her body, lengthening her spine as if to fill up every inch of her lungs with the fumes. Finally she unlocked her lips from the cardboard and looked up, her eyes bloodshot. Sweat glistened along her upper cheeks. She staggered a moment, then slumped against the base of a tree, her arms falling like heavy branches beside her body.

For a moment, I wondered if Libby—her eyes closed, her face serene—was still alive. Was this how the Dead Angels had looked when the fentanyl stopped their hearts? Or had they jolted awake gasping, clutching at life before they collapsed and suffocated on their own vomit?

Lester snatched the makeshift tube from Libby's fingers and handed it to Anna. He flicked his lighter and held the tinfoil for her. She inhaled several white plumes—hesitantly at first and then more voraciously as she gained confidence. After she sucked in a few more times, her eyes crossed and she looked like she was going to topple over but braced herself against Lester. She pulled the tube from her mouth and looked around. The wild dill weed rubbed at her sandaled toes. "It smells like pickles," she said and giggled. She again locked her lips onto the tube, her head rising and falling in rhythm with her breathing.

I shuffled my feet, stared at the dead grass and scratched where the nettles had chafed my ankles. It was happening so quickly. Over the girls' shoulders, the sky had turned blue-black. What more was there to see?

Anna stopped her cadenced gasping and offered me the tube. I shook my head. My stomach churned. Didn't she get it? I was just a *witness*.

Lester grinned. "Yeah. I want to see the reporter lady take a hit."

"No." I backed away. "I only watch."

Lester sucked in his bottom lip. "Uh-huh. Take a hit. Just so I know you ain't a *cop*."

I shook my head. "I'm not a *cop*. And I'm *not* doing a hit."

Anna grabbed Lester's arm, pulling him and the tinfoil toward her. "Leave her."

She pressed the cardboard to her lips, kissing its paper ends, inhaling, sucking, spreading the euphoria to the farthest reaches of her body. When just a small speck of tar was left, Lester crumpled the foil in his fist and put the lighter back in his pocket. Anna leaned back, her eyes closed. His hands free, Lester began moving his fingers across Anna's budding breasts.

Without thinking, I swatted Lester and heard myself yell: "Paws off! She's just a girl!"

Lester shot me an evil look. We both knew I'd crossed the observation line I'd so carefully drawn.

I shuddered and started to walk out of the woods. "I gotta go." Why had I thought this would be...*routine*?

Libby stumbled behind me, mumbling, then grabbed at the tail of my shirt. "Don't go. Please...don't leave her...with *him*."

I looked at her, then at the car. *Don't get attached*, Amy had warned. There was a fine line between remaining objective and responding with humanity, and I was straddling it. I wanted to get in my car and leave, forget about the girls. My internal voice was yelling at me to *get gone*. Something bad was going down, and if I stayed it would drag me under.

"Me and Anna were with Lester and his boys last night," Libby confessed, leaning against me. "They got handsy. Anna fell. Chipped her tooth. Don't leave her with him. It's why she wanted you to come. She's scared of him."

Beneath the black eyeliner and the tight clothes, Libby looked like a terrified girl. I remembered what it felt like to be that age, so vulnerable and insecure, dependent on adults to intervene. I walked back into the woods. To hell with objectivity.

Under the tree branches, Lester was kissing Anna, one hand down the front of her jeans. Rascal lay at their feet. He bared his teeth and snarled. Suddenly he looked like a guard dog.

I stood still, fingered the mace canister I carried on my key chain, wondering if it would discharge since I'd never used it.

Rascal began barking, saliva dripping from his mouth, his paws stomping at the ground. Then, in an instant, he charged at me. I turned my back and curled into a question mark.

His claws felt like jagged glass cutting into my back. Anna screamed. The dog yelped in a high-pitched cry. I turned around. Lester was holding Rascal off the ground by his collar and laughing, his face full of smug satisfaction. My shirt was ripped at the nape. I touched the scratches along my collarbone, my fingernails caked in blood. I felt my face burning with rage, my hands shaking.

"Let's go," I yelled.

Lester glared at me but didn't stop Anna. She stumbled toward me in the dark; I held her shoulders and guided her to the car. Lester followed with Rascal.

Libby stood by the passenger side, peering into my two-seater.

"One of you is going to have to sit on the other's lap," I announced.

The girls jostled into the seat while Lester stood next to their open door. For a moment I thought he was going to sic Rascal on us. Instead, he yanked on the leash; the dog whined.

"Close the damn door!" I yelled.

The girls could barely shut the door with both of them crammed in the bucket seat. I backed out of the parking lot, squealing the tires as I punched the gas. Anna was giddy, waving through the back window, though it was too dark for Lester to see her.

"God, he's so hot," she said. "He's such a good kisser."

The dashboard gauges lit up her face, her smile no longer fractured. A temporary cap on her chipped tooth hid the previous night's misadventure.

"That damn dog hurt you?" Libby asked, her eyes squinting at the scratches on my shoulder, her mouth contorted in a squeamish frown. "Lester's a mean, mean man."

"And what you know about men?" Anna snapped.

I touched the cuts on my back and wondered what other injuries Lester was capable of inflicting.

CHAPTER FIVE

June 13, 2008

CATALOGUE HEIRESS HANDS OUT NEEDLES

CHICAGO CELEBRITIES PLEDGE TO JOIN
FIGHT AGAINST POISON HEROIN

Chicago Sentinel

We drove in squared circles for an hour before Libby spotted the green roof of Morrie O'Malley's Hot Dogs in the shadow of Cellular Field, not far from her apartment. Libby's face lit up as she rolled down the window; the aroma of sizzling beef filled the car. Anna sang "Malley, Malley, O'Malley," like the radio commercial. The lights of Cellular Field were still burning, but O'Malley's front door was locked.

"Hey!" I pounded on the glass.

"We're closed," a bald man hollered. He flashed a sadistic grin as he turned over the "We're Open" sign.

Anna mashed her lips to the glass.

The man looked back and forth from Libby to Anna, then me. I pulled out a twenty and held it up behind the girls' heads. He blinked and yelled over his shoulder: "We've got stragglers." Then he opened the door.

Anna jumped up to hug his thick neck.

He smiled with embarrassment. "You got five minutes," he muttered, taking the twenty.

The girls ordered two red hots each: Anna's with "the works,"

Libby's with just ketchup. I wasn't hungry—my shoulders still burning where Rascal's claws had ripped my skin—and went to find the bathroom to clean the cuts.

The girls chose one of the round tables outside. We swatted at mosquitoes and shivered at the sudden chill in the night air, our faces illuminated by the synthetic sun of the ballpark. I smoked a clove cigarette and drank a beer as I watched them tear into their hot dogs, juice dribbling from the corners of their mouths. Sometimes they looked at each other and giggled. With each bite they seemed to come to life a little more.

"How come you're not married?" Anna asked, her mouth full.

"What makes you think I'm not?"

"You'd be calling him right now, all smoochie." She kissed her hand. "That's not a wedding ring." She pointed at the antique sapphire and diamond ring on my left hand.

"Well, you're wrong about that. This was my grandmother's wedding ring."

"She's dead, huh?" Libby chimed in.

"She died three years ago."

"My grandmother's dead, too." Anna's face was pinched with emotion. "She was the greatest. I could stay with her any time I wanted. And she didn't let my stepfather give me any shit. She said my mother deserved what she got—"

"You got kids?" Libby asked, cutting off her cousin.

"I'm not married." I didn't mention that I'd been feeling that old kick of wanting a child, a desire that came around occasionally, but lately more often and much more intense. Meeting Anna had awakened a curiosity, making me wonder what my child might look like.

"That doesn't mean you can't have kids," Anna said.

"Well, for me it's a requirement."

"My momma and daddy aren't married," Libby offered.

"Bet that's hard on you, huh?"

"My daddy raised me since I was a baby," Libby said. "My momma got pregnant in high school. She was seventeen."

"Not much older than the two of you now."

"That's what I tell her. She says girls in Indiana get married *young*," Libby said, not trying to hide her country twang. "That's why she wanted me to come to Chicago. She said she'd whoop my ass if I got *preggers*. My daddy, too,"

We all laughed. But inside I felt sad for Libby.

"Be a little late for a 'whooping' at that point, don't you think?" I prompted.

Libby shrugged. "Not gonna happen."

"Because you're careful?" I asked.

"'Cause there's no boy's dick I wanna stick in my v-g."

Anna rolled her eyes. "She's Little Miss Virgin."

"And you *ain't*?" Libby accused her cousin.

"A lady doesn't kiss and tell." Anna smiled and fluttered her lashes.

"You have a boyfriend?" Libby asked me.

I shook my head. "Not really. I did once, though."

There'd been a string of guys after Jake, but no one like him. Not even close.

The girls looked down at their hot dogs, like they felt sorry for me, a grown woman without a man.

"Can we go to your house?" Libby asked.

Both girls stopped eating and looked at me, wide-eyed with the thought.

"Maybe…some day." I wondered what kind of stunt they could concoct that would involve my apartment.

"You don't trust us, do you?" Anna said.

"You girls have to start telling me the truth."

"We haven't lied to you," Libby shot back.

"Oh yeah? Why'd you invite me? What's your game here?"

Anna pulled in her neck, aggrieved. "I thought you wanted to see what girls do for fun?"

"What's in it for you talking to me?"

Anna rolled her shoulders. "Thought I'd shake it up. You

know, see how some prissy woman like you deals with Lester. Pretty funny if you ask me."

"Yeah, his dog's a real laugh," I said.

"C'mon. Just admit it. This is like the best show you've ever seen, right? You got to watch white girls do H." She bobbed her head, mimicking the street cockiness of black girls.

"So tell me: what do you girls get out of that—smoking brown sugar?"

Anna swallowed and picked a stray piece of cabbage from her teeth. She closed her eyes, and her body swayed as she rubbed her palms up and down her stomach. "I felt all oozy and sparkly. Like I was standing in the middle of a rainbow."

Libby rolled her eyes. "I don't know what she's talking about. I didn't see no colors." She took a big bite of her dog, ketchup oozing between her lips. "It made me hot."

"Yeah!" Anna said. "It was like rolling around in a blanket. It just made me feel…*happy*." Her smile faded as she read the disbelief on my face. "What's so wrong with that?"

"Really? Let's review: Girls are dying. You saw the body bags today. I know it's almost impossible to OD smoking that shit, but smokers graduate to snorting and mainlining. Besides, do you really trust Lester? Why do you think he gave you brown sugar for free?"

"He's nice. He likes us. And he's cute." She got up and threw her half-eaten red hot into the trash. "Come on, Lib. We can walk home from here." Her eyes suddenly looked dull and brown, even in the bright lights. Jake used to say that when my eyes were green, he knew I was happy. But when they looked brown, he gave me a wide berth.

Libby stuffed what was left of her hot dog into her mouth.

I stood and held out my arms wide. "Hey, I'm just trying to be the grown-up here, doing my job. You didn't expect I'd approve, right?"

"We don't want anyone to know we tried smack. You can't put

that in your paper," Anna said, pointing her finger at the slender notebook sticking out of my bag. "No names."

I'd expected some negotiation. I exhaled with defeat. "Okay. No names. I promise I won't get you in trouble."

"Don't look so sad," Anna ordered, arching her eyebrows to match her tone. She tugged at Libby's shirt; the two turned to the sidewalk.

"Let me give you a ride home," I called after them. "It's nearly midnight. You shouldn't be walking in the dark."

Libby turned to her cousin. "We can't walk. *You said* if we let her come along…Daddy'll be home." There was dread in her voice. I wondered if this was the deal they'd struck: I'd be their ride and their alibi.

The girls folded themselves into my car. I drove slowly, following Libby's directions to a gravel lot behind a white four-story clapboard building. Neither girl moved to get out of the car, but stared up at the orange lights blazing from the top floor.

"Will you come tell my dad we were with you?" Libby asked in a little girl voice.

I didn't like lying for them. But I wanted them to let me hang around. They were the first solid lead I'd had. I was convinced they knew more than they were admitting about the Dead Angels. I was sure that once they knew me better, they'd tell me their secrets. I'm not proud of that moment. But I nodded, agreeing to cover for them.

Anna glared at her cousin. "Why do you have to be such a baby?" She opened the car door and pushed Libby off her lap.

We trudged up the three flights of stairs in a tense silence. The girls stopped at the door, wrestling over who should be the first one through. Then Anna opened the door and shoved her cousin inside.

A man at a table pushed back his chair in a huff and yanked himself up, blood rushing to his face. "Where the hell have you been?" He stiffened when he saw me.

Libby lowered her eyes and shrugged. "We were just driving around. She took us to O'Malley's." She wrenched her head toward me.

The man was wearing a nylon T-shirt that stretched across his broad chest, then narrowed at his small waist. He eyed me suspiciously, his mouth clenched, then, a toothy smile broke out.

"Hello, ma'am," he said, dragging out his vowels in that country lilt he shared with his daughter. "And who might you be?" He stretched out his hand.

I grasped his palm firmly, as my father had taught me, feeling the calluses at the base of his muscular fingers. He had hazel eyes that twinkled in the catch of the light and an affable demeanor that hadn't been crushed yet by the city. He grinned like a boy and scratched his fist across the stubble on his sunburned cheeks. His tawny hair, still wet from a shower, was slicked back, emphasizing the hard lines of his face—the rigid jaw, the flat lips. There was something overtly masculine about him. Maybe it was the way he smelled of old timey aftershave, or how stray chest hairs poked from the top of his shirt or how his jeans hung on his hips, or how he stood, his legs in a wide stance, his imposing arms crossed in a mass of strength over his chest. So many men in the city were delicate and sleek, polished and pruned. This man had sinewy contours and rough edges.

"I'm...uh, a reporter...for the *Times*." I suddenly felt dizzy from the climb and the bright lights and the overpowering presence of this strange man.

The only thing I knew about Libby's father was that he had been a farmer who moved to Chicago to make money as a union machinist. As he stood under the yellow light, I could picture him on a sunny day in a fresh-tilled field, kneading the soil between his fingers, smelling its earthy fragrance and scanning his eyes across the neat crop rows, his face glowing with contentedness. I guessed we were about the same age, which meant I was old enough to be the girls' mother, a calculation that made me feel spinsterish.

The girls left us standing in our awkwardness and slumped on the couch, clicking through channels on the television. Electronic voices of unfamiliar people filled the room. Libby's father waved his hand toward the metal kitchen table. I reluctantly pulled out a chair, scraping it against the dingy linoleum and sat down, unsure what I would tell him.

"I'm Danny. So, my girls gonna be celebrities?"

I forced a laugh. "Nothing like that…just doing some research. Cops found the bodies of three girls in Chinatown. Spiked heroin. I wanted to know what girls their age were thinking." My guilt for having watched them smoke heroin had only escalated since I'd walked in the door, my nerves making my voice sound scratchy and thin. Anna and Libby weren't street kids. They had someone at home caring for them. What was I thinking?

Danny picked up a smoldering cigarette from an ashtray and held out a pack of Marlboros. I took one, hoping it would ease my anxiety.

"They tell you what drugs they do?" He glared at the girls. They flinched. "Yeah, they think I don't know what they're up to when I'm working, how they slink around with boys and try everything they can." He stared at me hard. "I know."

I averted my eyes, trying not to confirm his suspicions.

"I've been reading those stories." He pulled that day's paper off a chair and held it up. Coffee stains blotted my story about the fentanyl heroin. "These girls better *not* be doing any of that smack."

Libby and Anna sank farther into the couch, their earlier bravado dissolved.

"So who do you think is killing those girls?" he asked, snuffing out his cigarette.

"That's what I'm trying to find out."

He rubbed one hand over the other, leaned his head across the table and lowered his voice. "I get scared for the girls." His eyes were wide and watery. "I work at night. Sometimes double shifts. I can't always be here to protect them, watch out for them, you know? They remind me of me at their age, curious as hell. Gonna do *whatever* they want. It pains me what they might be up to… what could happen to them. Two girls in a city—"

I stood up abruptly, the chair scratching loudly across the floor. "I should go." I was overwhelmed with guilt for covering for the girls. "I just wanted...to make sure that they got home all right." I took out my card and laid it on the table.

He stood, and I noticed for the first time that he was barefoot. I felt my face blush, as if he'd revealed something private.

"I'll walk you to your car."

"That's not necessary."

He slid on a pair of worn cowboy boots near the door. "Where I come from, a man doesn't let a woman walk alone at night. It just isn't done." He smiled and winked. "You wouldn't want to injure my reputation, now would you?" He gazed at me a little too long.

I smiled uneasily. "Of course not."

He opened the door and followed me out. The night air was cool, and a yellow moon hung low in the sky. Its elegance startled me, and I stopped to marvel for a moment.

"You don't often see such beauty in the city," he whispered, only he wasn't looking up at the sky. His hand touched my back, gently, and I could feel the warmth of his fingers spreading through my thin shirt. "Thank you for bringing the girls home. I'm not sure what kind of mess they're in. Lord knows...I can tell you're trying not to get them in trouble with me."

I started to object. He held up his hand in protest.

"You got your job to do, but if you could watch out for my girls, I'd really appreciate it."

Stay objective. Don't get involved. The words hammered inside my head. I clipped down the stairs, racing ahead of him. His boots thumped behind me. I moved swiftly to my car, then slid into the front seat. He appeared at my window and crouched down, his face eerie in the moonlight. I looked away, convinced he knew. I'd been played—outsmarted—by two fifteen-year-olds who'd used me as a cover for doing drugs.

I rolled down my window and waited for him to say something. But he didn't. It felt like he was lingering for my confession. We stayed suspended like that, listening to the night sounds of the city: a radio playing softly through a screen window, a motorcycle braying, someone laughing in the distance.

He tapped his knuckles against the door. "You take care now. Hope to see you again—Natalie."

I backed out of the lot, my chest thumping, my mind spinning, the car taillights casting him in a red hue in my rearview mirror.

I meandered through Bridgeport before jumping onto Lake Shore Drive—LSD as some Chicagoans called it—headed to my apartment in Lakeview on the North Side. Sitting up straight, I burrowed my eyes into the treacherous S-curves that wrapped around the shore of Lake Michigan. My mind, though, remained firmly entrenched in Jackson Park, recalling the pungent smell of hot tinfoil, the sizzle of heroin tar, the aroma of trampled musk weed.

I tasted an eggy, acidic liquid rising up my throat, a pungent cocktail of regret, fear, and shame. I hadn't planned on supervising teenagers smoking heroin. I thought we were just going to talk, hang out so they could explain their appetite for a substance that had already taken so many lives. But teenagers aren't into self-reflection. They wanted to *show* me. They wanted me to experience it. And they really didn't get this line I'd drawn around myself, this invisible boundary that let me be with them but not be *like* them.

That night I saw firsthand how malleable heroin was; its simplicity as a street drug didn't necessarily involve needles, but rather something as innocuous as a candy bar wrapper and a spent toilet paper roll. The abstract story of Poison had taken on human form in front of me. I couldn't get the image of Danny's twisted and pained face out of my mind. Even more chilling, Anna's description of heroin-induced euphoria reminded me of Jake. He felt more alive to me as I stood in the same woods we'd once made out in, the same park where we would secretly meet. Getting involved with Anna and Libby threatened my vulnerable objectivity. But in order to discover the answers that had eluded the cops, I'd have to insert myself into the girls' parallel universe.

CHAPTER SIX

June 14, 2008

COPS: POISON HEROIN DEALER SENDS MESSAGE

WHITE TARGETS COULD BE RETALIATION

Chicago Times

That night, I dreamt I was the one smoking heroin and instead of Lester, it was Jake who held the pipe. My throat burned as if I'd swallowed hot coals. Bright colors swirled in my head. The drug gave me supernatural powers, a kind of double vision. Jake and I floated above the trees; at the same time, I was on the ground looking up at the sky. We glided over the city and peered down on people in their homes, loving and weeping, fighting and alone. We saw them touching themselves, imagining their caresses belonged to someone else. Something pierced me, and I fell heavily to the ground. I was human again. Jake was on top of me. The leaves crunched as he pressed against me. I felt powerless but unafraid. I heaved with pleasure, gasped for breath.

Then the phone rang.

I sat up in bed panting, my hair drenched with sweat, the handset whining.

"Yes?" I eked out, choking.

"Good morning." The voice was chipper and unmistakable.

"Hello, *Mom*." I fell back onto the bed.

"It's nearly nine o'clock, sweetie."

I imagined her sitting at my parents' kitchen table, the newspaper spread out between her and my father, her long gray hair loose and wavy, suggesting something untamed. Her face at that hour would be nude, her skin pinkish and smooth, except under her eyes where wrinkles collected in soft ripples. My father would be finishing *The New York Times* crossword puzzle and half-listening to her.

My parents, professors at the University of Chicago, still lived in my childhood home, a faded Victorian in Hyde Park with a backyard overgrown with thistles and blackberry brambles. As a kid, I thought every neighborhood was like ours, a place where educated whites and blacks lived side by side. As an adult, I saw the neighborhood as a cocoon protected by the country's largest private police force, defending its residents from the *other* South Side, a place of boarded-up buildings, strewn trash, and men with hot sauce-stained T-shirts and missing teeth. That world, for the most part, didn't touch my parents. They plastered Greenpeace bumper stickers on their hybrid car and kept a perennial row of political placards in the front yard. That year, of course, the lawn was covered with the Hyde Park Senator's campaign posters for the White House.

"I was out late, working on a story."

"Are you doing this alone?"

My father coughed in the background.

"Mom, we are *not* getting into this."

She sighed loudly. "How about coming over tomorrow for dinner?"

"I'm working on a big story, Mom, and you know I can't stop." I had planned another go at Anna and Libby that morning.

I could hear water and dishes clanking. My father, apparently, was clearing the table, probably trying to usher my mother off the phone. He'd always been the more lenient parent. But even he had been adamant about the safety of my brother and me as kids, drawing a map delineating where we could go. The twelve blocks around the university were shaded in light green. A two-block ring outside of that was yellow, and the areas beyond were stop sign red.

Every time I looked at that map, I had an urge to sneak into the red zone just to see what would happen. Jake had been part of that fascination. And now, the heroin story was luring me deep into that forbidden territory.

"Not even for a few hours on Sunday?" She sounded defeated.

"They're street kids, Mom. If I leave them for even a day, they might not let me hook up with them again."

My mother had raised me to be career-minded, a choice she seemed to regret when I put my job first.

"Look, if I get a break, I'll stop by. Okay?"

"Fine." She sounded sullen. "Natalie...*please* be careful."

I touched the scabs on my back from Lester's dog. "I will, Mom, I promise."

No one talked about the dangers of the job. Few editors or reporters knew what it was like to interview drug addicts or street people. Reporters generally got their information through official channels: government flaks, corporate spokespeople, lawyers. The territory most crime reporters moved in, though, was unsanctioned and off the map. Beyond maintaining ethical boundaries, there were few rules, except to get the story and not get hurt.

No matter how hard I tried to explain to my editors—and my parents—they just couldn't grasp how paranoid people at the margins are, how once I'd gained their trust, I couldn't clock out at five p.m. I had to speed up time, make people feel safe to confide in me within a day or two. I usually tagged along until the novelty of my presence wore off and people acted like themselves, forgetting there was a stranger watching, listening, and scribbling notes about everything they did and said. It's what I'd planned to do with Anna and Libby that day.

I pulled on a pair of Lycra bike shorts and a T-shirt. My plan was to ride my bike over to Bridgeport, to show up casually and see if the girls were around. They may have thought they were done with me, but I had my own game too.

Standing at the kitchen counter drinking coffee and eating a granola bar, I scanned the front page of the morning newspaper.

My story on the Dead Angels was stripped across the top. So that was the reason my mother had called.

• • •

I pedaled south facing the sun and the wind. I felt like a teenager, my life as carefree as a Saturday bike ride. The air was sticky, hinting at an afternoon shower. The path was crowded with twenty-some-things. But once I got past downtown, the asphalt was mostly clear and the vistas of the lake broader. Just beyond Soldier Field, I turned off and headed toward Bridgeport, past its cigar-shaped shacks and crumbling warehouses. I rolled along the narrow side streets, weaving between Mexican girls carrying babies on their hips and past the taquerias, their signs adorned with images of Our Lady of Guadalupe, and inhaled the aroma of spicy pork that seeped through screen doors.

At the girls' white-frame apartment building, everyone was asleep. There were no voices, no angry words being hurled about, no hard footsteps over cheap linoleum—no noises through open windows. I sat on the front stoop and waited for signs of life.

I'd spent the past month leaning over yellow police tape, watching as the body of one heroin victim after another was packed into the coroner's black SUV. I talked to parents of the dead girls, their friends, their boyfriends, girlfriends, cousins, anyone who would venture to guess who was behind the killer heroin. I talked to judges and prosecutors. I interviewed drug counselors and former junkies, picking up some of the colorful slang.

On the street, heroin went by unusual monikers: schmack, schmeck, score, tecata, antifreeze, Big H, Henry, Hombre, Rambo, black pearl, brown sugar, caca, carne, Charley, China cat, dust, hell dust, heaven dust and—my favorite—Sweet Jesus. Back in the seventies when the heroin epidemic hit the United States, it cost thirty dollars for a bag that was about twenty-eight percent pure. In 2008, a baggie was eighty percent pure and sold for as little as five dollars, cheaper than a six-pack of beer or a couple packs of cigarettes. Modern heroin was so pure it didn't have to be injected, luring more people afraid of needles. With such purity, it was much easier to overdose, especially if the drug was cut with something as poisonous as fentanyl.

Even before Poison, Chicago ranked number one in the U.S. for heroin overdoses. Twice as many heroin users wound up in hospital emergency rooms in Chicago than in New York City, three times as many as Boston. Mo explained that Chicago was one of the first hubs for heroin, arriving from Mexico in its purest state before it was cut, repackaged, and distributed.

I thought about this as I picked at peeling paint on the stoop, wondering where the girls fit in this distribution pyramid. A group of guys strode toward me. Decked out in flashy sportswear—expensive sneakers, gold chains, baseball caps, and jerseys—they swung their arms, ready to take on the world. Lester led the pack, clearly the OG—original gangster. He recognized me, stopped, and smiled, the stones in his mouth glittering.

"Hey, boys. You wanna meet a celebrity? This here's an *in-vest-i-ga-tive* reporter. She's come to write *my* story."

The "boys" grunted approvingly.

"That's cool, Big Dog," said one.

"All right, my man. A lady reporter. Way to go. Honey, you want to take down my story?" Another one said, thrusting his pelvis near my face.

I leaned back on the steps. "Sorry, I've hit my quota of high school dropouts with sagging pants."

"What you say?" the guy yelled.

Lester laughed and pushed him away. "I'll see you niggas later."

As soon as they were out of earshot, Lester's come-easy attitude turned sharp. "What you want? Didn't you get enough last night?"

I turned away.

"Are you mad because my doggie hurt you?"

"Fuck off, Lester."

He sat next to me and toyed with a straw in his mouth.

"What you want to know, Snow White? I'll tell you." He leaned on my shoulder, whispering against my cheek.

I pushed him off me. "Straight up?" I said in a harsh street voice.

"Straight up. But if my name gets in the paper…" He lifted his jersey to reveal his rippled abdomen and the handle of a gun snug against his underwear. I tried not to flinch.

"You in a family?" I said, casually.

"You watch too much TV, Snow White. It ain't like that."

"Oh yeah? Gangster Disciples and Mickey Cobras run drugs on the South Side. Which are you?"

He wrung his fingers into fists, then let out a menacing laugh. "Snow White, you don't have a clue."

"So fill me in."

He frowned as if my questions pained him. "You're just as fuckin' stupid as Po-Po." He stood to leave.

"What good's it doing you?" I casually lit a cigarette.

"What you talking about?"

"You know. All that shit you got up there." I tapped a fingernail to my temple. "Nobody cares what you know. Not unless they're some wannabes, like those boys you got following you. How do I know *you're* real, anyway? Maybe you're just playing."

"You wanna see real?" He turned around and yanked up his shirt to reveal a six-pointed star with two pitchforks on his back, a crude prison tat.

"Jesus, that must have hurt."

"It ain't for pussies." He straightened his shirt.

"So you got cred. You're a GD. Congrats."

"*Was.* And it don't mean shit. My brother *was* a Mickey. Anyone can join a gang."

"So what are you now?"

"Let's just say I joined a different gang when I was inside, okay, Snow White?"

"You mean The Nation?"

"What do you know about that?"

"I know white guys go to prison and become disciples of Jesus or Hitler. Black guys go to prison and start quoting Tupac, Martin Luther King, or Malcolm X. So which is it?"

He hemmed and bobbed his head, but didn't respond. Then he pulled out a wad of money and peeled off a hundred-dollar bill, holding it to my face. "This be my religion, Snow White."

"And where do the girls fit in your *religion?*"

"I'm exposing them to the power of black supremacy." He smiled, biting on the straw. "It's difficult for white people to submit to black leadership because the white race was given dominion." It sounded as if he were quoting a text by memory.

"What's that from?"

"The Prophet."

"Which one?"

"You wouldn't understand," he scoffed.

"Right. Being white and all. You sound like Farrakhan."

Lester laughed. "He's old school. Ain't you never heard of Mohammed X? He's the new messiah."

"You mean the guy they call the Black Hitler? That guy's a terrorist."

"Call him what you want. A prophet is never accepted in his own city."

"What's all this got to do with Anna and Libby?"

"They're part of the *enterprise.* Soon the sweet stuff won't be so free, and they'll have to work for their Daddy Lest-*ah.*" He twisted the straw between his glittering teeth, forming a knot.

"And if they don't?"

"Oh, they always do. In the meantime, I get myself some nice, fresh boot-*ee.*"

"That is fucked up."

"Look." Lester pushed up his Prada sunglasses. "I'm just makin' a livin'. And these girls got nowhere to go."

I looked down at a dandelion growing in a crack of the sidewalk. "Why are you telling me this?"

He laughed his guttural *hey-hey-hey* and put his hand suggestively on my thigh. "Maybe I'm tired of Po-Po thinking they know everything. Maybe I'm bored, and I want a sweet thing like you to write my story. Maybe I just want to lick your *asssss.*"

I pushed away his hand.

"How do you know I won't go to the cops and tell them you're selling heroin?"

"And what would you tell 5-0 he don't already know?"

So some cop might be taking a cut, letting him know when he was on the radar. Or maybe he had a connected relative who was paying off a lieutenant to look the other way.

Lester quickly stood up. "I need some beer. Let's take your car."

I pointed to my purple Trek in the bushes, relieved I didn't have to haul around a felon.

"So we'll slap it." He pulled me up to walk.

I reluctantly got up, wishing in that moment that I were one of those reporters sitting in the air-conditioned newsroom writing my story from a press release. If Lester really was a heroin dealer on the South Side, he knew other dealers, and maybe I could cajole him into telling me what he knew about the Poison dealer.

• • •

The liquor store had steel bars on the windows and door. Inside, it was so dark I could barely see. Lester headed to a refrigerated case and grabbed a twelve-pack of Budweiser. I pulled out a six-pack of MGD. I didn't normally drink during the day, even with a source, but I knew the quickest path to friendship on the streets was through alcohol. Lester plunked his beer on the checkout counter, then demanded a couple packs of Marlboros. The cashier pulled them from the slot on the wall, tapped an old-fashioned adding machine, and announced the total. Lester looked at me, grabbed the beer, and walked out.

We barely spoke on the way back to Anna and Libby's. Instead of sitting on the front stoop, Lester looped behind the girls' apartment building toward a cluster of trees and spread out on his back under the largest one. He flicked the tab on his beer can and sucked the foam running down the sides. Someone had stuck a Democratic campaign bumper sticker on the base of the tree, and Lester glanced back at it approvingly.

"Here's to a brother in the White House." He raised his can.

"You think it'll make a difference?"

He shrugged. "Nothing matters until white people feel pain. Then they look around for answers. No one cared about how we're suffering down here on the South Side. Now, look. Cops all over the place. Everybody wanting to know who killed a few white girls. Didn't matter when they was hauling out black bodies."

I tossed my empty bottle at the base of the tree. Lester crinkled his beer can and hit mine, as if we were playing urban croquet.

"Where's your brother?" I asked.

Lester bit his lip and stared ahead as if he hadn't heard me.

"He's dead," he blurted. "H. Sold it. Snorted it. Killed him."

"I didn't know the Mickeys allowed their members to sample the product."

He turned toward me, a madness in his eyes, his hand tight in a fist. "It was spiked. A hotshot."

"So the Mickeys killed one of their own?"

"Don't know who spiked it. The mother fuckin' po-lice didn't do their goddamn job and in-vest-i-gate. He was just another dead nigga, the way they like it."

"So you blame the cops?"

"Snow White, there's things I wish I could tell you. But I gotta protect number one."

"You think the Poison killer is targeting white kids so cops will pay attention to crime on the South Side?"

"Makes sense to me. We got people dying every damn day. And nobody cares about them." He cocked his head. A strange grin spread across his face. "But then again, what if it's not? What if it was an accident and a few white girls just *happened* to get killed? What if it's just some weird coincidence, and now people are seeing things where there ain't things?"

It was nearly noon when the door to the girls' apartment

opened. Anna stepped out, lit a cigarette, and leaned over the railing. When she spotted us, she waved for us to come up.

The apartment shades were drawn, and the air conditioner spewed a constant mist of frigid air. The living room smelled of aftershave, Listerine, and smoke. I looked around, half-hoping Danny was there. The girls moved about in slow motion, drinking Mountain Dew, even refusing a beer Lester offered.

I gave him a dirty look and shook my head. "I can't be buying beer for minors."

"Ain't no big deal." He sunk into a leopard-print velvet chair, propped his feet on the coffee table, and opened his third can. I sat on a dank-smelling couch. We passed the afternoon in a haze of cigarette smoke, Lester regaling us with stories about dealing cocaine before he went to prison. I listened, taking mental notes.

After a few hours, Lester's posse trickled in and helped themselves to Lester's beer.

"How old are these guys?" I asked.

"It's my damn beer, Snow White. I'll do whatever the fuck I want with it."

I let out a heavy sigh. "I have to go." It was becoming harder and harder to draw boundaries.

Anna walked me to the door, a few feet from the living room. A sliver of sunlight slipped through the shades, lighting up her face. She ran a hand through her hair, a gesture I recognized as insecurity. "Can you come back tonight?" she whispered.

"This is all getting too strange. I have a story to write. I need to find some girls who have survived Poison."

She picked a stray hair off my shirtsleeve and held it to the light. "It's weird. It's like we could be related or something."

"You remind me of myself when I was your age." I'd had the same fickle mood swings.

"Right. I bet you were a cheerleader. Some goody-goody."

"Not really. I was too much of a tomboy." I couldn't tell if she was still raw about how I'd questioned Lester's motives the night before. He was staring at us from the living room.

"We could go do something fun tonight." There was an eagerness in her voice. "Maybe you could take us downtown. We could go to a club." It was the friendliest she'd been, yet I had the distinct sense I was being set up—again.

"They would never let you in, Anna. You're too young."

"Not if I was with you. There's this cool dance club called the Underground. They have these rooms like caves, and you dance in the dark and people wear these glow-in-the-dark neon strings. It would be so much fun." Her green eyes widened with excitement.

"I can show you fun, Anna," Lester shouted from his throne. He slouched on the couch, his jersey pulled up to reveal a wife-beater T-shirt. He fingered the fist charm on his neck chain as he stuck his other hand in the waist of his jeans.

Anna flashed him a smile. Though she was eager for his attention, she seemed uneasy around him. I wondered if he had done something to her or if she simply feared what he was capable of. She turned to me, her eyes pleading, and whispered in my ear: "I can show you some people. Like me. *Girls.*"

It was the first time she'd acknowledged she knew other white girls dabbling with heroin. Was this a set-up? She'd likely use me to get into a club, then desert me once she was inside. But this *was* the invitation I'd been waiting for, the passage into the secret world of girls doing drugs.

"Text me. I'll meet you there." I grinned at Lester.

He glared back in his menacing way. This was turning into a contest of loyalties. At that moment he was losing, and he wasn't the kind of guy who lost without putting up a dirty fight.

CHAPTER SEVEN

June 14, 2008

DEAD ANGELS' DEATHS SHOCK CLASSMATES

GIRLS WERE KNOWN AS STUDIOUS, NOT RISKY

Chicago Times

I was watching *When Harry Met Sally* on late night cable. My cat, Deadline, was curled on my belly. The film was a favorite, partly because Harry and Sally were University of Chicago students. The movie had reached its famous restaurant scene when Sally (Meg Ryan) loudly fakes an orgasm. My cell phone buzzed: a text.

"Warehse Prty-- 100 Clintn"

I slowly got up from the couch. It was nearly midnight, and I'd long written off Anna's invitation to join her at a downtown party as a bravado performance in front of Lester. I thought once I'd refused to drive her, she'd find someone else with wheels. But looking at the text, I wondered what Anna's game was now. I pulled on a long, sheer black skirt with short shorts underneath and chose a filmy burgundy blouse that barely veiled my black bra. Then I outlined my eyes with "Party Noir" and my lips in "Violet Vixen." I looked like a cross between a vampire slut and a Goth girl.

The West Loop bars were packed when the taxi dropped me off just after midnight. Music poured through open doors; people clustered together smoking in the cool night air. Kids sat on the curb wearing bright clothes—their faces painted blue and pink, their hair sparkling with glitter. I was about to ask a couple how to get into the club when an older man stepped from the building's façade.

"You want to go up?" He was thin with a craggy face.

"How much?"

He looked me up and down. "Twenty."

I pulled the bill from my tiny nightclub purse and headed toward the door.

"Wait, miss." He tugged at my arm. "I'll need to see some ID."

"You've got to be kidding." I pointed at the kids on the curb. One girl was hanging her head between her knees puking.

"Rules, ma'am. They have IDs."

"Fake IDs, I'm sure." I fished out my driver's license and handed it to him.

I could see him calculating my age. "You looking for someone? Your daughter, maybe?"

I snatched the license back. "That's none of your business."

He laughed and let me pass.

The foyer was dark. "This way, miss," another man called. He pointed a flashlight down a long, narrow hallway. I walked in step to the sound of his boots and a dull vibration from the music above us. The hall veered sharply to the left, then the right, snaking behind gallery storefronts, then ended abruptly at a set of swinging doors. I stepped into a cavernous but brightly lit receiving dock. Several kids were waiting by a freight elevator.

I stood behind them, listening to their talk about a band that was supposed to be playing. The three boys and a girl seemed to have coordinated their look: black hair dye, leather jackets with silver studs, black T-shirts, tight jeans, chains around their necks and chunky Frankenstein boots. They smelled like burnt grass. One smiled with a mouth full of braces.

A loud grinding noise signaled the elevator's arrival. The door rolled open and a tall, skinny black man motioned for us to get in. I walked tentatively toward him, all the while longing to be home on my couch. The man rolled the door closed, released a giant lever.

"Two or three?" he shouted.

"Two," someone responded.

I shrugged.

"Two then," he decided for me.

We lurched upward. I grabbed a railing along the wall. Then the man pulled the brake and rolled open the door. Sounds flew at us: a profusion of booms and the roar of people talking, screaming. The kids rushed around me, the hem of my sheath swirling in their wake.

The floor trembled from the thump, thump, thump of the screechy music. Arms punched the air to the beat. Rays of purple and red flashed across the ceiling and onto the bodies jumping and jerking. The floor glowed orange, and the air smelled of incense. Lighted tables offered various wares: T-shirts, CDs, Jell-O shots, neon-lighted headbands. A long line snaked to a table where they could buy balloons, filled with nitrous oxide. No one looked older than twenty, maybe twenty-two. Some of the girls wore lingerie, others bras and bodices with shorts or skirts. Several teetered on high heels with garters, their heads topped with towering wigs that had plastic animals peering out. Almost all were white.

Someone bumped me. I turned around to meet the hairy chin of a guy wearing a white tuxedo, his dirty-blond dreadlocks pulled into a ponytail. He looked tan, as if he spent his days walking North Avenue Beach selling beads and *'juana*. His eyes fluttered, and I wondered what he was on.

"Hey, *Momma*, what are you doing here?"

"I'm not your *Momma*. And I'm looking for someone."

"Some*one* or some*thing*? How about one of these?" He held out a handful of smiley-faced pills.

I shook my head.

"Come on, *Momma*. For you, it's free."

"Stop calling me *Momma*." I stood on my toes trying to spot Anna, then texted her: "2nd floor, b-loons."

"You seem a little lost."

"Why are you still here?"

"Is there someone I can help you find?"

"You know all these people?"

"Most. They're regulars. They show up wherever we do."

I felt a finger in my back and turned to see Anna in a tight leather dress that revealed her pale belly and back.

"You came!" she yelled.

"Is this your mother, Anna?" Dreadlocks asked.

Anna glared at him. "Let's go." She tugged at me. "The third floor is where we want to be." She dove into the crowd like it was water. The man disappeared in our wake.

"Who was that?" I asked once we'd reached the quiet stairwell.

"He's a *wigger*. His name's Rapper X. He's a drug dealer. Hangs out at all these parties."

"Why do you call him a wigger?"

"Because he's trying to act black when he's not. Says he's half or something. He's just there all the time, hanging onto people. He's creepy. But he knows *everyone*."

We started climbing the stairwell, illuminated only by tiny lights along the steps.

"I hope you have money," she said. "It's a hundred dollars to get on the third floor."

"What? Why so much?"

"You'll see."

"I only have eighty bucks. Maybe. And a credit card."

"Cash only."

She kept climbing the stairs, undeterred.

How could Anna afford this place? Having been at the paper five years, I had just reached top union scale for reporters, which wasn't a lot. But seventy-five thousand a year went pretty far in Chicago if you were single and didn't have kids. Even at that, I never went to clubs that charged more than a twenty-dollar cover.

At the top of the stairs an anorexic woman with tattooed arms in a skin-tight dress studied a clipboard as if tracking reservations at a four-star restaurant. The woman nodded when Anna held her wrist under a blue light revealing a dragon stamp.

I pulled out a wad of wrinkled bills that I knew didn't add up to the cover. The anorexic rolled her eyes and snatched the money. "Go ahead." She huffed and pulled back a black drape. Anna stepped through ahead of me. A faint light was enough to see the expanse of the warehouse floor subdivided into party rooms, each a canvas cube. We walked down an aisle peeking inside those with their doors open, as if we were touring an art show.

"Where's Libby?" I asked.

"She doesn't like my suburban friends. Besides, this is too rich for her."

"Where'd *you* get the money?"

She smiled. "It doesn't matter. Girls here all have cash—and lots of it."

We peered into open booths where occupants were in some state of undress, passed out or making out. Some people stared back, seemingly inviting us in with their eyes. I slowed, watching, feeling like a voyeur, but Anna pressed on with a determined stride, maneuvering me around clumps of people gawking at the erotic performances. The third-floor crowd was older, many in their late twenties and thirties. Finally, Anna stopped before a booth with its canvas door pulled shut.

"These are the girls you want to meet." Her face was strained. "You can't say you're a reporter. You're just a friend. Don't say anything stupid."

Before I could object, Anna flipped open the canvas door and the smell of menthol smacked me in the face. Five girls were stretched out on large pillows. Their glossy hair, smooth skin, and flawless makeup gave them that polished look of tabloid celebrities. Each had a designer handbag the size of a small suitcase attached to her hip. One girl was smoking a cigarette; another was dipping her fingers into a jar of Vicks and massaging it onto her chest—said to enhance the effects of ecstasy. Two others were sucking on medicinal-looking lollipops as they picked through the contents of a large bowl. A Goth-looking fifth girl lay on her back in a comatose state, a fixed expression on her face, her features etched in black.

The girls struck me as belonging to that hedonistic species of popular teens—the alluring, suburban girls with perfectly straight teeth and their fat in all the right places. They looked older than the Dead Angels, but they were definitely of that private school ilk. Everything about them—their clothes, their posture, and that entitled, aloof demeanor—suggested they were the cool girls, the kind who set the standards of what drugs and sex were acceptable among their peers.

"Girls, this is Natalie," Anna announced. "Her friends didn't show up, so she's going to hang with us."

"Hey," they said in a bored unison.

The girl with the cigarette waved for us to sit. The canvas walls dulled the clamor outside enough that we could hear each other with some effort. The rhythmic pulse of the music turned the tent into a womb, a safe and warm place.

"This is Cate," Anna said, plopping down on a pillow. I sat next to her.

"Hey," Cate said. She had fragile features: small facial bones, a tiny nose set off by a diamond stud, long blonde hair, and wispy pale eyelashes that fluttered like bug wings over bulging fly-like eyes. She stared at the other girls as if they were actresses in a live theatre and she a passive spectator.

Anna motioned to the girl with the Vicks jar. "That's Olivia—she's the boss."

"Oh, Anna. You can call me a bitch but don't call me a *boss*. That's so—*pedestrian...*" She rolled her eyes, waved her fingers smeared with goop, and gave me a frigid grin. Her gray eyes were dramatically outlined, swirled to a point, like an ancient Egyptian. She must have been the inspiration for Anna's eye flourish. Her bright red lips were so puffy they looked like an appendage. Her black hair, teased on top, cascaded down her back in long, soft ringlets. I tried not to stare, but she looked so familiar.

"And that's Rory." Anna pointed at the Goth girl, whose appearance didn't match the others. She was sitting now, combing her fingers through her tar black hair, an expression of boredom stuck on her face. Her eyes and mouth were shaded in an inky black. She wore black leather pants with silver chains looped around her waist and a gossamer blouse so thin that I could see piercings through her nipples. But the feature that really set her apart was the cerulean blue butterfly tattoo spread across the front of her neck. Beautiful and intricately designed, the tattoo reminded me of a large, garish birthmark.

"Those two girls, if you can't tell, are twins, Madison and MacKenzie." Anna continued with her introductions. The girls waved in tandem. They had identical features: chalky, pale skin, yellow-blonde hair, and iridescent green eyes.

The twins passed the bowl of brightly colored pills to Anna.

"Got any more lollipops?" Anna asked.

Everyone looked at Olivia. She smiled, as if amused by the idea, then pulled a plastic stick that looked like a giant Q-tip from her purse.

Cate snatched the lollipop from Olivia's hand. "No, Liv. She's too young." There was a sudden panic in her voice.

The twins held up their suckers and stuck out their blood red tongues, mocking Anna. "You're too young, you're too young!" they trilled.

"Cate's right," Olivia said. "You're not at that level *yet*. Soon, though." She blew Anna a kiss. "Don't worry. Cate can't be your babysitter forever." She flicked her long acrylic nails toward the bowl in Anna's hands. "Besides, there's some good stuff in there."

Anna sat back and pouted as she dug through the pills.

"What are these?" She held up a periwinkle blue oval.

"They're our mom's diet pills," one twin said.

"Good stuff. You get high, and you're not hungry," the other twin promised.

Olivia *ooohed* with approval.

I eyed Anna and shook my head. She made a face.

"Get over it," she whispered in my ear and handed me the bowl. "If you want to hang with us, you have to pick a pill. Rules."

"No way," I whispered back.

Someone passed around a bottle of cranberry vodka and each girl took turns washing down pills. It all seemed like a strange nightclub communion, and I laughed.

"I mean it," Anna whispered sternly. "You don't get to judge." She held out a yellow smiley face.

I fished out a blue diet pill. Just a little speed, I reasoned. I downed the pill with a slug of vodka. I didn't want to do drugs, but what was the harm in taking a diet pill, especially if it allowed me to hang with these girls who, Anna had suggested, were into H?

Anna, with her crooked smile and her toy tattoo on her shin, and I, with my diaphanous skirt and faux leather gladiator sandals, were clearly the interlopers.

"What cult do they come from?" I asked.

She giggled. "They're North Shore girls home from college for the summer."

Something about Olivia's face—the ghostly eyes and that regal nose—made me certain I'd seen her before. Anna saw me staring and said, sotto voce: "Olivia's grandfather is a bazillionaire. That's how she gets such good drugs. Her family owns Byrne Pharmaccuticals."

"Byrne? You mean her grandfather is Oliver Byrne?"

Anna shrugged. "Yeah, I guess."

Oliver Byrne was the pharmaceuticals mogul leading the drive to raise money for Chicago's bid to host the 2016 Summer Olympics. His monarchial image—shock of white hair, long, stately nose, piercing green eyes—appeared on the paper's front page nearly every day, as he and his cronies plotted what properties on the South Side were to be gobbled up as part of the proposed Olympic City. That's why Olivia looked so familiar: She had the family face.

"And the twins? Who are they?"

Anna squinted at them. "Their dad is some big hedge fund guy. He named his company after them."

"Let me guess: their dad is Richard Morrisey and the company is the Mad-Mac Fund?"

"Something like that."

"What's the story on Rory? She looks a little wild for this crowd."

"She's an heir to The Estate. You know, those hotels that don't have a name and you have to be a member? Mega, mega rich girl. Her dad wears earrings and lipstick." She rolled her eyes. "*She* could wear poop on her face if she wanted to, and no one would say a thing. She's kind of this wannabe bad girl."

I nodded. Her father—a cross dresser and heir to one of the largest hotel chains in the country—went by John or Joana Pretz. "And Cate?"

She leaned over. "Her dad was some big politician. Maybe he still is. He got caught fucking one of his interns. Don't say anything to her. She gets *so* upset if you mention it." She meant Senator Dixon, who had just been re-elected in a comeback campaign after having resigned in the middle of what was known as "Interngate."

I leaned back on a pillow, breathed in a mouthful of the menthol-laced air, and felt my mouth turning up in a wide grin, privately relishing my good fortune to have landed among the descendants of some of the most prestigious Chicagoans. These were exactly the kinds of girls who'd been experimenting with Poison. No reporter had gotten in with this kind of crowd. The question was: How did Anna, a girl seemingly living on the margins, end up with this crew?

Olivia jumped up and ordered us to the dance floor. Anna pulled me along, sidling up to Cate as we walked.

"Cate's cousin died from poisoned heroin," Anna volunteered.

Cate nodded without emotion. "She was one of the first girls."

"I'm sorry to hear that," I said in my most sensitive voice, knowing I'd need to press Cate later about the details.

We reached the dance floor, a visual assault of colored lights flickering along the ceiling and into the crowd. Olivia pointed to a group of girls, and the others joined them.

Anna pulled me back. "I don't like those girls," she said, nodding her head toward several tall blondes dancing with Olivia and the others. "They're from my old neighborhood."

"Which neighborhood?"

"Wilmette."

Anna didn't strike me as someone from one of Chicago's über wealthy suburbs.

"Didn't I tell you?" she asked. "My stepdad is rich. And he's fucking my mother, which makes him a rich motherfucker."

I stopped dancing and stared at her. When she brought up her stepfather, Anna's face darkened, as if there was something sinister about him.

"Cate was my babysitter," she hollered. "Her parents think she won't do anything illegal with me. She tells them we go to late-night movies." Her face lit in a mischievous grin. "If they knew she was with *those girls*, they'd never let her out of the house, especially after what happened to her cousin."

"Why wouldn't Cate let you have a sucker?"

Anna looked at me in disbelief. "You don't know?"

I shook my head.

"It was an F-stick."

"'F' as in fentanyl? Like a fentanyl lollipop?"

Fentanyl lollipops were used in hospitals to relieve intense pain suffered by cancer patients who didn't respond to other pain medications. The suckers had become popular, especially among clubbers who thought they were emulating movie stars.

"Olivia always has weird drugs."

Before I could ask what other drugs Olivia kept in her giant Hermès bag, Cate—Anna's former babysitter—and Rory—the Goth—were standing behind us. Cate jerked her head for us to follow. In a makeshift lounge, people were lying on beanbag chairs and smoking. Rory, her black makeup looking even more ghoulish in the neon strobes, lit a joint and handed it to Cate. I pulled out my clove cigarettes and offered one to Anna. We stood by open windows, feeling the breeze against our damp bodies, gazing at the Chicago River and the lighted drawbridges spanning its crooked banks.

"Why do you think your cousin did it?" I asked Cate.

She seemed introspective, staring out the window, but her mood turned harsh. "Because this is easy." She waved her arms at the crowd in their gaudy outfits. "Any girl with money can come here. It's like shopping at Bloomingdale's. Hardly an adventure. But going to the South Side and scoring the most dangerous shit? Now, that's an *adventure*." She spoke in a mocking tone, her face contorted. Rory, slouched against the windowsill, watched with spooky eyes.

"But they knew they could die, right?" I couldn't help myself. It was the first time I'd met anyone with genuine insight into why girls were willing to try such a dangerous drug.

Rory peeled herself from the window and straightened with authority. "Some girls want to do the most powerful stuff so they can *brag* about it, so they can say they *nearly died*; they know what it *feels* like to die, to be dead, and then come back. They think it gives them special powers to go to the other side and come back alive. It's like they're a little club of vampires, an exclusive sorority of the *dark side*." She laughed and stroked her fingers down her neck, as if she were petting her butterfly.

"And who do they let in?"

She turned to me with a snap of anger in her eyes. "Why? You want to join?"

"No. I just mean…aren't they afraid the stuff is going to kill them?"

Rory made a cynical, harsh sound that made me think she was making fun of me.

This time Cate spoke up. "My cousin said she felt invincible, that it was the most alive she'd ever felt because she knew she was risking everything. It's like playing Russian roulette, but instead of guns they use syringes. And—"

Cate stiffened; Olivia, flanked by the twins and several other acolytes, approached. There was a sour look on Olivia's face. "What's this? Having a private party, huh?"

Cate tried to hide the joint behind her back. "Just getting some air."

"What have you got there?" Olivia nodded toward Cate's hand. Cate shrugged and held up the nub.

Olivia reached over and snatched the blunt, taking a long drag before holding it out to the others. They shook their heads.

"Sure you don't want something stronger, Cate? I mean, we smoked weed in *high school*." A slice of laughter. The others' shrill voices echoed Olivia's.

Rory grabbed the nub, took a long drag, and exhaled a cloud into Olivia's face. "Don't be such a *cunt*."

"Let's go back," Anna said, pulling at Cate and me. Cate didn't budge.

"Go on. I'll catch up with you later," Cate said, her voice wavering.

"What was that all about?" I whispered to Anna when we were out of earshot.

"Old rivalries."

So there was division amongst the girls as to what drugs were cool. Olivia and the twins seemed the type who might experiment with H, an easy jump from sucking on fentanyl lollipops. But Rory and Cate appeared dismissive of the vampire girls, the ones shooting Poison. I wondered where Anna fit along that spectrum. With her cavalier attitude about heroin, her affinity for trying everything once, not to mention her penchant for imitating Olivia, Anna seemed likely to join ranks with the girls doing fentanyl drugs.

By the time we started dancing again, I was sweating, the room was spinning, and the lights felt like they were burning my skin.

"I don't think that was a diet pill," I yelled into Anna's ear.

"Of course not, silly. It was probably ecstasy or something. That's why they call it the mystery bowl. Everyone gets a little *surprise*." She winked.

I closed my eyes and imagined myself as a twirling dervish,

twisting and circling while this warmth moved into my feet, traveling up my legs, my torso, my throat, my scalp. For a moment I forgot where I was. I felt happy, twirling in the neon lights. But when I opened my eyes, I didn't recognize anyone.

"Anna," I screamed. "Anna, where are you?" I was met by a blur of strange faces. I scanned the dance floor; there was no Olivia or her fan club. I ran back to the lounge; they weren't there either. I ran through the aisles, listening for Anna's laugh. I couldn't remember which of the tented cubicles belonged to the girls.

Finally, exhausted and dizzy, I headed to the elevator. When the door rolled open, the operator smiled knowingly. After meandering through the maze of dark hallways, I stumbled out the front door, dazed and confused. The streetlights gave off an eerie yellow hue, as if a fog had suddenly descended on the downtown. A passing cab driver hit the brakes and backed up. I thought maybe Anna might have gone back to her cousin's apartment. I pulled out Libby's address I'd written on a scrap of paper and handed it to the driver.

The lights were off when the taxi pulled up. I paid him with my credit card, then climbed the stairs, feeling winded at the top, and knocked. Finally, I heard heavy footsteps and the clicks of the door unlocking.

Danny appeared bare-chested, wearing unbuttoned jeans, as if he'd thrown them on in a hurry.

"Natalie? What are you doing here?"

"Is Anna here?" My voice sounded panicked. Why hadn't I considered that Danny would be home? How stupid.

He squinted and shook his head. "At a friend's. Libby's with her mother for the weekend." He rubbed his eyes with the back of his hand. "It's kind of late."

I looked over the railing at the taxi pulling out of the lot.

He saw it too. "Wanna come in?"

It was dark inside except for a light over the stove. A half-empty bottle of Jack Daniels was on the table next to an overflowing ashtray and a smoldering cigarette.

"Bet you weren't counting on company this late, huh?" I tried not to slur my words. I needed to leave, but in my state, I couldn't calculate how to get home. I hadn't considered how showing up drunk and drugged might alarm Danny and threaten my access to the girls. But if Danny realized I was crocked, he didn't show it.

"Just got off work." He pulled out a chair for me. "Wanna drink?" He set two shot glasses on the table. I nodded and sat down mutely. Danny poured the whiskey to the brim. Then he held up his glass. "To strangers in the night." He seemed tired or drunk, maybe both, and eager for company.

I bolted mine, not wanting to appear a sissy, and felt the burn down my throat. Danny wiped his mouth with his thumb and lined up the glasses again.

"A girl who knows how to drink. I'm impressed."

He looked at me like he was daring me, his eyes laughing. I didn't have the good sense to back off. It didn't take long before the combination of the mystery drug and the liquor set in. The room felt wobbly, the objects wavering as if they were alive. I closed my eyes and wrapped my fingers under the metal seat.

When I looked across the table, instead of Danny's bristly cheeks, I saw Jake's smooth potato skin and the milky scar on his chin. He smiled back at me with those teasing malachite eyes that had always made my stomach flutter. God, how I missed him. I touched his forearm, leaning on him more than I'd meant. His skin felt warm, and when I looked up at his face, he was the Jake I remembered. He bent down, his lips dusting mine. It was a sweet kiss, not unlike our last.

CHAPTER EIGHT

June 15, 2008

ANGELS' FAMILIES HOLD MEMORIAL SERVICES
HUNDREDS PACK AREA CHURCHES
REMEMBERING POISONED GIRLS
Chicago Times

I woke to the "Marimba" jingle on my cell phone coming from somewhere in the apartment. Danny and I were on the couch, his arms wrapped around me, a throw cover draped over us. I squirmed under his arms, lifted myself up, and lurched toward the kitchen, answering the phone on its last ring.

A long sigh on the other end greeted me.

"Sorry to wake you." It was Amy, my editor. I wondered how long I'd been asleep. "We have a minor crisis. Shaqueta is sick, and she was supposed to cover the National Islamic Conference today."

Shaqueta was our latest urban affairs reporter. Any event that had an African-American connection was usually assigned to the urban affairs reporter—who was always black—as if to demonstrate the paper's diverse staff. But in truth, the *Times* had only a handful of black reporters, and they were even lower on the pecking order than The Single Girl With A Cat, often fielding assignments like Jesse Jackson Sr.'s speeches at Rainbow Push, public housing disputes, and community marches in gang territory.

Expecting a fight, Amy already had an argument prepared,

but I cut her off. "It's a big convention. What do you want me to cover?"

My voice was hoarse, raw. My teeth felt gritty, as if I'd been sucking on the couch lint in my sleep. I wasn't the type to show up at a strange man's house uninvited in the middle of the night. Nor did I know how to behave waking up next to him. Somehow I had thought I was with Jake. I knew he was a vision brought to life by the drugs and alcohol, but a small part of me had wanted to believe it was real. I'd given in to that part. Now my head ached. I was unsure what I would say to Danny and was hoping to sneak out without having to face him.

Amy stuttered for a moment, not expecting me to be so agreeable. "We were thinking maybe you could cover Mustapha's speech at noon." I could hear relief in her voice.

"What about Mohammed X?" I'm not sure why I suggested him, other than Lester had mentioned him the previous day. He was controversial, and he rarely spoke outside his mosque, where congregants were registered and passed through a metal detector.

"Uh…okay," she said, impressed. "But he usually only allows African-American reporters to cover his speeches. If you can get in, it would be a real coup."

• • •

After a quick stop at home to change clothes, my Indian Muslim taxi driver was only too happy to deliver me to the convention center.

"Are you interested in converting?" he asked me via the rear-view mirror, his dark eyes wide and his head wobbling. "Do you know there are many famous Muslims—like Jermaine Jackson, Mehmet Oz, and Kareem Abdul-Jabbar? Did you know Islam is the second most popular religion?"

"Yes."

"So why, my lady, are you going to the convention?"

"I'm going to hear Mohammed X."

The driver's lips turned down and his walnut eyes sagged.

"You know we don't endorse his kind of thinking. That's just a fringe group he's leading."

"Yes, a fringe group with millions of followers. Why would the organizers allow him to speak if he doesn't represent true Islam?"

The driver, looking troubled, bobbed his head. He kept speaking into the mirror, ignoring the road, nearby cars honking their horns. "Islam is about Allah, not hate. We welcome all people. I don't know why they are giving him an audience. Maybe because he's popular among young people."

"And ex-cons and drug dealers."

The driver frowned. "He's bad for us."

"Isn't this our exit?" The ugly, dark metal convention center loomed ahead. Yellow taxis queued outside. The driver veered the car off Lake Shore Drive.

"Sorry, madam. Please, please, don't listen to that man. I beg you."

I felt guilty for challenging the neat portrait of Islam the driver carried in his head. Chicago had long been home to controversial Islamic groups, including the anti-Semite Louis Farrakhan. Mohammed X was a younger, hipper version, who appealed to an even more radical generation.

"I'll try to keep an open mind." I handed him a generous tip.

The convention hall was buzzing with thousands of people moving between seminars, many wearing traditional Muslim garb. It was half an hour before Mohammed X's speech, but the guards were turning people away at the grand ballroom. I flashed my press pass, but the guard shook his head. "Sorry, miss, we've reached fire code capacity."

I was about to give up when I spotted the wigger from the warehouse party. He had on a white shepherd's robe and moved in and out of the hall, whispering to the guards as if he held a position of authority. His complexion looked darker; I spotted a makeup line on his neck.

I grabbed at his cloak. "Hey, weren't you at the warehouse party last night? This is a different crowd for you, huh?"

He studied me for a moment. At home I'd traded my club outfit for a black suit, and he didn't immediately recognize me. "You're Anna's friend, right?"

"I think you called me *Momma* last night."

He darted his eyes, embarrassed. "Yeah, sorry about that." He seemed more subdued in the daylight. "Glad you made it to the convention. Mohammed X is my mentor. I'd do anything for him." He pressed his hands together and bowed.

"That's a little strange coming from a white guy, isn't it?"

He laughed in a way that suggested I was simple minded. "Actually I'm just as black as our Hyde Park Senator. Like him, my mother is white and my father is black. But the color of someone's skin has nothing to do with Islam."

"Hmm. That's not what your leader preaches." Except for his dreadlocks and dark pancake makeup, he looked like a typical Irish guy.

"Look, three years ago I was just this punk kid in prison for selling meth. I had no life, and Mohammed X changed that. Now I have a spiritual father. I have a career. I have a family here." He held out his hands as if the people walking by were his relations.

"So you work for him now?"

"I'm a singer. My name is Rapper X. You might have heard of me?"

"Sorry, I don't know much about rap music." That was only partly true.

"I record on a small South Side label. Mohammed X is an investor. So you see how he looks out for people, how he tries to get people jobs once they get out of prison?"

"And selling drugs? That's part of your *religion*?"

"We all have our imperfections and our challenges," he said with agitation. "It was nice to have met you. Sorry I didn't catch your name."

"Natalie Delaney, reporter with the *Chicago Times*. You might have read my stories?" I handed him my card.

He tucked in his chin. "Were you writing a story last night?"

"Yes. But if you can get me a one-on-one with Mohammed, maybe I don't have to write about what I saw."

He pursed his lips, thinking. "Come on. I'll show you where you can stand."

The ballroom was packed. Dozens sprawled on the floor. Rapper X positioned me along the wall near the front, not far from the raised stage.

Mohammed X was late, and the crowd had grown restless. I squatted, tired from my lack of sleep, and still feeling the effects of the mystery drug. When I'd woken that morning next to Danny, I'd felt despondent, realizing it hadn't been Jake's shoulder I'd nestled against that night; it hadn't been Jake's neck that I'd kissed. Danny and I had both been too drunk to do anything but lightly paw at each other before falling asleep, cradled on the couch. It had all felt blissfully illusionary—my head resting on his chest, listening to his heartbeat. I had often dreamt of Jake, vivid half-memories as if we were still together. When I woke to the truth, I ached inside—a sad, longing sickness.

I still acted like Jake was going to walk through the door, and all would be forgiven. I guess that's why I was never able to stick it out with anyone for long. The truth was, I didn't need Jake as an excuse. I was always choosing my job over a man. When I first started dating someone, he was usually thrilled to be seeing a woman with an "exciting job" and her name in the paper. But the reality of missing dates and getting called out of movies and concerts got old fast for most guys. Only recently had I begun to calculate the personal costs of that choice. I was in my early thirties, prime baby-making time, but with no one special to make a baby with.

Then there was the psychological cost of writing about the ugliness of life: the mother who gave her children Drano, the teen-age rejects who drove around shooting strangers on Christmas. Chasing such stories had devoured my adulthood. After a while I'd become more comfortable chronicling other people's lives and less comfortable living my own. At first I was trying to prove I was as tough as "the boys," but as time went on, I found myself drawn to bigger and riskier stories.

That strategy, so far, had kept my name off the newroom's layoff list. But the threat always loomed. Some days we'd show up for work, and our colleagues would be gone, their desks bare, their chairs empty. No explanations. No goodbyes. No celebratory sheet cakes. It was like some biblical plague that overnight mysteriously wiped out a quarter of the staff. In the "good old days" people left for better jobs. Now there were no better jobs. Every newspaper in the country was bleeding. I worried that by the time they got around to letting me go, I'd be too old to have kids, too old to attract any normal guy. I'd just be unemployed and alone.

After an hour of waiting, a few people left the ballroom and others quickly took their seats. Organizers assured us that Mohammed X was about to arrive. Moments later, the metal ballroom doors swung open, and in strode a man wearing a tight-fitting, double-breasted, tan suit; a black shirt with gold cufflinks; brown wing-tip shoes; and a shiny gold watch. Everyone stood and cheered, even the old folks with canes and walkers.

Mohammed, who wore no Muslim garb, not even a skullcap, waved like a politician as he made his way to the bulletproof lectern.

"Good afternoon, my brothers and sisters."

"Good afternoon," the crowd roared back.

"I'll try to be as open as I can be today, but you'll understand if I'm more covert in my message." He stepped down from the podium and, with a wire-free microphone clipped to his lapel, began making his way into the audience. Women clasped their hands in prayer, young men bowed, others fell to their knees and peered up at him in awe.

"You see, today, in this ballroom, we have a reporter who has come here to write about what I say. I hope she tells the truth." He stared at me. "But that's not been my experience with journalists, especially those who are *unbelievers*."

People muttered to each other as he made his way toward me, his eyes silvery in the bright lights. I pressed myself against the wall as if I could blend into the wallpaper. I was the only white woman in the room. Mohammed stopped in front of me. His broad shoulders blocked my view of the audience, as if we were having a private meeting. He reached into his pocket and handed me his silk monogrammed handkerchief.

"You're sweating," he said, his fingers muting the microphone. He bent down and whispered in my hair: "I'm looking forward to our talk later." His attention felt intimate, sexual.

I stared down at the carpet, rattled, unsure how to react.

He turned and shouted to the crowd: "I'm going to be lambasted and called a racist. They'll say Mohammad X was up to his old tricks. Brothers and sisters, I preach a message of freedom. My mission is to release us from the chains white men have put on us. Emancipation occurred in 1863, and yet, we are still enslaved to the white race!"

Mohammed paced in front of the stage, nodding as if he were talking to himself.

"So now, our mayor, who is friends with all the white bankers and the white businessmen, says he is afraid we are going to lose our chance for the 2016 Summer Olympics because these heroin deaths are making people afraid to come to our city. He says religious leaders need to talk to their congregations about this drug, this poison that is moving through our communities, killing our children.

"But I say to you, this is nothing but a government hoax. There is no poisoned heroin. It's simply the white politicians and cops trying to convince white kids not to do drugs, to make them afraid to come to black neighborhoods, lest they be *poisoned*.

"Why can't white folks just admit their kids do drugs too? Heroin is a tricky substance, and no one ever knows the potency on the street. That's why black folks and white folks alike are dying of this drug. Black folks been dying of heroin for years. But those deaths never made the newspapers."

The crowd groaned.

He went on to challenge the politicians' claims that building an Olympic City on the South Side would create jobs for African-Americans. He dismissed the notion that the city would include black contractors beyond meeting a narrow quota. He challenged members of the audience to seek political office, to apply for city jobs, especially openings for police officers and firefighters. He told parents to encourage their children to attend college and become lawyers and judges so they could overhaul Chicago's corrupt system of forced confessions and trumped-up evidence.

I listened intently, surprised that I agreed with much of what he said, and wondered if he'd watered down his message for me. I could see why Lester had been so taken with him. Mohammed X was charming and charismatic and his message, at least what I heard, was not unreasonable.

"We cannot wait for the white establishment to give us token positions," he screamed. "No, no, no. We must stand up and demand to be counted!"

The crowd roared and stood, many of them jamming their fists in the air. Some yelled: "Yes, we can!"

Mohammed stopped and nodded. "Yes, we can. Yes, we can. I know you've all heard that. But do you believe it? Brothers and sisters do you believe a black man can run the country? Do you live like you believe it?"

"Yes, we can!" the crowd fired back. "Yes! We can! Yes, we can! Yes, we can!" The crowd chanted, getting louder with each refrain.

Mohammed stuck his palm in the air and lowered it to hush the audience. He took the microphone from his lapel and yelled into it: "Now, go make it happen."

The audience rushed to the stage. Suddenly Rapper X grabbed my arm. "Hold onto me." He led me through the crowd as we were jostled on all sides. Some shouted at me in a language I didn't understand. Finally, we reached the opposite wall of the ballroom where he opened a door concealed in the wall. A hallway led to an elevator. Rapper X pushed the button marked "P."

When the elevator stopped, Rapper X guided me toward a door flanked by a stout guard. Inside, several loveseats were stationed around a circular coffee table that held a large bowl of fruit. An old couple was seated. Rapper X sat down near them and began to make small talk. No one addressed me. I took a seat on the opposite couch and checked email on my cell phone. I studied my notes and jotted down questions, eager to meet Mohammed X and intrigued by how his convention speech hadn't correlated with his racist reputation.

Thirty minutes later, an adjoining door slid open. There stood Mohammed X in a white terry cloth robe, tufts of dark chest hair poking out, smelling of musky cologne. His short Afro was still wet and his feet were bare.

"Hello, folks. I'm sorry for my attire, but I had to take a shower. I was just drenched in sweat," he said, winking at me. He seemed even taller than he had in the ballroom, his personality filling up the hotel room. Around his neck hung the same clenched fist charm that Lester wore. "I hope you don't mind, Mr. and Mrs. Rauf, but I promised this reporter I would give her twenty minutes. I'll meet you for dinner shortly."

The couple hugged Mohammed and gave me a stern look before leaving. Rapper X remained seated.

"I can handle it from here, Randy," Mohammed said.

Rapper slunk out, seemingly disheartened Mohammed had called him by his Christian name.

Mohammed sat on a couch across from me and propped his bare feet on the coffee table, cinching his robe around him.

"I would have dressed, but I didn't care to protect your reputation. I'm only doing this as a favor to Randy. What did you think of our little show?"

He didn't wait for my response, but got up and began pacing in front of the television, much like he'd paced in front of the audience. "I hate that slogan 'Yes, we can. Yes, we can,'" he parodied in a tinny voice. "Sounds like someone playing a stupid game on *Romper Room*. 'Mother, may I? Oh yes, you can.' Who the fuck asks permission to start a revolution? We are *not* asking permission. The days of being polite are over."

I twisted in my seat and tried not to look stunned.

"But that's not why you came here, is it?"

I straightened. "Yes, thanks for meeting with me. I know you don't like to talk to reporters—"

"A lie! I don't trust *white* reporters. They twist what I say to fit their own purposes. I don't like *Jewish* reporters either, but I suspect with a name like," he pulled my card from his robe pocket, "Delaney, you're most likely Irish Catholic."

"What is it you have against Jews?"

He sat across from me, plucked a grape from the bowl on the table and rolled it around in his mouth. "I advocate for the protection of my people, who have been as abused and enslaved as much as Jews claim the Nazis enslaved and murdered them. You don't see anyone advocating that Jews stop talking about Germans, do you? What's the saying—'never forget'?"

"Do you know they call you the Black Hitler?" I couldn't believe the transformation I was witnessing. In a matter of minutes he had gone from reasonable social justice advocate to hate monger.

He sat up, spreading his legs, the robe opening. A bit of flesh dangled. His eyes followed mine, and he smiled.

"I find white women—certain white women—are very good in bed." He took another grape in his fingers and sucked on it, tearing off bits of skin, holding it on his tongue, between his teeth, making a slurping sound as he finally bit down and chewed. "Catholic women, the lapsed kind, are especially good. They know they're immoral and will never measure up to our Mother Mary, and so they are uninhibited. Saintly women, like devout Muslims, are not particularly good at pleasing their husbands. That's why some Muslims have multiple wives."

I averted my gaze and fumbled with my notebook.

"Many white women find me attractive." He stroked the hair on his upper chest, his gold ring gleaming in the soft track lighting. "Have you ever had sex with a black man?"

"That's really inappropriate, sir."

"Oh, it's very appropriate. You're sitting here with a married man in a hotel room and he's barely dressed. I'd say it's the elephant in the room. Or should I say the very large appendage?"

I sucked in air and closed my eyes.

"I personally enjoy cunnilingus." He wiggled his tongue before popping another grape into his mouth and rolling it around, sucking loudly. "I advocate all my male congregants try it. I teach a class at our mosque on how to please wives."

"I don't want to talk about this. *Please.*" I squirmed and wrenched my head away from him. I felt awkward and weak. It was like his eyes were raping me. I couldn't look at him, and I couldn't summon the inner strength to tell him to go fuck himself. He made me feel powerless and tiny, and I hated him for it.

"Oh? Is this making you uncomfortable? Isn't that strange, since you're the reporter? Aren't you supposed to make me uncomfortable, present all kinds of embarrassing details and get me to confess my sins? Isn't that part of your trickery?"

I shook my head, urging myself to respond.

"Then why don't you ask me what you came here to ask? You want to know why I called this so-called 'Poison heroin' a hoax?"

"You can't seriously believe the fentanyl heroin is a conspiracy by the government," I insisted, trying to regain my courage. "Isn't it possible someone has taken your hate speech as a manifesto to target white kids?"

"And why would I know this?" He stood and put his hands defiantly on his hips.

"Because many of your flock are ex-cons, you have prisons ministries, and you're very comfortable with a *certain element.* Some would say you have your hand in the underworld of crime, you have covert business ventures. In fact, I've seen that same fist you're wearing around the neck of a known heroin dealer. Are you running drugs with the Gangster Disciples?"

He laughed, but then his face turned rigid, and he walked toward me. He leaned down, putting his palms on my thighs, and looked me in the eyes. "Is that what the Jew cops told you? Let me tell you—and you can quote me on this—until someone cares about black kids dying from stray gunshots, I'm not going to lose sleep about some rich white girls who go down to the South Side to hook up with potent heroin, using their money to further encourage a criminal element in our neighborhoods that is destroying the moral fiber of our communities. Our kids are getting shot while doing homework at the dining room table. Those are the true victims."

He drew closer as if he were going to kiss me and whispered slowly, articulating each syllable: "Now, unless you're going to get on your knees, where every whore white woman should be, get out."

I glared at him. He backed away, and I walked out, imagining the story I'd write about him appearing on the front page.

CHAPTER NINE

June 16 & 18, 2008

MAYOR RECRUITS RELIGIOUS LEADERS
TO TALK ABOUT HEROIN
SUNDAY SERVICES FEATURE DISCUSSION OF POISONED DRUG
Chicago Times

On Monday morning, I went to the paper early, hoping to catch a source, an investigator with the medical examiner's office. He worked the weekend shift—when most murders happened—and I wanted to see if he'd slip me a copy of the three Dead Angels' autopsies, performed over the weekend. After a lot of pretty pleases, he reluctantly agreed to fax me the reports. While fax machines might seem antiquated in the age of the Internet, they were indispensable for people in government whose email accounts were monitored and subject to court subpoenas and open records requests.

I was standing at the bank of ugly gray machines when Julian stepped off the elevator. I watched him out of the corner of my eye as he strode deliberately toward me.

"Do you ever go home?" he asked.

I looked up at his freshly shaved face. His hair was slicked back, and he smelled like lavender soap. Though it was eighty degrees outside, he wore a dark pinstripe suit and carried an old-fashioned leather briefcase with a handle like Don Draper.

"I keep my bed roll under my desk."

Though we were the only ones near the fax machines, he leaned in and whispered: "Any luck on that arrest report?"

"I'm working on it." I felt self-conscious in my casual jeans.

He looked down at the fax machine furiously spitting out black and white pages and pointed at the reams piling up in the tray. "What's that?"

"Nothing." I pulled the last pages sputtering from the machine and held them to my chest.

Normally I'd arm-punch anyone who let their eyes drift to one of my faxes, but Julian's coy flirtation made the humorless newsroom a bit more interesting. Still, his intensity made me nervous about mispronouncing words or using the wrong verb tense. Most guys in the newsroom were overgrown boys who spent their weekends drinking beer and watching the Cubs. I knew how to manage *those* kinds of newsmen. But Julian was shrewd, urbane, and *fatherly*, like someone who spent his Saturdays cheering his kids at junior league soccer and Sundays hosting sophisticated dinner parties. I hadn't decided whether he could be trusted, and that uncertainty made him all the more dangerous.

"I'll let you know when I hear back about the *Kennan* arrest," I said loudly to annoy him.

He frowned. "You do that." He started toward the other end of the newsroom then turned around. "By the way, nice job getting the coroner's report on the Dead Angels."

I felt my mouth drop open.

"I was once a crime reporter, too. I know how to read upside down."

I hustled to my desk, eager to pore over the medical examiner's findings. It was the first time I'd obtained full autopsy reports on any fentanyl deaths. The ME had concluded that the Angels' deaths were homicides, unlike the earlier heroin deaths, which had been ruled as suspicious overdoses. I flipped through the pages, looking for the most helpful part of an autopsy: diagrams of the bodies, marked with injuries. Nothing conveyed atrocity like a body sketch marked with knife slits, entry and exit bullet holes, or a battered skull.

The Dead Angels' body diagrams showed where the fatal needle injections were administered. Two girls had tapped veins in their right inner elbows; the third girl had taken hers in the neck. That last detail suggested that either the other two girls had helped the third girl before they injected themselves, or, more likely, *someone else* had helped her. Besides fentanyl and heroin, the girls had no other drugs in their systems. All three had blood alcohol levels more than five times the legal limit; clearly *someone else* had driven them to the Chinatown house and left them to die.

The strangest markings were red stains across the Angels' faces on the diagrams, near their chins. I skimmed through the narrative and finally found the answer: "The subject presented with a red tint on her tongue, suggesting she had ingested a lozenge. Further testing revealed a trace amount of oral transmucosal fentanyl citrate (OTFC) in the subject's mouth."

So the girls were sucking on F-sticks before they injected Poison? How much fentanyl did they need? Were the girls dying of the combination of fentanyl sticks with poisoned heroin? Or were the fentanyl lollipops used to knock them out while someone administered a hotshot?

I thought about what Cate had said—that her cousin and her friends had sought out fentanyl heroin to take a trip on the dark side. Had that been the case for all the girls who had died of Poison? White girls, who weren't addicts, hunting for a specific brand of heroin on the South Side, seemed an unlikely scenario. How would they know where to go, and wouldn't there have been more witnesses? Girls like that stand out. Besides, the story line didn't correlate with what the cops were saying, that the girls had been targeted, lured—perhaps under false pretenses—to the heroin houses where they were injected with poisoned heroin, perhaps against their will. Mo suspected that the girls had already passed out when someone pumped them with drugs. But he'd never mentioned that the poisoned girls had been sucking on fentanyl sticks. If the girls were abusing narcotic lollipops, then they certainly weren't *drug virgins*—as Mo claimed. There was something calculated and intentional about these deaths. If the cops had lied about the girls' previous drug use, what else were they covering up?

. . .

Two days later, police brass summoned reporters to a press conference. I stood anxiously in the windowless conference room, exchanging theories with the TV reporters about what would likely be announced. We agreed it had to be something related to the Poison deaths. Maybe they'd caught the dealer responsible. Cops never had a press conference unless they'd nabbed someone. Most press conferences amounted to public brag fests where they displayed piles of drugs or guns cops had taken off the streets.

Our chatter halted when Adam Barkley, Chicago's barrel-chested police chief, marched to the podium. TV lights blared across Barkley's wide forehead. He licked his lips and brushed a hand through his shock of gray hair. Recruited from New Jersey, Barkley struggled for acceptance among Chicago's boys in blue who thought they should be led by one of their own. The mounting Poison deaths had only added to Barkley's troubles.

The chief cleared his throat. The only sound was the mechanical whirl of photo drives capturing his every twitch. A crowd of top cops, their jackets layered with shiny awards, stood behind him. Another group clustered to the side. They wore matching blue blazers and equally bad haircuts—FBI agents.

"This morning," Barkley said, leaning into the nest of microphones, his puffy cheeks straining to hold back his cheesy grin. "The Chicago Police Department, in coordination with the FBI and DEA, raided the Dearborn Homes housing complex and arrested forty-seven members of the Mickey Cobra street gang. The raid capped a months-long undercover operation. During the raid, officers and federal agents discovered a large cache of fentanyl heroin along with hundreds of glassine packages stamped with a distinctive brand—skull and crossbones. This particular strand of heroin is known on the streets as Poison and is connected to at least two hundred deaths in the greater Chicago area."

As Barkley continued to gloat, I felt my phone vibrate in my pocket. "Happy now?" it read. I scanned the room, my gaze stopping at the piercing blue eyes staring back.

• • •

He insisted we meet in East Chicago, which was actually in Indiana, at a dive near the steel mills. Mo didn't want to risk being seen with me in the city, but as a black man, he stood out even more amid the Hoosiers. The bar was full of guys with soot on their faces and hard hats under their arms. Just five miles outside Chicago, the joint was a holdover from another era: fake wood paneling, old-style country music, chipped enamel tables, and bearded men who seemed to have tumbled straight from the cover of a ZZ Top album. Cigarette smoke suspended like fog over our heads. Except for the bartender, a stout dyed blonde with black roots, I was the only female in the place.

I settled into a booth, leery of meeting Mo; I wasn't ready to share details about Anna and her friends just yet.

"You're grinning like you know something. What's up?" Mo said as he reached the table carrying a pitcher of Miller and two frosty mugs.

I shooed my hand at him. "Nah. Just glad they caught the Poison dealers."

He poured the beer then held up his mug: "To nabbing the Poison killers!"

We clinked mugs and stared at each other before chugging back mouthfuls.

"You don't believe the Mickeys killed those girls, do you?" He licked foam from his lips and offered a suspicious grin.

"And you do?"

"Maybe, maybe not. Seems a bit too neat."

"I could see the Mickeys settling scores by passing out hot-shots to addicts they didn't like. But white, suburban girls? The Mickeys weren't exactly advertising their wares at Macy's. How did those two groups mix? It doesn't make any sense."

"You got a better suggestion?"

"What if…" I lowered my head and whispered. "What if someone decided to take a play from the Mickeys, a copycat, someone who wanted to knock off white girls, knowing the Mickeys would be blamed? Maybe the Mickeys even sold their fentanyl H to this other player?"

Mo tightened his lips, trying to hold back a smirk. "The feds say the Mickeys acted alone." His voice was laden with mock authority. "They claim the Mickeys produced the fentanyl heroin to move into Gangster Disciples' territory."

"And the feds are always right." I spoke into the saltshaker as if it were wired.

"You're not giving up, are you?" He narrowed his eyes, matching his accusing tone.

"It doesn't make sense."

"So who's the copycat? Let me guess. You think it's the Gangster Disciples trying to get rid of their competition by framing the Mickeys. You probably think that loud mouth Mohammed X is somehow involved. By the way, that was a fucking great story you wrote." He tipped his mug toward me.

My front-page story about Mohammed X calling poisoned heroin a government hoax coupled with his inflammatory comments to me had provoked enormous reaction. The Mayor, the Governor, and even the Hyde Park Senator had denounced him.

"But?"

Mo sneered. "Mohammed X is a racist drug dealer. He's *not* a serial murderer."

"Was he ever a suspect in the fentanyl heroin deaths?" That was the real reason I had driven to Indiana to meet Mo.

"Mohammed X? For Poison?" He laughed and shook his head. "Sure, we've long suspected he's moving drugs in the state prison system. And the feds think he's laundering the Gangster Disciples' drug money. But manufacturing Poison? Or better yet, buying it from a rival gang and then framing them? That's quite the theory, Natalie."

"But look what happened. The Mickeys were arrested and accused of heinous crimes that are likely to break them up. Now the Gangster Disciples are the dominant dealer, and Mohammed X, their financial backer, stands to rake in millions more. Sounds like a perfect set-up."

The Mickey Cobras and the Gangster Disciples had been enemies for as long as anyone remembered. Usually they settled their differences with bullets—often hitting innocent kids in their spray. But this plot seemed more devious and had much more sweeping consequences. It was likely not the play of a street dealer, but the ambitious scheme of a brilliant mastermind.

I glanced at the empty pitcher, expecting Mo to buy another round. But he just stubbed out his cigarillo. When I wasn't buying, Mo's appetite for cigars and alcohol was more modestly tempered.

"What does a girl who went to the Lab School know about gangs and race?" It was an old argument Mo liked to pull out, how his Robert Taylor Homes childhood trumped mine in lofty Hyde Park.

"The Lab School was half white and half black—and the wealthiest kids were black," I countered.

"When you're rich, it doesn't matter what color your skin is. You become colorless."

"The clash between whites and blacks in Chicago isn't about money," I protested. "It's about education and class."

"Spoken like a privileged white girl. *Money* is what buys education and class."

"So now I'm the bad guy?"

"I'm just saying a lot of white folks can't understand why black folks are bitter. We don't start out with an even playing field. Even as a kid, you just feel like the world is stacked against you. You know what my nephew calls Chicago?"

I shook my head.

"Chiraque. Because he feels like he's living in a war zone. More than three hundred kids were shot on the South Side last year, almost one a day. Hell, some summer weekends there are more than sixty people shot—in two days. Many are just innocent bystanders. They have nothing to do with this gang warfare. If that happened anywhere on the North Side, it would be on CNN, Fox News, and in all the goddamn newspapers. They'd be calling it an epidemic. The Mayor would send in the National Guard. But when it's little black faces, it's like we're dispensable. Like we don't matter. Even in death."

I looked down at my beer. Rarely did Mo and I talk about the difference in our skin colors. I reached across the table and put my hand on his. We didn't say anything for a while, just waited for that awful feeling to sink beneath us.

Mo cleared his throat. "By the way, I checked out the Kennan arrest report. Actually, it doesn't officially exist anymore."

"And?"

"His name is Rex, and he was arrested, all right, in the early hours of June tenth." His voice was lively again.

"The night the Dead Angels shot up Poison?"

"The timing is suspicious, I'll give you that. He was clocked going over a hundred miles an hour on South Lake Shore Drive. They thought he was drunk."

"Was he?"

"Stone cold sober. They searched his car and found vials of prescription drugs and…syringes."

Mo was the master of dragging out the punch line. I motioned for him to get to the point.

"Naloxone—the heroin antidote."

We stared at each other. Had the Kennan kid been racing from the Chinatown house after helping the girls inject poison? Maybe he'd tried to revive them but was unsuccessful.

"He didn't have Poison on him?"

Mo grunted. "Don't you think I'd tell you? Just the naloxone."

"If he's carrying around an antidote, then he either is doing heroin or knows someone who is. What was his explanation?"

"He said he carried it in case his friends overdosed. He claimed he didn't know anyone who did heroin. It was just a precaution, after reading about all the deaths. Technically, it's illegal in Illinois to carry naloxone without a prescription, but we sort of look the other way."

"That's a fancy crowd for carrying naloxone. He didn't give any names?"

Mo raised his eyebrows. "Come on. The rich have their rules, too."

"So they let him off on the speeding charge as well?"

He grinned. "The Kennans are very generous donors to the state attorney's re-election campaign, not to mention the Mayor's."

"The city that works…" I said, mocking the city's advertising campaign.

"Your turn. Tell me what happened with them girls you hung out with the other night. They into Poison?"

"False alarm." I lit a black and mild I'd bummed from Mo. "But I'll tell you what I did get—the medical examiner's report on the Dead Angels." I bit my lip trying to hold back the smirk slowly spreading across my face.

"Where'd you get the report?"

"The ME's declaring the Poison deaths homicides. The report says the girls were sucking on F-sticks before they injected Poison. Why didn't you tell me that?"

Mo scratched his neck and sighed loudly. "We have to hold back certain facts so the killer can't recant and say that he confessed to some detail he read in the newspaper."

"How many white girls were sucking on fentanyl lollipops before they died of Poison?"

Mo shook his head. "Not going there." I could tell by the intensity of his eyes he was getting angry. Mo resented it when I dug up details he'd purposely withheld.

"How many white girls had red marks on their tongues when they showed up at the morgue? Tell me the truth, goddamn it!"

Mo pounded his fist on the table. "All of them!"

The bar suddenly got quiet, all those sooty faces staring at a black man screaming at a white woman. Mo looked uneasily at the crowd eying him.

"Happy now?"

CHAPTER TEN

June 18, 2008

MOHAMMED X SAYS POISON HEROIN A HOAX

CLAIMS POLICE SCARING WHITES

OUT OF BLACK NEIGHBORHOODS

Chicago Times

Mo's confirmation about the fentanyl lollipops and Rex Kennan's arrest were major exclusives, and I was giddy about the story I would write. From my newsroom computer, I clicked on Rex Kennan's Facebook page. His profile photo was sun-soaked: his shiny brown hair swept back, his skin bronzed, and his hazel eyes twinkling in the glare. His head was cocked slightly, providing a side profile of that pointy Kennan nose that had graced so many historic photos. His chin jutted out in a teasing way—his mouth half-open as if he'd been caught mid-sentence, mid-laugh. The image was slightly blurry, as if the photographer had been a paparazzo who had snuck up on him on some sunny beach somewhere.

I hoped Rex had inherited his family's ease with the media, and he would consider meeting with a reporter. I sent him a cryptic message on Facebook, mentioning his arrest on Lake Shore Drive, what he was carrying in the car, and asked to meet.

About half an hour later, my phone rang.

"Natalie?"

I had been wondering when she was going to turn up again.

"Anna, nice of you to call," I said, sarcastically, still bruised about her ditching me at the rave.

Her voice quivered; she sounded like she was on the verge of tears.

"Can…can you come over? Now?"

"Are you okay? Is Libby?"

"Just get here as fast as you can."

• • •

The apartment building looked deserted when I pulled up twenty minutes later. I raced up the back stairs, frantic about what I'd find inside. Libby opened the door and seemed genuinely glad to see me. Lester was sitting on the couch talking to Anna; his entourage, drinking from large brown Colt 45 bottles, was sprawled on the floor.

Lester started toward me. "Why the hell did you write that shit about the Prophet?" His eyes were fiery black stones.

I faked a laugh. "I merely quoted what he said."

"You made fun of him in that Jew paper."

"You don't strike me as a *Times* subscriber."

"You caused him…" He pulled a scrap of paper from his jeans pocket. "Ridicule."

"Where'd you hear that?"

"I know people." He puffed up his chest.

"Really? Well, tell your people to tell Mohammed if he wants to complain, he should call me himself."

Lester moved closer. His mocha-colored skin was peachy red. I backed away, but he kept coming toward me. The fierceness in his eyes reminded me of how he looked just before he released his dog on me.

I opened the back door and jogged down the stairs. I had just reached the car when I heard thumping behind me. Before I could get in my car, Lester and his crew surrounded me and grabbed the door.

"Where do you think you're going?" he said.

"We're done here." I sounded braver than I felt.

"I'll tell you when we're done."

I didn't see his fist until it smacked the side of my face. I fell back against the car, rolled to the ground, and lay there stunned, breathing in blood and dirt.

"Who the fuck do you think you are?" Lester screamed. He stood over me, his legs straddling my back. "Look at me, bitch!" He pulled my feet, dragging me across the gravel and away from the car. Rocks scratched at my face, my chin, the delicate skin under my forearms, my palms.

"What do you want?" I tried to get to my knees.

He grabbed a handful of hair and yanked my head back. My scalp burned in his fingers.

"Get off me!" I elbowed him in the face. He jerked back, more from shock than force.

His crew grabbed me, rolled me onto my back, and held me down, pinning my arms with their hands and feet, pressing my skin into the rocks. One of them wrapped his hands around my neck and squeezed. I coughed and gasped for air.

"Who's got the bottle?" Lester yelled.

I flailed wildly, kicking one guy in the mouth. The others jumped on me, grabbing my chest and arms, crushing my legs. Lester slugged me in the face again. Something cracked.

"Here, bitch, suck on this." Lester shoved a Colt 45 bottle into my mouth.

I wrenched my head away.

He backhanded me.

I tasted blood. My eyelids swelled. I could only see shadows. There was a buzzing in my ears. My face felt like it was on fire.

I heard her screaming from the deck above. "Stop! Leave her alone!" It was Libby's voice. Her feet hammered down the stairs. The boys loosened their grip. I could hear her shoes crunching across the gravel, charging at them.

"Get off her!"

"Come on, Libby. This ain't your business," Lester said.

"I said, let go of her!" Libby yelled.

"Yeah," Anna echoed. She'd followed her cousin; Libby leading the way for once.

There was scuffling and screaming. Someone grabbed Libby. She hollered. Anna cried. Then the hands around me tightened. They held my mouth open, while Lester poured beer down my throat. I choked and spit up. They sat me up and thrust back my head. One hand pulled against the roof of my mouth and the other hand pushed down my jaw. I tried to bite their fingers, but they pushed harder. I thought they were going to break my jaw. I was drowning. Beer was coming up my nose. I couldn't breathe. They kept pouring, pausing only to let me cough and gasp. I could hear the girls begging them to stop. Then they'd start again, their street version of waterboarding.

Lester finally ordered them to quit. I could feel him standing over me, blocking the heat of the sun.

"Get on your knees, bitch."

I didn't move. I didn't care if he punched me again.

"I said, on your knees!"

He pulled my hair until I crouched. I expected him to hit or slap me.

Libby yelled: "No! No!"

I felt something metal and cold lightly touching my cheek. He moved it slowly around the contours of my face, tickling the fine hairs.

"Open your mouth," he ordered. The girls were wailing now.

I was too beat to fight anymore.

He jammed the muzzle between my teeth.

"How does death taste?"

I was seething with anger. The guys were whooping and laughing, the girls sobbing. In a rush of noise, I heard a rumbling muffler and tires throwing gravel. A door slammed; a man screamed. Something cracked the air.

Then it got dark and quiet.

CHAPTER ELEVEN

June 18, 2008

MICKEY COBRA GANG MEMBERS
UNABLE TO MAKE BAIL

JUDGE SETS $1 MILLION BAIL IN POISON HEROIN CASE

Chicago Sentinel

I heard his lyrical voice before I saw him. It was a lulling voice, the voice of a dad, a protector, a man who shouldered responsibility. His melodic tone encouraged me to continue floating in the darkness. When I finally opened my eyes, I scanned his blond hair, his smooth, tanned cheeks, his sad eyes, and the pug nose he shared with Libby.

"Hell, that was a *nasty* scene," he said in his mush-mouth, Indiana drawl. "Y'okay?"

I nodded and closed my eyes. I didn't want to deal with this, the aftermath, the picking up of the pieces. We were in Libby's apartment, though I didn't know how I'd gotten there. He dabbed my face with a cloth. Libby and Anna were shrieking in the background.

"You gals be quiet!" he yelled. "And get me some towels! I gotta stop the bleeding." He turned to me and whispered, "Y'are gonna be okay. A little bruised. It'll just give your good looks a little character."

He blew softly on my wounds. The smell of the cigarette he'd smoked earlier made me want to smoke too, anything to distract me from my burning face. I wondered if Lester had disfigured me, moved my nose an inch or shattered my cheekbone. I poked my tongue around my mouth to check for missing teeth. All there, but a couple of front teeth seemed loose. Maybe my permanent retainer—the thin metal wires behind my front teeth—provided enough protection.

"This is gonna hurt." He pressed a wet rag to my face, and I could feel my skin splitting, as if Lester were tearing my flesh again with his fist. I breathed slowly through my teeth, short breaths like I'd seen women do in movies when they were giving birth. When he was finished, I reached up to touch the carnage, but all I felt were damp bandages. My head throbbed and my vision was hazy. Everything had three images.

He handed me a glass of cloudy liquid, wrapping my dirty fingers around its cold surface until he was certain of my grip. "You better drink this in case they spiked that beer with some kind of poison." His words were more an order than a suggestion. His thick fingers covered mine, guiding the glass to my lips. The concoction was salty and bitter.

"Hold it down as long as you can." He held out a plastic bucket. I retched with a sudden force, vomiting again and again until I could only dry-heave, the smell repulsive. I scrunched up my face and pushed away the pail. He wiped my mouth and told me to lie back on the couch.

"You want me to take you to the hospital?"

"Not if you think I'll live without it."

"Oh, you'll live. This'll just be some little white scar on your face, something you can tell a story about, something that in a few months won't matter at all." He grinned and winked.

"He was going to kill me." My body was shaking with the realization.

"What might've happened didn't. You're here. You're safe."

His voice was forceful. I wanted to believe him. Only I didn't feel safe. I was lying on a sheet on the same couch where only minutes earlier the girls, Lester, and his crew had all been drinking.

I worried Lester might come back with more guys and more guns. That's how gangbangers settled differences.

"I wish I'd gotten here sooner." His voice trailed off.

I closed my eyes. He'd placed an ice bag on one cheek, numbing my face. A vivid movie played in my head as he recounted what he saw: it was his day off and, after running errands, he'd stopped off at a neighborhood bar to have a few. "Probably, shouldn't a done that," he said sheepishly. He pulled his truck in the back lot and saw me on the ground surrounded by "hoodlums," two of them holding Anna and Libby by their arms as they screamed. Emboldened by the liquor, he jumped out of his truck, the engine still running, pulled out the sawed-off shotgun he kept behind his seat, and fired in the air. Lester and his boys stood back, holding up their hands. He ordered Lester to put his handgun in his pants. He assumed the others had guns as well, but they were no match for his sawed-off.

"'Get out of here, or the coroner will carry you out,' I shouted at them."

"What did they do?" I whispered, my throat raw from vomiting.

"Whaddaya think? They took off, like the cowards they are."

"You saved my life."

"Nah. I was just ridding the neighborhood of cockroaches." He let out a scratchy laugh.

I fell asleep, and when I woke he was still sitting on the couch softly singing a country song. He sang in that breathy way gentle men sing, almost like a whisper, as if he were telling me a secret. When he saw me stirring, he stopped his ballad and his voice turned rough again.

"You sure was snorin', girl. I guess you're gonna live."

I rubbed my eyes.

He handed me a glass of water. "Drink up, 'cause you got some decisions to make."

He wanted to know how I planned to live with "this brutality." Though I really wanted Lester and his boys to be punished, I knew if I called the cops, my attack would become news, and my editors would reassign me to safe—and boring—stories.

"I'm not snitching," I whispered hoarsely.

"Yep," he muttered, as if he already knew. "When you don't have the power, you have to outsmart 'em." He stood to get more ice, and I wondered how he'd hoisted me up three flights of stairs.

I could hear Anna and Libby talking in hushed voices in the next room.

"They feel responsible for what happened." He nodded his head in their direction. "I understand the leader is their friend."

"They didn't know he was going to do this. I certainly didn't see it coming. The girls tried to stop them. Libby was ferocious. I didn't know she had it in her."

Danny beamed. "When it comes to life and death and the things that matter, you can count on Libby. People underestimate her, but she has her own mind."

Libby peeked into the living room. "Daddy, can we come in?"

Danny waved her over. Anna followed. They knelt in front of the couch, cringing at the gashes in my face. Libby looked down at her lap and shook her head. But Anna couldn't look away. She pinched her lips and widened her eyes in horror. Watching her reaction was worse than looking in any mirror.

"Did it hurt?" Anna asked.

Libby glared at her cousin.

"It'll be okay," Anna whispered.

She pulled back a bandage and blew on a gash above my right eye. Then she pushed back the hair from my forehead and caressed the spot where Lester had yanked at my scalp.

"Were you scared?" She looked so young, not like the self-possessed girl who had ordered me to swallow a mystery pill only a few days earlier.

A blue vein across Danny's forehead twitched. He looked like he was going to yell at Anna. Then his jaw loosened and a smile re-emerged. He gently pulled back Anna's hands.

"Honey, it's time to let Natalie rest. How about you girls go get some food?" He pulled out a wrinkled twenty-dollar bill.

We listened to the girls clomp down the back stairs. Danny turned to me and smiled. "Sorry 'bout that. Her mother always said she wasn't afraid of nothing. She lacks some social graces."

"She reminds me of someone."

"Yeah? Someone with a death wish."

For the next hour or so, Danny talked about everything, it seemed, except the night we kissed. He held my head in his lap, occasionally stroking my hair. I wanted to bring it up, to tell him that I wasn't myself that night, that what he saw was something induced by chemistry. Admitting I'd taken a pill that turned out to be ecstasy sounded even worse. So I didn't mention it, and neither did he. Eventually it would surface.

Instead, he talked about how he was an imperfect father, a struggling man. He didn't know what to do about the girls. He grounded Libby because she had let Lester and his friends into the apartment without permission. He told Anna she'd have to return to her mother's house.

"It will last for a week," he said of their punishment. "And then they'll be back out there doing what they want. I can't stop them. Believe me, I've tried."

He told me Anna was on probation for shoplifting and minor drug possession. If convicted one more time, he said, she'd end up in juvenile hall until she reached eighteen.

I considered telling Danny about Libby and Anna smoking heroin. But how could I warn him without reneging on my promise to the girls?

"You know I'm writing stories about heroin, right? Stories about *young white girls* doing heroin," I said slowly, gazing at him through wet eyelashes, melting ice trickling down my face. He starred back with pained eyes, then dropped his chin to his chest.

"I don't know if Lester's involved or working for someone who is involved," I continued. "I wrote a story about Mohammed X that Lester didn't like. That's why he roughed me up." Lester had a number of reasons to scare me off besides what I'd written about Mohammed.

"Then you'd better think twice before coming back to this neighborhood."

I closed my eyes. My head ached too much to think about the future. "Is that because *you* don't want me here?" I sure didn't want to lose the girls as sources. Danny could ban them from seeing me. I also worried that Danny too, would refuse to see me.

"I don't know what I want right now. You better think about yourself. You might want to see a doctor. That man probably laced that beer they made you drink with heroin. I may be from the country, but I know how street thugs work. Excuse my French, but that kind of man shits with his mouth. If he'd wanted to kill you, he would have pulled the trigger. He was trying to scare you, make sure you didn't write any more stories."

He was seething, his lower lip twitching. I touched his shirt-sleeve, and he looked at me with reddened eyes.

"You're not going to do anything brave and stupid, are you?" I asked.

He stared into the distance, as if he were forming a plan, and shook his head slowly, but that didn't allay my foreboding that our clash with Lester wasn't over.

• • •

That night Danny helped me into my car and drove me home. He'd take the bus back, he said. The ride made me queasy. Danny drove slowly, reaching across the console and stroking my arm. When we arrived at my building, he guided me through the lobby and into the elevator. On my floor, he unlocked my door. We paused inside the entryway, a hallway light casting a shadow across his face. He rubbed his hands and glanced nervously into the hall.

"I heard what you said today, and I'm gonna deal with it." I could hear the strain in his voice. "Libby's no angel. None of us is. Hell, I was doing all kinds of shit at her age, and so was her mother. Guess it's in the genes. This hard stuff is new. I just got to get to her. And I will."

I leaned into him. He wrapped his arms around me. He didn't feel like a father anymore, more like a lonely man. We'd bonded that afternoon in the way that people who experience a crisis together do. He had seen the fear in my face, the kind of vulnerability I'd rarely shown anyone. Though we had little else to connect us, we had that day. I wondered if it would be the worst experience we would share.

CHAPTER TWELVE

June 19–22, 2008

MAYOR THREATENS TO CANCEL LOLLAPALOOZA

POISON HEROIN TAKES ANOTHER VICTIM

Chicago Sentinel

The next morning I emailed Amy that I'd been mugged, assuring her that it was a random attack, but that I wouldn't be coming in for a couple of days. I thought about calling my mother for help, but I knew if she saw my face, she would insist on calling the police. Instead, I phoned my best friend, Maggie, making her promise not to freak out when she saw me. It was a pledge she forgot as soon as I opened the door.

"For the love of God!" she screamed, her face crinkling at the sight of my purple and brown gashes. The oval thumb marks around my neck had darkened overnight and now looked like lips, forming a necklace of hickeys.

I buried my forehead in her neck and sobbed. It was the first time I had allowed myself to grieve the attack.

Maggie didn't go back to her public relations firm that day, or the next. She pleaded with me to go to the hospital. By the time I relented, it was too late for sutures. We left the emergency room with pain pills and trial-size tubes of salve to prevent scarring. I pulled out the prescription bottle from the bag and read the label: oxycodone, an opiate narcotic, similar to heroin.

"What's the problem?"

"Nothing," I said, reading the accompanying literature about side effects and addiction.

"Then take it." She held out a glass of water.

I eyed her with familial annoyance but swallowed the fat, white pill anyway.

Within half an hour, my face felt numb, even the wound where Lester had stuck his fist. The drug made me feel like I was floating in a tub of warm bathwater, my arms and legs loose, my fingers and toes tingling. I wondered if this was how Anna felt when she smoked heroin that night, if a sensation of peace washed over her body as it did mine, removing niggling doubts and offering in their place a synthetic happiness, an uncommon calm.

Days went by as I lay in a drugged-up dream state. I passed in and out of consciousness as if I were reliving my past in another world and then reviving to appear briefly in this one. It felt like I was swimming under water, surfacing only when I woke. Nearly every time I opened my eyes, Maggie handed me another pill. I resented her waking me, pulling me from my underwater world. She asked if I was having nightmares about the attack. I said no.

What I couldn't tell her was that I dreamt of Jake. They weren't dreams really, but memories of hazy days long ago when all we seemed to do was drink, listen to music, and lie in bed, sleeping and waking with our skin stuck to each other. It was many summers ago, and the last time Jake had materialized in my life.

That day I'd found him slouching against the *Times*'s cool, stone lobby walls, his guitar case at his feet, as if he were a Michigan Avenue street musician who might play for quarters. He looked much the same: jade green eyes, twisted, teasing smile, innocent freckles scattered on his nose making him look boyish. But what stood before me was definitely a man, or at least the shell of one. He smelled of cheap cologne, something from a rucksack bottle he'd splashed on his neck instead of showering.

It felt strange to have his full attention, to have him looking at me, waiting on me. I had always felt so ancillary in his life. I had been the one waiting on him, waiting for baseball games to end, waiting for the few moments he could spare, waiting for him to show up, waiting for years.

"What are you doing these days?" I'd asked. We mostly saw each other when he traveled through town on a gig; Jake appeared only when he wanted to.

He turned up his lips. "Not much." He was pale and Mick Jagger-thin; his hands twitched like he'd drunk too much coffee. He rubbed his eyes, his skin slowly filling with color, as if he were materializing into human form from a ghost of my past.

He strummed his fingers on top of mine. "Maybe we could get out of here?"

We walked down the street, his guitar case strapped across his back. In the sunlight his face was bony and angular, the rims of his eyes red.

Jake had insisted on hitting a dive where old blues players liked to riff, saying he was craving a beer. When we got there though, he ordered a Coke. A Velvet Underground song came on the jukebox, and I mumbled along. *"When I'm rushing on my run, and I feel just like Jesus's son…"*

"Do you know what you're singing?"

"Yeah. Sure. 'Heroin.'"

His eyes went vacant. He ran his fingers through dirty blond hair that was stringy and past his shoulders. His freckles had faded to mere specks. He pressed his fingers to his forehead and opened his lips to speak, then shook his head. Whatever it was, I knew it was bad. I wanted him not to say it. I swallowed hard and turned away.

• • •

Maggie gently rubbed my arm, waking me. "There's a guy named Danny who keeps calling. Wants to know how you're doing."

I sat up and wiped the sleep from my eyes, trying to remember what year it was. Then the awful memory of the Lester and his boys choked out the dreamy presence of Jake. It had been four days since the attack.

"He's the father of one of the girls I've been hanging with. I told you about him. He's the one…who rescued me."

She patted my arm. "I'm so sorry, Nat. God, I know that must have been awful." I'd spared her the worst details. Maggie was prissy and squeamish, a feminine girl who wore manicured nails, high heels, and pencil skirts.

"That guy—Danny—seems kind of sweet on you."

I gave her a sideways glance. We knew each other too well.

"Okay…we sort of made out," I admitted, shrugging.

Her face brightened. Maggie was always eager for someone to distract me from Jake. "And?"

"Let's just say: we'd both had too much to drink." I got up from the bed and began pacing in my small bedroom. Maggie might shove pain pills down my throat, but she was adamantly against illegal drugs. There's no way I could tell her I'd accidentally taken ecstasy. She wouldn't understand.

"Besides, he's not really my type. I mean he's good-looking, he has a great body…but…he…"

"What? Jesus, the guy saved your life. How romantic is that?"

I exhaled a long, exasperated sigh. "I don't know. We're just so…We come from such different places. I don't even know if he graduated *high school*. We have *nothing* in common."

She got up from the bed shaking her head. "You always have to find some fatal flaw in every man. Jake was a fucking drug addict, but that didn't stop you from falling for him."

She started to leave the bedroom, but stopped. "Oh, by the way, your boss, Amy, keeps calling, wanting to know when you are coming back to work. She says more girls have died of that bad heroin." She paused. "You're not going to keep covering that story, are you?"

"Maggie, it's my job." We'd been over this ground so many times. But this time she had real ammunition. "I can't just walk away."

CHERYL L. REED

"Is it so bad I want you to *live*? Why do you have to be the one who takes all the risks?"

"I am not going to ask for special circumstances just because I'm a *woman*."

"Jesus! You're always raising that feminist flag! It's not worth your life."

"There's a bigger issue. If I don't go back out there—" I pointed at the window, where bright sunlight flickered through the curtains. "I'll never go back out there."

At that moment, *out there* didn't just mean resuming my job. It meant leaving Jake in my dream world, staying above the water, and ditching the pills that had made me stop caring about returning to this realm. I'd failed at keeping Jake off heroin, a regret that tormented me, and I was determined to not let that happen with Anna and Libby.

CHAPTER THIRTEEN

June 23, 2008

MOHAMMED X MARCHES ON THE SOUTH SIDE

SAYS MORE HEROIN VICTIMS ARE BLACK

Chicago Defender

Five days after the attack, the bruises on my neck had turned sour green. I now looked less like a domestic violence victim and more like someone who'd survived a nasty car crash. I couldn't hole up in my apartment any longer.

It was time to visit the parents of the Dead Angels. A week had passed since the girls' funerals. By now their parents would have started ruminating on their daughters' behavior, searching for clues they'd missed. Some might have gone through the girls' bedrooms, sorted through their computers and cell phones, or even pierced their daughters' password-protected Facebook and Twitter accounts. They'd have tired of the evasive detectives who'd stopped promptly returning their phone calls. Their neighbors would have discontinued the string of casseroles they'd been bringing by. Some would have returned to work while others remained at home in a strange state of loneliness and anger, surrounded by memories and consumed with questions, including the most painful one of all: had they really known their daughters?

It was the perfect time for me to show up.

The most popular Angel, Harper Cabot, lived in suburban Evanston in a colossal Queen Anne on a tree-lined street not far from Lake Michigan and Northwestern University's sprawling campus. The squeals of children playing in a nearby backyard were the neighborhood's only sounds. I rang the doorbell. When no one answered, I went to the side yard and peered over the fence. At a patio table, a dark-haired woman was hunched over, reading something in her lap.

"Hello?" I called over the gate.

The woman looked at me with alarm. "Yes?" She didn't move.

"I'm Natalie Delaney with the *Times*? I wanted to talk to you about your daughter." There was no easy way to make such introductions, especially when the woman was fifty feet away.

She waved her hand dismissively. "We're not talking to the media."

"It's just that I read the medical examiner's report. And, well, there are things that I think you should know."

With an enraged look on her face, Mrs. Cabot rose from her chair and stormed toward the gate. "You think I'm going to fall for that *shit*? Who do you think you are, coming here, trying to trick me into talking to you?" When she was within a few feet, her pace slowed, and her eyes narrowed on my face. "What happened to you?" she asked, her voice softer.

"Drug dealer registered his displeasure on my face."

"What kind of drug dealer?" She studied me, probably trying to determine if this was part of the con.

"Is there more than one kind?"

She opened the gate, walked up to me, and, squinting, inspected my wounds, touching the purple splotches on my cheeks. I winced and stepped back from her.

She sighed with exasperation. "I'm just looking at your cuts. You need some ointment or you're going to scar."

I shrugged. "I went to the emergency room."

She laughed smugly. "I'm a plastic surgeon, and if you don't take care of those cuts, you will look like a battered wife the rest of your life. Then again, maybe that's what you really are."

"Do I look like I'm cowering?"

"This drug dealer, does he sell heroin?"

"He didn't like something I wrote."

She bit her lip, then sighed loudly. "Come in the house. I'll fix you up."

I tried not to smile. *I was in! I was in!* Finally, Lester's beating was worth something.

She led me past the yew hedges that smelled like cat urine, through the sliding glass door, into her faux country kitchen with distressed cabinets and high-end appliances, and pulled out a kitchen chair for me. From an overhead shelf she brought down a box of medical supplies and washed my cuts, then applied a cool, minty ointment.

"What's this drug dealer's name?" she asked, dabbing my cuts with a cotton swab.

"I don't know if he's involved with your daughter's case."

"That's not what I asked you." She scowled. "You've come here to ask me a lot of personal questions, correct? The least you could do is tell me the name of the man who cut up your face." She applied a bandage to the worst wound.

"Lester. Lester Williams." Anna had told me his last name.

"And how did you meet this Lester?"

"Through some girls who were doing heroin."

She sat back in her chair, holding a wet Q-tip. In the fractured light of the kitchen, she was pleasant-looking but unremarkable, a woman I might chat up briefly in the grocery store checkout and instantly forget. Her wispy brown hair drooped to her shoulders. She was thin, but had a pronounced wattle that swallowed her chin.

"What is it that you think I should know?"

"Well, you're a doctor. You read the ME's report, right?"

"I couldn't bear it." She shook her head and squeezed her eyes shut. "It's one thing to read the trauma done to a patient. It's entirely different to read what your daughter had to suffer."

I gritted my teeth. "Maybe I shouldn't tell you."

She put back the first aid box, then stood at the oversized

sink. "I don't want to know the extent of her injuries, if that's what you came here to tell me. I'm sure there was alcohol and other drugs involved."

"Did Harper have a drug problem?"

She looked at me with a furious intensity. "I wouldn't know. My daughter was very secretive about her life and her friends. Since her death, I've been trying to figure out what had been going on."

"Did you know the other girls she was with?"

"Not then. I've since met their families. They are just as mystified as I am. Harper was a straight-A student, in Advanced Placement classes. What do *you* know?"

I wondered if her generosity would turn sour once I voiced my theory: "I think there was someone else in that house with the girls." I waited for her to react, but she didn't flinch. "The girls' blood alcohol level was off the charts. That other person may have helped the girls insert the needles into their veins."

I still hadn't eliminated Rex Kennan as the other person. Private school girls like the Dead Angels were definitely in his milieu. And what were the chances that he just happened to be speeding away from the South Side about the time that the Dead Angels were convulsing from fentanyl heroin?

"And you believe this because?"

"You could infer it by the ME's report."

She cleared the table of her first aid scraps, then scrubbed her hands at the sink. She stood staring out the window, her gaze transfixed on something in the yard. "There *was* someone else there. They're calling her 'Ghost Girl.'"

"Who is calling who 'Ghost Girl'?"

"All I know is that the Streets & Sans crew found another person with my daughter and the other girls. That person was barely alive. The cops called her a ghost because she looked dead, but when they went to move her, she sat up and started gasping. They rushed her to the hospital. She *survived*."

I thought back to the Chinatown house and how, when I arrived, an ambulance with its light blazing was leaving. While it's possible the paramedics had been called to another emergency, it was just as likely they were ferrying a girl to the hospital.

Mrs. Cabot walked toward me, angry tears welling in her eyes. "Someone out there—" she jabbed her finger toward the window—"knows what happened to my daughter, and the cops won't even tell me her *name*." She sat down and rubbed her face in her hands. Then she jerked her head up, her eyes wide with an idea. "But they might tell *you*. You have...*connections*, right? Cops tell you things, off the record, and that sort of thing, right?"

I wanted to say that the police were more likely to divulge details to a victim's parents, but I just smiled. Ghost Girl was another piece of information Mo had withheld. Damn him.

"Any chance I could take a look at your daughter's bedroom? Maybe she kept a diary?"

Mrs. Cabot laughed harshly. "Oh yes, she kept a diary. They're all out there on the patio table." She pointed at black leather books stacked in a pile. "I've been going through them for days. Harper was prolific, noting every flaw I had, every personal habit of mine that annoyed her, every instance I failed her. I tell myself that she just wrote in her journal when she was angry, as a release, but there are so many horrific entries—*so much hate*—she must have been angry at me *all the time*." She quietly cried. I stood up and put my hand on her shoulder.

She snatched my wrist and pulled me down to her eye level. "Don't ever write that you hate your mother in your journal. Ever." Her lips stretched tightly against her teeth. "Someday she might have to read how much you despised her, and it will absolutely *crush* her."

I slowly pulled back my arm. "I would never do that. I don't hate my mother, Mrs. Cabot."

"Of course, you don't." She wiped her eyes and stood up, looking embarrassed. "Now, let me show you the little monster's room."

Harper Cabot had been an only child, and her room was a vast collection of designer clothes, handbags, electronic gadgets, hats, trinkets, and photos. Practically every inch of wall space was covered with snapshots of Harper and her friends or posters of thin, heroin-chic models, a painful irony given the circumstances. There was a walk-in closet nearly as big as the bedroom, filled with rows of expensive-looking clothes, some with tags still dangling from the hangers. Mrs. Cabot saw me calculating the exorbitance.

"This was my and my former husband's bedroom. When we divorced, I couldn't stand to be in here, so I gave it to Harper. She wanted to be a model. She needed more closet space." She sounded defensive.

"And your husband?"

"He lives near here. We tried to make it easy on Harper. We had an amicable divorce, shared custody and all that. Harper floated between our houses. We were never sure where she was spending the night. In retrospect, we were probably too permissive, trying to make her happy. Now, reading her diaries, it was clear she took advantage of our guilt. She often told me she was staying at her dad's when she was out with *those girls*, knowing that I wouldn't call and check with my ex. Parenting Harper had been a point of contention in our marriage. Bill was always accusing me of being too protective, too strict. He, on the other hand, gave her everything she wanted. He never once disciplined her."

I stared at Harper's desk, bare except for a computer cord.

"If you're looking for her computer, the detectives took it. They already had her cell phone and backpack. They said it would help them in trying to piece together that night's events. But I hid the diaries. I didn't know what was in them, but I knew it couldn't be good. And I didn't need a bunch of Chicago cops mocking me behind my back."

"Mrs. Cabot, why do you think Harper was mad at you?"

"Call me Wendy. Mrs. Cabot is my former mother-in-law." She pursed her lips, thinking. "I don't really know why. I suppose it stems from the long hours I spent at the hospital, the emergency calls that frequently took me away. According to her diaries, she blamed my job for ruining the marriage. I think she had this picture in her head of what a family was supposed to be, and when we fell far short of that, she blamed me."

I bowed my head, unsure how to comfort a wound that could never be mended now that her daughter was dead.

"I think," I said, "it might help if people knew there was a fourth girl, a living witness."

"That's what I told the cops. They told me to keep quiet, let them do their jobs."

"And how's that working out, now that other girls have been killed?"

"Can you keep my name out of it? I just want to close this sad chapter and get on with my life." She whimpered and swiped at tears with her fingers. "I should have paid more attention to what she was doing. I should have checked on her more. To hell with Bill and his criticism."

"All kids have secret lives. She *was* seventeen, Wendy."

She gave me a sad smile. "You're kind to say that, but I just don't think I was cut out to be a mommy."

We walked down the stairs and out into the front yard. It was nearly noon, and the sun was casting unflattering shadows across her face.

"You think the other parents will talk to me?"

She laughed sharply and sat down on her front steps, out of the glare.

"Not likely. Laila Wozniak's parents were deported last year to Poland. She lived with her grandmother, who only speaks Polish. I heard she is a hoarder. I doubt you'll get past the front door. And Emily Blake's parents aren't holding up too well. They have two other kids, toddlers. Her father yelled at a photographer at the cemetery. He strikes me as someone with a short fuse, a domineering kind of guy. At Harper's wake, the wife didn't even speak." She handed me a tube of medicine. "Keep applying this to your face. A pretty girl like you shouldn't have scars."

CHAPTER FOURTEEN

June 23 & 24, 2008

GOVERNOR THREATENS TO CALL
OUT NATIONAL GUARD

MAYOR ISSUES NEW CITY CURFEW

Chicago Social Scene

That night when I returned home, mail was piled on the hallway table, and Deadline was crying on the other side of my door. I cradled the mail and my bag and unlocked the door, only to lose my grip. Everything crashed to the floor with a loud *thwack*! I picked up Deadline, who had barely escaped the avalanche, and stroked her black fur. I was taking mental inventory of the contents splayed across the parquet floor, including two tiny bottles of booze, when my neighbor clicked open his dead bolts and poked his head out.

"You all right?"

"Fine. Just carrying too many things." I stooped to collect the bottles, but one had rolled next to his doormat. He leaned over and grabbed the miniature Johnnie Walker Red.

"My dad used to drink this." He licked his lips as if he were remembering the punch of malted barley. Then he handed me the bottle, our fingers touching briefly.

Sean Gardner was a high-profile criminal defense attorney. On occasion we had commiserated about our jobs—"bump-ins," as I called them—in the hallway. My tiny apartment was originally the maid's quarters to his. The owner of my unit was a family friend, an elderly woman who'd ended up in a nursing home but was convinced she would one day return.

"Sorry to have disturbed you." I quickly scooped up the rest of my possessions.

Except for the early-morning traffic out his door—all waifish blondes—I never heard a sound from Sean's apartment. Tonight he appeared barefoot in shorts and an oversized Bears jersey. His normally slicked-back hair was loose and curly. Mellow sounds of a jazz trumpet leaked from his spacious condo.

"The fentanyl-heroin stories keeping you busy?" he asked.

I sighed. "You could say that."

"Be careful. The cops don't have a clue."

From the sparkle in his eyes, I knew he wanted to tell me more. "Oh? And what have you heard?"

"It's not what I've *heard*. It's what I *know*."

"Which is?"

"My firm represents several of the Mickey Cobras. I can tell you they're not serial killers—at least not intentionally."

"I'm listening."

He laughed. "We can't have a reporter announcing our strategy."

"Don't you need to publicize some reasons why gun-toting drug dealers might be innocent? You might have a better chance in court if jurors felt the cops were scapegoating the Mickeys instead of finding the real culprits."

"True dat."

"So let me interview them."

He cocked his head and grinned. "I'll have to think about *that*."

He closed his door, and I counted one, two, three, as he latched his dead bolts. I slowly shut my own door, feeling the adrenaline from the possibility of snagging an exclusive interview.

• • •

The next morning, I was getting out of the shower when I heard a knock on my door, and saw Sean through the peephole.

"Yes?" I opened the door in my bathrobe, a towel on my head.

"Get dressed. We've got to get going."

"Where?"

"To jail. Didn't you want to interview the Mickeys? I like to get there after breakfast is served and before the guards get grumpy."

• • •

The line at the jail snaked out the front door and around the tall concertina wire fence. Sean waved toward another entrance for jail personnel and lawyers.

An officer escorted us to an interview room where three men, dressed in potato-sack coveralls, were chained to a table. Most of their exposed skin—parts of their faces, necks, upper chests, forearms, the tops of their hands, and even the delicate dermis between their knuckles—was needled in black and blue. I was used to seeing guys on the street with "sleeves"—whole arms inked—or a gang symbol tattooed on a shaved head. But these men looked freakish and grotesque, like circus oddities. I tried to focus on their faces.

Sean sat next to me, opposite the men.

"What are your names?" I asked, pulling out my notebook.

"Street names only," Sean insisted. "We can't afford to have you attaching their names to what they are about to say. It's too dangerous."

They took turns introducing themselves with creative aliases.

Elvis had a boyish face with pale yellow skin, sepia freckles, and amber eyes. His hair was twisted in long dreads. He had a man's muscular body but wore a childish grin, snickering at inappropriate times. Duke was a short, dark-skinned man with tight cornrows, a lazy expression, and eyes that wandered, as if the conversation bored him. The dominant character was Zorco, an oversized man with matching personality and ego. His bearish face looked puffy, and his hair was knotted in tiny spikes. He talked loudly, opening his mouth wide, showing off slivers of teeth.

"So what's this show about?" Duke asked. "I'm missing *Wheel of Fortune.*"

I started laughing, but Elvis widened his eyes and shook his head. No one else laughed.

"Guys, this is Natalie," Sean said. "She's going to write about your case for the *Times.*"

"A reporter?" Zorco asked. He seemed eager for the attention.

"Why would we want that?" Elvis asked.

"You want someone to tell your story," Sean said. "You want someone to counter what the DEA and the cops are saying. Everyone thinks you are serial killers who used drugs instead of guns. You're looking at life in prison without parole, and possibly the death penalty if they charge you under federal statutes."

Zorco held up his hand for the others to let him talk. "Okay. It's like this." He fingered the spiked braids that made him look like a crazed clown. "We got this thing going. It's a beautiful thing, you know. We're not fighting with no one, and we're just cool. We're doing our biz. We're making money, and life is a woman. But then The Man shows up with some new product he wants us to move, with skull and crossbones on it."

"Who's The Man?" I asked.

Zorco glowered. "He's our boss. The Big Man? We ain't here to squeal on him."

"But you knew the heroin was cut with fentanyl?" I asked.

"Seriously?" Zorco glared. "Lady, let us tell our story."

Sean tapped my knee under the table.

"So we start moving the shit, and it was the bomb. We couldn't sell enough of it."

"But people were dying, right?" I interjected.

"Always some motherfuckers dying of H," Duke said, defensively. "We tried to cut the stuff so it won't be so strong. But it didn't matter. That H was so fuckin' powerful."

"You knew you were killing people, and you just kept selling Poison?" Their tale of woe wasn't working on me.

"We wasn't sure at first," Zorco said, his voice rising. "But when lots of niggas started dying, The Man didn't care. He told us we had to keep selling it if we didn't want heat. But then those white girls turn up dead. We told The Man we need to cool it for a while. Them drugs was too hot. Cops was coming around."

"That's when the feds busted us," Elvis said.

"So how many people died?"

Elvis shrugged. The other guys looked down at the table.

"You act like we had a choice," Duke said.

"We gotta do what The Man says," Elvis protested. He had a tattoo of two drops at the corner of his mouth. I knew a teardrop tattoo under an eye symbolized each murder the bearer had committed, but I'd never seen drops near someone's lips. I hadn't meant to stare.

"You like my tattoos?" Elvis touched one at the corner of his mouth.

"They're unusual. Do they mean something?" I asked.

He laughed and licked his lips. "My girlfriend's juices." He puckered his mouth and gave me an air kiss.

I tried not to look shocked.

"C'mon, man. Stop flirting with the reporter," Zorco snapped. Then he turned to me. "Ma'am, we wasn't the only ones selling Poison. There was people dying we never sold to. Somebody else was out there doing it too."

"Another gang?"

"Don't know. But we've been in here, and the killing ain't stopped," Duke said. "But we *never* sold to no white girls, that's for sure."

"You never sold to a single white woman?" I didn't bother hiding my doubt.

The men looked at each other and vigorously shook their heads. "I don't know. Some whores maybe? But no girls," Zorco said. "Skanks sometimes. Never no girls."

"Man, I ain't *never* sold to no white woman," Duke reiterated.

"You think you were set up?" I'd done a lot of stories on drugs dealers who snitched on their competition to eliminate them.

"Who knows? There was this one dude who bought five grand a week," Duke said. He bit the head off a pen I'd placed on the table, and the ink was turning his lips blue, matching the rest of his body.

"What's the name of this big buyer?" I asked.

For the first time Duke laughed. "Lady, you don't ask names. We called him 'Locks.'"

"What did he look like?"

"Dude was white," Elvis piped up. "He carried this gun on his hip, like he was fucking Clint Eastwood."

They all laughed.

"He was crackers, man," Duke said. "Fuckin' crazy. He would say 'I'm wearing protection. If you fuck with me, they'll come in and fucking kill you all.' We thought he was funny, and we liked him because he always brought clean cash."

"You think he was an undercover cop?"

Zorco bunched up his lips. "Nah. He was some kind of rapper or something. It was like he playing being a bad dude."

"Any more questions?" Sean asked abruptly. He seemed nervous about the level of detail the guys were providing.

"Why'd you call him Locks?" I asked.

"'Cause he was a real pretty boy," Elvis said, as if that made perfect sense. "He called me 'brother' and told me he was black." He snickered. "Dude used to rap. He called it freestyling skittle-scat. Made us laugh. White dude, long blond hair—but with dreads."

"Dreads?" I grabbed Sean's cell phone on the table and googled Rapper X images. I held up the phone. "This him?"

The guys leaned in and squinted at the small screen.

"Yeah, that's him," Zorco said. "Hey, dude's really a rapper? Who knew?"

"A rapper who sells heroin," I clarified. "He works for Mohammed X, patron of the Gangster Disciples. Why is he buying Poison from you?"

CHAPTER FIFTEEN

June 25 & 26, 2008

MICKEY COBRAS GANG CLAIM THEY
NEVER SOLD TO WHITE GIRLS

ALDERMEN QUESTION VALIDITY OF GANG ARRESTS

Chicago Times

When I called Mo to see what he could tell me about Ghost Girl, he said that I'd have to go through official channels—meaning I'd have to talk to his boss, Captain Detective Tim Nickles. Unlike Mo, Detective Nickles had never taken a liking to me. He was a crude man who openly despised women and frequently made sexist jokes. Nickles was so secretive and paranoid that he refused to talk on the phone with his own detectives, much less reporters.

When I showed up at his office, Nickles made me wait in the lobby for an hour before he appeared in the doorway chomping gum and nervously clutching at his wrists. In his early fifties, he had a comb-over of wispy, flyaway hair that sometimes covered his square black glasses. His long, angular face was set off by a Fu Manchu mustache. When he opened his mouth, his distinct nasal slur gave him away as a native South Sider—actually a *former* South Sider, someone whose family moved during the city's white flight that made the South Side majority black and created a racially divided Chicago.

"So you say a girl survived at the Chinatown drug house, and you want us to identify her?" We were standing in his office now.

He kept his blinds closed and used a low-wattage desk lamp for light, which cast menacing shadows across his face. His black eyes, behind thick glasses, bore into me while his teeth gnawed angrily at the wad in his mouth. "That's just not going to happen."

"Then can you at least confirm that they found a survivor with the Dead Angels? I hear they're calling her 'Ghost Girl.'"

"And just where are you getting this information?"

"I can't tell you that, only that it's a source who doesn't want his or her name used."

He leaned across his desk and motioned for me to come closer, as if he were about to share something confidential. "The next time your 'source' decides to share his ejaculations with you, my advice is that you swallow, don't spit."

• • •

That afternoon, still reeling from Nickles' insult, I mindlessly clicked on my Facebook page and felt a surge of adrenaline: Rex Kennan had replied to my message from a week earlier.

"Ms. Delaney," he wrote, "I apologize for not answering your message sooner. I don't often check my Facebook page. I'm writing now to let you know that I fear you have been misinformed. I am willing to meet with you to clear up any misunderstanding, but I'm afraid I have to insist our conversation is off the record. If you're agreeable to those terms, I can join you at Riccardo's tonight at ten."

How many twenty-one-year-olds would have the presence of mind to insist upon ground rules or would suggest Riccardo's? He was showing his roots as the scion of one of America's famous political families. Riccardo's was an upscale bar downtown where geriatric journalists hung out, reliving their better years over hard liquor. Rex had probably heard his father or relatives talk about meeting reporters there back in the day. It was a safe bet on his part, knowing there'd be plenty of witnesses if he needed them.

I arrived at nine-thirty and chose a table facing the door,

wanting to get a good look at him before he saw me. I ordered a Jack and Coke, turned down the "no smoking" card stuck inside an ashtray on my table, and lit a cigarette. Chicago was six months into a smoking ban, but many bars, like Riccardo's, didn't bother enforcing the law. At about ten o'clock, I received a text: *turn around.*

I had to squint, but in a dark corner I could make out the familiar contours I'd first seen on the Internet. He'd been there all along, watching me.

"Clever boy, aren't you?" I pulled out a hi-boy chair across from him.

He nodded at my bag. "I'll need you to turn off your phone. Can't take any chances that you're recording this."

"Okay. You have your conditions, and I have mine. No more messaging through your Facebook account. I need a real cell number."

He bore a look of surprise. "Sure." Then he took out his phone and called mine. When it rang, I nodded and shut mine off.

By then, my eyes had adjusted to the darkness, and I could see that Rex was actually much more handsome than his Facebook photo allowed—his square jaw and intense gaze conveying an inherited confidence not so evident in a snapshot.

"So why'd you agree to meet me?"

"My father always said: 'Make friends with the press. They're going to print what they want, but at least it will be harder for them to go negative if they know you.'"

I laughed. "He's right."

He returned a smug smile. "I came here because I wanted to let you know what you heard about my traffic stop on Lake Shore Drive was wrong."

"Okay, so fill me in."

He sat back in his chair. "It's not what it seems. I carry the heroin antidote because I've had friends who have overdosed, and I just want to be prepared in case something happens to one of them."

"So you're often present when people are doing H?"

He shook his head. "Now, don't go twisting my words. I've never watched anyone do heroin. But I have received more than one panicked phone call after someone got a hotshot."

"Yeah? And what did you do when you got such a phone call?"

He bit down on his lower lip. "I didn't come here to talk about that. I just wanted you to know that I wasn't doing anything illegal except speeding on Lake Shore Drive."

"And where had you been until three a.m. that night?"

"With friends."

"Did any of those 'friends' include the Dead Angels?"

The confidence drained from his face. "If you must know, my father gave me a Jaguar XJX for college graduation. I was just testing its limits with a couple of friends."

"Yes, it's called drag racing, and it's *illegal*." I lit a cigarette, knowing it would annoy him.

"Noted."

"So what was your relationship with the dead girls from Queen of Angels?"

He sat up rigidly. "I've told you my story. Don't link me with those girls. I don't know them. There's nothing nefarious about my traffic stop. And that's what I came here to tell you."

"Then why'd the police drop the charges? Why doesn't the arrest paperwork exist anywhere?"

He stood. "Now that, Ms. Delaney, is hardly a mystery." He tipped his head at me as if he had a hat and headed toward the door before I could articulate my next question.

• • •

An hour later, I nervously stood on the deck in front of Danny and Libby's apartment. I had to find out if Anna—or her friends—had heard of Ghost Girl or if they knew anything about Rex Kennan. Lights glowed from the windows, and I could hear the television. If

Danny appeared at the door, I was unsure what I would say. When the door cracked open, I could see Libby had been crying.

"Oh, it's you." She unlatched the security chain. Her face was pasty, her black hair mussed and tangled.

I entered hesitantly, my heart hammering inside my chest. Only six days had passed since the attack. I followed Libby into the kitchen. McDonald's and Popeye's wrappers were strewn across the table. Bent pizza boxes sat atop an overflowing garbage can. But it was the crushed beer cans stacked on the counter that stopped me.

"Don't worry. They're not here."

Anna stumbled out of a back bedroom, looking wild-eyed, clutching a small silver canister.

"Hi, Natalie!" she yelled, then lost her balance and lurched forward, the carpet cushioning her fall.

Libby and I lifted her from the floor and guided her to the couch. From her hand fell a canister known as a whippet, a dispenser for nitrous oxide, used by huffers for a cheap high. Anna mumbled incoherently. Her head slumped. Using her own shirttail, Libby gently wiped a string of drool from Anna's mouth.

"Damn, Anna, are you trying to sample every drug out there?" I asked.

"Looks like it, doesn't it?" It was the first time I'd heard Libby side against her cousin.

Libby left Anna on the couch and sat down at the kitchen table, her head in her hands.

"I don't know what to do." Libby seemed exhausted and much older. I knew that look, that fear in her eyes. It had been me at the end with Jake, unable to sleep for fear he'd sneak out and score.

"What's going on?"

Libby looked down, her hair covering her face. "Anna decided she wanted to try whippets. Out of nowhere. She gets this burr up her ass and runs off to the park."

"I thought you all were into heroin?"

Libby wrinkled her face. "Who said that? Anna's into whatever she can get her hands on." I'd been so focused on Anna, I hadn't considered where Libby stood in all this.

"Have you told your dad?"

"You mean about her tripping on whippets?"

"Any of it. This, the other night?"

She looked down at the dingy linoleum floor and shook her head. Ratting out Anna was against the cousins' code of secrets. "You can't tell him neither. You promised you wouldn't get us into trouble." Black mascara smudges rimmed her eyes. "I know my dad likes you. But…"

Anna stirred in the living room, then jumped up and began running in circles, her arms outstretched, her mouth making buzzing noises like a toy airplane.

I started to get up, but Libby grabbed my arm. "She'll get tired and fall asleep. That's what she needs right now."

For the next hour, Anna bounced between looking alert, her eyes wide and excited, to practically comatose, her head drooped to her shoulders. I had seen girls inhale nitrous oxide from balloons at rave parties and guys huffing in parks, but that hadn't prepared me for how Anna was acting. Libby wasn't sure how many whippets Anna had huffed or whether she'd consumed anything else.

I debated taking Anna to the emergency room. The effects of inhaling nitrous oxide were brief, usually lasting no more than a few minutes. But Libby didn't know what other drugs Anna might have consumed. I knew showing up at the emergency room meant filling out forms, Children's Services would be called, and Anna might wind up in foster care or juvenile detention, especially since she already had an arrest record. I also knew calling Danny meant reneging on my promise to the girls.

I decided to drive to a hospital in case Anna got worse. We could sit in the parking lot and monitor her condition. Libby objected, insisting Anna just needed to sleep it off, but helped me load her into the car anyway. Anna slumped on her cousin's lap in the passenger seat. I made wider and wider circles around various hospitals, studying Anna for some overt change. She seemed to come a little more to life the more we drove.

When we passed the red light district, I recognized a few of the prostitutes I'd interviewed for stories; their ghoulish smiles and missing front teeth made them look like zombies in the headlights. I parked the car and turned to Anna. She was resting her head against Libby's shoulder; I knew she wasn't asleep.

"Is this what you want to become, Anna?" I asked. "Do you want to suck dick so you can get high? Look around, because this is your future if you don't quit that shit."

Anna shook her head but was unable to look away from the women who bent down to peer inside our car for potential customers. "That's not me. I'm not addicted."

Knuckles rapped against the passenger window. I pushed the button and the window opened. An old woman squatted down to meet us at eye level. She had flaming, dyed-red hair with an inch of gray at the roots and waterfalls of wrinkles under her eyes. Seeing the girls, she laughed. It was a smoker's cackle, as if she might spit up chunks of her lungs.

"You babysitting tonight, hon?" she called to me over the noise of the nearby traffic.

"Just driving."

"You need a school bus for these girls." Her lipstick bled above her mouth. The whites of her eyes were red and her low-cut blouse revealed two leathery, jiggly breasts.

"You see something you like?" she asked, following my gaze.

The girls fidgeted, uncomfortable with the woman so close, spraying them with her spit as she yelled to be heard.

"You got a cigarette, hon?"

I rifled through my bag and handed her a couple.

She stuck one in her mouth and stashed the other in her bra. "Hey, them's sweet."

"They're clove," I said.

"I meant the girls," she said, careful not to exhale smoke into the car. "Better never catch you out here, girls. I don't need no young pussy like yous for competition. Got it?"

Anna flinched and sat up straight. "I want to go home."

The woman stuck her arm into the car and stretched out her palm. "You got some change, hon? It's been a slow night."

I handed her a twenty.

She winked. "Hope you got what you came for."

By the time I arrived at Libby's apartment building, Anna was asleep, her head curled into her cousin's neck.

"Can you take her? Just for tonight?" Libby begged. The circles under her eyes had darkened. Clearly, this was not the first time Libby had cared for her cousin while she was high.

I closed my eyes and sighed. *Don't get attached. Remember, you're a reporter, not a social worker.*

"Yeah, sure."

. . .

The next morning, I stood over the couch and watched Anna sleep. She was wearing an old pair of my pajamas, and her red hair and pale skin in the morning light reminded me of my childhood pictures. Deadline jumped on the couch and stretched out next to Anna purring loudly. Anna opened her eyes and grinned widely at the cat, picked her up, and stroked her head.

"I wish I had a cat."

"She comes with a litter box and a scoop for poop."

She wrinkled her nose. "What's her name?"

"Deadline."

"That's a weird name for a cat."

"I found her while working on a story about a woman who had been murdered in her apartment and no one found her until a week later. The cat was nothing but fur and claws by that point. I took her to the newsroom. She kept jumping on my lap, eager to be petted, nudging my fingers while I was typing. I kept saying: 'I'm on deadline. I'm on deadline. Deadline. That's how she got her name. I had hoped my friend Ben would take her, but it turned out he's allergic to cats. Since I don't have any kids or a husband, I took her home."

"Hey, maybe you and Uncle Danny should get together." Her face beamed with the thought.

"I'm on a man hiatus at the moment."

I moved a stack of newspapers from a kitchen chair for Anna, then fixed her a bowl of milk and cereal.

"We need to talk about last night."

"Is this the part where you say you're 'concerned' and all that shit?" she asked, spooning stale Cheerios into her mouth.

"I don't know. I've never had this conversation with anyone before," I lied. It was one thing to plead with a lover about getting off drugs and another to preach the dangers of illegal substances to a girl young enough to be my daughter.

"Uh-huh. Well, I'm just experimenting. Everyone does it. I'm sure you did drugs when you were a teenager. Pot is still illegal you know."

I eyed her with annoyance, but didn't respond. I was uncomfortable in this role of quasi-mother. I knew firsthand how ineffective speeches about drugs were.

"Thought so," she continued. "It's just something I have to do. I know what addiction is. My dad was a dealer, remember? Women used to come around all the time. Dad called them *chromers*. Said they'd suck the chrome off an exhaust pipe for drugs. I'm not going to wind up like that. So save the speech."

I scanned the morning papers, pretending to read. Anna got up and put her hands on my shoulders, and the tension between us dissipated. She craned her neck to see what I found so intriguing—a story about Rev. Jesse Jackson caught on a live microphone saying he wanted to cut off the nuts of our Hyde Park Senator for "talking down to blacks." It clearly didn't interest her. Instead, she pointed to a picture of the Senator stumping.

"My mom is related to some politician," she blurted.

"What's his name?"

"Don't remember. I only met him once. His wife gave me this Easter outfit that was way too tight and stank like moth balls."

We both laughed.

"My mom is always saying we are related to famous people, like Elvis or Bill Clinton or the Governor. I think she makes it up. We never did do too much with relatives. I mean, my dad was always in jail, and my mom used to drink a lot."

That afternoon, Anna and I watched *Sex and the City* reruns and ate Moose Tracks ice cream while still in our pajamas. I thought if I spent more time with her, maybe she'd open up about what was driving her to experiment so aggressively. Or maybe she'd trust me and tell me what she knew about girls doing Poison.

I waited until late afternoon before bringing up the Chinatown bodies. "I talked with one of the mothers of the Dead Angels, and she says there was a girl who survived. They are calling her 'Ghost Girl.' Any idea who she might be?"

Anna shrugged. "Why would I know?"

"Because those Dead Angels were sucking on fentanyl lollipops before they died—just like your friends the other night."

Anna rolled her eyes. "Those are everywhere at raves. It's no big deal."

"The girls who died were sucking on F-sticks. Why doesn't that terrify you?"

"Can you stop acting like somebody's mother? I already told you, you have to know who is giving you stuff. Those dead girls probably bought drugs from some dealer they didn't know."

"It's that simple, huh? And how many dealers do you know *personally*?"

"I have friends. They take care of me."

"Do your friends give you H?"

She glared at me. "I'm *so* not going to answer that."

Anna seemed her sarcastic self, not edgy or nervous, just a typical teenager. I thought if she were truly addicted she wouldn't be able to go a day without getting wasted. Still, I had to be sure. While she was in the shower, I searched her purse. I found a vial of lip gloss and a small leather wallet with a little money inside. In the wallet's plastic photo pockets she'd stuck snapshots of her parents and a recent photo booth shot of her and Libby. Tucked in the back was my card. On top she'd written, "in case of emergency."

I felt a pang in my chest, as if she'd written "I love you."

I was rifling through her jeans when Anna walked out of the bathroom wearing a towel. "What are you doing?"

I stood there with her pants in my hands, pockets inside out.

She snapped the jeans away. "You don't fucking go through my shit. Ever." She stormed into the bedroom and slammed the door.

On the way back to Danny and Libby's apartment, Anna pouted, refusing to even look in my direction. When we reached the building, I pulled into the back lot next to Danny's truck, my belly a twist of nerves, knowing I'd probably have to lie to Danny about why I took his niece home. Anna hesitated before getting out of the car.

"How come you don't have kids?"

"I told you before: I need to be married first."

"So you wouldn't want to adopt a kid unless you were married?"

"What are you saying? You want me to adopt *you*? Is that what you're asking?"

Anna looked away and shrugged. "Just wondered, that's all."

She opened the car door and bolted up the stairs. I dawdled, rewinding our conversation again and again in my head. We barely knew each other. Was her talk of adoption a way of toying with me—getting me back for digging through her jeans? She had no idea how much her suggestion would open old wounds. She didn't know about Jake and what had happened between us. She didn't know that when I looked at her, I often wondered if some part of the universe was showing me what our child might have looked like.

I stumbled out of the car as if I were drunk, my mind strung out on thoughts of Jake and Anna and what it all meant. As I neared the top landing, I saw amber threads of his cigarette in the dark. He was leaning over the railing.

"You all right?" His voice was rough.

I wondered where to begin.

"The girls get into trouble last night?" he asked, not waiting for my answer. "That why you took Anna home, huh? You didn't want me to see her?" He straightened his back, flexed his arms, and cocked his right eyebrow as if he'd caught me in a lie.

"Danny, this is all too complicated." I grabbed the railing to steady myself.

"What's wrong?" The edge in his voice disappeared. He brushed his thumb over my split lip. I flinched. His touch felt electric, synapses twitched up and down my body. The gentleness of a strong man had always been my undoing. His calloused fingers glided over my cheeks, my bruised eyelids.

"You're like a wounded cat, cowering and skittish," he whispered. His breath made my skin tingle. I closed my eyes, and he pulled my face toward his. His lips were soft and timid. I could taste the sweetness of beer on his tongue, and for a moment I forgot about all the conflicted feelings I had and gave in.

Anna and Libby shrieked with laughter inside the apartment, breaking the spell. I pushed him away. His face looked wounded in the half-light of the porch.

"The girls tell me secrets—secrets I can't tell you. I've promised them."

"You have a job to do." He moved closer. "I get that."

"No, you don't." I walked to the far end of the landing. "This is all muddled. I shouldn't have…I mean, I have to stay objective. We can't…"

He slowly edged toward me and reached for my hand, his warm fingers grasping at my palms. If the girls knew about Danny and me, they'd never include me in their adventures. I needed them more than I needed him. But, God, did I want him in that moment.

I pulled back my hand. "Please talk to Libby. She needs to be the one to tell you."

CHAPTER SIXTEEN

June 27, 2008

CRIME RATES THREATEN U.S. OLYMPIC BID

CHICAGO HEROIN DEATHS CITED AS DAMAGING 2016 HOPES

New York Times

I left the apartment that night knowing what I had to do. I couldn't remain an observer, watching as Anna spiraled out of control. At least Libby was starting to come around about how dangerous her cousin's taste for drugs had become.

I called a long-time source, a firefighter and paramedic who had often tipped me off about people rescue workers couldn't resuscitate, including Poison victims. He agreed to meet me at Emmit's Irish Pub, a firemen hangout just west of downtown, a place with tacky knickknacks—brass spittoons and ceramic dalmatians—mounted to the walls and ceiling. By the time I arrived at five, guys in official blue Chicago Fire T-shirts were standing shoulder to shoulder. Mark was at his usual table, a nod away from the bartender, his hands gripping a mug of Black and Tan. When he saw me, he broke into a toothy grin.

"Nattie!" He swung an arm around my neck. "Good God. You're looking skinny. What the hell's happened to you? Not trying to fit in too much with those heroin addicts, are you?"

He yanked at my arm, pretending to look for track marks.

"Fuck off, Mark!" I rubbed the milky skin of my inner elbow where his calloused fingers had tugged.

Mark was an awkward sort of guy, over six-feet, four-inches tall with a mashed-up, adolescent face, a bulky frame, and social gawkiness that made him a frequent target of fellow firefighters. He liked meeting me in front of them, pretending I was his date. But they all knew the score.

"Aw, come on. I'm just teasing you." He patted my shoulder, looking around to see if anyone had seen me push him away.

"It's not funny, Mark. You think I want to put Poison in my veins?"

"Nah, Nattie. You can't blame me for wondering. You look like you haven't eaten in a week. And what happened to your face?"

"It's nothing. Hazards of the job."

"So how's your story coming?"

"I'm in the thick of it now."

"I can tell. Who is *she*?"

"What are you talking about?"

"With you, there's always some victim, some down-and-out sad sack case you're trying to save."

My thoughts flickered to Jake. "What's your point?"

The bartender slammed down two foaming mugs; beer sloshed over the rims.

"Thanks, Ted," Mark said, tucking a ten-dollar bill into the bartender's belt loop.

Firemen often struck me as outwardly homophobic but secretly curious. Mark and his firehouse buddies were almost too familiar with each other, a little too generous with the backslaps and shoulder hugs, sleeping in the same rooms, showering together. Their conversations were full of insider jokes, personal jabs, and politically incorrect remarks, like frat boys who never grew up, still laughing at farts and penis sizes.

"There's this girl who is dabbling with H." Saying it out loud made me realize that Anna had become less integral to the story and more important to me personally. Instead of writing about Ghost Girl—which was what I should have been doing at that moment—I was trying to find ways to protect Anna.

He scratched the stubble on his chin. "How old is she?"

"Fifteen. She's smoked heroin and she was high on whippets and something else the other night. She seems to be trying as many different drugs as possible. I'm worried Poison is next."

"Well, there's naloxone. It works like magic. One minute they're on death's doorstep, and the next they're wide awake and wondering what happened. Then they get pissed when they realize you spoiled their high. I always feel a little like Dr. Frankenstein bringing them back." A crazy grin spread across his face.

"Does it always work?"

"Sometimes you have to inject them a bunch of times, especially if the heroin's strong. I remember we injected this one guy, and we were talking to him and we thought he was fine, but then a couple minutes later he went under again."

"Did you revive him?"

He shook his head sadly. "If they've done a lot of dope, then you have to inject them like every ten minutes. You just never know." Mark slugged back his beer. "C'mon. I've got some in my truck you can have."

I chugged my beer and followed him, wondering how Rex Kennan had come by his naloxone shots.

When we reached Mark's truck, he turned to me. "You seem different, Nattie. Are you sure you're okay?"

"I'm fine. Just worried about this girl. That's all."

Mark opened the truck door. "Get in."

He only had a single vial of naloxone and a needle left in his emergency kit. His instructions were brief: stick the needle into the vial, then pull the syringe back to fill to the 1 cc mark. Then inject it into the thick of a muscle.

"The butt is the best." He giggled.

I laughed, too, and, for a moment I forgot we were conspiring to save a young girl's life.

• • •

When I arrived at the girls' apartment that night, the door was unlocked. Libby was watching television alone in the dark.

"Hey, Lib, what's up?"

"Anna's not here."

The place smelled clean for once. "Where'd she go?"

Libby peeled her eyes from the television and gave me a stiff look. "Don't know."

"You guys have a fight or something?"

"Maybe."

I sat on the arm of the leopard print chair and leaned toward her.

"What happened?"

She pivoted away from me: "You don't want to know."

"Yeah, I do."

Libby clicked off the television and stared at the black screen, the street lights filtering through the shades. "She's with Lester."

"What?" I jumped up. Just the mention of his name made my face hurt.

"He came around today. There's no way I was going with him. But you know Anna, always sniffing for a hit." There was a newly acquired disgust in her voice.

"She's with him now?"

Libby shrugged. "Look, I can't keep up with her all the time."

"But I thought you guys were close?"

"We're cousins, not twins. I'm tired of all that shit!" She jumped from the couch and began pacing. "Besides, my dad and I have been talking. I don't want to do this stuff anymore. Anna— she doesn't have a mom and dad around. They don't give a damn. She just gets her little envelope every month. The guilt check, she calls it."

"Why?"

"'Cause her stepfather's a fuckin' creep, that's why."

"There's got to be more to it than that."

Libby sighed dramatically. "He used to get all handsy with her. That's why she ended up in Children's Services. She can't live with them. Dad didn't know until he tried to send her back home, and her case worker said she'd go to a foster family if we didn't keep her. I think her mom sends her money just so she won't tell the cops everything her stepfather did to her."

"Anna's stepfather molested her?"

"She won't talk about it, but if Anna told him no, that fucker made up shit about her to her mom, like Anna was being mouthy or he found pot in her room. Stuff like that. He made Aunt Patty not believe anything Anna said. Who does that shit?"

"What's she doing with Lester?"

"What do you think?"

"And you let her go alone?"

"Anna does what she wants. I can't stop her."

Minutes later we were cruising the back streets of Chinatown, looking for Anna. It didn't take much to convince Libby to tag along; I suspected she felt guilty for letting her cousin go alone with Lester. I wasn't sure what I was going to do if we found him. Libby directed me to the house where we'd met that first day—where they found the Dead Angels, the yellow police tape long since removed. I parked a few houses away, and we watched as a trickle of slender figures, many wearing hoodies, came and went.

I pulled out the vial Mark had given me. "I want you to have this."

Libby studied the glass container and the blue-capped needle in my hand and took it.

"Do you know how to use it?"

She nodded reluctantly.

"How do you know?"

Libby clamped her eyes shut. "Me and Anna came here last week to hang out. You know, just to watch. We didn't have any money. We were upstairs in this room smoking a joint when this guy passed out and shit started coming out of his mouth. This big black dude took out a needle and stabbed it in the guy's leg, and the guy sat up like some freakin' zombie. It was fuckin' spooky. Scared the shit out of me. But not Anna. She started asking the guy all these questions about what it felt like to be dead and to come back. He got mad at her. Told her to shut up, but she kept on. Then he holds out a needle and some H and says, 'Find out for yourself.' I pulled Anna out. If she fuckin' wants to kill herself, she can do it alone. I'm not gonna watch."

I looked over at Libby, red-eyed and gnawing at her cuticles. Anna wasn't the only one who needed help. I pulled her hand away from her mouth.

"You know you can call me anytime," I said softly. "You don't have to do this alone."

CHAPTER SEVENTEEN

June 28 & 29, 2008

CHICAGO MEDIA OFFERING REWARD FOR GHOST GIRL

COPS REFUSE TO RELEASE IDENTITY OF POISON SURVIVOR

Chicago Reporter

Amy was circling my cubicle every few minutes, anxious for anything new about the Dead Angels. If I didn't get something soon, she'd likely assign me some pathetic story, like a seven-hour education board meeting, or a county zoning commission meeting, or—perhaps the lowest—an obituary. You knew you were on an editor's shit list when you were assigned an obit.

"Whatever you got in that reporter's notebook," Ben said, eyeing me from his cubicle, "you'd better start dumping it into the computer, because that woman keeps nosing around here like she smells something dead, and it *ain't* those girls."

I nodded nervously. "It's coming."

Despite texting Mo for several days, I still hadn't heard back. I had tracked down the sanitation worker who found Ghost Girl. It wasn't hard since he'd blabbed to half of City Hall. He agreed to talk to me because he was considering suing the city for worker's compensation, claiming he had suffered grievous emotional distress. The coroner investigator was a bit harder to convince, but eventually he gave me a brief—and harmless—quote. I decided to hold back the details about the Dead Angels' flaming red tongues for a future story and possible bargaining chip with Mo.

My Ghost Girl story ran as the lead article online that afternoon, with a giant headline:

"GHOST GIRL" SURVIVES POISON HEROIN WITH DEAD ANGELS

CHICAGO POLICE WON'T DISCLOSE
GIRL'S IDENTITY OR WHAT SHE SAW

By Natalie Delaney

When a Chicago Streets & Sans worker found several female students lying in an abandoned Chinatown house earlier this month, he thought they were all dead—until one stirred. The sanitation worker believed he was seeing a ghost, but then the girl opened her eyes.

She was barely alive.

"I just couldn't believe it," recalled the worker, who asked that his name not be used, because he had not been granted permission to speak to the media. "She was so pale and her lips were shriveled like grapes. It scared the sh— out of me, and I just started screaming."

Police have not released the identity of the survivor, known as "Ghost Girl," to the families of the three Queen of Angels students who died of heroin poisoning. Their bodies were found on June 13. The Cook County Medical Examiner has ruled their deaths homicides. Previous deaths by fentanyl-heroin, known as Poison on the streets, have been ruled as suspicious overdoses.

While the Medical Examiner's office refused to comment on the ruling, an investigator with the office said they'd collected enough evidence to conclude that someone had helped the girls inject the fatal heroin and then left them to die in the abandoned house.

"It was a miracle that she lived," the investigator said of the Ghost Girl.

The Dead Angels were juniors at the Queen of Angels Academy in Rogers Park who on the last day of school went to the Chinatown neighborhood and injected heroin. They were later identified as Harper Cabot, 17, of Evanston, Laila Wozniak, 16, of Chicago, and Emily Blake, 17, of Skokie. Their families did not wish to speak on the record.

One of the girls' mothers said she was angry that the police had not revealed the identity of the mysterious survivor or what details the girl had provided police. The girls had been dead for three days when someone called 311 and complained of rats in an abandoned building in Chinatown. Police now believe that anonymous caller may be linked to the deaths.

A police source said the suspect in the killings may not be a drug dealer. Last week, an FBI-DEA-Chicago Police Department task force charged 47 Mickey Cobra gang members with multiple counts of second-degree murder, saying they manufactured and sold tainted heroin that has killed dozens of people. At their arraignment, the judge set bail of $1 million per defendant, citing the number of victims.

Mickey Cobra gang members, in an exclusive interview with the *Chicago Times*, adamantly denied they had ever sold Poison to any white girls. Gang members contend police are using them as scapegoats.

The story generated a flurry of emails from people who offered their own ideas about the identity of Ghost Girl. And even though it'd been scooped, our tabloid competition, the *Sentinel,* shamelessly launched a contest with a thousand dollars in prize money for the person who correctly provided Ghost Girl's identity. Local radio and television talk shows were abuzz, even featuring therapists who talked about the psychological damage Ghost Girl might have suffered lying next to her dead friends.

Mo's reaction, delivered via text, was predictable and succinct: *F U.*

• • •

Minutes later, I was leaving the *Times* building when someone caught my elbow.

"Fucking great story," Julian said, his face more friendly than I'd remembered. I rarely saw Julian because the business news department was in a different part of the building. I'd emailed some information about Rex Kennan's arrest, but I hadn't mentioned that I'd met him. I wanted to make another go at Rex, but I didn't need Julian hounding me until I did.

"Thanks. Sorry I haven't done more on Kennan. But the cops didn't think much of it. And since there were no charges…"

"Since when do you believe the cops? Did you believe them about the Mickeys? What do they say now that their main suspects are behind bars and the bodies keep dropping?"

"They claim there are copycats eager to take up where the Mickeys left off."

"And you believe them?"

I didn't like the way he was goading me. "You really want me to step back from a front-page story about Ghost Girl and chase something I've already reached a dead end on?"

"A Kennan carrying syringes and a heroin antidote…hmm… Doesn't sound like a dead end to me."

He pulled out a stack of papers from his bag. "I had one of my reporters do some research. Turns out Kennan went to New Trier High School. Do you know how many girls from New Trier or recent grads have died of poisoned heroin? Maybe he knows something."

I felt a sharp pang in my side, the kind I got when I'd missed a key detail in reporting a story. I'd been so focused on the Dead

Angels I hadn't pressed Rex about other girls who'd died. He said he had friends who'd overdosed. He'd received panicked phone calls from friends who'd suspected they'd gotten a hotshot.

Julian read the alarm on my face. "It's okay. Check it out before somebody else does." He handed me the stack and left.

As I glanced at the papers, another question nagged at me: why was Julian so fixated on Rex Kennan? Was it just a journalistic hunch or did he know something he wasn't telling me?

• • •

The next afternoon, writing at my desk, I looked up to see Mohammed X, flanked by an entourage of men in expensive suits, being escorted into the newspaper's editorial boardroom. While it wasn't unusual to have controversial figures speak to the editorial board—the folks who wrote the paper's unsigned opinion pieces— it was unusual not to invite reporters to attend.

Amy's office door was cracked open and she was squinting at her computer—too vain to wear reading glasses—when I barged in.

"What do you know about Mohammed X speaking to the editorial board? Why the hell wasn't I invited?"

She waved for me to sit down. "We thought his visit would be less contentious if you weren't there. He seems to have a particular enmity for you. It seems very personal. He complained that your stories about him were unfair. The paper is simply giving him an opportunity to voice his point of view."

"His side? Does he deny that he called Poison heroin a hoax perpetrated by a white mayor? He said that before a packed convention hall. Is he now trying to take it all back?"

Amy shifted in her chair. She'd recently lost weight and had her hair straightened so that it hung to her shoulders, curving at the ends. She wore a snug dress with a chunky gold chain necklace and earrings. Her designer high heels lay under her desk, kicked to the side, her toes spreading out in her nude nylons. She didn't seem like a rumpled city editor anymore but had morphed into a corporate-looking vice president. In a newsroom, upward ambition can be dangerous. It often requires hijacking good journalism in order to reap more profit for the paper, something that ink-stained wretches are supposed to not care about. But with Amy, it was all she talked about—the paper's bottom line.

"Natalie, focus on the Poison girls and forget politics, okay?"

"But he's involved. The Mickey Cobras identified Mohammed X's drug guy as the man who'd been buying their Poison. Mohammed X has close ties with the Gangster Disciples. Supposedly they run his drugs in prison. So what's Mohammed's guy doing buying lethal drugs from a competing gang? You have to get me into that room. He needs to explain these connections."

"You want to ask a Muslim imam why he's buying drugs from a rival gang in front of the editorial board? That's not going to happen. Now go find out who Ghost Girl is so we can sell some more papers." She turned her back to me.

I left Amy's office in a huff and staked out the hallway near the boardroom. Half an hour later, Mohammed X rounded the corner right into me.

"And here she is, the conniving little bitch who wrote those lies about me in the paper," he said, taking a step back.

His men closed in around him, forming a wall of muscle. Mohammed X gently pushed through them. "It's all right. I'm not afraid of this newspaper whore. Her editors are coming to understand her tactics." He walked closer to me, peering intently at the wounds on my face. "Looks like someone was unhappy with one of your stories." The bruises were still dusty brown under my eyes and along my cheeks.

"And you wouldn't know anything about that, right?"

He smiled perversely.

"Why'd you have Rapper X—Randy—buy Poison from the Mickeys? How is Lester Williams involved? What was the purpose in giving Poison to white girls? Were you trying to make the Mickeys the scapegoats or were the girls the real hits?"

"Hmm. With forty-seven arrests, the Mickeys aren't doing so

well. I hear the GDs have taken over some of their territory. It's tragic all around. Young girls dying. Black men again being arrested on trumped-up charges. I agree with you. Our justice system is completely racist and biased—almost as much as your reporting."

An elevator door opened; he and his men got on. Mohammed X stared out, his head cocked to one side, his face lit with some private pleasure. He curled his fingers in a dismissive wave as the elevator doors closed.

CHAPTER EIGHTEEN

June 29, 2008

GOV ORDERS CRACKDOWN OF STREET CRIME

CHICAGO POLICE ON OVERTIME, CANCEL VACATIONS

Chicago Sentinel

Queen of Angels Academy was on the golf course-like grounds of a Benedictine convent in Rogers Park, the most Catholic of Chicago neighborhoods, home to Loyola University and a number of other Jesuit institutions. The selective all-girls school was still run by habited nuns and was the alma mater of a number of Chicago's most notable women, including the Governor's wife.

Ten blocks from the school, on a side street lined with oversized Chicago bungalows, stood Paulina Wozniak's two-story brick home. The front porch was enclosed, but when I peered through the plastic sheeting, I saw piles of newspapers, bottles, and Tupperware.

"What do you see in there, darling?" Ben asked. I'd convinced him to come along and serve as my translator. Ben's parents had been Polish immigrants, and he was required as a child to take language classes on Saturdays.

"It's nothing but junk."

He pulled at the thin metal screen door. It budged enough that we could shimmy through the opening. Inside, we followed a narrow path between stacks of empty milk cartons, piles of newspapers in blue plastic wrappers, and scooted our way to the front door.

"My mother always said the Polish were the neatest people," Ben said, widening his eyes at the mounds of trash. "I guess she never met Mrs. Wozniak." He fanned his fingers in front of his face, moving around the stale, hot air, and pushed the doorbell. There was no sound. He tapped the door's glass window. I was about to give up, but Ben insisted we wait a little longer.

"She's an old lady, hon. It may take her awhile to get to the door."

We huddled in the suffocating space between the newspaper stacks. Ben dabbed his damp forehead with a monogrammed handkerchief.

"Guess I can skip the sauna today." He hung his tongue like a dog.

I giggled, but then suddenly the curtain on the door parted, and a withered face with large, black eyes peered out. I screamed and jumped back, losing my balance on the blue plastic newspaper wrappings underfoot.

Ben grabbed my hand to steady me. Then he waved at Mrs. Wozniak and jabbered something in Polish. She slowly clicked open the door locks. A stooped old woman appeared wearing a large crucifix and a faded babushka wrapped around her head.

Ben bowed. I smiled awkwardly. Mrs. Wozniak and Ben exchanged a few brief courtesies in Polish, then their sentences became paragraphs. He nodded and smiled, and she fluttered her eyes. I'd only occasionally heard Ben speak Polish when he was interviewing someone on the phone. It was a skill that came in handy, since Chicago boasts one of the largest concentration of Poles in the U.S. Watching the guy I sat next to, a flamboyant man with a high-pitched voice, abruptly transform into a foreigner—sounding deep-throated and masculine—was disturbing.

I tugged at his elbow. "What's she saying?"

He held up a finger for me to wait.

At first, I was giddy Mrs. Wozniak was talking to us—well, to

Ben. I'd tried to get Emily Blake's parents to talk to me, but her father was just as Wendy Cabot had described—angry and suspicious. When I mentioned Ghost Girl, he snapped and threatened to call the cops.

But the longer I continued to listen to Ben and Mrs. Wozniak talk, the more anxious I became. They acted as if I wasn't standing there. Ben didn't even bother to translate. He seemed entertained by the woman and at times laughed and offered her that charming grin of his. In response, Mrs. Wozniak smiled sheepishly and stroked her scarf as if it were the long hair of her youth. I recognized those flirtatious mannerisms: smoothing her dress, tugging her necklace, hooding her eyes, and cocking her head. Then, all of a sudden she disappeared, and Ben and I were left standing in the doorway.

"What's going on?"

"She's telling her story. She and her husband immigrated to Chicago two decades ago, shortly after the fall of the Soviet Union. You might not remember that, Natalie, but it was a momentous time…"

"Skip the history lesson, Ben. We're in a hurry."

"Okay. Okay." He waved his hands at me. "Geez, I didn't realize you were so demanding. Mrs. Wozniak and her husband ran a Polish deli in Rogers Park. When Mr. Wozniak died, her son and his wife came over from Poland on emergency visas but ended up staying. They never became U.S. citizens. Laila was born here.

"Mrs. Wozniak says she doesn't trust the police because they deported Laila's parents last year," he continued. "When the Chicago P.D. came to collect her granddaughter's things, Mrs. Wozniak wouldn't give them anything. So they came back with a search warrant." He simpered. "They didn't find a damn thing. How could they?" He held up his hands at the boxes that lined the porch and the interior walls. "But she likes me." He winked. "And she'll let us look at her granddaughter's computer."

"Why is she talking to us? I mean *you*?"

He beamed. "I have that effect on older women, hon."

"Oh God. She does understand we're reporters, right?"

"Of course. She says she loves to read the paper." He gestured to the carpet of bulky blue plastic sleeves.

The old woman waved at us to follow. We wended down a narrow pathway through ordered stacks of plastic crates piled to the ceiling. A tidy hoarder, who knew? The place smelled moist and rancid, like milk curdling on a hot day. Pill bottles lined a metal kitchen table where several icons and candles were displayed. Mrs. Wozniak pointed to metal chairs. We sat down.

She handed Ben a shiny silver laptop, which looked out of place amid the gray walls of debris. He slid the computer to me. I opened the screen and immediately saw the blinking cursor.

"Shit!"

Ben peered at the screen. "What's the problem?"

"It's password-protected."

He shrugged. "So? How many times have I forgotten my password? Just do your magic, hon." He flitted his fingers in the air as if he were sprinkling fairy dust over the laptop. Ben, like some reporters of his generation, barely surfed the web, let alone understood how to manipulate the innards of a computer. Waiting on the tech guys to fix a computer on deadline was wishful thinking. So he often turned to me to override the system for him.

I gritted my teeth and pushed restart, holding down the control and S keys. The screen went gray, then black. I typed the string of letters and numbers I'd typed numerous times into Ben's computer. The computer responded, prompting a password change. So far, so good. I rebooted, whispering a prayer over the black screen. When the normal screen returned, I slowly typed in "deadangel" for the new password. The computer hummed for what seemed an eternity, then the screen filled with software icons.

"Yes!" I pumped my fist in the air. Ben looked over at me and rolled his eyes. Mrs. Wozniak didn't lift her eyes from Ben.

I still needed passwords to access her email and social media accounts. I searched her documents, finding one named "Pzzwords." It listed several accounts. I clicked on Laila's bookmarked Gmail account and typed the password in the document—her mother's name.

"Don't tell me they have Wi-Fi here?" Ben asked.

"Looks like Laila was using the neighbor's." I watched the brightly colored symbol—which I called the Spinning Pizza of Death—whirl and whirl, wondering if it would stop. Suddenly the screen filled with Laila's private life.

"Fuckin' A," I whispered to myself. There were pages and pages of emails, more than 11,000 in all. Laila stored emails like her grandmother hoarded paper and plastic. Then I clicked on her Facebook account. This time, bright red letters appeared, announcing I'd entered an incorrect password. No problem; I'd have a new one sent to her email account later. I skimmed through the faces of her friends on her public timeline. They looked like the same girl repeated over and over: glossy long hair, sparkling eyes, flawless complexion, and pearly straight teeth. As Ben babbled on, I furtively pulled a flash drive from my purse, inserted it into the laptop and downloaded Laila's files.

"Where's her cell phone?" I asked Ben.

He jabbered something to Mrs. Wozniak. She waved her arms, looking exasperated.

"She says the police have it. They have everything that Laila had on her at the time."

I continued to dig through Laila's postings and emails. My flash drive was filling up with Laila's electronic detritus. "Can you ask her why she thinks her granddaughter was trying heroin?"

Ben wrinkled his forehead. "You sure you want me to go there? She may kick us out."

"Ask about the girls she was with, Emily and Harper, or about any other friends she spent time with."

He gulped. "Okay, but so far she's avoided talking about her granddaughter. She just keeps talking about her husband and Poland."

Ben slowly began a different tact, stuttering as if trying to find the right words. His tone became softer, at times almost a whisper. Mrs. Wozniak pulled an embroidered handkerchief from her sleeve and dabbed her eyes. Her voice more gentle and tender, she stopped occasionally to compose herself. Then, she turned back to Ben, always Ben. Her clenched features relaxed, her rheumy eyes widened, and her arthritic fingers expanded as her hands sliced through the air. Ben listened intently. When Mrs. Wozniak began to cry, he gently placed a hand over hers.

"It's time to go," he said, standing.

I ejected the flash drive and concealed it in my hand. Then I grabbed Ben's arm. "What about Laila's bedroom?"

"Really? You think she's going to give us a tour through her *treasures* to her granddaughter's most intimate space? I can see why you get good stuff. You sure are pushy."

"I think she'll do it for *you*. Please? Can you ask?"

He sighed loudly, and I could feel Mrs. Wozniak's eyes on me. They talked in low tones. Finally she nodded and, with her shoulders hunched, walked past me. Ben motioned for me to follow. We climbed the stairs to the second floor.

The narrow, gray hall seemed expansive because of its bareness. A dim light bulb hung from the ceiling. We followed Mrs. Wozniak to the end of the hallway, where she pulled a key from her apron pocket, and opened the door.

Light flooded the hallway. Ben and I walked in slowly. The sun shined through a slightly opened window, the light reflected by the white floor and pink walls. A breeze made the sheer curtains move like spirits. An expensive scent hung in the air. A single bed with a pink fabric headboard, bedspread, and pink side tables were in the middle of the room. A corner shelf held elaborately framed photos. The room seemed disconnected from the rest of the house. It was as if Mrs. Wozniak still lived behind the Iron Curtain and her granddaughter's bedroom was in West Berlin. Ben and I gave each other anxious Twilight Zone looks.

"You have to ask her," I whispered. "How is it that her granddaughter's room is so...so..."

"Clean?" he whispered back. "Hon, I'm getting goose bumps just standing here."

Ben cleared his throat and Mrs. Wozniak stood erect, tilted her head at him and grinned. He struggled with the words, and I could see her jaw tightening. They talked in a clipped volley.

I walked over to get a closer look at Laila's pictures. A photo of her parents looked recent. I recognized the other Dead Angels—Emily and Harper—in another framed photo. There was a portrait of Laila at a formal event wearing a tight-fitting red gown flanked by Olivia Byrne, the pharmaceutical heiress who I'd met at the rave, and another girl, who looked familiar but who I could not place. Standing next to her was a face I did recognize—glossy brown hair swept back, hard jawline, and that unmistakably patrician nose—Rex Kennan. I pulled out my phone and snapped a few photos. What was Laila, the daughter of illegal immigrants, doing at a formal event with the sons and daughters of Chicago's elite?

"Ask her how she knew these people." I held out the photo of Rex with Laila. Mrs. Wozniak rushed over, snatched the frame from my hand, and gently placed it back on the shelf.

"She says this was at the Governor's Ball."

Mrs. Wozniak stood solemnly in front of the photo shrine.

"I don't get it," I said. "Why'd she let me pry through her daughter's computer but doesn't want us to touch her photos?"

"She sees the computer as a game box Laila used to play with her friends. These photos are real to her. They're like religious icons." He looked over at Mrs. Wozniak kissing a photo of her granddaughter and tugged at my sleeve. "We need to go."

Silently, Mrs. Wozniak led us down the stairs and to the front door. I bowed to her and Ben offered her his hand, but she threw her arms around his chest. Then we slid out the screen door and into the sunlight, where we breathed in mouthfuls of fresh air.

"Don't say anything until we get out of her sight," he ordered out of the corner of his mouth. We walked to my car in silence.

I drove slowly down the block, sensing we were being watched by eyes peering from behind that Eastern bloc wall. After turning the corner, I pulled to the curb.

"What did she say?"

He sighed heavily. "Oh, Lord. She told me I reminded her of her dead husband."

"Sorry." I patted his arm.

"It's heartbreaking." He shook his head. "She said Laila was devastated when her parents were deported. She kept saying she was going to get them back."

"What else?"

"Mrs. Wozniak had no idea what kind of drugs Laila was doing or where she went. She said Laila came home late at night and often drunk."

"She was a teenager."

"There's more." He gulped in air trying to calm his nerves. "Mrs. Wozniak says her granddaughter was convinced that these girls' parents somehow were going to help her obtain citizenship for her mother and father. She told her grandmother that she was working with—*the Governor*."

We looked at each other with wide eyes, my scalp tingling.

The web of powerful people connected to the Dead Angels now included the state's most powerful politician, the grand-daughter of the city's biggest political donor, and the scion of the country's most famous political family. Was Laila merely an outlier who'd gotten swept up with a group of rich girls? I hoped the trail she'd left on her computer would answer those questions. Still, one detail gnawed at me: if Rex Kennan had lied about something as innocuous as knowing girls from Queen of Angels, then he was likely trying to cover up something much more serious. How deep was Kennan involved with the Dead Angels?

CHAPTER NINETEEN

June 29 & 30, 2008

POLICE TO SWEEP KNOWN DRUG SPOTS

WILL BE TESTING DRUGS FOR FENTANYL

Chicago Sentinel

Piecing together Laila's life from her computer files, emails, and Facebook entries made me feel like a psychiatrist trying to unravel multiple personalities. In Facebook photos she wore stylish outfits at venues far too sophisticated for high school students. She and her friends, especially Emily and Harper, emailed about downtown clubs and shopping at high-end stores on Michigan Avenue. At least twice, the girls talked about shoplifting outfits, apparently as a dare. Her voice in those emails was catty and superficial.

But in emotional emails addressed to Mommie and Poppie, Laila wrote about how much she missed her parents and how she had worked hard to befriend girls whose parents had the political clout to help them return to America. She recounted meetings with an immigration lawyer, Mr. Blake, who I recognized as Emily's father. Occasionally she sounded desperate and talked of moving to Poland. In more recent emails, Laila seemed more hopeful. The Governor, she said, had taken an interest in her case. She thought this was the break they needed.

Among the email addresses that showed up regularly in Laila's inbox was someone called ThrillGirl29. A few days before she died, Laila wrote to ThrillGirl29 and addressed the girl by name:

Bethany,

I'm so glad we're friends!!! Sometimes I don't know who I am anymore. ☹ ☹ I feel so lonely. ☹ Not a minute goes by that I don't think about my parents and the responsibility I feel in getting them back, in taking care of my grandmother, who is losing her mind. This morning I found her digging through the neighbor's garbage. I can't babysit her 24/7. Emily and Harper say I'm lucky because I don't have to report to anyone. They hate their parents. They don't want to hear about how I miss my mom and dad, how sad I am. Sometimes I think maybe if my parents lived here, I might resent them too. I might be just like Emily and Harper. Sometimes I think I *have* become just like them. B, I think we've gone too far. I'm not liking what's happening. ☹

Who was Bethany and why was Laila so trusting of her? I sent ThrillGirl29 an email and asked if we could talk about Laila.

The most stunning revelation on Laila's Facebook was the large number of friends she had who'd died of Poison. I spent the day cataloguing Laila's Facebook posts, trying unsuccessfully to figure out how the poisoned girls, who went to different schools, were connected. I was about to stop working for the night when I recognized a face in a blurry photograph. I closed my eyes and thought back to the day I stood outside the Chinatown house—the day they brought out the Dead Angels in black bags—the day I watched *her* walk by. When I opened my eyes, a face similar to my own stared back.

• • •

The next morning when I arrived at Libby's apartment, she and Anna were still in sweatshirts and pajama bottoms, eating cereal out of coffee cups while watching *Ren & Stimpy* cartoons. Sometimes I forgot they were just kids.

"Hey, girls," I announced.

They both grunted "hi" but kept their eyes locked on the TV, mindlessly spooning Froot Loops into their mouths.

"We gotta be quiet," Libby said. "Dad's asleep."

The mention of Danny made my chest tighten.

"I brought some Dunkin' Donuts, but I guess I'm too late."

"No way!" Libby whispered loudly, grabbing the paper sack. "Chocolate Cake. My fav!"

Anna didn't get off the floor.

"I hear you saw our friend," I said to her.

She shrugged and looked away. "We just went for a ride."

I handed her a glazed doughnut.

She finally looked up at me. "You're not mad?"

"You don't need him. And you don't need that shit." I crouched down, wrapped my arms around her shoulders and held her. She didn't flinch. It was the first time I'd hugged her, the first time I'd touched her in an overt way. Libby stared at us, fidgeting with discomfort.

Ever since Anna had suggested that I adopt her, the idea had gnawed at me. It was a crazy notion, and I knew she was probably toying with my emotions. But some small part of me enjoyed the idea and wanted to believe her feelings were genuine. No one had ever said they wanted me to be their mother. If you were an aggressive woman, someone who was good at her job, people judged you as *not* mommy material. Why were passive and soft-spoken women deemed better mothers? I believed what kids needed most were passionate advocates, people who loved them and would do anything to protect them.

"He's got a sports car now," she said, wiping her eyes. "It's all tricked out with big wheels and shit. He asked about you, but I wouldn't tell him where you live. He said he wants to tell you he's sorry." And in the next breath she added: "If he ever comes around here again, Uncle Danny says he'll kill him."

"Then why you hanging with him?" Libby half-shouted. She'd been so quiet I'd almost forgotten she was there.

"You know it's not like that. I had to get some stuff straight with him." There was something in her voice I'd heard before, a lilt of fear.

"Did he threaten you or do something to scare you?"

She looked down, her flame-colored hair covering her face, and whispered: "No. Not like that…"

"What happened, Anna? What did he do to you? Did he hurt you?"

She shook her head.

I sat on the floor next to her. "Okay. If you don't want to talk about Lester, let's talk about how you know Laila Wozniak."

Anna looked at me with shock but then quickly feigned a cool demeanor. "We went to the same school."

"You went to Queen of Angels Academy?" I couldn't believe this had never come up. "Why didn't you tell me?"

"You never asked. Besides, I got kicked out. I'm never going back," she said in a disinterested voice.

"How well did you know Laila, Emily, and Harper?"

"I don't know. Saw them at clubs and stuff."

"Like what kinds of *stuff*?" It angered me that she was taking this so lightly, that she hadn't admitted she'd known the Dead Angels from the day I met her and Libby walking by the Chinatown drug house.

She heard the irritation in my voice and turned from the television to face me. "I didn't know it was them that day. I swear." She bit into a doughnut.

"But when you did, why didn't you tell me?"

She gave me a one-shoulder shrug. Flakes of sugar stuck to the tiny hairs around her mouth. "I don't know."

"Is that the only phrase you know? Anna, I need you to tell me how well you knew those girls and why they did Poison. And why you were at that house the day I met you."

She stared ahead as if she hadn't heard me.

"Okay. If you won't tell me, maybe Libby knows."

Libby looked over at her cousin, seeking permission, but Anna shook her head.

Anna got up from the floor and went into the kitchen. I followed her and watched as she poured herself a glass of milk. "They were curious, like everybody," she said, finally. "They wanted to try it. Not everyone dies. There are lots of girls who do it, and they say it's great. Best high ever."

"Really? Like what girls?"

Anna fidgeted and glanced about the room. "Olivia and her friends. But there are others."

"Why don't you introduce me to these girls?"

"I have. They think you're creepy. They don't want to talk to you. It's *our* world."

"How can you keep this a secret when Laila, Emily, and Harper are dead? Doesn't that make you angry? Don't you want the guy who is selling this stuff to be caught?"

Anna threw her head back and let out a haughty laugh. "There is no one *guy*, stupid. Poison is everywhere."

I let that thought settle for a moment. "Are they getting it from Rapper X or Lester?"

"Are they like the only drug dealers you know?"

"Why were you at the house in Chinatown that day?"

She smirked and trudged back to the living room.

I sat next to her on the floor and feigned interest in the cartoon. But when Ren did something over-the-top funny, no one reacted. Something had changed. It was as if we were unsure how we were supposed to act with each other. I wasn't only hanging around them for a story anymore, and they knew it. I wanted to protect them, but I was sounding like a parent, checking up on them, pleading with them, circling them, eager to step in if they'd only let me.

I heard Danny rustling around in his bedroom and knocked on his door.

"Lib, what you want?" he called out. "Daddy's trying to get ready for work."

"It's me. Natalie."

The door opened. He was standing in faded jeans, his face expressionless.

"Can I come in?"

He silently backed away from the door. The room felt spare, populated only with an unmade bed and an old wooden dresser. The closet held just a few hangers of clothes.

I sat down on the rumpled sheets. He remained standing, his arms crossed over his bare chest. I expected he'd be angry at the way I'd rebuffed him the last time I saw him.

"I'm sorry about the other night." My voice sounded hollow and scratchy. "I don't expect you to understand. There are just these rules. We're not supposed to be friends with the people we write about, and we certainly shouldn't be romantically involved with them."

He listened, chewing on the inside of his cheek. I expected him to say something, but he didn't.

"I'm getting closer to finding out who the Poison dealer is."

Danny nodded.

"Aren't you going to say anything?"

"Didn't know I was part of your story."

"Well, you're not, but your niece is…well, she might be. She knows a lot of these girls who have died of Poison. I can't help think that she knows more than she's letting on."

"And Lib?" His voice cracked.

I shook my head and tried to swallow. "I honestly don't know."

He sat next to me, smelling of day-old cologne, a scent that felt intoxicating. The chemistry between us once again ignited my baser instincts. And yet it wasn't really Danny who excited me. It was the memory of Jake that he evoked. They didn't look much alike, but they were both fearless. After that first night on ecstasy when I'd mistaken Danny for Jake, I'd merged the two in my mind. Since then, I somehow felt closer to Jake every time I saw Danny. It was as if he were channeling Jake and didn't know it. None of it made sense. And I felt dishonest about my true affections.

He patted my leg. My throat tightened with emotion.

"You do what you gotta do. You're a career woman. You put your job first. Never dated a gal like that."

"Is that what we did the night I fell asleep on your couch? Dated?"

He chuckled. "Guess we didn't exactly go to dinner."

We both laughed awkwardly. I felt like I was suffocating, as if there wasn't enough oxygen in that tight room. My head was reeling, my mind sorting through what Anna had just told me—wondering what else she had kept from me—and this hold Danny had on me.

"By the way, Lib showed me what you gave her," he said.

"The naloxone…was…was that okay?"

He shrugged. "What are you gonna do? I can't be there all the time. I gotta make a livin'—sort of like you."

"Yeah. Sort of like me." I sighed heavily. He wore such a pained expression, as if he felt a similar regret.

I'm not sure who made the first move. But in the next instant I was flat on the bed, his crumpled sheets pinching the small of my back, his lips locked over mine, his pelvis bones pressing into me. I was panting for breath, wanting him in a way I hadn't wanted another man since Jake.

And then we heard the knocking. "Daddy, are you in there?"

CHAPTER TWENTY

July 3, 2008

DOZENS STEP FORWARD CLAIMING
TO BE GHOST GIRL

POLICE REFUSE TO REVEAL IDENTITY OF
THE FENTANYL-HEROIN SURVIVOR

Chicago Times

It was the day before the Fourth of July, and the city felt deserted. Everyone, it seemed, had gone to their lake homes. The newsroom was nearly empty, too, except for a handful of reporters, including Ben and me. I was ostensibly writing a story about criminal mobs attacking tourists on Michigan Avenue. In reality, I was combing through Laila's emails trying to determine Bethany's identity. Queen of Angels Academy's online roster listed three Bethanys. (At least Anna had given me the code to log on to the school site.) I immediately eliminated the first one, a geeky freshman who wore braces and bobby pins. The second, a distance runner on the track team, was a possibility. The third, a daughter of a prominent politician, held the most potential for being the mysterious Bethany.

Eager to share my little nugget, I looked over at Ben, but he was busy writing several columns to run over the long holiday weekend, his desk littered with wrinkled yellow legal paper. Though Ben tended to be chatty by nature, when on deadline he was studious and prickly. When he had that crazed look in his eyes, I gave him a wide berth.

Instead I tried to summon the courage to call Rex. The trick was to point out his lies without sounding like I was impugning his character. Part of me felt relieved when he didn't answer. I left a message: "I saw your photo in Laila Wozniak's bedroom. I snapped a picture of. I'm wondering why you told me you didn't know the Dead Angels, but mostly I'm wondering why you denied being at that house. It'd be best if you told me the whole story before someone else does."

Around three o'clock, Julian showed up in the newsroom. He was wearing jeans and a tight, black T-shirt, as if he'd stopped by on his way to a barbeque. Trailing behind him were two kids with similar black hair and beige skin.

"Hiya." He peered over my cubicle. "You're doing great work on the Dead Angels case. Loved the piece on Laila Wozniak and her grandmother. Very detailed, and yet, so sad."

I grinned, waiting for "the ask" that I knew was coming. No one in the newsroom dished out compliments without then seeking a favor—not that I wasn't relishing his praise.

His kids, a boy and a girl, had discovered the tchotchkes lining the barrier between Ben's desk and mine. The boy, about six, pointed at the Star Wars stormtrooper, and the girl, about four, screamed for the purple-haired trolls.

I shot Julian a wry smile.

"Do you mind?" He jerked his head at the kids.

I shrugged. "Why not?"

Ben raised his eyes above his half-glasses, but went back to writing.

Julian handed the action figure to his son and the family of trolls to his daughter.

"What do you say when someone lets you play with their toys?" he asked them.

The boy looked at the white armored soldier in his hands. "Thanks," he said quietly.

"This is Nate and this is Alex," he said to me, then bent down

169

to their eye level. "Can you say hello to my friend, Ms. Delaney? She's a really important reporter."

Alex waved and Nate smiled before they went back to playing with the tchotchkes.

"Hey, I know you are probably on deadline, but I have to talk to Odis. It's important. Do you mind?" He gestured to the kids and grimaced. "It'll just take a few minutes."

"No problem."

Focused on playing with the figurines, the kids didn't notice their father walking away. I cleared newspapers off a nearby desk—the former workspace of a reporter recently let go—and told Nate he could sit down in the swivel chair. His face brightened, and he got up off the floor. Alex had already staked out a part of my desk and commandeered paper and office supplies to draw pictures for her troll family. "I'm making a house," she announced, then detailed each aspect.

Ben kept his head down, but I could see by his shoulders, drawn up to his ears, that Alex's babbling was distracting him.

I pulled Alex on my lap. She resisted and whined, her arms grabbing for her trolls. Then I found a YouTube video from the show *Barney & Friends*. I put earphones on her, so Ben wouldn't have to hear the tedious sounds of kids singing "Barney is a Dinosaur." Alex giggled and squealed, jiggling on my lap. Ben gave me an annoyed look.

Eventually both kids got bored and hungry. I took them to the vending machines and punched in enough quarters for orange juice and cookies, praying that neither had food allergies. Alex ate hers and immediately fell asleep in my lap. She felt good in my arms, and even when my legs went to sleep, I didn't put her down, but watched her breath faltering as she snored. Nate put his head down on his desk, the stormtrooper still clutched in his fist.

An hour later, Julian returned looking sheepish. "I'm so sorry it took so long. Geez, I didn't realize he was going to talk so much."

"It's all right." I handed him his sleeping daughter. She whimpered, then buried her face into her father's chest.

He ran his fingers through Nate's hair, hoping to rouse the boy, who continued to make soft whistling noises through his nose.

"Did you have a chance to check out that Kennan file I gave you?" he whispered.

"Sorry, I haven't had time to chase down any more details."

Julian's smile faded. "Keep the file a while longer. Maybe you'll have a slow day."

"The thing is, I don't think that's going to happen any time soon."

"What have you found?"

"What makes you think I got anything?"

He peered at me in a way that made me uncomfortable. "You're too confident. Most reporters hit a wall after a few days and are eager to chase other leads."

"Maybe I do have something," I teased.

"Can I ask what?" He leaned over and pretended to look at my screen.

I turned my computer away from him. "No! Don't look!"

He grabbed my hand to stop me, still cradling his sleeping daughter in his other arm. His fingers felt warm and soft. I stopped laughing and looked up at him, my hand still in his, our faces so close I could see the afternoon stubble on his cheeks.

Ben coughed loudly, and Julian let go of my hand. "Maybe the two of you could take your *lovely* conversation down to the Goat?" Ben's face was pinched and his eyes dark with anxiety. "Your little dance would sound better over a couple of beers. But for those of us who have to fill the paper for the next *four days*, your chatter is *distracting*." Ben propped his reading glasses on the top of his head, underscoring the seriousness of his complaint.

"So sorry, Ben," I said, and winked at him.

Julian frowned and gently pulled at Nate, who got up wiping his eyes. Then, as an afterthought, he turned to me. "You're good with them. You'll make a fine mother someday."

"Thanks." I smiled sadly, wondering if I would ever have the chance to find out.

CHAPTER TWENTY-ONE

July 4, 2008

CITY ON ALERT FOR HOLIDAY DEATHS

POLICE WARN OF GROWING FENTANYL OVERDOSES

Chicago Sentinel

The morning of the Fourth, Danny called and invited me to join him and the girls at the 31st Street Beach. They wanted to make a day of it, swimming, barbequing, and hanging out until the fireworks display that night. I was still in bed, having stayed up late sorting through Laila's emails—only another thousand to go. I tried to justify that Danny's invite had come at an opportune time. Maybe Anna could identify who Bethany was. I had suspicions that she might be Ghost Girl. What I tried to deny was that I was aroused by Danny's voice on the phone.

"Let me guess." I sat up in bed. "This is your first Fourth of July in Chicago?"

"How'd you know that?"

"Because you seem like a sane guy and only insane people go to the beach in Chicago on the Fourth, *especially* the 31st Street Beach. Every year there's a gang shootout and some kid gets killed."

"Hell, I didn't know."

"I know a beach that's not on anyone's radar. It's not even on city maps. We used to go there when I was a kid. We called it the Secret Beach."

"Well, that sounds pretty enticing. Where is it?"

"Now, Danny, if I told you, it wouldn't be a secret, would it?" My voice was playful and suggestive. I hadn't stopped thinking about him since Libby had caught us making out on his bed. Actually, she hadn't seen anything. But I'm certain our faces belied our lust when Danny opened his bedroom door.

He crowed a smoker's rasp. "You're just playing me, aren't ya?"

"Nope. I'll swing by and pick up you and the girls. That is, as long as you swear you won't tell anyone where I take you."

"Aw, hell, no. I won't say."

We hung up, and I lay in bed thinking of him. I knew I needed to put some distance between us. And here I was encouraging the opposite.

It was nearly eleven when I showed up. He and the girls were sitting on the back stairs next to a mound of supplies: a giant bag of charcoal briquettes, a Weber grill, beach chairs, an oversized cooler, beach bags, and a sun tent—enough equipment and food to camp for a week.

"Guys, we can't exactly drive up to this beach."

Anna and Libby pouted at the thought of carrying all their stuff, but Danny playfully slapped their backs. "No problem. These girls are as good as mules."

He even gave in to using the hibachi I'd packed in my tiny trunk instead of his backyard griller. Libby said she'd ride with her dad in his pickup, and Anna jumped in my convertible, immediately striking a pose: her chin jutted out, her dark sunglasses reflecting the bright sun, her hair pulled back in a jiggly ponytail—just like mine.

I was still angry with her for keeping secrets. But seeing her look so eager, so full of possibility, made me feel alive. She'd awakened something inside me that had lain dormant, a desire to belong to someone else, not just to a man, but to a child. How could I not feel connected to her when she smiled at me in that euphoric way I used to smile, believing that life was one big adventure?

Once we neared Hyde Park, I pulled off and rambled around the one-way streets that only a native could maneuver until I found a little-known free parking lot. Draped with supplies, we made our way through the dark and musty pedestrian underpass that carried us to the lake trail. A quarter mile down, we climbed over a short cement wall to a pebble beach where there were no lifeguards. As soon as Danny climbed over the barrier, he stood, grinning, taking it all in.

"Well, you weren't shitting me, were ya? What a beauty."

The sun shimmered off turquoise waters that stretched to the horizon and joined the blue sky somewhere out there, as if you could swim forever. A man and his dog played along the shore of pale sand mixed with white speckled rocks. A family had staked out a far corner, near the break wall. But otherwise, we were alone on a vast empty beach, nothing but sand and water and the twinkling metallic spires of the city skyline peering at us in the distance. We climbed onto a collapsed cement breaker, a flat slab that looked like a giant raft, and pitched our tent on the nearby pebble beach. I built a mound of briquettes in the hibachi.

"Girl, you act like you know what you're doing," Danny said. "Never seen a city girl build a fire before."

I stood back, my hands on my hips. "The number one rule of the Secret Beach is that you can't make fun of the city girl who brought you here."

"True 'nough." He handed me a cold bottle of beer from the cooler.

I wiped the sweat from my forehead and looked out at the girls, already swimming to a rock a hundred yards out. Danny lit cigarettes and handed me one. We quietly smoked, smelling the charcoal smoldering.

"You came here when you was a kid, huh?"

"Doesn't every kid have a secret watering hole?"

"Guess so. I had a crick in the back woods. Sometimes after summer rains, it was like a river. We used to tie a rope and swing out and jump in. Damn! Scares me thinking about it now. How stupid we were."

"But no one could tell you that then, right?"

We clinked beers.

The girls had reached the break stone, slimy with moss. They slithered onto the rock on their bellies, then tried to stand but lost their footing and fell in. Then they clambered back on. Anna managed to stand for ten seconds, waving her hands to balance. Libby, clinging to the side of the rock, pulled one of Anna's legs. Anna fell on top of her cousin, both of them shrieking.

Watching the girls reminded me of my own mother sitting on that beach peering out at my brother and me jockeying for control of the rock. While my father would drink a single beer and doze off in the sand, my mother sat alert, perched in her scratchy nylon chair and watched us through theater binoculars.

"How's she doing?" I sat down in a beach chair. Danny placed his next to mine.

"Anna? She's doing better. I told her momma to stop sending her money since she just burns it on drugs."

"Why is she living with you and not her mother?"

He looked at me warily out of the corner of his eye. Though Libby had told me about Children's Services and Anna's stepfather, I wanted to hear how Danny characterized the situation.

"It's just for the summer." He pulled back his shoulders. "Figured I'd give my sister a break. She's got three little ones. Besides, Anna'll go back to school in the fall. Everything'll be all right." He slapped his hand on my thigh.

"Libby said Anna couldn't go back home. Something about Anna's stepfather molesting her." I looked at him over my sunglasses.

"Damn, girl, you're really digging up the dirt. I'm sure my sister will convince Children's Services that Anna made it all up."

"You think Anna's lying?"

He sucked in his bottom lip. "You have a way of making a man talk about things he doesn't want to talk about. These are family secrets. They shouldn't be aired." He looked out at the horizon reflectively. I waited, knowing he would tell me. "If I thought Anna was lying about that son-of-a-bitch stepfather, she'd be living with her mother right now."

"So why aren't you afraid of her mother getting custody of her?"

"Those awful things happened when she was younger. She's not going to take it—not from him or her mother."

"Why don't they get along, Anna and her mother?"

He sighed loudly. "Why does any girl fight with her mother? Libby's going through a hard time now, too—moving, her mother ignoring her. I thought it would be good for the two cousins to have some time together. Libby'd do anything for that girl." He pointed with his bottle at Anna wavering on the rock. "They need each other. I just worry about them when I'm not around. Hell, I could've worked double time today. But those girls need a father."

"They also need a mother." It was out of my mouth before I could stop it.

Danny wrenched his head to me. "You volunteering?"

I smiled nervously. "I'm just the *big sister*, remember?"

He smirked. "Sure, sure you are."

When the girls finally came to shore, huffing from their swim back, I put the chicken breasts and brats on the hot grill and watched the heat sizzling the skins. Anna, still damp, casually wrapped her arms around my neck.

"Whatcha doing?"

"Making lunch."

Seeing the brats, she giggled. "What are we having, peniswursts?"

"Yessiree, that and chicken boobies." We both laughed.

"Why don't you come swimming with me?"

"And burn this meat? How about you keep me company while I cook?"

Danny and Libby disappeared, walking along the shore. Anna grabbed a beer from the cooler. I raised my eyebrows at her.

"Uncle Danny said we could have one because it's a holiday."

She plopped into the chair Danny had been sitting in and stretched out her long legs. Her skimpy two-piece showed off a pale belly and the gentle curves of her breasts. She wiggled her toes, sifting sand between them. Freckles, the color of henna, flickered on her shoulders. Red splotches on her face warned of a sunburn. I sat back and smoked a clove cigarette that Danny called "smoke weed." We both stared at the sailboats rocking in the distance.

"So I have to ask you something."

She pulled down her sunglasses and gave me a pierced look.

"Who hung out with Laila, Emily, and Harper?"

She grabbed a handful of wet sand and started molding it into a castle. "Are you asking me who Ghost Girl is?"

I smiled. She'd read my story. "You know, you are smarter than you let on."

She grinned proudly. "Give me a drag." I handed her the cigarette. She took a long pull as if it were a joint. "There was a girl who hung out with them all the time."

"Yeah? What's her name?"

Anna tilted her head and smirked: she wasn't *that* easy.

"Laila got a lot of emails from a girl named Bethany. Ever heard of her?"

Anna stopped her hands in the sand. "You looked at Laila's email?"

"It's a long story. Ever hear of this girl?"

She shrugged. "Maybe. Is this for a story?"

"No, Anna, I thought I'd ask to be friends on Facebook." The remark stung her more than I'd intended, and she turned away. "Come on. You know this is what I do."

She continued building turrets on her sand castle. Without looking up, she asked, "Who do *you* think it is?" She loved the tease, more than anyone I'd ever met.

"Really? We are going to do this? Why can't you just tell me straight up?"

She threw sand at me. "That wouldn't be any fun."

"Okay, what do I have to do?"

"Swim with me out to the rock and stand up for fifteen seconds. I get to count."

"Oh, for Christ's sake." I stood and brushed off the sand before checking on the meat—still pink. She held out her pinky finger. I wrapped mine around hers, taking the bet.

The water was icy cold. I stood on tiptoes and waded. Anna swam ahead, kicking water towards me.

"Cut it out!" I screamed.

She turned around and crawled in the shallow water, circling me like a crab, tugging at my thighs, nearly pulling me down.

"Just dunk your head under! Get it over with!" she screamed.

I took my time, wading in deeper. She wrapped her arms around my waist and let me pull her as if she were water skiing. I dunked my head underwater and began furiously swimming.

"I'll beat you!" I yelled.

I could hear her cutting the waves behind me. I reached the rock, panting, and heaved myself up, my belly teetering on the rock's hard edge. Slippery green moss covered its surface, just like I remembered. Anna clutched my back and tried pulling me down.

"No fair!" I yelled.

"Wah! Wah!"

I gently pushed her off then slithered farther up the rock, the moss cushioning me as I reached for the peak. Anna hooked her arm around my ankle. I flinch-kicked her off. She treaded water, watching while my feet gripped the rock on both sides by memory. I crouched low, my arms outstretched, as if I were surfing.

"Start counting!" I yelled.

"I said 'stand.' You're not standing!"

"I really hate you right now."

I gradually straightened, teetering. Anna started counting, slowly. At ten, a wave crashed against the rock, dragging me with it. I hit my head, then rolled to the sandy floor. I couldn't see in the stirred-up muck, and thrashed around, fearing I'd never surface. Then something tugged on my arm. I emerged from the water, gasping. Anna held onto me, leading me to shore. My eyes hurt. I couldn't stop spitting up water. At the shoreline, I lay down in the sand, still hacking. Anna slapped my back, coaxing out more water.

Danny ran down the beach.

"What happened?"

"She got hit by a wave," Anna said.

"More like...I got hit...with a hundred pounds of stupid... for taking your bet."

Anna stood up. "And you *lost*." That meant she wasn't going to tell me *shit*.

The chicken breasts were charred and the brats had shriveled—making them look even more like penises—but no one complained. The sun and water had made us famished. Afterward, Anna and Libby stretched out on beach towels and fell asleep. I pulled out a book and eventually dozed off.

I woke to Anna screaming and jolted upright. She was splashing in the water as Libby—sitting on Danny's shoulders—chased after her, dousing and dunking her. When Anna saw that I was awake, she begged me to join them. I waded up to my chest. Anna swam over, and I hoisted her onto my shoulders. Now Anna held the advantage, and Libby and Danny fell backward. When they got up, we went several rounds until Danny suggested we take a break.

On the beach, Anna knelt in front of me, and I rubbed her back and shoulders with sunblock. Her face was beet red. I spread sunscreen over her pointy nose, across her cheeks, on her forehead—the places where her reddish-tan freckles were clustered more densely. I'd flinched when my mother had daubed sunscreen on me. But Anna sat with her eyes closed, her neck outstretched, her face serene, relishing my touch, like a puppy getting its head rubbed.

The rest of the day we seesawed from the water to the beach, swimming and racing, then sleeping, then back to the water, returning to the beach exhausted. By late afternoon, the Secret Beach was getting more crowded as locals staked out spots to watch the fireworks detonated from boats. After Danny cooked a dinner of burgers, Anna and I climbed into the beach tent to take a nap.

• • •

The booms of the first fireworks roused me. When I opened my eyes, Anna was sitting up, watching me. The colored lights outside the tent cast strange shadows on her face, making her appear ghoulish, her eyes intense, her mouth taut, as if all the joy from the day had drained from her. I shuddered.

"How long you been awake?" I asked.

"Awhile," she whispered hoarsely.

"We should go outside or we're going to miss the show." I started to get up.

Anna grabbed my ankle. "I'll tell you what you want to know."

CHAPTER TWENTY-TWO

July 7–10, 2008

MAYOR LAUDS SAFE HOLIDAYS WITH NO DRUG DEATHS

CREDITS NEIGHBORHOOD PATROLS
FOR DROP IN POISON DEATHS

Chicago Times

It didn't take long for Mo to return my phone call.

"Pretty clever of you." His voice was tinged with pride, as if he'd taught me everything I knew. "I still don't know how you figured out that Ghost Girl was Bethany."

"Just to be clear, you're confirming that ThrillGirl29, also known as Bethany, also known as Ghost Girl, is indeed…the Governor's daughter?" I could feel a good story coming on; my scalp tingled.

He exhaled loudly, then laughed. "Off the record, on deep background, and I mean *fucking* deep background. Yes, ThrillGirl29—the girl you contacted via email—is, indeed, Bethany, the Governor's daughter. But you can't *ever* print that."

"Then why the hell are you confirming it?"

"The Governor wants to make a deal. A little horse trading in exchange that you keep the identity of Ghost Girl a secret."

"And what's in it for me?"

"The interview of the year: a one-on-one with Ghost Girl herself." The eagerness in his voice unnerved me. He sounded as if he were trying to sell me a set of Ginsu knives.

"You better not be shitting me."

"Nope. You found her. You get the interview. But in exchange, you don't reveal or hint or suggest or provide clues as to who she is. Capeesh?"

"Why would the Governor agree to let a reporter near his daughter? And don't you think it's only a matter of time before other reporters figure out who Ghost Girl is? Her classmates will talk." That night in the beach tent, Anna told me that she'd seen Bethany with Laila, Emily, and Harper at clubs, but that they rarely hung out together at school. Bethany had a reputation as a good girl; the others did not.

"The Governor knows your paper is likely to reveal her identity—even without official confirmation—or at least print enough that any Chicagoan could figure it out. He doesn't want his daughter's name associated with fentanyl-heroin. He is running for re-election. Deal?"

I still wasn't convinced. The better story, in my mind, was that the Governor's daughter survived lying beside her friends' corpses for three days before the sanitation crew found her.

"It's not a deal if she clams up."

"She'll pony up to what happened."

"Why should I trust you? This could be a trap to assure that the paper never publishes her name, when in a few more days I'd have her classmates on the record identifying her."

"Wow. You must really think we're manipulative."

A few minutes later, the Governor's spokesman called, cheeky and friendly, as if he'd personally vouched for me to the Governor. But I knew it was all Mo. The interview was set to take place in three days at the Governor's house.

Amy was on the train headed to her suburban mansion when I reached her. She was about to pack up her toddler daughter and husband and head to her parents' cabin in Wisconsin for a long-awaited summer vacation. I expected her to be annoyed by my phone call. I'd forgotten how much of a company woman Amy was. Within minutes, she was on a train back to the paper.

Amy, Odis, the publisher, and the company attorney holed up in Odis's office, haggling over the interview terms on speakerphone with the Governor's attorney. Eventually they emerged, the men walking past me without a word. Amy smiled and nodded.

"Good job, kid." She patted my back. "I think you've impressed Odis. Just get the girl to spill her guts."

• • •

I spent the next three days combing through Laila's emails, practically memorizing anything pertaining to Bethany. I barely slept. On the day of the interview, I was bleary-eyed and over-caffeinated. If Bethany didn't reveal much, I would be seen as a failure, and my job would again be in jeopardy.

A security detail was standing outside the Governor's blonde brick home when I arrived. The Governor greeted me at the door, wearing sweatpants and sneakers as if he'd just come in from one of his famous jogs the TV stations loved to film.

"I'm not happy about this," he said. "My family—especially my three daughters—have been off limits during my entire political career. Bethany is only fifteen. You vultures won't be happy until you destroy every modicum of privacy my family has."

"I understand, sir."

He led me to a formal living room with monotonous beige décor. The stage for the interview had been set: a tan couch across from two faux Louis XIV chairs.

"I swear to God, if anyone finds out that my daughter was with those girls, I will sue your paper and you personally. Do I make myself clear?"

"I understand, sir."

"I was just sick when I read your stupid emails, trying to coax my daughter into talking to you. Those things you said to her—private things. I don't know how you know. It's a good thing my wife took over Bethany's computer after the incident. Do you have any idea how hard this has been on our family?"

"Sir, with all due respect, ThrillGirl29 suggests someone… *much older.*"

"Don't get smart with me, or I'll call this whole thing off."

A tall man wearing a pinstripe suit appeared, clasped the Governor's elbow and whispered in his ear.

"Okay, okay." The Governor pointed his index finger at me. "Don't try to be clever. My attorney will be sitting in to make sure you behave. I can't bear to hear the details." As he and the attorney walked into the hall to talk privately, I took a seat on the far end of the couch, hoping Bethany would sit next to me.

Despite his protests, the Governor couldn't sit in on the interview and then later insist he didn't know what Bethany and her friends had done. He had to maintain plausible deniability.

A few minutes later the attorney returned, escorting a pouting teenage girl. She wore a hoodie, sweatpants, and socks, and plopped into the chair farthest from me. Seeing her in person, I suddenly realized she was the mystery girl in the picture with Laila Wozniak, Olivia Byrne, and Rex Kennan. For much of her childhood Bethany had been a pudgy, shy girl who hid behind her father's pant leg at news conferences. She'd gone through an ugly duckling phase when she was about thirteen and had avoided public appearances. But six months ago, Bethany emerged as if from a chrysalis, her face smooth and her legs long and slender. She'd frequently been photographed accompanying the Governor on his long runs. That's why the image in the photograph with Laila had seemed familiar but not immediately identifiable: it was taken in the midst of Bethany's metamorphosis.

"Hi." I scooted closer to her.

"Hi." She gave me a flimsy wave of her hand. Her shoulders slumped, and strands of hair hooded her face. From her Facebook pictures, I knew Bethany was a social, outgoing girl. This interview was the equivalent of being force-fed broccoli.

"Bethany, why don't you start by telling me how you, Laila, Emily, and Harper ended up at that house in Chinatown?"

She slid down in her chair and gazed at the carpet. "Some guy took us," she mumbled.

"What guy? Where did you meet him?"

"I don't know." She rolled her shoulders and kept her head drooped.

"What did he look like?"

"I don't remember."

I looked at the attorney. "You guys promised me she would cooperate."

"She is," he said, smugly. "She can't help it she doesn't remember everything."

"Well, if she doesn't start *remembering*, the interview is off and her name will be in the paper. Her choice." The paper had stipulated that Bethany had to give a detailed account.

The attorney rose in a huff and went to track down the Governor.

Bethany kept her head bowed. I moved closer and leaned toward her.

"I need you to tell me what really went on. Who else was there with you? I know you are protecting someone."

Bethany sat up straight and looked me in the eyes for the first time.

"I know your dad was trying to help Laila's parents get citizenship," I said. "And I'll be sure to include all those good things in the story. But you have to tell me who was there."

An anxious look replaced the sad, wallowing expression on Bethany's face. She glanced nervously at the living room door. "Laila was a good person," she whispered forcibly. "She just got caught up with *those girls*. At first it was all about getting her parents citizenship, but then she sort of got hooked on their games, you know?"

"Why were you with them?"

"I guess I was kind of curious, too. I'm supposed to be the poster child—the goddamn Governor's daughter. Sometimes I have to let loose. Even my father has his releases…he says politicians are risk takers. Well, what the hell does he think their children are?"

We heard the attorney's hard footsteps coming down the hall and moved away from each other. He walked over to Bethany and whispered into her ear. She squeezed her eyes shut.

"She'll tell you what she knows," he said. "But no names. She's not going to incriminate other people."

Bethany began describing that night. They'd met at Emily's house, where they'd told their parents they would spend the night watching movies. What they didn't tell them was that Emily's parents were out of town. About ten o'clock they went to several downtown bars. Wearing designer clothes, they looked much older, she explained. Then they moved to a rave in the warehouse district. At about three a.m., a guy offered to take them to the South Side to score some Poison. They were drunk. Bethany rode in the backseat of the guy's car and couldn't see where they bought the drugs. Then they drove to the house in Chinatown, where he dropped them off. They had planned to cab it back to Emily's house. She didn't remember much after that, just waking up when the sanitation worker screamed. And that was her story, as I'm sure she'd rehearsed with her father and his lawyer. Too bad they had done what amateur interviewers do—think they owned all the secrets.

"Why were you sucking on fentanyl sticks before you injected Poison?"

Bethany's jerked back her head. "What?"

"The medical examiner found that the girls had all been sucking on fentanyl sticks."

Her attorney stiffened as Bethany struggled for an answer.

"It's supposed to make you more tolerant of Poison," she said eventually, her voice increasing in confidence.

"Urban legend. The medical examiner also found that the girls' alcohol content was five times the legal limit. How did you manage to find a vein within a millimeter of accuracy to inject yourselves if you were so intoxicated?"

"Okay. So *he* was there." She raised her hands as if she were submitting to an arrest.

"Who?"

"The guy from the club. He took us to buy Poison. He helped us cook it, inject it."

"And who was *this guy*? Had you seen him before? What did he look like?"

"I'd seen him at other raves. He was white but he has these long dreads."

"How do you explain why *you* survived and the other girls didn't?"

She wiggled on her chair and wrinkled her nose, then exhaled loudly. "I was last. He injected me last."

"Did someone call for help? Did someone come to revive you?" It was the only plausible explanation.

Bethany's eyes turned watery. Her voice rose with emotion. "I was so scared. I didn't know what to do. Stuff was coming out of their mouths. I could barely see."

"Who did you call? You called someone, didn't you?"

"How the fuck do you think I survived?" She stood, spit spraying from her mouth.

"Did that someone inject you with an antidote?" I stood too, stepping toward her.

"Yes!"

"Except he or she didn't get there in time. Isn't that it? Is that why the fentanyl didn't kill you but you didn't recover immediately?"

Mark had warned that naloxone sometimes takes several injections before it revived someone completely. If that had happened with Bethany, it could explain why she'd lain unconscious and barely alive, next to her dead friends.

She crumpled to the floor, sullen, her hair hanging in her face.

"Who was it?" I said, bending over her. "Who gave you the naloxone?"

"That's enough," the attorney interjected, holding his hand

out as if he could stop me from talking. "The police told us not to give names."

I grinned. "Okay. Then let me give you a name: Rex Kennan."

Bethany sat up suddenly. Her eyes met mine, a long fearful stare.

"Is he the one who tried to save you?"

Mascara-stained tears streamed down her cheeks. I thought I saw her nod, but I couldn't be sure. Then she let out a piercing wail.

The attorney stood. "That's it. That's absolutely the end of this interview."

CHAPTER TWENTY-THREE

July 13–19, 2008

GHOST GIRL SAVED BY DRUG SAMARITAN

MADE FRANTIC PHONE CALL WHILE THREE ANGELS LAY DYING

Chicago Times

There's nothing quite as inebriating as having your story and byline at the top of the Sunday morning paper for more than a million people to read. That Sunday, the only story people were talking about was my exclusive interview with Ghost Girl.

The article ignited frenzied speculation over who had saved Ghost Girl. In a city where people can feel anonymous and insignificant, the notion that someone was out there rescuing young girls in trouble—well, it melted the heart of the most rigid cynic. This urban hero was straight out of comic books. After so many senseless deaths, people were ready to entertain the idea. Columnists even started calling him the Heroin Superhero. Newspaper artists drew him as a cross between Spider-Man and Superman, a tights-wearing nerd with a needle and a vial of antidote.

If I thought snagging the interview with the Governor's daughter had plucked me from the layoff list, it had only raised Odis's expectations. He became fixated on finding the Heroin Superhero, convinced he had revived other girls. It wasn't the first time an editor concocted a story and dispatched troops to find it, though they all knew they'd come back empty-handed.

The premise was ridiculous: no one was going to step forward and admit they'd left four girls in a heroin house in Chinatown. It was a waste of time, a major distraction from finding the killer. Besides, I was convinced Rex Kennan had tried to save Bethany, but somehow botched her rescue, then panicked and left her body there with the others. I just needed confirmation. And Bethany's vague nod was not enough to publicly accuse a Kennan. For that, I would need *ironclad* confirmation.

I pressed Anna for Rex's connection to the Dead Angels. She claimed she didn't know, but her tone suggested otherwise.

"It would be kind of cruel if he was Bethany's boyfriend, and he left her for dead, don't you think?" she said. "Maybe he wants to be a senator like his uncles, and he couldn't be caught with a dead girl, huh?"

"Do you know for sure they were dating?"

"People say stuff. Doesn't mean it's true."

"Anna, this is really important. Did girls at school know they were a couple?"

She turned away, refusing to say anything else. But her comments nagged at me, the way she said it, with authority. I felt she was again playing me, as if she derived some sort of sinister pleasure from making me beg her for information, only to tease me with bits and pieces.

• • •

By mid-July, Danny was working double shifts, and the girls seemed lonely and bored, the worst combination. Danny asked if I would occasionally stop by and check on them. With our crazy work schedules, Danny and I hadn't seen much of each other. It was better that way. We could be *just friends*. That didn't mean I'd stopped thinking about him. He was like some folklore character who'd emerged from the woods to protect me. And in his presence, I felt safe. My heart sank just a bit each time I pulled into the back gravel lot of the girls' apartment to find an empty space where Danny normally parked. For days, I'd shown up at the apartment with bags of food. The girls and I watched bad TV, ate greasy burgers, pizza, or fried chicken. It was as if we'd formed our own urban, underprivileged sorority.

One night I drove them downtown in my convertible, and we splashed in the reflecting pool at Millennium Park, then walked along the rocky shores of the 31st Street Beach, smoking and admiring the skyline, telling stories. Feeling the warm breeze off the lake and the lasting affects of the sun on our skin, the girls seemed more relaxed and talked about feeling abandoned by their mothers.

Anna's mother had insisted Anna live in the dorm at Queen of Angels with the international students, even though the school was seven miles from her home in Wilmette. Anna said it made her feel like she'd been exiled from her family. That spring, shortly after Easter, Anna was kicked out of school for repeatedly skipping. After that, she refused to return home. She'd been living with Libby since she and Danny had moved to the city in May.

Libby told a similarly heartbreaking story. Her mother, she said, hadn't remembered her birthday for three years. She'd given up parental rights when Libby was a baby. Libby had been excited to move to Chicago to be closer to her mother, who lived in the city's western suburbs. But when Libby called, her mother made one excuse after another about why she couldn't see Libby. Libby had seen her only once—the weekend of the rave—since she'd moved to Chicago.

I wanted to believe my presence was having a positive effect. Anna had stopped experimenting with drugs, or so she said. Chicago police had swept up dozens of suspected drug dealers in yet another crackdown. There hadn't been a Poison death in a week. The police claimed that whoever was peddling Poison after the Mickey Cobras went to jail had either been arrested or had gone underground.

One night the girls called asking for Buffalo wings and drumsticks, the hot kind. I was only too eager to kick back and pretend we were having a slumber party. I arrived with an added treat: Lil

Wayne's newly released CD. When I pulled out the disc, the girls screamed and jumped up and down. Anna snapped it into Danny's stereo and cranked up the volume.

When their favorite song, "Got Money", came on, the girls struck poses in front of the kitchen counter, glamming with drumsticks as microphones. On the chorus, they threw napkins around the room like cash.

White paper rained down on us. I snapped photos, paparazzi-like; the girls hammed it up, jutting out their hips and flicking back their hair. When the song ended, we sat at the kitchen table, giggling, our faces glistening with sweat. Libby grabbed my cell phone and shot a photo: Anna cuddled against my shoulder, her lips forming a serene smile. My eyes sparkled with that in-the-moment trance.

We had just sunk our teeth into the Tabasco-laden chicken when someone banged on the door. Libby held a terrified expression as she darted for the door. Anna threw down her drumstick and raced ahead of Libby.

"Let me in!" insisted the male voice on the other side of the door.

Keeping the security chain on, Anna opened the door and quickly slammed it shut. "I have to see this guy."

Before I could say anything, she opened the door. A man brushed past her.

"What the fuck? You slammed the door in my face!" He was tall, thin, with shaggy white-blond hair hanging past his collar. He talked fast and twitched his shoulders. Despite the humid summer heat, he wore a tattered army jacket. Plastered across his right earlobe was a Daffy Duck Band-Aid.

He noticed me looking at his ear. "Freak accident," he said, then flashed two fingers and a thumb—a gang symbol. From the dried blood on his jacket, I guessed the wound was fresh.

"She's my sister." Anna pointed at me.

The man shrugged. "Could be your momma for all I care."

I sat there, my mouth agape, trying to process what was happening. The stranger, Anna, and Libby quickly disappeared into the girls' bedroom. I remained at the avocado-colored tabletop, surveying the food wrappers and the wadded napkins smeared with wing sauce.

"I'm not cleaning up this mess!" I yelled, as if it mattered.

I tapped my fingernails against the table and remembered Amy's directive: *you're a reporter, not a social worker.* I wasn't supposed to intervene or change the course of events.

I heard Anna giggle, and I laid my ear against the bedroom door; their voices were muffled. Someone shrieked.

"Open up!" I slammed my fists across the door. I tried the handle, but it was locked. "Anna! What is going on?"

"We're just smoking a joint," she screamed. I knew she was lying.

I paced outside the door. I hated the way the girls kept secrets, how it made me feel used, powerless to stop their self-destruction. And yet every day I spent with them, I became more attached, more sure of this ridiculous notion that I might save them.

The bedroom door swung open. The stranger stopped in the doorway to zip up his pants.

"You look a lot like Anna," he said, then laughed. His open mouth revealed decaying teeth—stalagmites that rose from his gums, like a cartoon character. He grabbed a drumstick from the table and gnawed at its red skin as he walked out the door.

Anna lay crumpled on the bed she shared with her cousin. Libby was sitting on the floor in a corner, her face creased, her eyes burning with anger.

"Why'd you do it?" she demanded of Anna. "Why'd you do it?" she repeated, louder. Libby ran out of the bedroom. The back door slammed. Anna lay still on the bed, a faraway, vacant look in her eyes.

"Anna?" I touched her leg gently. She didn't move. "What'd he do to you?"

She sat up, her face oddly naked without her usual thick mascara. Her eyes held a tortured look. "He didn't do anything to me. It's what I did to *him*." She licked her lips and her mouth formed a pink O, for shock. She pulled a wad of bills from her pocket and splayed them on the bed. "I wanted to know what it felt like to be a whore. Isn't that what you said I'm going to be?"

"You're twisting my words."

"I must have been good, because he gave me some great shit." She wiped her nose.

"You're high. You don't even know what you're saying."

She laughed, a harsh cackle. "I don't want you coming here anymore."

"Anna, come on."

"I know you like Uncle Danny. I see the way he looks at you. That's really why you come around—to see him, not us. As soon as you guys get together, you'll want nothing to do with me and Libby, just like my mother when she married my stepfather."

I looked at her blankly. "That's not true. I care about you, about what's happening to you." I leaned over her and wrapped my arms around her shoulders.

She flinched and threw me off. "I don't need you preaching at me. Get out of my face."

"You don't mean that."

She looked at me with a grown-up expression, eyes narrowed to slits and her lips pulled back with contempt. "You don't even know who I am."

And in the moment, I didn't.

"I'm not giving up on you." I slowly backed away.

I knew Anna was testing me, putting me through the rigors that kids use to torment their parents—tugging them closer, pushing them away, assessing the limits of their unconditional love. It's fair to say I hadn't worked out exactly what she meant to me. Maybe if I'd never had Jake in my life, I could have closed my notebook on Anna and not felt a pang of guilt. But I already carried so much regret about how, ultimately, I had failed him. I couldn't walk away from her, too. There was this gravity about her that kept pulling me back, that made me believe she could change, that made me think that I mattered to her. In the same way I had wanted to save Jake, I longed to rescue Anna. Saving her was my second chance at redemption.

CHAPTER TWENTY-FOUR

July 19, 2008

CITY BEGINS NEW ANTI-HEROIN CAMPAIGN

POSTERS OF HEROIN USERS POSTED
IN TRAINS, BUSES, PUBLIC SPACES

Chicago Monthly

That night I dreamt of Jake. It was one of those fierce, colorful dreams, the kind that leaves you aching in the morning, wondering what it all meant. I woke crying, longing for his touch, feeling empty and mournful because, after all, it had not really been a dream, but a reflection of our last days together.

It was the summer after I graduated from U of C. I'd just started a coveted internship at the *Times,* my head brimming with big plans. Then Jake showed up without so much as a phone call. He looked as if he'd just stepped from an album cover: long hair, shirt unbuttoned to the middle of his chest, and pencil tight jeans, the kind that only look attractive on musicians.

We were at the apartment I shared with Maggie near campus, sitting on the couch drinking beer, the air conditioner belching warm air. I was sweating, but Jake seemed cold. He pulled me close and wrapped his arm around me.

"Baby," he whispered. "Wouldn't it be great if we were always together?" He pressed his lips lazily against mine, not a kiss but a marriage of lips, and held them there gently. I started to pull away. "Didn't you miss me? All these years?"

"I thought you'd moved on. Geez, I haven't heard from you in two years." The truth was I'd thought of him constantly.

"How could I ever get over you? You were my first love." He knelt on the floor, took my hand in his and bowed his head as if he were praying to me. "I want us to get married. I want us to be together forever." It was a prophesy, not a proposal.

The girl in me had longed for this moment for years. But those fantasies belonged to a teenager, not a young woman on the cusp of a bright career. I didn't know what to say. I started crying. He took that as a yes.

I holed him up at the apartment, insisting he get clean. Maggie was predictably hostile, protesting that I was using our apartment as an outpatient rehab. She hadn't understood my attraction to a college dropout, a heroin addict.

I'd spent so many nights kissing my pillow as if it were his lips. And then, there he was, all mine. I could have as much of him as I wanted. And he wanted me. How could I not give in?

For the first two days, all he did was sleep, waking in a sweat. I knew he was detoxing. I made him soup, but he just rolled over and pulled up the covers. Late at night, I'd hear him retching in the bathroom. In the morning, Maggie looked at me askance. It was the same look my mother gave when she restrained herself from saying: *I told you so.*

But a few days later, Jake seemed better. He pulled me onto the couch amid his cool sheets, pecking me with kisses, speaking in that low murmuring voice that wilted my reserve. Somehow I hadn't seen it coming. Jake had always pulled back, as if I were some kind of aging virgin he wanted to preserve.

"We're going to be together, forever," he whispered then rolled on top of me. He was wearing only underwear; I could feel his erection between my thighs. He held my hands above my head and pushed himself against me.

My skin quivered as he pulled off my nightgown. His fingers gently caressed between my legs. All the while his lips traveled down my body, leaving little hickey marks I wouldn't see until I stood before the mirror the next morning—pink dots scattered along my collarbone, my breasts, my stomach, as if he'd meant to mark me as his own.

His eyes tracked mine, and, if I tried to look away, he brought them back. He grasped my hands and held them at our sides while he moved in and out, slowly. It was like he was making love to my mind more than my body. But my body felt it, shuddered. Jake panted and then collapsed on top of me, holding me tightly. For a minute I didn't hear him breathing. Then he gasped and laughed and kissed me.

We lay there a long while, enthralled. For a fleeting moment I would have moved anywhere to be with him, joined a roaming band of groupies to share a fraction of his life. But when I tried to imagine what that life might look like, I could only picture a vast grayness, a fog of uncertainty.

More than a week had passed when I cut Jake's long, sun-bleached locks. I sat him on a kitchen chair like a little boy, draped him with a beach towel, then snipped his long strands, tapering his hairline to the back of his neck. The thin, flyaway hairs scattered about the floor. Some strands floated in the air and clung to my damp skin, coating my body, as if I had rolled around with some gigantic shedding cat. Weeks later, I'd find stray hairs in odd places, in the clasp of a necklace, in the crevices of my toes.

Jake's hands stopped shaking, his eyes cleared, and his feet didn't constantly tap the floor. He'd been there several times before, he admitted, on the doorstep of sobriety, as he called it. But he'd always lost his footing. He was certain that with me, he wouldn't. He called me his rock of stability, his savior. We could have a life together, he said. He could form a band in Chicago.

I wanted to believe him. But neither of us had considered how the ambition of a young woman trumps the lusts of a young girl. As much as I wanted him, I didn't want my life to revolve around a man, let alone one so unstable. And I had a longing desire to experience life *out there*, beyond the confines of Chicago, as if life were some foreign country I had to visit. I dreamed of working as a journalist in New York, London, Paris, or Berlin, traveling the world, pursuing one adventure after another. Those ambitions didn't include—at least not then—staying in my hometown, getting married, and having kids. Of course, I couldn't have known then how the journalism industry would tank just when I'd achieved enough experience to land an overseas assignment, making my personal sacrifices pointless, and leaving me convinced that the universe—or God—was punishing me for putting my career first.

We never argued about him leaving. Even parting we strove to keep our image of each other pure. He said he knew I wasn't ready, implying that someday I would be. I doubted that was true. I was convinced we had a sliver of time to make it work, and once that chance was gone, we'd never get it back.

I quietly cried and he held me. He was sober. I had given him that much. He picked up his big duffel and strapped his guitar across his back and walked out of the apartment.

That was the last I saw him.

CHAPTER TWENTY-FIVE

July 21, 2008

HYDE PARK SENATOR LEADING POLLS

CRITICS QUESTION ABILITY TO LEAD

WHEN CITY CRIME RATE IS SO HIGH

Chicago Reporter

Anna wouldn't answer my calls. Libby claimed she didn't know where her cousin was. I spent my evenings driving around neighborhoods popular among heroin addicts, searching for the girl with fiery hair and freckles whose shininess had tarnished overnight. It was then, staring out at the bleary faces, that I came up with a plan to save Anna.

• • •

"It's just in case things don't work out for Anna at Danny's place," I said to Maggie as we ate at our favorite sushi place. "I don't want her to wind up with strangers in foster care."

"Are you still kissing her uncle?"

I shook my head. "It's…too complicated."

"So this isn't an attempt to get back with him?"

"No…not at all."

Maggie looked at me with arched eyebrows, taking frequent sips of sake.

"The situation isn't sustainable for Danny or for Anna. He can't control her and he doesn't have flexibility in his schedule to check up on her like I do. The main problem is that my apartment isn't conducive for a full-time foster kid. For that, you have to have a bedroom completely devoted to the kid. But as an emergency foster parent, I could have Anna live with me for a while."

Maggie stared at me blankly. She chewed slowly, took a sip of water, and wiped her mouth with her napkin.

"Are you fucking insane?" She looked angry, her eyebrows pinched, her lips stretched thin. "Why would you want to add a drug-addicted teenager to your already erratic life? Kids like that need round-the-clock surveillance. You'll come home some night, and your TV and stereo will be gone." She laughed at the thought.

I sulked, mad at Maggie for not seeing the beauty of my plan. Her life was too conventionally safe. Why had I thought she'd understand?

"People always say they hope they make the right decision when it comes along." My voice quivered. "But that's just it. Making the right decision doesn't announce itself with some clouds-parting, trumpet-wailing sound. You live by truth in small moments, making the right decisions instead of the ones that selfishly benefit you all the time. Unfortunately, most people are lazy, fucking cowards."

Maggie pushed away my sake cup, as if alcohol were the root of my anger.

"I don't want to become one of those people," I continued. "I want to matter to someone, Maggie. I want someone to depend on me, to need me. I want to step up. I want to do the Right Thing. And this is it. What's so wrong with that?"

Maggie grabbed my hand. "Nat, is this about Jake, about what...*happened*?"

I exhaled loudly. "This is about me doing something significant with my life. I don't want to be some gray-haired lady still on the police beat knocking on the doors of gangbangers. Fuck, I'm thirty-three. Didn't Christ save the world at our age?"

"Yeah, but he was crucified."

"Don't make fun of what I'm saying."

She smiled sadly and tilted her head. "Nat, I know you are still grieving for *him*, but Anna isn't just *any* teenager. She's a drug addict. She should be in a juvenile facility."

"This isn't about *him*." My voice was more forceful than I'd intended. I hated it when Maggie brought up my past as if it were a map for everything that was unfolding in the present. People at neighboring tables turned to stare. I lowered my voice and bent over the table. "Maybe Anna wouldn't be so bad if she had someone who really *wanted* her. I'm not naïve. I know it would be difficult. I could help her get off drugs. I've helped *other people* get off drugs."

Our eyes met.

"One person doesn't constitute 'people,' Natalie. Besides, you can't have a meaningful relationship with someone who is always looking for their next hit."

I looked away, fiddled with my chopsticks. My throat thickened. Heat was building beneath my eyelids.

Maggie licked her lips and coughed. "Don't take this the wrong way, but, Nat, you are not Christ. Anna isn't Jake, and you can't save her like you tried to save Jake. He wanted off drugs—or at least he said he did. Anna doesn't. Men will do things—or say things—to get a woman that no one else will say or do—not even a fifteen-year-old girl who says she wants a mother."

She patted my hand. "You weren't suited for a life with a musician, Nat. And even if you had stuck it out with Jake, it doesn't mean he would have stayed off drugs, and it doesn't mean he'd be alive today." She paused, then softened her voice. "What you had with Jake was a fling, a romantic intoxication. Addicts seem to be your drug of choice. Just like Anna is now. And you've got to get over it."

CHAPTER TWENTY-SIX

July 22, 2008

HEROIN SUPERHERO MAY HAVE SAVED MORE GIRLS

OTHER "SURVIVORS" COME FORWARD

Chicago Sentinel

When I walked into the newsroom Friday morning, reporters were clustered about, some with looks of shock, others wiping stray tears. At my cubicle, the tchotchkes that once lined the ledge between Ben's desk and mine were gone. And so was Ben.

I'd had an early morning interview and had missed the theatrics, according to a clerk who saw me gaping at Ben's empty cubicle. Ten reporters had been summoned, one by one, into Odis's office, where a woman from human resources handed them a severance agreement: one week for each year of employment in exchange for their promise not to sue the paper. Ben had been the last, he said. Each victim was led back to his or her desk by the HR woman and allowed to take one box of personal items. Ben slid his tchotchkes into his box, walked up to Odis's glass office, pulled down his pants, and mooned him and Amy.

"It was hilarious," the clerk said. "The whole newsroom was watching."

"What did everyone do?"

"Are you kidding? They didn't do a thing. They don't want to risk losing their jobs."

I found Ben's old Rolodex on my desk with a hastily penned sticky note: "Perhaps these people will help you get out of here."

I sat down slowly in my chair, feeling as if Ben had died, because in a way he had. He wouldn't be sitting across from me, making those kooky expressions, giving me his take on the latest crime suspect. I looked over at the senior crime reporters who were yukking it up, telling jokes, as if nothing had happened.

I closed my eyes and tried to blot out their belly laughs, their blustery language, that tone of assurance and cockiness. But in my head, they just kept getting louder, their boastful stories sounding more raucous. I wrung my hands and pressed my fingers to my mouth, as if I could hold in the anger, the way I'd held it in all these years. But the loss of Ben, along with Anna's disappearance, was more than I could take.

I climbed on top of my desk and screamed: "SHUT THE FUCK UP!"

The murmur of the newsroom abruptly stopped. People turned to stare at me.

"Ten people just lost their jobs!" I shouted. "How can you be so fucking callous?"

Someone tapped me on my leg. I turned to see Julian offering me his hand.

"Come down," he whispered. "You don't want to make a scene."

"Too late for that. I want these assholes to know," I pointed at the next row where the men were gawking at me, "that they can't be so oblivious to everyone else's pain."

"You've succeeded at that."

Julian took my hand and pulled me down. Everyone stood gap-mouthed and staring.

"Get back to work," Julian shouted. "There's nothing to see here." He then escorted me to the hallway.

"Look, I know you are upset—"

"Upset? No, I'd say I'm clinically insane at this moment. It's a damn good thing I don't have a gun."

"Don't talk like that."

"They fucking let Ben go! He was one of the hardest-working and most proficient reporters in this fucking place! They just shoved him out the door. After *thirty fucking years*."

Julian put his arm lightly on my back. "Did you think Odis had a choice? The revenues just aren't there anymore. Somebody had to go, you know that, right?"

I pulled away from him. "I'm not a child, Julian. The thing is, most of us have had to suck it up. We've not had a raise in four years, and yet the people at the top keep getting longer and longer titles and more and more bonuses. And their friends—like those assholes—get raises and bonuses. But if you're not kissing ass and playing politics and just do your job, well, there's not a lot of reward in that, is there? There's plenty of dead weight around here. They didn't have to pick Ben."

"You're right. And everyone knows you're right." Julian patted my back. "Keep your head down, keep writing your Poison stories. That's what matters. Don't let the politics here get to you. You'll be okay."

"I'm not going to be *okay*." I jerked away from him and marched back into the newsroom.

The senior crime reporters had retreated to their desks, where I assumed they were sending snarky emails about me to each other. I was sick of them, how they picked and poked for weeks and months at "high-minded" investigative pieces of their choosing. Meanwhile, people were dying of Poison, Anna was missing, and I didn't have enough time in the day to track down all the places she might be.

Something inside me had altered. I no longer cared about finding the Poison killer solely for a story. I wanted to stop the deaths. I was embarrassed that I'd been part of the newspaper's silliness, turning victims into cartoon characters with names like Dead Angels and Ghost Girl. And who could forget Heroin Superhero? In the beginning, the girls were just bodies at the morgue. Now I knew them. I'd stood in their bedrooms. I'd read their emails and diaries. I'd studied their Facebook accounts. They had become more real to me than most people in the newsroom.

I felt I was suffocating under the glares of my coworkers. I stared at my computer screen unable to focus. When my phone rang, it startled me out of my miasma of pity. It was Rex Kennan saying he wanted to meet.

"I have something to show you."

• • •

The Executive Hotel, its name prominent in giant green neon letters, was a crumbling Japanese-owned relic that rented rooms by the hour. The star attraction on the ground floor was a three-star steak house featuring booths where business could be conducted privately.

Rex told me to ask for the booth of Mr. White, apparently a reference to *Breaking Bad*, a television show about a chemistry teacher-turned-drug dealer. If Rex was trying to be funny, he missed the mark. A tiny Asian hostess escorted me to a back booth where Rex was already chewing on a steak.

"Ms. Delaney." Juice glistened on his lips and his cheeks ballooned with meat. "I'd give you a kiss but my mouth is already preoccupied."

"Save it for someone who cares." I was not about to play nice this time, since he'd lied at our last meeting. It was just a matter of time before I found the irrefutable link I needed that placed him at the Chinatown house the night the girls died. I was guessing Rex knew that too. and that's why he'd asked to meet. Only this time I'd insisted that the meeting was on the record.

He wiped his mouth with a linen napkin and studied me. "Okay. I can see you're angry. I admit I lied about knowing the girls. You can see why. You're trying to tie me to their deaths."

"And why should I believe you?"

He slouched lower in the booth and swallowed hard. This was

not easy for him, humbling himself. There was something more dear than his reputation he risked losing.

"Bethany told me what you said."

"So you admit to being her boyfriend?"

"How do you define boyfriend?"

"I don't have time for games." I scooted to the end of the booth and pulled back the curtain to leave.

He grabbed my hand. "Wait." I felt the power shift in my favor. "I didn't kill them."

"So why were you there?"

He looked around trying to decide the right words that would convey his message without incriminating himself. "*Hypothetically*—I could have been there to *save* them."

"Then—*hypothetically*—why didn't you?"

"Maybe, the antidote wasn't working. Maybe, *hypothetically*, I panicked, okay?"

"If you'd called 911, they might have been able to save them. You could be charged with manslaughter, spend twenty years behind bars."

There was a flash of anger in his eyes. "With the Kennan name? Not likely."

"You think you're so special, huh?"

He licked his lips nervously. "It may surprise you, but I'd like to track down the fucker who sold them Poison as much as you would."

"Only so you aren't charged for your negligence."

"I'll admit that's part of it, but there are other reasons." He ran a hand through his hair. "This guy killed several of my friends. I want him stopped."

"And what are you doing about it?"

He slid a manila file across the table. "My family hired a private investigator. It looks like the killer is a South Side drug dealer."

I laughed cynically. "That's what the Kennan money buys? I could have saved you some dough and had your investigator read my stories. Then again, maybe that's what he did."

Rex gritted his teeth. "I'm giving this to you to help your story."

"Oh…you're such a good Boy Scout."

"Yeah? You print that I was at that house, and you'll find out just what a good Boy Scout I am…"

I snatched the folder and darted to the door. Standing on the sidewalk, I took a quick look at the file. It contained a list of South Side heroin dealers, including Lester and Rapper X. Kennan's investigator had stopped short of determining which dealer sold Poison to the girls. So they'd reached the same dead end that I had. That's when I knew I'd have to take an even riskier course.

CHAPTER TWENTY-SEVEN

August 3, 2008

MAYOR ASSIGNS SPECIAL TASK FORCE ON HEROIN
INVESTIGATORS TO DECIDE WHICH
DEATHS ARE LINKED TO SAME SOURCE
Chicago Times

Wiry, with gray eyes and rivers of white coursing through his cropped Afro, Eli seemed harmless in that way older men can be disarming. Drug dealers confided in him. But his grandfatherly demeanor was deceptive. When he got desperate for cash, he sold information to the police: Eli was a snitch. He also was a source of mine.

The downside of asking Eli for help was that he always wanted something in return. But I was running out of options. I needed someone inside the South Side's drug scene, someone who could provide a shortcut through Kennan's long list of dealers.

Eli agreed to meet me at a "gentlemen's club" called The Excalibur. We sat at a back table, the chairs covered in plastic, and yelled over loud eighties music. A disco ball twirled, showering the room with dizzying shades of purple and red. Besides the dancers on stage, strippers sauntered from table to table, offering drinks and private lap dances. At the bar, clumps of men in loosened ties and others in T-shirts and work boots hunched over drinks, fingering stacks of singles they kept ready for tipping.

"Hey, doll, how about I buy you a lap dance," Eli said. He

held his cigarette between his forefinger and thumb like a joint, its worm of ash threatening to singe another hole in his pants. His drooping eyelids and slack posture made me want to keep him engaged in conversation, lest he dozed off.

"No thanks, Eli. I like guys."

"Indulge an old man, doll. Maybe I want to see a beautiful woman dancing naked on another beautiful woman."

"I'm wearing clothes."

"My dick may be dead, doll, but my imagination *ain't*."

Eli waved over a leggy brunette in a G-string and chocolate pasties. He tilted his head towards me. She grinned as she stepped onto my chair, a foot on either side of my thighs, her glass high heels crunching the plastic seat covering.

"Hi ya, girlfriend. I'm Dara." She squatted low over my lap and opened her legs wide to show me the bare pink skin between them.

"Can we hurry this up?"

"Sure, sweetie. I'll quit whenever you put a big tip on my kitty." She touched herself between her legs.

I pleaded with my eyes for Eli to stop the performance, but he was mesmerized, his eyes wistful and dreamy, his jowls hanging loose. I couldn't reach my purse without coming in contact with some private part of Dara. And I knew the rules: no touching. Dara didn't look like she'd mind, though, writhing her pelvis inches from my face. She was laughing, her mouth wide open, her tongue wriggling. I clamped my eyes shut, angry, the heat rushing to my face. How much was I willing to endure for some scrap of information from this guy? Just when I thought I couldn't take it anymore, Eli wrapped a twenty around Dara's G-string and pulled her away.

"What was that?" I demanded, wiping the sweat from my face.

"Initiation."

I stood up indignant, ready to leave.

Eli pushed me back down.

"No sissy girl could stand another woman's pussy in her face." He laughed. "Come to think of it, I can't say I know too many women who'd put up with it, unless they were *dykes*." His face stiffened, then he waved his hand. "Come on. I'll show you what you want to see."

I wasn't sure whether I'd demonstrated that I wasn't a prude or that I was a lesbian. Either way, Eli seemed convinced I was tough enough to go "undercover," as he said. We got in his old pickup truck and rode down Martin Luther King Drive. Eli tapped his fingers on the steering wheel, listening to a blues station.

If we didn't have history, I probably wouldn't have gotten in that truck. But I owed one of my biggest stories to Eli. Mo had introduced us two years earlier when I was writing a story on drug informants. After weeks of following him around strip clubs where he sold OxyContin to young dancers, Eli introduced me to the mother lode: drug snitches immersed in Chicago's underworld of drugs, sex, guns and crooked cops.

When those stories hit the paper, the police chief resigned in disgrace. U.S. Attorney Fitzgerald launched a federal investigation of the police department, resulting in the convictions of several cops for drug trafficking. It was probably the only reason I wasn't laid off with the first batch of newspaper kills. Since then, police antagonism toward me hadn't waned. At times I wondered why even Mo talked to me.

I gazed out the window, still stewing about my "initiation." I wasn't exactly dressed for going to a drug house in my designer black jeans, high-heeled boots and a blouse decorated in gold sequins. If Eli was worried, he didn't show it. He hummed along to the radio. At Forty-Seventh Street he turned right and, just past the El tracks, took a left down a side street lined with vacant lots and boarded-up houses. He pulled to the curb and cut the engine.

"See that house there on the right?" he whispered. "The one with the lights shining from the upstairs windows?"

I nodded.

"That's where we're going. But when we get in there, you can't be no reporter, doll. You'll be my girl. Understand? That way they won't question you."

"Why are you doing this, Eli?"

"You earned it, didn't you? Hell, maybe you liked Dara?" He laughed and patted my hand. "Stop worrying, doll. Sometimes a man just wants to kick it, feel alive."

"Let's be clear. I'm not shooting smack and you're not getting any of this." I waved my hand over my body.

"No big deal. You watch me. Act a little stoned. And no fancy words. Think white trash because tonight that's what you are. Trust me. You'll pass."

"And what if I don't?"

He raised his pant leg, revealing the gun strapped to his shin. "That's when we initiate the Smith & Wesson plan, doll."

I rubbed my face. Fuck. What was I doing? This was some heavy shit.

Before I had time to reconsider, I felt Eli pulling me from the truck. We stepped through the chunks of concrete and lumps of soil where a house once stood. I staggered behind him, tripped on a knot of tree roots, but Eli didn't look back. When we reached the back of the house, a man coughed loudly from the shadows. Eli pulled out a ten and mumbled something. The guy handed Eli the stub of a candle.

Eli struck a match and lit the candle as he gingerly stepped over debris—old dolls, toys, children's books, clothes—heaped on the floor. When he held up the candle, the flame, coupled with the streetlights that filtered through the broken windows, revealed charred walls and drywall drooping from the ceiling. He pointed the candle toward a staircase. The steps were narrow, the railing missing. Eli tugged me along wordlessly. We mounted each stair slowly until we reached a landing where we heard voices and music. He directed me up another flight of stairs. At the top, we met a hallway where people were milling around, smoking and taking swigs from big brown bottles.

"Came to see Theodore," Eli announced.

A young man wearing a White Sox cap sideways and a

thick gold necklace drooping to his waist pointed listlessly to another room.

Staged around the room were dripping candles. A dozen people were inside, mostly clustered near the window. They sat on stools or crouched on the floor, stacked like stadium seats. Some were folded up together, as if asleep. Most were older men, but there were three white women. One cried in the corner, stabbing herself with a needle, searching for a vein. In the dim candlelight, her pale skin contrasted sharply with the crimson stream running down her arm.

Scanning the room, I realized people were organized into a makeshift assembly line. One man stood in the middle. He kneeled, helping an anxious man find a vein, prodding the man's forearm with his fingertips. When he'd successfully sucked blood into the syringe, he yelled: "Got one!" He pushed his thumb down on the needle head; the man's eyes closed and he let out a long sigh.

The man in the middle rose to his feet, grabbed a basket he kept beside him, and approached us with a twisted grin that showed off a single jagged front tooth. He was short and bony with tangled dreads dangling at the back of his head. Though it was warm, he wore a tattered ski vest, grime collected at the collar. A string of candy beads hung around his neck, and occasionally he'd scrunch down his chin and with his tongue pull the string to his mouth and chew off a bead with his bare gums.

"Theodore," Eli yelled and clutched the man's hand in a fist.

"Hey ya, brother? What are you slumming around here for?" The man's eyes shifted to me, as if I was the one for whom the question was really intended.

"Got me a woman and thought I'd get me some happy." Eli swung his arm around my neck. "Going to take her to Lee's Unleaded. Thought I'd stop off, see some folks, party a little. Got room?"

Theodore glanced over his shoulder at the clutch of addicts. No one looked back.

"Sure, over there." He pointed at a bed against the wall.

The bedspread was made of a scratchy nylon material, the design of roses bleeding into the tucked corners. Eli positioned me between them. The two men talked over my lap. They traded details about friends and dealers, people who were in jail, people who were dead. I slouched and casually glanced around with half-closed eyes, trying to convey boredom instead of curiosity. The air smelled of vanilla and vinegar. Flames from the candles radiated a yellow cast and made the floor seem as if it were on fire. Shadows flickered along the walls, making the faces around the room look sinister, evil. Eli appeared different, coarse. He spoke more street and kept flaring his nose, as if anxious for a hit, a tic that was probably intentional. Theodore kept his basket on his lap, and to my surprise, I recognized the contents. It was all stuff they handed out for free at the county needle exchange: syringes in sterile plastic wrappers, tiny cotton balls, little metal "cookers," blue plastic bottles filled with distilled water and alcohol swabs.

A couple of times Theodore got up to help a customer find a vein. Once he shook a guy slumped over until he slowly came to. Occasionally someone would come in, asking to buy a needle after they'd bought their stash from the guys in the hall. A young black girl stumbled in and asked Theodore if he could help her cook her stuff. She was afraid it might contain Poison.

"You new at this, huh?" Theodore asked her.

"Just got back in town. Heard people be dying of bad dope. Don't fucking want to die." She handed him a five-dollar bill.

Theodore took her baggie and sprinkled the powder into the metal canister, mixed in some diluted water, and held a candle under the concoction.

"See how it don't change colors? If there'd be fentanyl, it be changed purple. You safe." He handed her the metal cooker.

The woman made the sign of the cross on her chest, then found a spot on the floor.

"So what you hearing about this fentanyl?" Eli asked.

"Well, it sure as hell ain't the Mickeys," Theodore said. "I don't fucking believe them feds. And why the fuck would the Mickeys want to kill off their buyers? It don't make sense."

"It's fucked up, all right." Eli took a drag on his cigarette. "Some fucker up at Dooey's says it be one guy doing all this shit. You fucking believe that?"

"Yeah? People says lots of things. Everybody thinks they know something."

Eli growled a laugh. "Brother, you *always* know. You the one who knows the truth."

Theodore smiled with pride, revealing a dark hole around that single shiny fang. "Well, can't say what I know *be* the truth. That's all. Don't like spreading rumors, you know?"

Eli nodded. "Sure, sure."

"Heard he's some former gangbanger just got out. Did some time for coke or some shit. The Mickeys, they be looking for him after their boys got locked up."

"No shit? One nigga killed all them people?" Eli lowered his voice and leaned over my lap and whispered to Theodore: "You know who it is, don't you?"

Theodore wrinkled his mouth as if he'd smelled something rank and pulled back from Eli. "Can't say for sure. Ain't never heard no name, just a nickname. Dog? Big Dog? But I believe it. Heard too many folks buy shit from some *nigga* named *Dog* and turn up *dead*."

I wracked my brain trying to remember if Lester's boys had ever called him Big Dog. The nickname was hardly unique.

"Word be he a Gangster. Has some grudge against the Mickeys. He be taking out his revenge through the po-lice," Theodore continued.

"He workin' alone?"

Theodore looked around nervously to see if anyone else was listening. Most people had their eyes closed or were busy trying to find a vein. Then he leaned in, his head hovering above my lap. Eli did likewise.

"I hear he be connected. High up." Theodore widened his dark eyes.

Eli shifted his head. "Whatcha mean, brother?"

"Don't know. Just heard he got *protection.*"

Eli took out a bag of heroin and ran two lines of white powder on a large hand mirror Theodore had given him. He handed the remains in the bag to Theodore, his take. Theodore handed him a broken straw, and Eli moved his big nose slowly up the mirror, sucking in one of the white lines. Then he handed the mirror to me.

I glared at him, pushing it back, scattering the neat white line. "No! I told you."

"You said no shooting. This ain't no injection, doll."

Theodore smiled. "That's right. Enjoy it, sister. Go on."

They were both staring at me, eagerly waiting. The conversation had drawn stares from the others in the room.

"It's just a little H, doll. Ain't gonna kill ya." Eli's voice warbled with nerves.

A few dealers from the hallway came in to see what everyone was gawking at. They stood in the doorway, watching. Watching me.

Eli handed me the broken straw. My hand shook. I swallowed hard. This was far worse than the lap dance, and I couldn't see a way out. I put the straw to my nose, as Eli had. I held one finger against the other nostril and bent my face to the mirror. But what I saw in the fractured light were green gimlet eyes staring back. They didn't look like mine. They looked like *hers.*

I screamed and dumped the mirror on the floor, charging through the people in the hallway. I wanted away from those eyes. Maybe it was the hysteria of the moment, maybe it was the alcohol I'd drunk that night. But that night I swear I saw Anna in the mirror. She held a terrified expression, a panicked look.

In the dark stairwell, I tripped, then tumbled into a big man. Without a word I got up and staggered the rest of the way down, past the charred bits of ceiling hanging above my head, and beyond the eerie white baby doll lying at the foot of the stairs, the streetlight highlighting tufts of her synthetic red hair and the gaping hole where one of her green marble eyes used to be. I stepped sideways to avoid crushing her face with my boot. At the back door, I pushed past the guy standing guard and kept running, past the hookers under the El, past the liquor stores, and the dive bars with patrons spilling out into the street. At the corner, taxis were lined up outside the Harold Washington Cultural Center, and I jumped into the back seat of the last one in line.

"Ma'am," the driver said turning around, "you got to go to the one in front." That's when he must have seen the crazed look in my eyes. "Are you all right? Did somebody hurt you?"

A large cross hung from his rearview mirror.

"If you love Jesus, sir, you'll save me from this place."

He jammed the car into gear.

Once home, I poured a large tumbler of scotch, sat on the balcony, and smoked half a pack of cigarettes, my hands shaking. Like a skip in an old record, my mind played and replayed snags of conversations, desperately trying to remember what Lester's boys had called him. One thought nagged at me: If Lester really was *the* Big Dog, why had he spared Anna and Libby? I texted Anna but she never answered. Finally, I crawled into bed but could not forget that face in the mirror, the shock in her eyes. I lay awake for hours, sensing something tragic and horrendous had happened.

CHAPTER TWENTY-EIGHT

August 4, 2008

GOVERNOR'S DAUGHTER IS IDENTIFIED AS GHOST GIRL

CLASSMATES SAY BETHANY WAS ALWAYS WITH THE DEAD ANGELS

Chicago Sentinel

The next morning I was running on my treadmill near my bedroom window that overlooked the shops along Broadway. My favorite sushi chef was sweeping outside his restaurant when two young girls in short skirts and flip-flops whisked past him, reminding me of that steamy day I'd met Anna and Libby. For a minute my chest hurt, longing to see the girls again. The window was open, and the air was already thick with heat, southwest winds swirling leaves and trash in the street, reigniting sullied smells of summer.

Above the hum of the treadmill I heard the phone ringing. I slowed down, expecting to hear on the answering machine the desperate voice of a clerk assigned to track me down. TV news and the tabloid *Sentinel* had identified Ghost Girl as the Governor's daughter, quoting Queen of Angels students who said the four girls frequented clubs together and jokingly called themselves "Sex in the City." Odis was probably having me summoned to follow the story.

But the voice on the answering machine was muscular, one that was using all its strength not to break.

I ran to the phone.

"I'm here, Danny," I said breathlessly. "What's up?"

"Nat, something awful happened."

He took a deep breath; so did I.

"I...I...don't know...I just...can't." His voice broke off and I thought I heard him sob. He covered the receiver, and there was a scratchy noise.

"Are you all right?"

He was blowing his nose and sniffling.

"This is...I just don't...I don't know how to say..."

"Danny, I can't hear you. What's wrong?"

"Anna was shot last night," he blurted.

"What? What are you saying?"

"Her and Libby got into something. I don't know." He moved the phone away from his mouth. "Goddamn it!"

"What happened?"

"Libby, Anna, and a bunch of girls went down to Woodlawn to buy drugs, or something. I don't know. I didn't know Lib was with her. This is all such shit!" He was suddenly talking fast. "This group of black girls didn't take to them coming down there. Said they were trespassing or something. Libby and Anna should've known better. Goddamn it!" He dropped the phone and I could hear him crying. I'd never heard him so unhinged. Finally he picked it up. He was breathing heavily.

"Danny, *please*, tell me what happened."

"One girl, she took a gun to Anna's head. She said Anna was disrespecting them...Oh God...she shot Anna right in the face. Right in the eye! She's dead, Natalie. Anna is dead."

My knees crumpled, and I slumped to the floor. I imagined Anna's freckled face, a face like my own, marred by a gaping hole. Scenes from last night flashed in my mind: Anna's brilliant green eyes in the mirror staring back at me; the red-haired doll with its missing green marble eye. Then I remembered the first day we met, Anna's gap-toothed grin, and her strange explanation: "A girl's gotta do what a girl's got to do. Too much fun last night and well, here I am with a hole in my head."

I shuddered. I couldn't concentrate on what Danny was

saying. Something about Anna's mother donating parts of Anna's body: her liver, her kidneys. It sounded so clinical, so morbid.

"She said she would give it all away, but not the heart. That's because, despite all her shortcomings, Anna had a good heart."

Then the line went quiet.

"Danny…I'm so sorry."

"I know you really cared for her. I know you tried to help her. There are just some people you can't do for, you know?"

I felt guilty for having failed Anna, just as I had failed Jake.

"She thought she was invincible, that nothing could hurt her," I said quietly.

"That kind of foolish thinking is what got her killed, Natalie."

"Was Libby hurt?"

"She got sprayed with her cousin's blood. She saw it all…"

"Oh, God."

He started choking up again. "I gotta go."

After he hung up, I held the phone in my lap. I couldn't move. I sat there, stroking Deadline. At that moment all I could picture was Anna's limp body, blood coursing down her face, her one eye wide open, stunned at how her adventure had ended.

I counted on my fingers. It had been ten days since I'd last seen Anna. I'd found her in a heroin house, a needle sticking in her arm. I begged her to leave with me, but she wouldn't. After that I didn't call her again. I didn't check in with Libby. Now that silence was eating at me, choking me with guilt.

I starred out the window, listening to the *thunk, thunk, thunk* of cars rolling over a manhole cover, an ambulance blaring its siren, kids yelling. It all seemed magnified as if someone had cranked up the stereo. Anna was dead. I was alive. Anna was dead.

• • •

An hour later, my hair still wet from a shower, I stood in Amy's office doorway. Amy jumped up, engulfed me with her arms and rubbed my back in circular motions, my snot smearing her tailored suit jacket. She smelled of hair spray and Chanel No. 5. She stroked my hair and, for a second, I was reminded of my mother cooing to me on sleepless nights. I whispered: "She's dead."

Amy didn't have to ask who "she" was. As I lifted myself off her shoulders, I saw the upward curl of her lips and her eyes widen with an idea. I left her standing there, with that strange sparkle in her face, and headed into the newsroom where the hum of computers and the racket of reporters oddly comforted me. Though a teenage girl had been tragically shot and killed, the world I'd known had not changed.

I walked in a daze, forged on with the weight of knowing what I had to do. I had a story to write. There were police and autopsy reports to track down. There was a mother I had to find.

CHAPTER TWENTY-NINE

August 4, 2008

GIRL DEAD AFTER GANG FIGHT

RACE AND DRUGS BLAMED

Chicago Times

When I arrived at Anna's home in suburban Wilmette, Pam appeared at the door expectantly. A petite woman, she clung to a cigarette in one hand and a tissue in the other, blotting at the mascara smudged under her eyes. She looked like any other housewife aged by failed dreams. I stared awkwardly at her, comparing the image in my head of a drunk and stoned mother with the sober and contained woman before me.

"Not what you'd envisioned?" she asked in a scratchy smoker's voice. "Anna always painted me a boozer. I've been in AA since Anna was a baby. Her father's the drunk. But somehow Anna always found it in her heart to forgive him."

Pam led me through the cavernous foyer and into a formal sitting room neatly arranged with white velour couches and pale plush carpet. Every surface was lined with pricey bric-a-brac. Among the cluster of gold frames along the mantel was a portrait of Pam with Anna in pigtails.

"She was five in that photo," Pam offered, following my gaze. "Full of wonder and amazement even then. Danny said you knew Anna?"

The mention of Danny's name made my uneasy. How much

had he told her? I hadn't worked out how I would describe my relationship with Anna. Somehow I thought I'd approach Pam as I would any other mother whose child had been tragically killed. But, of course, this was different.

"I met her while I was reporting the stories about the fentanyl deaths."

"So, Anna was into heroin, too?"

"I think she was into a lot of...stuff." My voice was wobbly with nerves.

Pam clicked her French-manicured nails against each other and studied my face. "You don't have to obfuscate on my part. I'm painfully aware of what my daughter was capable of."

She moved from the mantel, sucked in a long breath, smiled to compensate for her harsh tone, then swept her white frosted nails over the couch. "Please, have a seat."

At our knees was a glass coffee table stacked with photo albums.

"The funeral home asked me for some photos to include in the program." She flipped one of the album's yellowed plastic sleeves, and a child with fiery red tufts and fair skin peered out. A combination whimper and laugh emitted from Pam's throat. She grabbed her mouth. Tears bubbled up at the corners of her eyes.

"She so much wanted this pink taffeta dress." She shook her head with the memory. "Its little acrylic hoop slip made her break out in a rash. But no, she insisted on wearing it, even though she had the dress hiked up, scratching her rear end the whole time." She laughed and blew her nose. "That was pure Anna. She had to figure out everything in her own way." She looked at me, curious. "I guess you already knew that."

While Pam narrated Anna's life, prompted by the photos, I pulled out my phone and quietly snapped pictures of the mother and the frozen images of her dead child. Anna had never said anything charitable about her mother. Anna claimed as soon as her mother remarried she wanted nothing to do with her. Pam told another story, one of heartbreak and betrayal. Over and over, she said, she had tried to parent Anna, but Anna wouldn't have any of it. Anna, she said, had splintered their family by making up stories about her stepfather.

"How do you know they weren't true?"

"Because I took Anna to a doctor, and he said she was still a virgin!" She sobbed into her hands.

I didn't know whether to hug her or pat her arm. But, suddenly, Pam composed herself, dabbing a wadded tissue at her eyes.

"Anna was always trying to escape responsibilities," she said. "I called her 'Peter Panna' because she never wanted to grow up, and, at the same time, she wanted to be free. Once she had been out in the world, there was no bringing her back home. Nosiree. She didn't listen. She didn't obey rules, and she wasn't going to do anything I told her to do."

"Why did you send her to Queen of Angels?"

She waved her cigarette at me like a wand. "Oh, honey, that's a long family tradition. I went there, so did my cousins. I thought it would be good for her, give her a solid religious foundation." She smiled awkwardly.

"Did you not want her to come home? I mean, you put her in the dorm."

She gurgled a laugh. "Is that what she told you? That was *her* demand. She said if she had to be taught by 'old wrinkled virgins' that she deserved to live in the dorm. She knew what she was doing. It was one foot out the door. She wanted to be as far away from us as she could."

Pam continued flipping through the album. Most of the newer photos were the official variety: school photos, dances, political fundraisers—Pam's husband had donated to a number of Democratic campaigns, she said. As Anna aged, there were fewer and fewer photos with her family. The last photo in the album caught my eye. It had the same background—the city skyline at night silhouetted by sparkling skyscrapers—as the one in Laila's bedroom. Only in this photo, it was Anna standing next to Rex Kennan.

"How did Anna know Rex?"

Pam blinked. "School events and political parties, I suppose. I think this was taken at the Governor's Ball last fall." She pulled out the five-by-seven and held it up to the light. "His mother went to Queen of Angels with me." She turned silent, as if recounting some memory, then pivoted to me. "Are you surprised I was friends with a Kennan? My family wasn't always poor, you know. My father at one time owned hundreds of acres of farmland. By the time Danny came along, well, it was the farm crisis. They'd lost it all. I guess I felt I had nothing to lose running off with Anna's father. I could say it was the biggest mistake of my life, but then I wouldn't have had Anna."

She quickly changed the subject, recounting another story of Anna as a young child, but I couldn't concentrate. I kept thinking about the photo of Anna and Rex. Anna and the girls from Queen of Angels hadn't been casual acquaintances, as she'd claimed. And then there was the mysterious relationship they'd all had with Rex.

Pam looked exhausted. Her red-rimmed eyes creased at the corners. She'd nervously twisted a tissue until it dissipated into tiny white scraps on her lap, like snowflakes. Though we had connected that afternoon on an emotional level, I was startled when she reached over, stroked a strand of my hair and touched my cheek.

"You remind me of her," she whispered.

My skin tingled, and I had a strange sensation that we were being watched.

"I'm sorry, but I have to get back to the paper."

Pam shuffled to the door in her white velvet slippers. Having unburdened herself of Anna's story, she seemed more at ease, but I felt more confused. Had her stepfather really molested her? What kind of person uses rape as a prop? What kind of person lies so horrifically about her mother? I felt embarrassed I'd ever believed this woman would have allowed me to be a guardian for her only daughter.

As I made my way down Pam's limestone walkway, the weight of all I'd heard, the lack of sleep—coupled with the guilt and the grief—pulled at me. Pam called out after me, and I turned to wave at her. A flicker of intensity appeared in her face. Gone were her dull brown eyes. Instead I saw slivers of green reflecting chards of light as if they belonged to Anna.

• • •

As I stepped off the elevator and into the newsroom, Amy practically accosted me. She'd convinced Odis to devote the entire front page to Anna's murder. So this was what she was conjuring up earlier. Though Anna didn't die of heroin, Amy was linking her murder to the Poison deaths. The fentanyl stories needed a poster child, she said, someone whose narrative was sympathetic. The problem had been that most families were too embarrassed over their daughters' deaths to provide details. Anna was different. I'd been there from the beginning when Lester introduced her to brown sugar. Her story and pictures were the "hook" the newspaper needed to personalize how girls were overdosing.

At my desk I struggled with what to write. I had so much information and yet not enough. My mind catalogued the images of Anna and weighed their veracity. Had I seen the real Anna or the one she'd invented? Images flashed through my mind: her mouth twisted in grown-up ecstasy as the heroin rushed through her veins; her childlike face imploring me to adopt her; her eyes full of rage after the drug dealer with the stalagmite teeth left her bedroom.

After a few minutes Amy appeared at my desk with a plastic cup of coffee. "This might help," she said, handing me the cup. "How's your story coming?" When she saw the blank screen, her face fell. She motioned me to her office.

"I know this is tough stuff." She shut the door. "But you're a professional, and you have to put aside your personal feelings right now. You can mourn her later. Right now you need to write your ass off. Your job depends on it and maybe even mine."

"But once I write Anna was doing drugs, no one is going to care about her. She'll be a stereotype."

"Readers will care about her because you're going to show why you cared about her." Amy gently stroked my arm, then sat down at her computer. "Okay. Tell me about the first time you met Anna."

I recalled how Anna had seemed ghostlike as she strolled past the house with the Dead Angels, laughing in a way that made me shudder. I could still see her fingering her chipped tooth, how she marveled at the cartoon snake on her ankle. I recounted how only hours later I'd watched Anna smoke heroin in the woods, how excited she'd been, how she'd giggled and said the wild dill weed smelled like pickles.

Amy kept typing. "It was her first time?"

"Supposedly, for H. There were other drugs before that."

Amy swiveled around, her eyes aflame. "This is incredible stuff! You know that, right? I mean, how often do we get to know these kids before they wind up on the other end of a gun? How often do we get to witness the course of addiction?"

One time too many, I wanted to say. My head ached, my eyes hurt. I wanted it to be over. The story. The guilt.

"Here, you drive." Amy stood.

The fine lines under her eyes wrinkled in sinister delight, probably factoring how such a story might get her promoted. As much I hated her in that moment, I grudgingly took her seat as she left the room. She'd compared Anna's first experience smoking heroin as if it had been her first kiss. I didn't change those words. Maybe I should have. I recounted what Anna's mother had told me, and the gory details from the police. The story I wrote was the truth as I knew it. I showed how Anna—at least the Anna I'd gotten to know in two months—was a clever girl with an insatiable curiosity. I also wrote about Anna's dangerous side, how she stood under the cover of trees and pressed her lips to a cardboard toilet paper roll and breathed in a cloud of heroin. I wrote how I watched, how I didn't know what to do, how I did nothing. I wrote how Anna seemed desperate to try other drugs, how drugs fueled Anna's obsession for living, how that obsession led to her death.

I also wrote that it was Lester Williams who had supplied Anna her first hit, that he was the one who heated the brown sugar and held the tinfoil while Anna sucked in its fumes. Despite my promise to keep Lester's name out of the paper, I wasn't going to protect a man who had contributed to her death. It was one journalistic oath I felt comfortable breaking.

But I didn't write about the last time I saw Anna; I didn't detail how listless she looked lying on the floor amid fast food trash, how when I approached her, she sat up with a rage in her eyes. That last image served as my own private torment.

I filed the story and drifted back to my desk. I answered a few minor questions from Amy and the copydesk. A version was sent to Odis, who signed off on publishing it. A half-hour later, Amy held a printed copy in her hand.

"Powerful," she said softly.

I shrugged. Unlike other homicide stories I had written, this one said "I" throughout. I saw. I watched. I did nothing.

"Let me buy you a drink," she offered.

The "second newsroom," as we called it, was the Billy Goat bar, only steps underground on Lower Michigan. Yellowed news clippings papered the walls. The late John Belushi made the bar famous with his *Saturday Night Live* skits showing a short-order cook yelling: "Cheezbooger, cheezbooger, no fries, chips, no Coke, Pepsi."

As soon as Amy and I ducked inside the bar, my lungs filled with its familiar stale, smoky air, putting me at ease. The place was nearly empty except for regulars propped up at the bar watching TV.

Amy ordered two Old Styles.

"To a reporter who is going to go far!" She raised her bottle.

"No. To Anna, a life snuffed out by desire."

Amy frowned but clinked my bottle. "Yes. Let's first pay tribute to the dead."

Amy heaped on the praise: the story on Anna was "excellent work"; I was now ready for the "big leagues"—the *Los Angeles Times* or the *New York Daily News*. I just listened and drank. After several beers, I hailed a taxi. At home, I fell into bed, fearful of opening my eyes and seeing what I imagined was there in the dark: Anna's single gimlet green eye gleaming from the shadows.

CHAPTER THIRTY

August 5, 2008

REV JESSE JACKSON DEMANDS POLICE
ARREST HEROIN DEALER

CLAIMS POLICE FRAMED GANG FOR HEROIN DEATHS

Chicago Sentinel

"Have you listened to the radio?" Amy demanded, having awakened me with her call.

I rubbed my eyes. My head hurt. Too many beers.

"They're talking about your story," she said.

I sat up in bed.

"Every radio and TV station in town has called asking to interview you, asking us to defend your actions."

"What? What actions?" The conversation felt like an absurd dream.

"They are saying you shouldn't have let Anna do heroin. You shouldn't have stood there and watched. You should have called the police." Amy spat out the criticism with such vigor it felt as if she were accusing me herself.

"That's ridiculous. How could I stop her?"

"Tell that to the judge."

"What are you talking about?" I scrubbed my hands over my face, urging myself to wake up.

"The judge who arraigned Anna's killer this morning accused you of contributing to Anna's downfall. He said you and the paper—*we!*—had 'blood on our hands.' He's calling for a police investigation." Amy's voice was growing more hysterical. "You need to come in *now*."

• • •

Forty-five minutes later, the newsroom greeted me with a not-so subtle disapproval. People clustered together and spoke in hushed voices. As I passed, they looked away.

A news clerk ran up behind me. "Is it true what they're saying? That you gave that girl drugs to make your story better?" His face was animated with the possibility.

"Is that what they're saying? You think I got kids addicted to heroin to get a story?"

"No. It's just…they just said you bought kids booze and stuff. And…"

"And what? What are they saying?"

He shrugged and dropped his eyes. "You know, that you sort of…well…that you had sex with some of the boys?"

As journalists we were trained not to believe gossip until we'd checked out the facts. But many reporters engaged in *schadenfreude*—taking pleasure from others' troubles. The staff was only too eager to spread such rumors. I could imagine their condemnations: She shouldn't have been hanging out on the street anyway. Serves her right to think she could solve murders.

I tried to ignore the anger rising within me. At my desk, a crowd was shouting at Amy.

"Why did you let this happen?" an older copydesk editor demanded.

Amy stood with her arms crossed. When I appeared, the crowd glowered and parted.

"In my office," she ordered, then stormed off, her high heels pounding the floor.

I sat down at my desk and buried my face into my palms. The

senior crime reporters must be gloating at my troubles. But when I looked up, I found only Julian, hanging over my cubicle.

"How are you holding up?" He sounded concerned.

"Swell. Don't you know I'm the new pariah? You might want to avoid talking to me."

"They'd better be backing you up. They should have had better sense than to run that story the way they did."

"What do you mean?" Editors didn't normally criticize other editors.

"You so much as admitted to committing a felony on the front page. You wrote that you watched a fifteen-year-old do drugs. In this state, it's a felony if you don't report it to the police. The journalist shield law might protect you from having to reveal your sources—the girls' names—to the cops but that's a stretch. Amy should have known better. She should have had the good sense to have the story lawyered before she slapped it on the front page. It's like waving a red flag in front of the cops, who would like nothing better than to bust your ass."

"Amy couldn't help herself," I said with irritation. "She's so driven, she never thinks of the consequences, only what it will net her. It's her fatal flaw. It doesn't matter anyway. Even if she hadn't insisted I use first person, it was obvious that I was there when they were smoking in the woods." I looked up at him bleary-eyed. "Everyone thinks I should have been the school monitor. Somehow I was supposed to wrestle the drugs out of a drug dealer's hands or call the cops and turn in Anna."

Julian rocked on his heels.

"What do you think?" I pressed.

He rubbed his goatee. "When you are a crime reporter, you hang between two worlds, the bad guys and the cops, and some-times they are the same people. No one understands that unless they've been out there. I was a crime reporter for ten years. They'll come after you. They did for me—the cops, I mean.

"The cops are going to come down on you hard now that they've been given license to do so from a sitting judge," he continued. "They'll try to blame you for that girl's death, and maybe others. No doubt the spineless powers here will distance themselves from you. But if you can find who is responsible for the murders… well, that's a different story. You'll have the public on your side."

"How am I going to find evidence pinpointing one drug dealer when every cop out there, not to mention the feds, is looking for this guy?" I heard the panic rising in my voice. I still couldn't connect Lester and Rapper X. I assumed their relationship triangulated around Mohammed X.

"You're going to need protection. The only people the corner office types want to shield are themselves. If they sense in any way that the sleeves of their starched shirts will get dirty from this mess, they'll sell you out in a second. They only care about their careers, their paychecks, their perks, their stock options—how much money they can siphon off from a sale of the newspaper. Don't forget that. You, my dear, are an afterthought."

I slumped in my chair. Julian was right. The police would use the judge's mandate for an investigation as a means to dish out retribution. My stories on the fentanyl deaths had further infuriated the cops who were already furious over my previous drug snitch stories. It didn't help that the Governor was pissed that the *Sentinel* had outed his daughter as Ghost Girl. I'm sure he blamed me for that as well.

Meanwhile, the rest of Chicago demanded justice for the hundreds who had been murdered with spiked heroin. TV news was repeatedly airing an interview Danny had given in which he insisted Lester should be charged for providing drugs to Anna. Some politicians demanded the police question Lester as a suspect in what everyone was now calling "the Poison murders." Community leaders were calling for an investigation into the police department's mishandling of the case. Overnight, those who had died of poisoned heroin were suddenly regarded as hallowed murder victims. Family members of the dead insisted detectives had botched their investigation by refusing to look at any evidence that didn't corroborate charges against the Mickey Cobras. The police had put out an arrest warrant for Lester, ostensibly for parole violation, but the reality was that they feared vigilante justice would get him killed before police had a chance to interrogate him.

Normally, any reporter would have been thrilled to have written a story that stirred up so much controversy, especially if it led to the arrest of a serial killer. And yet I couldn't find any joy in my front-page story. Nor, seemingly, could my editors.

Amy emerged from her cramped office, her hands firmly pasted on her hips.

"If you don't mind, Julian, I'd like to have a word with Natalie. Isn't there some company filing for bankruptcy?"

Julian and I exchanged pained looks. I trudged after Amy to her office.

"Could you be a little more supportive, Amy?" I sat down on a pile of newspapers stacked on a chair. "For Christ's sake, I lost Anna yesterday, and now every reporter who's never been south of Roosevelt Road is judging me. These people don't know what it's like to cover anything that isn't handed to them in a press release."

"I do support you." Her voice was calm with a practiced civility. "I know this is hard. But you've got to realize how this looks, and how this makes the paper look."

"If these concerns are so obvious, then why didn't someone bring them up yesterday?"

Before she could respond, her door opened. Odis directed his instructions to Amy. "We'll be meeting with the publisher and the company lawyer in fifteen minutes."

"Yes, sir." She stood at attention like a good soldier. "We'll be there."

Then, without acknowledging me, Odis shut the door.

"What's happening?"

Amy cleared her throat, clasped her hands together: "There's concern…the girl's parents may sue us…The judge's comments are all over the news. He's saying…you should have yanked the drugs out of Anna's hands."

"Which judge?"

She gnawed on her lip, debating whether to tell me. "Walters."

"You mean the judge I wrote about in my drug snitch stories? The one our editorial board declared 'the worst judge in the city'? That Walters? Oh, yeah, he's *really* objective."

"We know his bias. But readers don't remember that. All they see is a judge on the news blaming a *Chicago Times* reporter for a fifteen-year-old white girl's death." Amy averted her gaze. I sensed there was more she wasn't saying. In that moment, I knew Amy would side against me to protect herself. "This isn't going to play out pretty, okay? This is going to get a lot worse before it gets better."

I leaned over her desk. "What aren't you telling me, Amy?"

She shuffled some papers. "The police have requested your records."

"What? Have they ever heard of the First Amendment?"

"Natalie, it's not that easy. They're not asking for your note-books—that we could defend. They are asking for your expense reports as part of a criminal investigation. They think you bought drugs for Anna and expensed them somehow. I know it sounds ludicrous."

I started laughing, this eerie, madwoman howl. Surely no one was buying this intimidation?

Amy waved her hands at me to calm down. "This is the game they are playing. We've got to be very smart in how we respond."

I felt a sharp pang in my gut, a knotting and twisting that I suspected would not unwind for a very long time.

• • •

We met in the wood-paneled office of publisher Jack Jones. Jack sat center stage behind his marble-topped desk. He'd been a small-town newspaper man who wound up running one of the country's biggest newspapers—after the *Chicago Times* acquired his little weekly and Jack became a drinking buddy of the board chairman. The paper's corporate attorney, Thomas Spielman, pulled up a chair next to Jack's desk. Amy and Odis shared the leather couch. There were no other chairs except an antique wooden one stacked with books in the corner. I perched on its edge precariously.

Jack held court, exploring the pros and cons of turning over my financial records. Normally newspapers don't turn over anything voluntarily.

"I've gone over the reporter's expenses with Spielman," Jack said. "We don't see any reason not to comply with the police department's request."

The men volleyed about *how* and *when* the paper would release the records, as if I weren't present. Still hungover, my head hurt, and everyone's voices seemed way too loud.

Finally, Amy chipped in: "Perhaps we should wait for a subpoena."

The men shifted in their seats, then stared at the floor.

"We want to avoid the publicity that would involve," Jack replied. "Handing over the records keeps the matter out of court and, more importantly, out of the court of public opinion. In the politest of terms, Amy, this is damage control." His implication was clear: You got us in this mess, Amy, and now we're having to clean up after you—again.

Jack turned to me: "Just what *was* your relationship with the children you interviewed, Ms. Delaney? Did you ever give them money? Even if it was for some innocent thing, like to buy candy or ice cream?"

I was surprised Jack even remembered my name. We'd never engaged in anything other than elevator chitchat. The man unnerved me. He had a judgmental demeanor and harsh, black eyes. He'd grown up in the wafer white suburbs and attended an elite boarding school out East—about which he never stopped yakking. It was unlikely he'd ever spoken to a street kid.

Looking around the room, I realized, to my horror, that they were all so insular in their suburban worlds of comfy McMansions, shopping malls, and big SUVs. Their urban experience was limited to the Magnificent Mile's capitalist glitter, Gold Coast manors, or Wrigley Field's historic charm, never venturing beyond those friendly confines, except inside the protective metal of a train or a limousine.

"I never gave money to anyone," I said adamantly. "I didn't buy drugs. You know what kind of reporter I am. I don't cut corners. How much of this is concern about the sale of the paper?" I was feeling braver as I sized up the situation. "Is this about protecting good journalism or protecting your stock options?"

Amy chewed on her lip; Odis sat up stiffly. Jack leaned back in his chair as if I had taken a swing at him.

"It is our fiduciary responsibility to keep the interests of our shareholders in mind," Jack said, arrogantly. "If the police find fault with our reporting, if we have overstepped our ethical boundaries here, it will surely affect the sale of the paper. We can't ignore the consequences of that. Even though our stock is thinly traded, we still have to think about our shareholders and our nearly one million readers, Ms. Delaney. This is bigger than you. I'm not sure if you can comprehend all the ramifications."

"I don't want the records released," I said loudly, standing.

Everyone looked at me.

"It sets a bad precedent that the cops can just willy-nilly demand certain records under the guise of a criminal investigation if they don't like a story we're pursuing. Besides, my sources are listed in those records. We have an ethical duty to protect them." I thought of all the times I had taken Mo out for drinks and dinner.

"There's nothing that says these are your sources," Jack said, then turned to the attorney as if the matter were closed.

"Hardly," I objected, stepping closer to him. Amy shot me a look of desperation. "These people aren't supposed to even talk to me in any official capacity, let alone go to lunch with me. They'll be ostracized, perhaps demoted or lose their jobs."

"We'll consider that when we make *our* decision," Jack said and stood, as if he had dispatched an unseemly task.

And with that, everyone headed to the door.

"Wait!" I shouted. "Isn't there anything else we could offer them?"

Jack and the company attorney, Spielman, looked at each other.

"Well, there is one thing," Spielman said. "But I hesitate to bring it up."

Everyone turned toward him.

"What if you agreed to talk to the police? We could see if they would go for that instead of handing over the expense reports."

Odis shook his head vigorously. "Too risky."

"I don't know," Jack said. "Sounds like a good idea to me, particularly if it stalls us from having to release the records. Would you be up for that, Natalie?" His voice was suddenly friendly.

They all looked at me, realizing that, unlike turning over the records, an interview with the cops required my consent.

"I guess I could do that," I said tentatively.

Spielman whispered in Jack's ear, then Jack and Odis nodded at each other.

"All right. Then it's settled," Jack said and clapped.

We were nearly out the door when Jack yelled after us.

"One more thing. I'll be going on WTTW tonight to debate Judge Walters."

I turned around in disbelief. Privately, they were debating about outing my sources, questioning my judgment, grilling me about my contact with kids, and deciding to offer me up to the cops for an interrogation, while publicly Jack was prepared to tout the ethics of my reporting. That's when I knew for certain this was a campaign for profits, not principles.

CHAPTER THIRTY-ONE

August 5, 2008

JUDGE BLAMES REPORTER FOR GIRL'S DEATH
ALLEGED KILLERS ARRAIGNED; THREE ARE JUVENILES
Chicago Sentinel

That night as I turned the key to my apartment dead bolt, I heard a crash inside. On the floor, I found a vase in pieces. My balcony door stood open. I was sure I'd closed it that morning. I tiptoed through the apartment, flipping on lights, taking inventory to see if anything might have been stolen. The place mirrored my life for the past two days: utter chaos. Clothes were strewn about my bedroom, newspapers had fallen from the kitchen table, reporter's notebooks were scattered over the living room floor. I found Deadline swatting flies on the balcony, picked her up, cradled her in my arms, and stroked her black fur.

"Was someone here, Deadline? Did you see anyone? Did you knock over the vase?" I whispered in her ear.

As I rocked on the glider, Julian's warning rang in my ears. *You are going to need protection. They'll sell you out in a heartbeat.*

I dragged myself inside, contemplating calling 911. Then I realized the intruder might have been a cop, a detective, or someone working with them. I was beginning to resemble one of those paranoid conspiracy types who were always calling the newspaper. If there had been a break-in, it certainly hadn't been orchestrated by an ordinary burglar. My unused checkbooks remained in the bottom drawer of my desk; my grandmother's heirloom crystal sat untouched in the kitchen cabinet. Even my desktop computer was still there, though it was impossible to tell if they'd gone through my files.

It was nearly nine o'clock and Maggie, no doubt, was preparing for bed in order to make her six a.m. Pilates class. My call hadn't finished its first ring when Maggie picked up.

"Nat?" She sounded panicked.

"Maggie, someone broke into my apartment. I think—"

"I'm there." She hung up.

Not knowing whether my mystery intruder would return, I opened the door and sat on the threshold, knowing if I screamed, my neighbor, Sean, would hear me.

Only a few minutes had passed before I heard Maggie clomping up the stairs.

"Oh dear God." She kneeled and threw her arms around Deadline and me. "What have you gotten into?"

"Mag, I gotta believe it's the cops. They're looking for anything they can get on me. Today they demanded my records. Everyone thinks I'm a child murderer."

"I know, sweetie. I called you after I heard about it on the radio. You seriously need to listen to your voicemail."

I watched her wander around my apartment, stepping over the shattered vase, surveying the detritus of my life: the dirty dishes, the film of dust that covered everything. She hunched over my stereo, adjusting its knobs and switches, then flipped a switch. Music blasted from the speakers.

'Cause I'm a dirty white boy...

"Oh fuck!" Maggie screamed. "Why can't you listen to music from this era?" She held her hands over her ears.

I reached to turn it off.

"Don't! If they bugged your apartment, the music prevents *them* from hearing *us*," she yelled into my ear. Now *she* sounded paranoid.

"Sorry. About the music—"

"It's *his* music, isn't it?" She grabbed my arm tight and pulled me under the speaker. There was an intense look in her eyes.

"Is this really necessary?" I screamed.

She yelled back, "You, of all people, should know: you can't trust Chicago cops."

Just then the front door creaked open. Maggie and I screamed and grabbed each other, squishing Deadline between us. The cat meowed and darted from my arms. Sean stood in the entryway, wearing a bathrobe, his hair sticking up on one side.

"Do you think maybe you could turn down the music? It's a bit late and a school night, I might add." His voice was loud but monotone, tinged with sarcasm.

I burst out laughing. It all seemed surreal: the shattered glass, the balcony door standing open, Maggie and I screaming over bad eighties music. And then there was Sean, this high-priced attorney, looking rumpled with his matted hair and bed sheet lines across his cheeks. I doubled over and slid to the floor, shrieking like a crazed woman.

CHAPTER THIRTY-TWO

August 6, 2008

POLICE OPEN INVESTIGATION INTO HEROIN DEATHS

INTERNAL AFFAIRS LOOKING FOR COP CONNECTION

Chicago Sentinel

Maggie had already gone; the sheets on her side of the bed were pulled up neatly. I found my cell phone buzzing under the newspapers on my bedroom floor. Sorting through the papers, I shuddered when I saw a picture of Anna and me accompanying my now infamous front page story. Seeing her head resting against my shoulder, that dreamy smile on her face, made me wistful.

Anna's funeral was in two days.

I hadn't gone to Jake's funeral, and it had always troubled me. I'd heard it was a small family affair, his parents embarrassed by his overdose. Strangers who last saw him told police he was distraught because his girlfriend refused to marry him. The police report suggested Jake's death was a suicide. The idea that Jake had killed himself because of me hit me hard at the time. I'd never stopped blaming myself for his death.

My cell phone buzzed again.

"Yes?"

"Well, honey, if you aren't the talk of the town. How's it feel to be getting your fifteen minutes of fame?"

There was no mistaking the voice: energetic, high-pitched, and confessional bitchy.

"Hi Ben."

"I wished I'd been there to defend you in front of all that sorry suburban trash in the newsroom. Jesus, show some loyalty and defend your own. I heard what you did for me when I was summarily dismissed. Nice performance. Sorry I wasn't there to clap. I would have egged you on for a while before your boyfriend made you get down."

"He's not my boyfriend."

Ben chuckled, as though he knew these things. "In any case, how are you holding up, dear? You want me to call out the faggot brigade to defend you? A few phone calls…"

"I'm fine. Just a little shaken."

"Hell, don't give me that puffery. I sat next to you for four years, watched you duck under your desk all weepy-eyed when the editors hacked your stories. I know how you put on a fancy face. So, tell Uncle Ben how you're really doing."

"Don't make me cry." I choked up. "These have been the shittiest days of my life."

"I know, dear. You loved that girl like she was a daughter. I could see it. Don't say I didn't warn you not to get attached. So what's on the agenda now, your public hanging?"

"I have an interview with the cops this afternoon."

"Oh, Natalie, don't talk to the cops. Nothing good ever comes out of talking to those shitheads. You know, dear, you can't trust them. Did you learn anything as a crime reporter?"

"I need to know where they're going with this investigation. Besides, I'll have an attorney with me."

. . .

I arrived at Jack's office that afternoon. His door was cracked. Men were laughing and talking in low tones—the conspiratorial discourse that I had long associated with the shared misogyny of the good-ol'-boys' clubs that thrived at newspapers. I pushed the door open, my pulse quickening in my ears. Jack was on his couch with his back to me, his arm casually draped over a pillow, his left leg crossed and nervously kicking against the coffee table. Odis and Spielman were seated across from him in wingback chairs.

Spielman saw me. "Well, hello, there, Ms. Delaney." It was the kindest voice I'd heard him use. "Have a seat."

I tried to appear casual.

"Natalie, we just wanted to go over a few things before the police interview tonight," Jack said. "We'd like to give you a chance to tell us anything you might have overlooked or thought insignificant. Maybe you want to practice what you'll say?"

I sank back, trying to discern which Shakespeare play best mirrored the drama being performed in front of me.

"We already went over this. I told you everything. There's nothing left to tell."

The men looked at each other, as if communicating telepathically. That was part of the charm of the good-ol'-boys' club: they always knew what the others were thinking. And, as if on cue, Spielman and Odis stood up. Odis shook my hand and offered me a hearty "good luck," a genial entreaty that sounded phony. Spielman said he'd see me later. Then they walked out, leaving me alone with Jack, who smiled awkwardly.

"Natalie, I want you to know that we are supporting you one hundred percent. I just want to make sure there's nothing else, perhaps something you've forgotten, maybe even something you might be embarrassed to bring up. Really, anything."

"Oh yeah. I just remembered I bought a bag of heroin and slipped it to one of the kids on the street. I forgot to expense it, though."

Jack's lips turned down. "Not funny, Natalie."

"Come on. There's nothing, Jack. Really." I felt no reason to repeat what I told him during our first meeting. Perhaps I should have questioned why the attorney hadn't offered me advice on which land mines to avoid or at least provided talking points. But I didn't know enough then to be suspicious.

Jack's watery blue eyes bore into me. "If you say you didn't give kids money, or buy them drugs or alcohol, I'll believe you. But it would be better for you—and for the paper—if you told the truth now, before you talk to the police. If you've done anything illegal, I will do everything in my power to get you the best deal."

For a few moments, neither of us said anything. I tried to project confidence. But what he was intimating was true. There was something I hadn't told him, hadn't told anyone. I was still trying to get that image out of my head—those droopy eyes, her head hanging slack against her shoulder, her pale arm, the plastic needle dangling from her inner elbow. Could he see that in my eyes, that slight hesitation, that twitch in my gaze? Could he sense the torment I was enduring by holding back?

CHAPTER THIRTY-THREE

August 6, 2008

COPS SEEK DEALER WHO GAVE DRUGS TO GIRLS

WARRANT ISSUED FOR PAROLE VIOLATION

Chicago Times

Spielman and I stood on Michigan Avenue, hailing a cab to take us to police headquarters near Chinatown. Though it was still summer, the nights were cooler. Spielman offered me his suit jacket, but I insisted I was fine. I wasn't cold, just nervous, very nervous. I'd been to police headquarters hundreds of times, but never as a suspect.

The halls were empty except for the Polish cleaning ladies speaking in their high-pitched word stew. Spielman and I were ushered to a waiting room where a prominent photo on the wall depicted a detective handcuffing the city's most notorious serial killer, John Wayne Gacy. So far the heroin killer had trumped Gacy by more than two hundred victims. Spielman made small talk in an attempt to calm me, but his chatter had the opposite effect.

After ten excruciating minutes, Detective Nickles finally appeared and directed us through the squad room. I expected to run into Mo—he reported to Nickles. More than anything I yearned for one of Mo's winks and his smiling assurances. But his chair was pushed in and his desk bare.

Nickles opened the door to a small room with a two-way mirror.

"Wait a minute," Spielman objected. "This is not what we agreed upon. This is a holding cell."

"No. It's an interview room," Nickles countered.

"You mean interrogation room," Spielman corrected. "This will not do. Ms. Delaney isn't being interrogated. She's come on her own to volunteer information that may be of use in your investigation."

Detective Nickles threw up his arms and led us back to the waiting area. At first I thought Spielman was trying to defend my honor, but then he muttered under his breath: "I will not be put into a common criminal cell. Who do they think they are dealing with?"

A few more minutes passed, and we were guided into a large conference room. In the corner hung an American flag next to President Bush's portrait.

"How's this?" Nickles asked, not bothering to conceal his contempt.

"This will be fine," Spielman responded smugly.

Detective Nickles sat across from me, and a female detective took a seat across from Spielman. After I signed a standard waiver of my Miranda rights, Nickles started with simple questions, then his inquiry became more specific.

"Did you ever have any dealings with Lester Williams?"

"Yes, he was the one who supplied heroin to Anna and Libby."

"And did you ever buy him beer?"

"Yes, once."

"Did you ever buy beer for other people while you were reporting this story?"

I ticked off the names of parents for whom I'd bought beer as a thank you for letting me hang out at their houses or for referring me to people in the neighborhood.

"So these were street bribes, huh?"

"No." I rose from my chair and looked over at Spielman. He tapped my hand and I sat back down. "I gave beer as a token of my appreciation. There was nothing sinister about it. I also took them buckets of KFC, but I suppose you don't care about that?"

Nickles shuffled papers and exchanged looks with the female detective. If they were playing good-cop, bad-cop, Nickles had clearly assigned himself the role of asshole.

"So, Lester didn't have money to buy himself beer, but he had money to supply heroin for Anna and her cousin? Isn't that strange? You say he's a big drug dealer, and yet he doesn't even own a car?"

"Do all drug dealers have to drive decked-out SUVs? I believe he did buy some sort of low-rider. You might want to check that one out. Maybe he's playing you."

"The only one playing here is you," Nickles said, glaring at me. "Except what's at stake here is your life, Miss Delaney. You've already caused the death of one girl—"

"That's enough," Spielman said, holding up his hand. His objection was loud and forceful, almost personal. It made me wonder if he had a daughter who'd gotten into trouble.

Nickles looked at his paperwork and stroked his mustache. "Let's talk about what else you bought for people. What did you give the kids you were interviewing?"

"Sometimes, I bought them food or pop. Little stuff."

"Did you ever give them money?"

"No."

"Are you sure?"

"Absolutely."

"Did anyone ever try to sell you anything?"

"Oh, you mean like glassine packets branded with skull and crossbones?"

Nickles's thin lips tightened. "Young lady, this is a serious police inquiry. We have been ordered by a judge to investigate your actions."

"It's convenient that a judge gave you permission, but you didn't need that, did you?"

Nickles ignored me. "So how many times did you watch kids do drugs?"

"I don't know. I didn't count." The truth was I did know. But I didn't want to have to detail any of those painful circumstances to Nickles, especially the last time I saw Anna.

"You never felt compelled to tell them to stop?"

"What I said to them is none of your business."

"A court has made it my business."

"The court didn't compel me to come here today."

"No, a demand for your records did. So, you'll need to be more forthcoming. This interview may determine whether charges are filed against you."

I looked over at Spielman, expecting him to say something. He remained quiet, doodling on his yellow legal pad—bigheaded stick figures with bulging eyes and spidery hair that looked like him. That's when it occurred to me that Spielman might not be there to defend me. More likely, he was a spy. His job was to report back to the paper. Julian had been right. The men at the top would sell me out. I swallowed hard and felt a painful hollowness in my stomach—the realization that I was truly alone.

"Your attorney can't answer the questions for you," Nickles said.

"You keep dodging around. What is it exactly that you want to know?"

Nickles coughed and leaned back in his chair, studying me. "Why'd you give drugs to Anna? Why'd you get her addicted? Was advancing your career worth a girl's life?"

Spielman sat up straight and for a fleeting moment I thought he was going to object. Instead, he looked at me intently, curious of my answer.

"I never really knew when Anna was going to do drugs. She was…" I searched for the right words, but they were elusive. "She was intent on doing whatever it was she thought would make her happy. I couldn't stop her no matter what I did, no matter what I said."

"Hmm. Well that's all very touching. But what would you say if I told you we have your fingerprints on a bag of heroin found at Anna's uncle's house? What would you say if I said that we have a long list of witnesses who saw you snorting and smoking heroin with Anna?" Nickles locked eyes with me. "What would you say if I said your fireman friend says you sought out naloxone from him so someone could revive you when you overdosed."

"That wasn't for me! That was for Anna."

"Really? Why did you need naloxone for Anna? Because you'd gotten her so addicted you were in over your head and couldn't stop her?"

I blew out a long breath and shook my head. My knees bounced up and down. I craved a cigarette. The acid in my gut felt like it was burning a hole in my intestines.

"Well, for starters, I've never been arrested, so how could you have my fingerprints?"

Nickles laughed. This time it sounded genuine.

"You have a Chicago Police Department press ID, correct?"

"Yes, as do most reporters."

"Uh-huh. And what did you have to supply in order to get those credentials?" He stood and began pacing the room. The power had suddenly shifted in his favor, and he could hardly contain his self-satisfaction in the grin that spread across his face.

"My fingerprints," I whispered. "But it says right on the application that the police can never use those against journalists in a criminal case." My voice sounded shallow and weak. The room suddenly felt humid, the air sticky and static.

"Oh really? Didn't read that section. We take them, by the way, to *rule out* journalists' fingerprints at a crime scene. Only in this case, yours ruled you in."

"That's absurd. I've never touched a bag of drugs. You are fucking lying."

"Oh, am I?" He leaned over the table inches from my face. "And your little friend Libby? Is she lying too? And all those kids you thought were so trustworthy that you quoted them in the paper, but now they aren't trustworthy enough to testify in court?"

I looked at Spielman, but he just continued doodling his Charlie Brown characters.

Nickles continued. "You even had the gall to ask Detective Mobley to reveal classified information about the case. And when he questioned you, you knew details that the police had not released, details that only the killer could have known."

I knew he was twisting Mo's words, but it still stung that Mo had even talked to Nickles about me. My ears were hot. I could barely concentrate, I was so angry.

"That's what reporters do. They ask detailed questions, and they have sources who provide them classified information."

It began to sink in. Everything I'd done as a journalist could be turned around and used against me. My routine of observing kids and hanging out with them could be presented as if I were intent on poisoning them—all for the vainglory of a story. I scrubbed my hands against my face, ordering myself not to cry.

"No matter what I say, you are going to twist it to fit your needs," I said. "I know how this works, Detective."

He bent down near my face. I could smell the spearmint gum he was chewing: "Then why did you agree to come talk to me, Ms. Smarty Pants?"

Before I could answer, Spielman looked at his watch and abruptly stood up. "That's enough. She's answered all your questions." He closed his legal pad. He was probably worried he'd miss *Dancing with the Stars*.

Nickles smiled with a sinister relish. Somewhere in my answers, he'd gotten what he wanted, something he could bend and reshape to make it look like I'd admitted to a heinous crime. He walked over and held the door open. Spielman and I scuttled out; the only sounds were the echoes of our shoes against the faux marble floors.

Out in the cool night, the streets near district headquarters were empty. There wasn't a cab in sight, so we walked, the rattle of the El train overhead relieving us of our awkward silence. Spielman lit a cigarette and offered me one. I took it, my hands shaking as I pressed it against the burning end of Spielman's.

How could I have been so naïve? Both the police and the

newspaper would use the interview for their own purposes. Spielman would scour his memory to see if there was anything unethical or illegal that could be used as evidence to fire me; Nickles would construct his evidence into what might become a grand jury indictment.

"I'm glad that's over. But probably not as much as you are," Spielman said, forcing a laugh to break the tension.

"Why didn't you object to his questions? Why did you let him badger me and push me into a corner?"

"It all seemed pretty routine to me," he said, not meeting my eyes.

On the next block, he touched my arm and pointed to a neighborhood pub. "I really need a drink right now, and I imagine you could use one too."

The bar was empty except for a couple of twenty-something guys throwing darts. Spielman ordered a shot, and I asked for Dewar's on the rocks. Spielman took off his suit coat and loosened his tie. When the barmaid set the drinks in front of us, he drank his whiskey in one gulp and asked for another.

"Listen," he said as he nursed his second drink, "I feel really awkward about all this. I'm supposed to be representing the paper."

"Then who is representing me?"

"Well, I am—sort of. I mean, I represent the interests of the paper. I am a corporate attorney, not a criminal attorney."

I had downed most of my drink and was feeling bolder. "Shouldn't you have told me this *before* the police interrogation?"

He took a drag on his cigarette and exhaled through his nose. His skin was ashen, his teeth stained. He seemed like so many gray-haired men past their prime, skittish and desperately clinging to a job that he no longer was qualified to possess.

"You need a criminal attorney. Someone who knows criminal law, who can represent your interests. That's all I can say, okay? I'm just trying to help you."

I looked at my empty glass. The alcohol burned my insides. I could taste defeat.

CHAPTER THIRTY-FOUR

August 7, 2008

GIRL KILLED IN HEROIN-RELATED
SHOOTING IS BURIED

FUNERAL IS A POLITICAL WHO'S WHO

Chicago Sentinel

Maggie loaned me a black dress—Donna Karan—and agreed, somewhat jokingly, to act as my bodyguard in case I encountered hecklers at Anna's funeral. After the judge's comments, I wasn't sure how people would treat me, especially Anna's family. Danny suggested I sit in the back of the church to avoid attention. His sister Pam was upset about what I'd written and furious at her brother for having allowed me to hang around.

In death, Anna achieved a kind of celebrity status, and her funeral mass was being held at Holy Name Cathedral, the largest Catholic church in town, to accommodate the expected throngs of mourners—and gawkers. Maggie and I took a cab downtown but encountered gridlock several blocks from the church. We got out and walked. It was a hot, sticky day. The sun hid behind opaque clouds. Our dresses clung to our damp bodies, and our makeup beaded on our foreheads. As we neared the church, funerary organ music drifted from its massive doors, triggering a wave of immense grief. My knees buckled, and I grabbed Maggie.

"I can't do this." My head was spinning, my vision blurry.

Maggie wrapped her arms around my waist and lifted me.

"Nat, you have to. Just breathe." She wiped my eyes with a tissue and smiled. "You need to say good-bye. It feels like shit, but I'm right here." She squeezed my hand. I couldn't help but smile back, tears trickling down my cheeks.

"All those people think I killed her, that I'm responsible for her death. Yesterday the cops said—"

"Since when do you care about the damn cops? As I recall, you hadn't seen Anna for two weeks before she died, and you'd told her uncle she was doing drugs, and you gave her cousin a heroin antidote. Come on, Natalie, fight back. These people want a scapegoat. They want someone to blame instead of having to face the cold hard fact that young, beautiful girls are choosing to do drugs that will kill them."

I sucked in a long breath, then slapped down my sunglasses from the top of my head. "Okay. Let's do this."

Inside, the cathedral was cool and dark. Maggie handed me a candle. We stepped tenuously up the center aisle, our heels clacking against the slick marble floor. At the altar, Anna lay in a closed cherry wood coffin. On top rested a photo of her as a child playing with her mother. I lit my candle and dropped to the prayer kneeler, mumbling a little plea—not to God or any saints—but to Anna, asking her to forgive me for not saving her.

I'm not sure how long I was kneeling. Maggie tugged at my sleeve. A long line had formed behind us. We scurried down a side aisle and chose a pew behind a marble column. The melancholy sounds of the pipe organ dislodged a powerful longing. My chest hurt as if I'd been holding my breath. The light streamed through the stained glass windows, exposing a spray of dust motes and casting rays of amber, a color I associated with Anna. I hadn't been to Mass in so long; I'd forgotten the cool darkness and the smell of incense and melted wax.

Maggie jerked her head to a cluster of mourners making their way to the casket. Leading the group was the Governor, his wife, and Bethany, looking virginal in a white lace dress, her hair tied back in a white satin ribbon as if she were nine years old. She saw me staring and winked. After the *Sentinel* had identified her as Ghost Girl, her picture had been all over the news. Not far behind her trailed the Mayor and his wife in a wheelchair, followed by several aldermen. Anna's Queen of Angels classmates brought up the end in their gray and blue uniforms, which matched the gray habits and short blue veils of the nuns who escorted them.

I scanned the pews, spotting several familiar faces. Olivia Byrne, the pharmaceuticals heiress, was dressed in a stylish black dress with a high-back collar and long, silk gloves that extended to her biceps. Her face was covered by a short, black lace veil. Rex Kennan draped his arm over Olivia's shoulder in a consoling pose. Rex's hair was moussed into a single egg-whitey wisp. He wore a charcoal-colored suit with a white shirt, looking as if he were the lead singer in an eighties band. In the same row were Cate, Anna's former babysitter, and Rory, the Goth girl. Cate had chosen a conservative dress that accented her pale features while Rory was dressed in Goth regalia—garish makeup and a large Germanic cross that hung beneath her gaudy butterfly tattoo. The entire row looked like a group of heroin-chic models, their faces pale and maudlin.

The organist played "Ave Maria," while Danny, looking glassy-eyed, his face red with emotion, escorted Pam to the front. Libby, wearing a simple black smock, her face wan and her eyes lifeless, faltered behind. A tall, bespectacled man with three boys, scattered in stages from toddler to preteen, followed. I assumed he was Anna's stepfather, the auburn-haired boys her stepbrothers.

I felt angry so few of the "mourners" had actually known Anna. Amid the pageantry of the service, their pious looks seemed disingenuous. Thwarting the urge to scream, I closed my eyes and squeezed Maggie's hand.

When the service ended, Maggie nudged me to stand. The family filed out of their pew and one by one laid white roses on the coffin. When Pam, her shoulders heaving, reached the casket, she collapsed and emitted an inhuman wail. Finally, when Danny and Libby started down the aisle, I made my way toward them.

Danny simpered and hugged me. He smelled of whiskey and Old Spice. I missed him, aching for us to be alone, away from this officious crowd, to privately mourn our loss. In that moment, I felt we were the only adults in that cavernous church who really knew her. Then I had this harrowing thought that maybe I'd never known her at all.

"Come over tomorrow," he whispered. "There's something I got to tell you...something Libby said."

I stared into his ruddy face, silently urging him to explain.

"Tomorrow," he promised.

Libby, standing behind her father, glared at me.

"Hi, Lib."

She jutted her chin and looked past me.

Pam, moving slowly down the aisle, clutched her husband's arm and raised her tear-stained face to me. "How could you have written those ugly things about *my* Anna?" She looked monstrous, her eyes bloodshot, her makeup caked in her wrinkles.

"I'm very sorry about Anna."

"You'll be more than sorry by the time I'm done with you." She whisked past.

I slumped against Maggie, blind with guilt, trying not to break down. Maggie quickly led me from the church through a back door. The heat hit as soon as we stepped outside. She hailed a cab. Not until we were in the backseat, the cool air blowing in our faces, did I notice my hands shaking. She wrapped her long, manicured fingers around mine and pulled my hands to her heart.

"Anna wasn't *you*. And she wasn't *your* daughter. I know that's what you think. I see it on your face, the way you're grieving. No matter what miracles you think Jake can wield from the afterlife, he didn't send you Anna. She was not a gift from the beyond."

We'd managed so far not to mention *him*. But somehow he always came up. I glared at Maggie, angry that she'd opened that emotional vault I tried so hard to keep shut. I'd coped with Jake's death by telling myself I was living a parallel life with him in my dreams. Then I met Anna. The rational part of me knew we weren't connected. But sometimes it made me happy to pretend, to wonder if Anna could be the child I'd never had. It was a private joy, and Maggie had no right to crush it. Anna's loss meant so much more than the murder of a teenage girl I'd known for a few short weeks. Her death was the end of all magical thinking, a cruel awakening that left me hollow and hopeless.

As the taxi wound around Lake Michigan, the clouds retreated to reveal a brilliant summer day, extravagant and shimmering, like colorized film. Maggie asked the cabdriver to pull over at the North Avenue Beach. We took off our shoes and waded into the water up to the hems of our dresses. Then we scampered back and lay on the sand, our eyes leaking salty, wind-blown tears, and clung to each other. Our sorrow felt all too familiar.

We lay there a while, Maggie's breath in the narrow of my neck, the sun sparkling off the silky blue water and the heat tingling our wet skin. The sounds of the waves rolling in were broken only by cawing seagulls, chasing each other in the foamy water. It all reminded me of that halcyon Fourth of July with Anna.

That day she'd seemed guileless and expectant, splashing in the waves, teasing me, the sun awash in her face. By evening, in the shadows of the tent, she had matured from childhood to someone cunning, shrewd, and detached. She'd delivered the secrets of the Dead Angels in a flat, colorless voice, as if their deaths didn't matter.

Aware of the emotional power she had over me, I'd asked her why she had allowed me into her life. It was a question that had been gnawing at me for some time.

"Are you playing me?"

She laughed dismissively, then her voice grew serious. "Yeah, maybe. At first."

"And now?"

Fireworks erupted in the sky. Streams of yellow and red flashed across her face, as if she were a hologram that would quickly disappear.

"What does it matter? As soon as you're done with your story, you'll be done with me."

I wanted to argue that wasn't true. But no matter how attached to someone I became, someone else in another story always came along to replace them.

In two quick steps, she flitted away, and I was left alone in the dark, bracing for the next explosion.

CHAPTER THIRTY-FIVE

August 8, 2008

SUSPECTED POISON HEROIN DEALER ARRESTED

SHERIFF SAYS DEATH THREATS AGAINST
DEALER TAKEN SERIOUSLY

Chicago Times

I showed up at Danny's a little after ten with a carafe of coffee and a bag of bagels. Minutes passed before he appeared at the door wearing only jeans. He squinted and shaded his eyes with his hand.

"Now that's what I call rise and *shine!*" He choked out a gravelly laugh, then ushered me inside. When he shut the door, the apartment closed in like a cave, the shades drawn, the only light a flicker of orange at the windows. We stood awkwardly in the darkness. Slowly Danny enveloped me in his arms. I collapsed into him, muffling my cries against his warm skin. His chest heaved but he emitted no sound. Finally, he pulled back, wiped his face with the back of his hand, and ran his rough thumbs under my eyes.

"It's gonna be okay," he said. "We'll get through this."

He pulled on a shirt hanging from a kitchen chair, then sat down and lit a cigarette. The door to Libby's room was closed and for the moment I felt relieved I didn't have to be subjected to her rage. I got two coffee cups out of the cabinet and poured him a cup. He dug the palms of his hands into his eyes.

"Pour a little holy water in my cup, hon." His voice sounded like a scratched country music record. He pointed to a lower cabinet where I found a nearly empty pint of Jim Beam.

"Really, Danny?"

He brandished a crooked smile. "Now don't go picking at me. I just need a little help this morning. Nothing wrong with that."

I gave a generous pour into his coffee. "How was the dinner at Pam's?" I pulled out a chair and sat down, remembering the fast food the girls and I had shared at that shiny table.

"Oh, Lord. She had it catered. The Governor was even there. We're distant relations to the Governor's wife. Our mother and her mother were cousins."

"Anna mentioned something about that."

"Yeah, well, none of those people knew Anna from a hole in the wall. It was all show. I knew Pam was torn up, but part of her must have been tickled to have all those famous people at her house, kissing on her…" He shook his head with disgust. "I love my sister, but there are sides of her I just don't understand. I have the awfulest hangover. Hon, will you get me aspirin? It's over the stove."

I got him the aspirin and a glass of water. "Eat a bagel. You'll feel better." I pushed one toward him.

He lit another cigarette and spun his silver lighter on the table. "The scene at the graveyard was enough to break your heart. Pam fell apart, laid in the dirt. It took me *and* that slimy husband of hers to get her into the limo." He exhaled, fanned the cigarette smoke, and stared at me wide-eyed as if he were about to say something profound. "I tell you who I'm most worried about—Libby. She hasn't cried at all, as far as I can tell. She's been real quiet ever since that night. I guess she's in shock. You think I should take her to a shrink?"

I shrugged. "Couldn't hurt."

He waved away the thought. "I don't want her thinking something's wrong with her."

"Did you hear about Lester getting arrested?"

"Yeah, slept better hearing that piece of trash is locked up. I hear there's some death threats against him." He winked.

"Danny, you didn't?"

"I had nothing to do with phone calls to the jail threatening to kill him. I know some folks who might want him dead, but I was *engaged* at the time." He sounded playful, then his tone got serious, and he tapped my hand gently with his sandpaper fingers. "How are *you* doing?"

"I keep thinking about things Anna said, trying to piece it together. It just doesn't make sense. She always told me she never took drugs from people she didn't know."

"That's just it." He turned and coughed. "Her and Libby didn't go there only to get drugs—not really." He studied me for a reaction.

I motioned for him to continue.

"Damn, it's some kind of story." He shook his head and crushed out his cigarette. "I just don't know if it's the truth. Maybe Libby's covering up something."

"What did she say, Danny?"

He rubbed one hand over the other. "She told me her and Anna and some other girls went to Woodlawn that night because some girls dared Anna to buy drugs there. Does that sound like something girls do?" He shook his head in disgust. "I don't fucking get it—excuse my language."

"Was Libby involved?"

He lit another cigarette. "Who the hell knows? She said she wasn't, but you and I both know how those girls cover for each other."

The air conditioner buzzed, but the room was sweltering. I wiped my forehead with a paper napkin. The cigarette smoke made it hard to breathe.

"You don't look so good, hon." He leaned over and caressed my forearm. "You okay?"

"What else did Libby say? I need to know, Danny."

"It's the damnedest thing. Anna got kicked out of school, but

Libby said she went to the *library* every day. Down the block." He pointed his arm at a nearby window. "The thing is, she didn't strike me as no bookworm, and I can't say I ever saw her reading."

"Do the cops know about this?"

He croaked out a laugh and whispered, "The cops don't know shit." I could smell the liquor on his breath. His words were slurred, and his country accent was stronger than I'd ever heard. He'd been drinking long before I showed up. He sat back and sucked on his cigarette, contemplating. "They never asked when they came around that day—the cops. Nothing about no dare, and Libby sure as hell didn't tell them."

"You know the police interrogated me? They told me they found a bag of heroin here with my prints on it."

"Ah, Jesus. What a bunch of sorry-ass liars. They didn't find shit. Wanted to take half the apartment. I told them to come back with a warrant."

"Did they?"

"Does it look like anything's missing?" He grinned.

I stood up. "I need to talk to Libby."

Danny tucked in his chin. "Don't know about that. Pretty much hates your guts. She says you lied to her, promised her and Anna you wouldn't ever say they'd done drugs."

"I didn't put Libby's name in the story," I protested.

He shrugged. "You might as well have. Libby is Anna's shadow. Or *was*, I mean. Where one went so trailed the other. Anyone who knows Anna knows Libby was the other girl in that article you wrote." He shook his head. "She *ain't* going to talk to you."

"What about you? You mad at me too?"

"That judge pretty much made you out to be a murderer."

"You think he's right? That I should have grabbed the drugs out of Lester's hand or yanked that makeshift pipe from Anna?"

He glared at me. "How can you ask me that? I saw that gang-banger put a gun in your mouth."

I flinched at the mention of that brutal scene.

"I can't be mad at you, Natalie, because then I'd have to be mad at myself!" He jumped up from the table, his hands clenched at his sides. "I was a witness too. Hell, I lived with her. I knew she was doing drugs, and no matter how hard I tried, I couldn't stop her, neither."

The bedroom door creaked open. Libby stood in a T-shirt and cut-off shorts, her hair ratted and her eyes red. "Daddy, what's wrong? Why are *you* here?"

Danny walked over to Libby and put his arm around her. "Lib, I asked Natalie to come over. I wanted to tell her what you told me." His voice was suddenly quiet and gentle.

"Why? Why does she have to know?"

"Now, Lib, maybe Natalie can find out if someone was pressuring Anna to do drugs."

"Anna did it on her own," Libby said, flailing her arms, pushing away her father. "She liked doing stupid stuff."

Danny motioned Libby toward the kitchen table. "Hon, please come talk to Natalie." His voice quavered, and I realized why he'd really told me: he was worried Libby was more involved than she'd let on.

Libby walked tentatively toward us. One sock hung several inches off her foot, the other foot was bare. She sat down and clutched her knees to her chest. "Anna made me swear I would never tell you." She stared at me with dark and angry eyes.

Danny put a hand on her knee. "Lib, Anna's gone. She'd want you to help figure out who put her up to it—going to some god-forsaken neighborhood in the middle of the night. That's just not like her—or you." Danny turned away and smothered a moan into his forearm.

"Daddy, I told you I tried to get her not to go. She wouldn't listen." She turned to me. "You made everything worse. The whole world knows Anna was doing heroin."

"I thought about it a lot, Libby," I said slowly, looking at Danny to offer amends. "And I decided that I couldn't get Anna into trouble when she was already dead. Don't you think it was better for me to write the truth so that maybe we could catch the Poison dealer?"

She laughed. "How's that working out for ya?"

"You have a right to be mad at me, Lib. You do."

"People think I am just like her, an H-head." She stood up from the table and banged her chair against the floor. "Daddy has to keep a shotgun by the door. Oh yeah, and we're moving. All because of you!" She stomped off to her room, slamming the door.

The apartment echoed, and Danny and I winced at the noise.

"It's gonna take some time for that one," he said. "I meant to tell you about the move. It's for the better."

"I'm surprised you're even talking to me."

He closed one eye and squinted at me with the other. "It's the strangest thing to feel so connected but disconnected to you." He exhaled a long sigh. "But I now know we can't...not after Anna and all this business over her death. It's too muddy for us." He shook his head and his voice cracked with emotion. "I know you had a job to do. But did you have to spoil her name in public? My sister isn't ever getting over that. And it doesn't sit well with me. I'm not mad at you. Just hurt."

The oppressive sadness in the room reminded me of the day Danny nursed me after Lester's attack. We sat for a while without saying anything. Then he sprang up as if he'd remembered an urgent task.

"I got something I want you to have." He left the room, came back with an object wrapped in newspaper. "I thought about giving it to her momma, but she won't miss what she never knew existed, right?" He winked.

I peeled back the newspaper to reveal a brilliant red and purple silk scarf.

"I saw her wear it once. I think her daddy gave it to her. She cherished it. Anyway, it's yours now. I know she'd want you to have it. Something to remember her by."

I held it to my face and breathed in Anna's scent, a sweet jasmine smell, and closed my eyes. For a flickering moment she was alive, her glittering green eyes playful as she stood at the beach, her hand extended, her voice begging me to join her in the luminous water. I was about to reach out and touch her fingertips when the image went black. I slumped in my chair, drained. When I opened my eyes, tears dripped onto the scarf.

Danny poured a shot of whiskey. "Hon, you best drink this. You don't look so good."

I downed the shot and licked my lips. When I finally spoke, my voice was raw. "I'm sorry, Danny. I don't even know where to begin."

He squeezed my shoulder then went to the sink and splashed water on his face. I stood behind him and wrapped my arms around his waist. At first, his body felt rigid. Then he turned around and gently pulled me to him. I buried my face in his shirt, breathing in his smell. Since Anna's death, I'd felt more drawn to him, as friends who shared the same regret: we had been the only adults in Anna's life when she died, and that plagued us with a tremendous guilt. It was a strange sorrow, a private, excruciating anguish, each wondering how we could have saved her.

CHAPTER THIRTY-SIX

August 9, 2008

CITY HOSTS LOLLAPALOOZA AMID TIGHT SECURITY

POLICE ARREST SEVERAL FOR HEROIN POSSESSION

Chicago Sentinel

The next day, I found a small package stuffed in my mail slot at the *Times*. I rarely checked the mailroom because no one sent letters these days. I wondered how long it had been sitting there. Wrapped in brown paper, the package had no return address. My name and the *Times* address were written in bold capital letters. The post office cancelation stamp was marked Aug. 3, the day before Anna died. Inside I found a moleskin journal, three tubes of medicine, and a handwritten note.

> Dear Natalie,
>
> I'm sending you one of Harper's journals that contains her Internet passwords on the back cover. I've made my way through three years of her journals and can't bear to read any more of her secret life. I thought this might help you further piece together what my daughter and her friends were up to. Of course, I send this with the caveat that you not report any of the spiteful things she's written about me. I'm leaving for Africa as part of Doctors Without Borders. I don't expect to be back for months. The memories are just too great to stay in

this house. I've failed as a mother, and now I'm going to do my penance in parts of the world where my skills are needed most. Perhaps the journal will be more of use to you. My hope is that you'll find something that may spare another parent from going through what I've endured these last few weeks. Good luck on your search. Be careful. You may not like what you find.

Sincerely,
Wendy Cabot

P.S. I'm sending you several tubes of BioCorneum because I suspect that you never got that prescription filled, and I'd hate for your face to scar.

I flipped through the journal, its pages filled with large, loopy cursive writing of a teenage girl. Most pages catalogued how much she ate, how hungry she was, and how beautiful she thought she'd look in certain designer outfits if only she were thinner. She devoted an enormous number of pages complaining about her mother's nagging her to eat. Wendy Cabot had taken Harper to several pediatricians specializing in eating disorders.

The most helpful parts of the journal were the website logons and passwords. She'd tried to disguise them, but "F" clearly stood for Facebook and "G" was for Gmail. There were others I couldn't figure out, including one she'd designated with the letter T. I couldn't find any Twitter or Tumblr account associated with Harper. "The T site" was listed in Laila's Pzzword document, and I wondered if it was the same website.

Harper's Facebook pages mirrored Laila's. They had similar photos and friends, went to the same parties, and posted similar fashion pieces. Harper's emails, though, disclosed a complex network of politically connected kids. Messages from Olivia Byrne, the pharmaceuticals heiress, and Bethany, the Governor's daughter, revealed their families frequently socialized together. Harper exchanged messages with other girls whose names I didn't recognize, discussing what they would wear at various political fundraisers. Wendy hadn't told me her ex-husband was a high-end real estate developer—and a major Democratic contributor.

I ran the unfamiliar names of Harper's friends through the newspaper's various databases and learned many of their families were major political contributors. I was starting to see a web of affluent girls who didn't necessarily attend the same schools or live in the same cities or suburbs, but who'd met through Chicago's esoteric system of politics.

That afternoon I obtained a complete list of female fentanyl victims from the coroner's office and ran those names through the same databases. A pattern emerged: half the victims' families had donated to the Senator's presidential election campaign. That detail in itself wasn't surprising since most Chicagoans had donated *something* to their hometown's White House contender. But these girls' parents were giving the maximum allowed under the law and then joining political superpacs to donate and raise even more money. Politics was not my area of expertise and neither was math, but I knew that fifty percent of any group was not an anomaly.

I knocked on Julian's office door. He looked like he was on deadline—his eyes fixed on his screen, his forehead wrinkled. But his face brightened when he saw me.

"What's up?"

"Could you take a look at this list and see which victims' names stand out? About half are from political donors. I just can't figure out how the others are connected."

Julian read the list, checking off names and circling others. He turned to his computer and pulled up a spreadsheet, then volleyed from the computer to the list I'd given him, typing in the dead girls' names.

"Your mystery girls are from families who have contributed to the city's Olympics bid. Not all of them, for sure, but about forty percent."

"And the other half have given to the Senator's campaign. Not likely a coincidence," I said. "The victims had to have been targeted. But who's against Chicago winning the Olympics and the Senator winning the White House?"

Julian emitted a cynical laugh. "Only about half the city."

I laughed, too—the first time in days. It felt like such a release. We both fell into a convivial mood, briefly forgetting that we were researching girls' deaths. He told me his kids kept asking about me.

"They want to know why I don't have toys on my desk." He sported a hurt look. "They think that *you* get to play all day, watch Barney videos, and eat cookies. I'm jealous." We both smiled, and for a few seconds there was this recognition of each other, not as colleagues, but as people who might have more in common than the newspaper.

That momentary insight was interrupted by a knock on the door. Before we could say anything, it swung open.

"I thought I might find you here," Amy said, harshly. "Natalie, you need to get down to the South Side. Mohammed X is having a press conference at his mosque."

"I thought you didn't want me near him?"

"Yeah, well, that was before the latest layoff. We don't have anyone else to send."

• • •

When I arrived at the gilded dome, reporters and TV satellite trucks had already clogged the parking lot. A stage had been set up at the mosque's entrance, and everyone was jockeying for space near the podium microphones. Right on time, Mohammed X walked out, surrounded by his entourage. Trailing was Rapper X, this time wearing a dark suit, his dreads gone, his hair clipped short and gelled back.

Mohammed tapped his fingers on the mic, the sharp static pricking our ears. "I've gathered you here today because a grave injustice has been done." He scanned the crowd, a glimmer of recognition when our eyes met. "I'm normally not a friend of the media, but in this instance I believe your megaphones can right a terrible wrong."

Women in long dresses, their hair tied back in colorful scarves, began handing out flyers. Mohammed held up a copy showing a picture of Lester, his face beaten, his eyes swelled shut.

"His name is Lester Williams. He's been arrested in connection with the Poison killings after certain media reports *erroneously* identified him as the drug dealer who sold fentanyl-heroin to white girls." He glared at me, prompting other reporters to turn around and stare as well. My exclusives hadn't won me any friends among my competitors.

"This man was sitting in a prison downstate when people started dying of this brand of heroin. He is in no way connected to these murders. I'm asking you to do your jobs and look into this man's case. He has been severely attacked since he was arrested and placed in the Cook County Jail. The police have already charged forty-seven members of the Mickey Cobras for these crimes. They can't just keep locking up every black man on the South Side. The Mickey Cobras will kill him before there's ever a trial. Please investigate this miscarriage of justice."

He turned from the microphones, reporters shouting questions at his back. I had positioned myself near the doors, predicting he would bolt.

"Did you poison those girls to stop the Olympics land grab?" I shouted as he made his way toward me. "Or to discourage contributions to the Hyde Park Senator's campaign, or so you and the Gangster Disciples could take over the Mickey Cobras' territory?"

His men grabbed my arms and tried to move me from the doors, but Mohammed stopped them, his face beaming with some private thought. He bent over and whispered in my ear: "You'll soon be joining Lester." Then he stormed past me, the reporters following.

I told myself it was all bravado. But something about his tone needled me. He was too confident, too sure of himself. It wasn't a bluff. It was a warning. He knew something I didn't.

CHAPTER THIRTY-SEVEN

August 11, 2008

HEROIN KILLER TARGETED CHILDREN OF WEALTHY

VICTIMS HAD TIES TO SENATOR'S
CAMPAIGN OR OLYMPICS BID

Chicago Times

My story revealing how white female heroin victims had been targeted because of their parents' political affiliations appeared above the fold with a screaming headline. The story was garnering the most hits of any online. Amy and Odis praised me, and Jack, the publisher, sent a congratulatory email. Chicago television and radio stations followed my angle. But the praise was short-lived.

Two days later, our competitor, the *Chicago Sentinel,* broke a story with the headline "Heroin Girl was Gov's Kin" over a grainy picture of Anna, her mother, and the Governor's wife. Anna looked like she was eight years old.

Within an hour, the Governor's face appeared on the newsroom's bank of plasma screens. He stood behind a wooden podium, grasped its sides and, like a TV evangelist, stared directly into the camera, smiling a mouthful of pearly whites. His grin, along with his iconic black pompadour, made him look like a genetic mix between Elvis and Alfred E. Neuman, the *MAD Magazine* boy mascot. Problem was that the Governor couldn't stop smiling, even while he detailed the gruesome events around Anna's death. His wife and Anna's mother, Pam, flanked him. Both appeared somber, their eyes downcast. Pam quietly sobbed into a tissue.

"That reporter—Natalie Delaney—had no business keeping such important details from this young girl's family," the Governor insisted, shaking his mane to make his point, and pointing his finger at the cameras. "If she had alerted the police, our little Annette would be alive today."

His wife, whom reporters called "The Mrs.," discreetly elbowed him, but the Governor didn't notice.

"I gotta tell you. My wife has been so upset." He shook his head, and strands of hair fell into his face for effect. "Annette was one of her favorite little cousins. This tragedy is even more appalling when you consider the forces that could have been brought to bear by this office if that reporter and her newspaper had simply alerted us to Annette's drug addiction."

By then Pam was glaring at him. Each time the Governor misspoke Anna's name, the reporters in the newsroom laughed; it was like watching a parody on *Saturday Night Live*.

Finally, the Governor's wife pushed her way to the microphone: "We're saddened by *Anna's* death. Some of us, like my husband, called her by diminutives. We miss her and believe her death could have been avoided had the paper been more interested in preserving life than chasing Pulitzers."

A reporter at the news conference yelled, "When was the last time you saw Anna?"

It was a seemingly innocent question, but The Mrs. looked startled. She batted her eyelashes, then glanced at Pam, who appeared equally stunned. The Mrs. stammered, "I'm not sure…It could have been at her eighth-grade graduation?"

"She was kicked out of school," a reporter at the news conference yelled. It was a fact detailed in my story about Anna's death.

The Mrs. was clearly rattled. "It could have been a spring choral concert…I—I…just don't remember."

Those of us standing near the newsroom's TVs howled. I

almost forgot Anna was dead and that the police, a judge, and now the Governor were holding me responsible.

I hadn't noticed the young editor who walked up behind me until I felt his breath against my neck. "Even a blind pig finds an acorn once in a while," he said.

I spun around. "What's that supposed to mean?"

"Looks like you caught a lucky break. Seems the Governor's more incompetent than you are." He smirked and walked away.

The young editor's comment enraged me, but I knew it was too much to expect him to see beyond the prejudice of our profession.

The fact that the cops believed I had done something wrong was all it took for many in the newsroom. As journalists, we made our living by believing that the accused were guilty because the police said so. We prominently displayed their mug shots and wrote vivid stories about the crimes they supposedly committed. Rarely did we publish stories of police arresting the wrong person or dropping charges. As a crime reporter, I had been just as guilty of trusting the cops. Arrests were the bread and butter of my beat. I had bought into the police lore that if the person wasn't guilty of what he'd been arrested for, he was guilty of at least three or four other crimes he hadn't been charged with. While it's true the paper had run my stories about police corruption, they had done so only after I had acquired irrefutable evidence—internal memos and leaked video footage. In general, most reporters believed the police, unless it was fashionable not to. Newsroom jealousy made them especially disposed to believe a reporter who'd netted so many exclusives had cut corners.

A clerk summoned me to Amy's office where she and Spielman, the company attorney, were seated at a small conference table. When I walked in, she laid her ice-gray gaze on me with a prophetic heaviness and ordered me to shut the door. Her office was stifling. The afternoon sun blared through her windows as the building's air conditioner sputtered in the vents. I sat down, my palms beginning to sweat. Amy tented her hands on the table and smiled a little too energetically. Spielman sat cold-faced, his skin gray and his eyes dull, black marbles behind thick glasses.

"Natalie, I've asked you here because, well, we believe we need to make some changes." She spoke in a cool monotone. "The judge's comments—and now this business with the Governor—has caused the paper irreparable damage. Your position with the company isn't tenable anymore."

I felt a surge of despair and looked over at Spielman, his eyes fixed on the table.

"What are you talking about? I've had front-page stories nearly every week. I've broken some of the biggest exclusives on the Poison heroin case. How can that be *untenable*?"

She wrinkled her nose. "I think you know."

"Know what? That you've been telling me what a great job I'm doing, that I'm 'ready for the big leagues of LA and New York'?"

"Not everyone sees your work the way you do."

"So that's it? You're firing me?"

She pushed back from the table, a sign that the mute man should speak. Spielman cleared his throat and pushed his glasses up the bridge of his long, pointy nose. "If you resign and sign a non-disparagement agreement, we'll give you three-month severance."

"And what would I say is the reason for resigning? I wanted to spend time with my *cat*?"

"Don't make a scene," Amy chided. "It would be better for your career if you went quietly."

"My career? Really? There is no career after this, Amy. Newsflash: the newspaper industry is in the toilet, which is where you've just pushed me." I looked away, anxious and confused, my thoughts jumbled.

"So let me get this straight," I continued. "The Governor has a press conference, looks like a complete buffoon, throws out some hollow threats, and you all fold?"

"This...*your departure*...has been in the works for a while," Amy said spitefully. "The Governor's press conference...well, that was just the last nail in the coffin."

Spielman slid the legal agreement across the table. "You have a week to sign. Enough time for you to consult your accountant and your attorney."

"Well, you *were* my attorney. That is, before you told me you weren't qualified to represent me after escorting me to a police interrogation."

Spielman pressed his lips together. Amy's jaw tightened. They were ready to be done with this unpleasantness. I stood, but took my time leaving. They both looked apprehensive.

"Don't worry," I said. "I'm not going to pull a Ben move. If you want to see an ass, look in the mirror."

CHAPTER THIRTY-EIGHT

August 11 & 12, 2008

GOVERNOR BOTCHES PRESS CONFERENCE

CAN'T REMEMBER NIECE'S NAME, BLAMES PAPER

Chicago Sentinel

A woman from human resources was waiting for me at my desk, holding one of those white boxes that screamed "I've been fired." I told the HR drone she could keep her goddamn box, but she hung around watching me stuff my Rolodex—inherited from Ben—into my giant bag. After Ben's firing, I packed up the files I valued and took them home. I can't say I was surprised the editors fired me. I was just amazed there hadn't been more warning. How can you applaud someone, send them congratulatory emails, praise their work in public, then hours later kick them out the door? The newsroom was a mercurial beast, one that cannibalized its best people.

I slung my bag over my shoulder, winked at the HR woman, and walked out of the newsroom. No one looked up or wished me well. The rumor mill would be churning within minutes. For legal reasons, Amy wouldn't be able to publicly confirm I'd gotten the boot. But people would know. Anyone who resigns receives a cake, a good-bye party, and when they leave the newsroom for the last time, a standing ovation. My clout as a reporter was gone. Without Mother *Times* backing me, the police would now come at me even harder.

When I steered my car south instead of north on Lake Shore

Drive, I knew where I was headed. I didn't know if he was home, but I thought it was best to catch him off guard. I hadn't seen Danny in four days and worried he might have adopted a less forgiving attitude toward me, especially with his sister grousing about me.

He answered the door wearing cut-off jeans and cowboy boots. White paint was splattered across his bare chest. *The man never wore a shirt.* Hank Williams whined in the background; the place smelled like a brewery.

"Wanna get shitfaced?" I asked.

Danny handed me a beer, and we stood admiring his work in the living room.

"Gotta get my deposit back," he said. "We were a bit rough in here. Thought I'd touch it up. Whataya think?" The afternoon light caught the slant of his cheekbones and his two-day stubble. He looked like a male model in an underwear ad. The man simply had no bad angles.

"Looks good." I clinked my bottle against his. "Where's Lib?"

"I made her mother take her for a few days while I got the place ready. That woman hasn't done shit for Libby. Didn't even come to Anna's funeral. I gave her hell."

Danny handed me a brush, and we spent the rest of the afternoon painting, the music eventually lightening our mood. When "Honky Tonk Blues" came on, Danny grabbed my hand and tried to teach me how to two-step. We ended up falling backwards over the couch, giggling and half drunk. It was there, lying next to each other, staring at the wet walls, that I told him I'd been fired. He hugged me, smearing paint on my shirt and in my hair, then disappeared into the kitchen, returning with a bottle of whiskey and two squat glasses.

He held up his glass: "To a helluva life. It kicks you in the ass, and you have to kick it back." We slugged back our first shots.

A sad love song came on the radio. Danny reached over and touched my hand. His fingers felt gooey with paint. "I've missed you."

"I've missed you, too. But isn't this better—just being friends?"

"Friends with benefits?" He pumped his eyebrows.

I couldn't help laughing. He shrugged reluctantly. The liquor and the music were making us mellow.

I refilled our shot glasses. "You gotta promise me one thing."

"Anything."

"You'll write to me in prison."

We both pretended to laugh.

About one a.m., Danny kissed me on my forehead and put me in a taxi. We were both too drunk to drive. He'd drop my car the next day, he promised. At home, I fell into bed with my clothes on.

• • •

A pounding on my door the next day woke me. Thinking it was Danny, I ambled to the door and flung it wide open.

It was Julian, wearing his usual dark suit and tie, holding one of those stupid white boxes.

"My God, what happened to you?" His voice was rough but concerned.

I looked down at the paint streaked across my shirt and ran a hand over the top of my head, my fingers catching in knots. "Oh, yeah. Art therapy."

"I brought you what the vultures didn't take from your desk." He held up the box.

I sighed and invited him in.

"You want some coffee?" I asked making my way to the kitchen. Deadline circled at my feet and meowed for breakfast. I hadn't managed to pick up cat food—or any food. I set a can of tuna on the floor. Then dug through the freezer looking for coffee.

Julian sauntered into the kitchen. His eyes surveyed the pizza boxes piled on the counter, the ballooning bags of trash. "Forget the coffee. What are you doing for lunch?"

"I was thinking of buying some rope." I cocked my head and stuck out my tongue.

"How about chopsticks instead?"

"Death by chopsticks? That's a new one."

• • •

The hostess seated us at the back. I pretended to study the menu. I'd rarely lunched with editors, and certainly never alone with a male editor. Julian was a self-contained and guarded man whose default posture was an intense silent brooding. He still hadn't explained the real reason he had shown up at my apartment in the middle of the day. We weren't friends.

"How about getting a couple beers? I love Thai beer," Julian said, licking his lips.

"You mean this beer?" I pointed to a picture on the menu of a green bottle with the label Phuket. "How do you pronounce that?"

"How do you think?"

"Fuck it?" I giggled.

He laughed, rich and raw and at odds with his sophisticated persona.

"I think I'll have the Fuck-It beer!" I said, feigning a male announcer's voice. "Are you sure this is Thai beer, because Fuck-It beer sounds very American!"

"Fuck-It! That's exactly what we need right now." Julian held his water glass as if it were a beer mug.

We were still snorting and squirming on our straw seat covers when the waiter arrived.

"To drink?" the waiter asked.

I pointed to the menu. "We'll have two bottles of this."

The waiter lifted his pencil from his menu pad and wrinkled his forehead. "Which one?"

"This one." I stabbed the picture. "Fuck-It beer."

The waiter giggled and held his hand to his mouth. "*Poo-ket* beer," he corrected.

Julian tried to hide behind his menu, but I could see his eyes tearing up.

When the waiter walked away, I threw my napkin at Julian. "You fucking knew!"

In a falsetto voice, he mimicked me, "Yes, I'll have the Fuck-It beer, please."

I doubled over, my stomach pinching from laughter.

We continued to riff on the *Poo-ket* beer until our green bottles arrived. Then we strained for some common interest that didn't involve the newsroom.

After a long silence, Julian cleared his throat. "I'm really sorry about what happened yesterday. Jack and Odis are fucking idiots." He spit out the words with such hostility, it startled me. "They're worried that this business with the cops is going to ruin their chance to sell the paper. Then the Governor made it worse. I wanted to see how you were doing. And…to let you know that the paper turned over your expense records to the police."

Heat was building behind my eyelids. The catch in my voice gave me away. "They were so eager to wash their hands of me, weren't they?"

"Whatever you do, don't sign the paper's settlement agreement. You may have to denounce them publicly in your defense. Have you hired an attorney?"

I shook my head.

"The cops are likely to get a search warrant for your apartment. Is there anything there that shouldn't be?"

"What? You think I'm hiding drugs?"

"No! I mean anything pertaining to the case. Any papers that were leaked to you—like those autopsy reports?"

I closed my eyes and thought of Harper's journal that Wendy Cabot had kept from the police.

"You can keep whatever you want at my house."

"That's convenient. You can go through my stuff and tell Jack and Odis what I have."

Julian winced. "If I were spying for Jack, would I be urging you to get your own attorney? Good God. I can understand why you're worried. But I have my own mind. I'm not going to sit by and watch a reporter end up in prison."

Until then no one had mentioned the P-word. Saying it out loud suddenly made its possibility more real. Maggie had delicately suggested I see one of her attorney friends, but I'd outright dismissed the idea. I didn't want to let the paper off that easily from defending me. Now it was clear losing my job was the least of my worries. I'd need to find a good criminal lawyer. I looked down at my plate, afraid I might burst out crying.

Julian leaned over the table and gently touched my arm. "I'm going to give you some free advice. Odis and Jack are terrified of the police and the Governor, but they're more terrified of that girl's parents suing the paper. A lawsuit would jeopardize the sale of the paper. The lawyers would settle, admit anything, dish out any amount, to end a trivial case that could stand in the way of reaping millions for stockholders, and lots of money for Odis and Jack. In this era of failing newspapers, getting a buyer is more important than winning awards, more important than defending ethical standards. The top people at the *Chicago Times* aren't about to let good journalism get in the way of a windfall in a sale. So you, Natalie, need to get your act together, hire an attorney, tear up that agreement they gave you, and, with your free time, find out who killed those girls. It's your only sure way of staying out of prison."

I sat immobile, stunned. "I don't have the money to hire an attorney." I sounded so feeble.

"I'll loan you the damn money. Don't you get how much trouble you're in?"

Who was this guy? And why did he care about me?

"Natalie, you're so naïve about what they could do to you."

"I know very well what the cops could do to me."

"I wasn't talking about the cops."

CHAPTER THIRTY-NINE

August 13–16, 2008

TIMES REPORTER FIRED

CANNED MINUTES AFTER GOVERNOR'S PRESS CONFERENCE

Chicago Sentinel

Without work or any place I had to be, I quickly fell into a disturbing pattern: sleeping until the little screamers at the nearby elementary school woke me during their noon recess, watching back-to-back episodes of *Law and Order*, then *Judge Judy*. Promptly at five o'clock, I poured my first drink, like a civilized person—a civilized person who was still wearing her pajamas and hadn't brushed her teeth or her hair.

My mother left multiple messages on my answering machine. Maggie and Ben called, too. I didn't have the energy to talk to them, to hear their platitudes that everything would work out. I had a feeling things were going to get a lot worse.

My firing had been leaked to the *Sentinel,* which ran the story in its Page Two gossip column. "The reporter who broke the Ghost Girl story" was how they described me. Gossip columnists and investigative reporters were filling up my answering machine with conspiracy theories that my firing was part of a cover-up involving the Governor. You couldn't live in Chicago without eventually believing government corruption was at the root of every ill in the city. Only in this case, they'd be right.

A malaise invaded my body like the flu, leaving me dizzy, achy and weepy. Everything felt too raw, too painful to think about in specific terms. My grief had rolled into one dark black cloud—the loss of Anna, the loss of my career, and the pending loss of my freedom if I went to prison. I kept the curtains closed and the lights off, as if I could hole up in the cocoon of my apartment for the rest of my life. Even now when I think of that time, I'm overcome with a suffocating despair.

By the fourth day, the place smelled like burnt popcorn and microwaved mac and cheese. Even Deadline smelled like dead fish, mostly because that's all she was eating. Despite the August heat and humidity, I felt cold and feverish. I stood in the shower for half an hour letting the hot water beat down on my skin, just to feel something. Then I opened my mouth and wailed, a horrid, ugly sound. I was afraid I wouldn't be able to stop. But finally, my tear ducts ran dry and my throat became hoarse. I napped for hours afterwards.

• • •

That night a supermoon dangled over the city's tallest buildings as if drawn by a child. It pulled me to my balcony, where I sat enthralled, rocking back and forth on my glider, hugging Deadline, and drinking liberally from a bottle of Johnnie Walker Red. Why bother with glasses? They were all dirty anyway. My neighbor, Sean, who rarely used his balcony, quietly stepped out, his face bathed in the light. From time to time he glanced in my direction.

"How are you holding up over there?" he finally asked. He'd kept a respectful distance since the night Maggie and I had jarred him awake with loud music.

"I was fired." My voice was flat, detached.

"Yes, I read about that. I'm sorry. Did they give you a reason?"

"Even if they had, it wouldn't have been the truth."

He climbed onto the partition between our balconies and swung his legs around. Perched there in the wan light of the moon, he seemed so delicate, so haunting with his pale blond hair and his colorless skin. I wondered for a moment if I were imagining him, this person reaching out to me when it seemed the whole world had turned their backs. Besides Julian, not a single colleague had called to offer condolences or sympathies.

"What are you going to do?"

I shook my head and sighed. "I just keep thinking that if I'd tried a little harder maybe Anna would still be alive."

He laughed gruffly. "You can't force people to do something they don't want to do. One thing I've learned from my clients is that there are only two sure ways to quit drugs: jail and death."

"She was just a kid."

"What you should be worried about are the cops. From the state of your apartment the other night, it wouldn't surprise me if they were the ones behind your break-in. If they really want to arrest you, there are a million ways to frame someone."

The fact Sean was seeing the situation from my point of view made me feel like I had someone in my corner. I detailed my police interview, how Spielman hadn't objected to Nickles's questions, even advising me to get my own criminal attorney. Once I was finished, we sat quietly, a pall washing over me as I considered the grimness of my situation.

"Have you seen a transcript of that interview? Did the cops tape record the interview? Certainly the attorney did, right?"

I shook my head no, realizing how naïve I'd been to believe that the paper and its attorney would protect me.

"Without a recording, the cops could claim you said anything." Sean paced the balcony. "I hope your attorney at least took good notes."

"He spent the whole time doodling. Besides, he's the paper's attorney. Not mine anymore." I suddenly felt embarrassed by the whiskey bottle at my feet. "After the cops interrogated me, he admitted this was way out of his league."

"Yes, as well he should have. He could be disbarred for claiming to represent you when he doesn't."

"I have a…friend—an editor friend—at the paper who

advised me to get an attorney." I struggled for the right word to describe Julian. I still had reservations about him, but given that he was the only one in the newsroom who'd shown any concern, my suspicions were waning.

"Good advice."

"Do you think you could take my case?"

Sean nervously ran his hands through his hair. "I don't know Natalie. My firm represents the Mickey Cobras. There's a potential conflict."

"How so?" I sat up, suddenly charged with the thought. "My issue is with the cops framing me. I don't think the Mickeys were targeting white girls because their parents were Democratic contributors."

"I'll have to talk to my partners. In the meantime, how about getting a good look at those Democratic contributors?"

"What do you mean?"

"I have two tickets to a fundraising dinner for the Senator. They cost me over ten grand, but my date can't make it. You want to take her spot? Maybe I could introduce you to someone who could help you. And, frankly, you look like you need cheering up."

CHAPTER FORTY

August 17, 2008

SENATOR HOSTING EXCLUSIVE PARTY AS FUNDRAISER

PRESIDENTIAL HOPEFUL'S COFFERS REACH HIGHEST LEVEL YET

Chicago Times

We were standing in line outside the nightclub Studio Paris, pressed together amid glittery gowns and tuxedos, a whir of photo drives catching every angle as though we were on the red carpet at the Academy Awards. Sean wore a tux with a periwinkle blue bowtie that paired well with the blue and silver cocktail dress Maggie had lent me. Unfortunately, the heat was melting the intricate makeup job she'd done. I dabbed my face with a tissue; Sean fanned himself with the palm-sized VIP cards that would eventually get us a seat inside and a private audience with the Senator. I was less interested in the photo-op with the presidential candidate and more curious to see who would fork over thousands of dollars to spend mere minutes with Chicago's man of the hour.

"Hope it's worth the money," I said, trying not to dampen Sean's enthusiasm.

"Oh, it will be."

The line crept along. I wobbled in my borrowed stiletto heels. I hadn't worn heels this tall since my high school prom. Finally, we reached the entrance and were led to a roped-off balcony overlooking the dance floor. Only VIPs were allowed on the second floor where a private reception with the Senator and his high-end donors was taking place. Sean was handed a ticket with our appointment time. We moved among the clutches of people waiting their turn, all nervously looking at their watches and silently practicing what they would say.

I spotted several state senators and city aldermen and their wives including Illinois's senior U.S. Senator, with whom I'd had many off-the-record conversations. His eyes passed over me as if I were a stranger.

The older crowd congregated near the Senator while a young group, mostly blonde-haired young women in tight gowns, had converged at a back bar. Some draped themselves over lounge chairs, holding flutes of champagne, striking poses as they snapped pictures with their cell phones. I heard a shrill laugh and turned to see Olivia Byrne, the pharmaceutical heiress, at the center of the group, flanked by twins MacKenzie and Madison. Nearby, wearing a slinky peach dress, stood Cate, Anna's former babysitter. Next to her, slouched against the bar, was Rory in a black leather cocktail dress.

Sean introduced me to colleagues at his firm. I tried to seem likable, hoping they would either agree to take my case or refer me to someone who would. My eyes kept drifting to the girls at the back bar. Eventually, I excused myself and stepped toward the younger crowd, remembering what Anna had said about her friends being "creeped out" by me.

I touched Cate lightly on the elbow. She turned around and squinted. Finally a big grin emerged. "You're Anna's friend, right?"

"We met at the rave…"

"Oh my God. I'm so glad to see you." She threw her arms around me.

"Wow." I stepped back, surprised by her emotional response. "Nice to see you too."

She looked stunning, yet harsher. Her pale hair was swirled like an ice cream cone, falling tendrils framing her face. Her satin dress was the same hue as her skin, which made her look nude at first glance. Gone was the nose ring. Instead, she wore a strand of pearls and diamond earrings.

"Anna...God, I miss her so much." She fluttered those long eyelashes. She seemed high or tipsy, her pupils twitching. She grabbed my arm to steady herself. "Hey, Rory," Cate yelled. "Remember Natalie, Anna's friend?"

Rory turned around, her eyes thickly outlined in black, and held up a fist for me to bump. "Anna's death was cruel. Real cruel."

I awkwardly bumped my fist against hers.

"God, I need a smoke. This place is fucking lame," Rory complained.

"Why'd you come?" I asked.

"Let me guess. You've not been to one of these monkey spankings before, eh? The old farts stay at one end and drink their scotch and smoke their cigars. The wives congregate and talk about their latest redecorating projects and how their husbands can't get it up anymore—at least not with them. And the people under thirty with all their real parts? Well, we're dragged here because the law says that a person can only give $5,300 per candidate. So, to increase their donation, everyone brings their kids. Hell, I think they'd bring their dogs, if the law would let them. Point is, I have to come so Daddy can write an even bigger check."

I scanned the room for Bethany. Clumps of people stood around the bar, their backs to me. One tall guy turned around. His sandy blond hair was swept back from his forehead, accentuating those captivating eyes and that brash smile. When he saw me, his face faltered.

Rory saw us staring at each other. "That's Rex Kennan," she whispered, "He's Olivia's toy. Olivia made sure of that. He used to be Bethany's boyfriend—before he left her for dead."

I wrenched my face to her.

"Oh, I thought you knew." She raised her eyebrows, and her face perked up at having caught me off guard. "Bethany said you'd mentioned Rex during your interview with her. Just so you know, Rex felt terrible about what happened to Bethany, but what was he supposed to do? I mean, he did try to revive her. He didn't know she was still alive when he left. Besides, he plans to go into politics, and he couldn't have a dead girl hanging over his head like his uncle—the press constantly bringing up that car wreck eons ago that drowned a townie girl in Maine as if it were a conspiracy instead of an accident. But Bethany wasn't all that forgiving. Who could blame her? If you can't count on your boyfriend to save you, who can you count on?"

She continued around the room providing snippy commentary. I'd stopped listening, my mind stuck on her admission about Rex and Bethany. And then there was this other question nagging at me: How did Rory know I was the reporter who interviewed Bethany? I'd met Rory once, briefly, at the rave with Anna, who made sure I never said I was a reporter.

"Have you ever met her?" Cate asked, gesturing at a girl encircled by a dozen people.

I shook my head. I recognized her as the Senator's seventeen-year-old daughter, Regina. Her hair had been straightened, and she wore a modest white lace dress, which seemed out of place amid the girls' designer outfits revealing cleavage and midriffs.

"Her mother usually keeps her away from these events," Cate said. "This is the first one where Mommy doesn't have her on a leash."

We watched as Olivia handed Regina a small flat tin, the kind that normally held aspirin.

"Olivia loves this," Cate said. "Everyone's kissing up to her grandfather for money and she's dispensing his drugs."

"Isn't that risky, especially with all the cops and the Secret Service hovering?" I asked.

"Oh, but that's what makes it fun," Rory said, her face excited. "Sucking on an F-stick in the same room as a presidential candidate, well, now that's precious, isn't it?" She nodded her head toward Madison and MacKenzie. Both were licking red suckers.

I blinked. "Is that really…?"

"I'm not going to defend everything they do," Rory said,

stroking her fingers over the wings of her butterfly tattoo. "These girls are like my family. We grew up together. No one on the outside gets this life, what it's like. The pressures…My dad—*when he was still John*—more than once went missing. We thought he had been kidnapped. Turned out he was on a coke bender. Holed up in one of our hotels fucking the staff. Why? Because he could. He owned the company. When the cops showed up, he called our Senator. We give wads of money to the Senator just so he can clean up such messes. And that's how it is."

"See Becker over there? Her stepdad got caught diddling an intern—same as Cate's daddy—and everyone wonders why he risked his reputation. Well, it wasn't about the sex. That's what people don't get. It's the thrill of risking it all, the rush of getting away with it. And look at Madison and MacKenzie. Fuck! Their dad is a high-riding hedge fund guy. He makes more in a minute than most make in a lifetime. The man is wired, like he spoons his coffee with coke. With a dad like that, you think those girls are just going to do a *little weed*?

"We're the descendants of a bunch of adrenaline junkies, risk takers, players, and hustlers. And you know what? We're just like them."

I stared at Rory, unsure of how to react. Her *Rocky Horror* makeup, garish tattoo, and self-absorption had disarmed me. Before I could ask more questions, I felt a hand on my shoulder.

"There you are." Sean's eyes were wide, his forehead beaded with sweat. "It's time to meet The Man."

I reluctantly said goodbye to Rory and Cate and followed Sean to a cordoned-off area where the Senator was sitting with several couples. Sean handed his ticket to a guard and the red velvet ropes opened.

CHAPTER FORTY-ONE

August 17 & 18, 2008

POISON DEALER BEATEN

REQUESTS TO CHANGE JAILS

Chicago Sentinel

On the ride home, I was still basking in the excitement of meeting with the Senator. He'd called me by name and said he was sorry I wasn't at the *Times* anymore. It was an uplifting moment amid so many dark days. Sean—equally hyped up—waved the private card the Senator had given him.

"He said I could call him anytime," he bragged. "Yep, that's what ten grand gets you. Five minutes with The Man and his private cell phone number—not that I'm complaining."

Minutes later, standing at the landing between our apartments, we awkwardly lingered, not wanting the night to end. I took off the stilettos and stood in my bare feet, my ears still ringing from the buzz of the club.

"Was it everything you hoped it would be—the party, I mean?" he asked, still beaming.

"It gave me real insight into what it's like for the kids who grow up in that political realm. They're much more isolated than you think, clinging to each other in a creepy, *Lord of the Flies* kind of way."

"My partners were impressed with your story, your character.

They're *appalled* at the injustice of your situation. Natalie, they've decided to take your case, *pro bono*."

"Oh my God." I threw my arms around his neck and hugged him.

"You'll be my first innocent client," he mused.

• • •

The next afternoon, Sean arrived at my apartment with a stack of witness statements, a coup given that Spielman had gotten nothing after his negotiations. We sat on my couch reading them, my hands trembling. From poorly typed statements, riddled with spelling errors, I learned I had provided much of the South Side with heroin, that I was probably the one who had spiked the heroin with fatal amounts of fentanyl, and that I was also providing beer and alcohol to kids. One girl even intimated I was having sex with gang members.

"Surely the prosecutors don't believe this crap?" I yelled.

"They're attacking your most coveted possession: your reputation. They'll paint you as an unscrupulous journalist who provided drugs so you could get a story about kids doing heroin. They'll claim these kids weren't doing drugs until they met you, especially Anna. They'll use your own words against you. You did admit on the front page of the newspaper that you watched Anna do heroin for the first time."

I flung the witness statements across the room. "The cops pressured these kids into making false statements. They're probably all on probation."

"Natalie, sworn statements—even if they conflict with each other and put you in different places at the same time—are all the prosecutors need to get an indictment."

"But this is fucking *me* we're talking about. Not somebody with a long rap sheet. Hell, I've never even been arrested. For *anything*."

"We're going to fight this. This is why you have an attorney. We don't want them to get an indictment. Once they charge you, the game is over. Your reputation is ruined, even if the charges are baseless."

We sat in an awkward silence. He pretended to read more statements, but I suspected he already knew their claims by heart.

"There were a couple of kids who said you never did anything illegal, that you only talked to them." He handed me several pages he'd tagged with yellow stickies.

"Why'd they give you these?"

"They're obligated to by law."

"Like they follow the law."

"You realize the detectives on this case are the department's premier homicide team—Nickles, McNamee, Mobley, Cook, and Smith." Sean's eyes met mine.

I knew their names. Detective Mobley, of course, was Mo. He'd complained occasionally about a few of the detectives on this squad, especially Nickles, saying they operated above the law—demanding subpoenas when there wasn't probable cause, focusing manpower on people they wanted to take down while ignoring killings they didn't care anything about.

"Yeah, I know Mobley well."

"How's that?"

"Attorney-client privilege, right?"

He nodded.

"He *was* my number one cop source."

Sean patted my arm. "You've got to steel yourself for what's ahead. This is rough. But you'll come through it. The truth is on your side."

I took a visual inventory of the statements scattered across the coffee table, couch, and floor. The enormity gave rise to a deep sorrow within me, a loss of what I'd worked so hard to attain. These lies would become fact because someone said them, because someone swore to their veracity, because someone would put them in the paper and because someone would read them and believe them.

CHAPTER FORTY-TWO

August 19, 2008

BYRNE'S OLYMPICS GROUP RAISES HALF BILLION

PHARMACEUTICAL GIANT LEVERAGES CLOUT FOR OLYMPICS BID

Chicago Sentinel

Early the next morning a jail guard texted me that Lester was about to appear in court on an emergency petition. I raced to the courthouse and snagged a front row seat as Lester sauntered into the packed courtroom. In his jail-issued orange jumpsuit, his hands cuffed behind his back, he shuffled slowly in leg irons. His eyes were little more than slits between swollen eyelids and purple cheeks. Lester squinted in my direction, only twenty feet away. His attorney tugged on his elbow, forcing him to face the judge.

I leaned forward to hear the discussion at the bench. Junked-up women in the back row talked loudly. A baby cried. The clamor from the hallway leaked in as people periodically opened the door.

Lester's attorney was seeking to have him placed in a neighboring county jail for his safety. The attorney told the judge that Aryan Nation inmates had repeatedly meted out their own justice on Lester.

In less than three minutes, the judge approved the motion. As the judge pounded his gavel, a bailiff guided Lester toward the door leading to a holding cell. Lester kept his eyes on the floor, but just as he rounded the judge's bench, he elbowed the bailiff in the gut and limped toward the courtroom seats—and me. His leg chains rattled as he hustled forward, glaring at me with his bloated and bruised face. Within a few feet of me, he let loose an eerie guttural wail, then scrunched up his mouth, extended his neck, and projectile vomited.

I ducked behind my bag, the watery puke barely missing me. The bailiff knocked Lester to the floor; two other bailiffs rushed from the back of the courtroom. Amid muffled cries, Lester shouted, "You bitch! You fucking bitch! I will fucking kill you!"

One of the bailiffs fired a stun gun at Lester's leg. He shrieked, then went limp. Within seconds, he started wiggling and thrashing on the floor. The bailiff stunned him again. Finally, he stopped resisting. It took all three bailiffs to remove Lester's slack body from the courtroom. As they carried him away, Lester twisted his face toward me, his eyes exuding a harrowing rage.

• • •

Still rattled by Lester's threats, I was driving home when my cell phone rang. It was Sean, his tone distant, all business. He'd already heard about Lester's attempted attack and, after making sure I was okay, chided me for showing up at the courthouse.

"I'm your attorney now. You need to talk to me before you do *anything*." He hesitated briefly. "I just met with the prosecutors about your case. We need to talk."

"Can't you tell me now?"

"Nah, I can't, Natalie. I'm standing in the hallway of the courthouse. I'll see you later."

• • •

By the time he arrived hours later, I was mentally exhausted. I practically tackled him as he came off the elevator.

"I can't take the suspense. What did the prosecutor say?"

He sighed. "Come in." He unlocked his door. I followed.

I perched rigidly on an ottoman. Sean sat back in a leather lounger and loosened his tie. The tiny crow's feet under his eyes appeared more pronounced; his eyes lacked their usual sparkle.

"We have some decisions to make." He slapped his palms against his knees. "Natalie, I don't want you to panic, but the prosecutors are convening a grand jury to ask for an indictment against you."

"What? Why all of a sudden?"

"They say their witnesses are credible. I explained to the prosecutor that there is bad blood between you and the Chicago police. The prosecutor didn't budge. I told him before he embarrasses himself, he might want to give us a chance to counter any bogus claims in those witness statements."

"But how? How do I prove I *didn't* do something?" My voice cracked.

He studied me, as if assessing my character.

"By taking a polygraph."

At first I thought he was joking. But his face was stern.

"I thought polygraphs weren't admissible in court. I thought they were unreliable."

"Yes and no. Defense attorneys and cops use them all the time before charges are filed. You are innocent. You're one of the only innocent clients I've ever had. You're the perfect candidate for the polygraph."

"I don't want to take it from the cops."

"We use a private polygrapher. He used to be a cop and administered the polygraphs for the police, so they trust his results. I've used him many times."

"I thought you said you didn't have any innocent clients."

"Well…sometimes they are innocent of one particular aspect of the crime they are charged with." He grinned. "I limit the scope of the questions. I don't need to do that with you."

I had started to get up when Sean cleared his throat.

"That's not all. Anna's father, Kent Reid, filed a civil suit against you and the paper today. That's why I was so mad you were at the courthouse this morning. The last thing you need is a bunch of reporters sticking microphones in your face, making you look guilty. He's suing you and the paper for reckless disregard and asking for twenty-million dollars, including five million in punitive damages. He's claiming that you got Anna hooked on heroin for your story."

I felt dizzy. The room wobbled.

"In some ways, this is good. It will require the paper to help in your defense—unless, of course, they settle. But let's hope they take the ethical high ground and back you up."

CHAPTER FORTY-THREE

August 20, 2008

OLYMPIC DONATIONS DOWN

DONORS SAY THEY ARE AFRAID THEY WILL BE TARGETED

Chicago Times

The next afternoon we met at the polygrapher's office. A stocky man with a blunt moon face and a much too short tie greeted us at the door.

"Hey, Carl," Sean pumped his hand. "This is Natalie."

Carl's most distinctive feature was a menacing black monobrow. He looked straight out of the 1970s. His beige shortsleeve dress shirt stretched over a middle-age paunch and partially revealed a military tattoo on his left bicep. The two men engaged in friendly banter. Occasionally, Carl glanced in my direction, sizing me up through thick square glasses.

When Sean left, Carl motioned me into another room where a gray machine, the size of a laptop, sat on the table. The anticipation was akin to sitting in the gynecologist's exam room, eyeing the cold metal speculum, knowing I was about to be splayed and probed.

Carl handed me several forms to sign. He asked if I was on any drugs. I told him my doctor had prescribed antidepressants after Anna's death.

"*Illegal* drugs." He looked up from his clipboard and arched his monobrow in annoyance. "The test doesn't work if you're under the influence of alcohol or drugs. You've had neither in the last twelve hours, right?"

I counted the hours (twenty) since my last glass of scotch. "No."

"I'm going to ask you some questions about yourself before we get started."

At first the questions were basic: Where was I born? What did my parents do for a living? Then the questions became increasingly personal.

"At what age did you lose your virginity?"

"Eighteen."

"Have you ever had an abortion?"

"No."

"Are you sexually active?"

"What does sex have to do with this?" I scooted to the edge of the chair, ready to bolt.

"Just answer the question, please. We're setting a baseline."

"What was the question?"

He looked down at his clipboard again and coughed. "Are you sexually active?"

"How do you define 'active'?"

"How many sexual partners have you had?"

"That is none of your business. Move on or I'm leaving. I'm not here to titillate you."

"I assure you, miss, these questions are all very standard. It's just to get to know your personality."

"You mean you want to know my deviant traits to see whether I'm more likely to lie?"

He ignored me, but skipped the question. After thirty minutes of grilling, Carl put down his clipboard. He reached over me to wrap a wire around my chest. His breath was sour. Awkwardly holding my hand, he adjusted a thimble-like pouch around my middle finger, then wrapped a blood pressure bag around my bicep. Flushed, he sat back in his chair, wiped the sweat from his brow, and flipped the machine's switch. The needles jumped up and down as if registering an earthquake.

The air around me was sterile and inert. The only movement came from the machine with its bouncing needles and large white scroll of paper.

"Pick a number between one and ten, but *lie* when I ask if that's the number."

I watched the red needle jump and sucked in a slow breath.

Carl asked whether it was one, then two, until he reached ten.

"It was seven, wasn't it?"

"How did you know?"

"It's the machine. Look." He pointed to lines on the graph paper made by three different needles. "Here is where you said six wasn't the number. Here is where you lied and said seven wasn't the number."

The needles had practically shot off the chart when I lied—about a number. How high would the needles jump if I lied about something of consequence?

"You're not a good liar." Carl smirked with the prowess of an expert.

He started with the obnoxious questions he'd asked before, changing them slightly so I'd have to answer in a different way. Eventually he focused his questions on my case.

"Did you ever provide alcohol to teenagers?"

"No, not intentionally."

"Did you ever provide drugs to anyone?"

"Never."

"Were you ever present when drugs were consumed by teenagers?"

"Yes."

"Did you ever provide the money that was used to purchase those drugs?"

"No."

"And did you ever take anyone to buy drugs in your car?"

"No."

"Are you sure?" He scrutinized me over the rims of his glasses.

"Yes, I'm sure!"

"The machine is showing that you're unsure; you're hesitating. It's showing possible deception."

"Are you saying I'm lying?"

"I wouldn't necessarily say that you are lying. But there's something you're not being wholly truthful about. What happened?"

I looked up at the ceiling, trying not to cry. I didn't have any other way to release my feelings with Carl's wires squeezing me. Carl hunched over his machine, waiting. I looked at my fingers strapped to his gauges and felt sad. This was what my life had come down to. The words I had lived by, cultivated, were no longer credible. I was seen as a fraud. A hypocrite. A liar. The epithet was unexpectedly sharp, like the edge of a fresh newspaper.

Carl stared at me through his square glasses smudged with fingerprints. His eyes—no more than tiny dark holes beneath stubby eyelashes—were fixed in a permanent glare. He raised his wormlike eyebrow, urging me on.

"I was all alone out there." My voice quivered. "Sometimes I knew the girls were up to something, and other times I didn't. They used me as their personal body guard and chauffeur."

I took a deep breath.

"Take your time." Carl turned off the machine.

"I had been looking for Anna for days. She wasn't returning my phone calls. Her cousin claimed she hadn't seen her. Then one night Anna texts me. I go pick up her and Libby and take them to get tacos. Anna seemed normal. When I asked her where she'd been for the past week, she said she had been staying with Cate, her old babysitter. I was so happy to see her, I didn't press her for details.

"On the way back to Libby's apartment, Anna told me she needed to drop something off at a friend's house. Well, she *said* it was a friend's house. She directed me to this apartment house in Bridgeport. Libby and I sat in the car while Anna went in. I don't know what I was thinking. Clearly, I wasn't thinking. Sometimes the girls just seemed like regular girls, you know? I would forget that they were always scheming.

"We were waiting and I was checking my email on my phone. I was distracted. After a few minutes I said to Libby, 'Who is she seeing?'

"Libby looked away and shrugged. That's when I knew. I screamed at her, 'Why did you let me come here? Why did you do this?' Libby claimed not to know what Anna was up to, but admitted she'd seen her take money out of my purse at the restaurant.

"I jumped out of the car and ran to the back of the building where I'd watched Anna go in. The door opened to a back hallway. Loud music came from the upper floors, screeching hard rock. I followed the noise. A dark staircase led to a door slightly cracked open. Behind it I could hear women laughing—an eerie, wicked sound.

"I pushed on the door and it swung open. Fast-food wrappers and beer cans covered the floor. I smelled an overwhelming pungent odor, like vinegar and vomit. Dark buggy eyes looked up at me from the listless bodies spread out on couches and mats on the floor. I spotted Anna slumped in a corner. I started toward her. A big black guy stationed himself in the middle of the room, daring me to pass. No one said a word.

"I yelled at her: 'C'mon, Anna, let's go. Let me take you home.'"

"Anna looked at me, her eyes rolled back, and her head drooped to her shoulder. That's when I saw her fingers clutching at a needle in her arm. I yelled again, but she didn't respond. I stepped toward her, ignoring the man in the middle of the room.

"Anna sat up and opened her eyes. 'Oh, hey,' she said, and smiled dreamily. 'What are you doing here? Following me? You following me Natalie?' Her words were slurred.

"'Why'd you come here?' I called out. The man held out his hands, stopping me from moving any closer.

"'Needed a little juice. Didn't think you'd mind.'

"'You knew what you were doing. You wanted me to find you, to see you like this. Why?'

"'You still want to adopt me, make me your little *princess*?' She snickered.

"'Anna, please. Let's go. Just leave. Leave with me.' I was yelling, angry.

"She shook her head. 'You don't care about me. You only liked me when I was fun. I'm not so fun now, huh?'

"'Anna, please. We'll work this out. I need you to come with me.'

"'You know, you keep following me, Natalie, and you're gonna wind up in hell.' She laughed viciously. 'See you in hell, Natalie.'

"I didn't try to get by the man. I kicked the plastic wrappers on the floor. Then I ran down the stairs and out into the night air. I was angry, fuming. She'd betrayed me and used me. I flung open the car door and got in.

"'Why didn't you tell me?' I screamed at Libby. 'How could you do that to me—to *her*?'

"Libby looked at me blankly. I backed out of the driveway and jammed the gearshift into first. Libby screamed at me to stop, to go back. She tried to unlock her door, but I kept pressing the master lock. It was awful. Ugly. I punched the gas and took off— leaving Anna alone with those strangers, in a shooting gallery, with a needle sticking out of her arm.

"It was the last time I saw her."

I sobbed, pressing my free hand to my mouth. Carl stared at the floor, nodding. When I stopped weeping, he let out an empathetic sigh.

"You've never told anyone that, right?"

I shook my head.

"Thought so." He handed me a tissue.

"I didn't know what to do." I pounded my fists against my thighs. "I should have kicked that guy in the chin, grabbed her and pulled her out to the car. I should have called her uncle and told him where to find her."

Carl chuckled. "You've watched too many movies."

He handed me a glass of water. I gulped it down. He waited while I composed myself, breathing and dabbing at my running mascara.

"Let's try this again," he said.

He flicked on the machine and zeroed in on the night I'd driven Anna to the heroin house.

"Did you know you were taking Anna to a drug house?"

"No."

"Did you know that she was going to buy or get heroin inside that house?"

"No."

"Did you try to get her to leave when you realized what she was doing?"

"Yes."

There were a few more questions. Then, without warning, Carl stopped. He disconnected the wires around my chest, pulled off the blood-pressure bag, and extracted the monitor on my finger. He pointed at the waiting room and asked me to sit there while he studied the results.

I curled up on the couch, feeling raw, exposed. I wanted to sleep, to forget about what had just happened. The only thing keeping me awake was anticipation over whether I'd passed.

Carl finally came out and took a seat across from me. I still couldn't decide whether I hated him.

"You passed. All the questions the state's attorney wants to know, you told the truth. You didn't have anything to do with giving drugs or alcohol to those kids, and you didn't have anything to do with Anna's death."

My shoulders dropped, and I let out a long stretch of air.

"What about the part where you said I was being 'deceptive'?"

"That's guilt. It's normal. But you weren't lying. I'll write up a detailed report for Sean."

I stood up to leave.

"Good luck to you." He sounded more considerate than he'd let on during the testing.

I was about to open the door when Carl cleared his throat.

"I did the polygraphs on Anna's killers and on Lester Williams.

You should know she had been doing all kinds of drugs—and maybe even heroin—long before you ever met her."

I turned around and stared at Carl. He'd put me through this emotional wringer, and all the while he'd known the truth.

"I had to," he said, as though he were reading my mind. "It's my job."

CHAPTER FORTY FOUR

August 21, 2008

POL'S DAUGHTER FOUND DEAD
NEAR PROPOSED OLYMPIC PARK

POISONED HEROIN CLAIMS ANOTHER VICTIM

Chicago Sentinel

The next morning, I was jolted awake when the newspaper hit my apartment door. As I mindlessly pulled the paper from its blue plastic sleeve, my eyes darted to the headline stripped across the front page: POLITICIAN'S DAUGHTER FOUND DEAD; POISONED HEROIN SUSPECTED. A homeless man had discovered Cate's body in Washington Park, near where the proposed Olympic City was to be built.

I instantly regretted not talking to Cate more the night of the Senator's fundraiser. I had wanted to ask her how Anna had seemed when she was staying with her. Then it occurred to me that that too could have been another of Anna's lies.

Cate's death revived that haunting sense of powerlessness and guilt entangled with my memory of Anna. Determined not to read about another death of a girl I knew, I dragged myself from the apartment with renewed conviction, dead set on getting answers.

Danny's truck was gone when I pulled into the lot behind the apartment building. He hadn't said when they were moving, and I worried I was too late. I rushed up the stairs to the fourth floor and knocked. When that didn't get a response, I started pounding. The door cracked open, and one of Libby's dull green eyes peered out.

"I need to talk to you."

"I don't want to talk to you." She sounded groggy.

"You don't have a choice."

We both knew I could call her father. I hadn't told Danny I was coming over, but he wanted answers as much as I did. Finally, she unlatched the security chain and the door opened.

Wild-haired and squinting at the sunlight, Libby wore a cropped T-shirt that revealed her belly button and white cotton underwear. She shuffled into the living room and curled up in a blanket on the couch. The TV was turned to cartoons, the sound muted.

"Dad's not here." Her skin looked sallow in the dim light. *Did they ever open the shades?*

"Do you think you can get over being pissed at me? It's really getting old." I didn't have time or energy to cajole her into talking to me.

She buried her face in the blanket, ignoring me. The apartment smelled of fried onions and charred burgers. Ashtrays on the coffee and side tables were full. A tumbler with a spit of liquor remained within an arm's reach of the couch.

I sat next to her. "What do I have to do to make it up to you, to get you talk to me?"

She sat up slowly, knitting her eyebrows as if it had just occurred to her that she could have things *she wanted*. Libby had stood in the shadow of her cousin for so long, I wondered if she even knew what she wanted. I regretted I hadn't spent much time talking to Libby about anything other than getting her cousin to stop doing drugs.

"Libby, it wasn't your fault. She had secrets—even from you."

Her bottom lip trembled and her eyes teared up. Her voice was faint, whispery, and I had to lean in to hear her: "I want you to take me to her grave."

I pulled her to me. She wrapped her arms around me and

sobbed. It had been nearly three weeks since Anna died. Libby no doubt had spent much of that time alone. Though she might be angry with me, she didn't have any other friends. After a while she pulled away and wiped her face in the blanket.

"I really want to find out what was going on with Anna. Can you help me?" It sounded like baby talk, but Libby had never been as sophisticated as Anna.

Curled on the couch gnawing on a thumbnail, Libby looked like a fragile kid, a motherless child in need of nurturing.

"What happened that night? Why did you girls go down to Woodlawn? Why did *you* agree to go?" Much of what happened still didn't make sense.

She looked at me with eyes huge and glassy. "We were with these girls, friends of Anna's. I don't remember their names, but one girl had this giant butterfly tattoo on her neck and the other girl had super long black hair and eyes like an Egyptian."

So Rory and Olivia had been with Anna that night. Their fathers must have used their political connections to keep their names out of the police report. All the witnesses' names, except Libby's, had been blacked out of the police report.

"I wasn't gonna let her go without me, not with *those girls*."

"Why? What was wrong with them?"

She cringed. "They gave me the creeps. I didn't think they had her back, you know?"

"How'd you get there?"

"Butterfly Girl drove. Me and Anna sat in the back." She stared into the distance, her eyes focused on something, remembering. "Butterfly Girl kept making fun of Anna, saying she didn't have the guts to buy heroin, that she was a poser. She kept saying that: 'Poser! Poser!' So Anna says she'll do it. Butterfly Girl drove us to a house in Woodlawn. We didn't even get out of the car before these black girls surrounded us. One said she was Lester's girlfriend. But I didn't believe her. She wanted to know what we were doing there. She took one look at Anna and didn't like her. But Anna was too high to see that—"

"High on what?"

"They had these pink suckers with medicine in them. Made them goofy."

"Where'd they get those?"

"The Egyptian girl. She tried to give me one, but I said no. Something about those girls." She shook her head. "I knew I had to have my wits about me that night. Anna asked the black girls if they had any H. That's when the leader took out her gun. She was waving it around, saying we were 'disrespecting' them by coming to their neighborhood to buy drugs. Anna said we were really looking for Lester. That made the girl even madder. She said Anna was fucking Lester. Anna said no, but the girl didn't believe her. The girl pointed the gun at Anna's head.

"I yelled at the girl to leave Anna alone, and she pointed the gun at me. 'Oh, so you want some of this?' She was hopped up on something. Her eyes were big and scary. Anna told her to leave me alone. I was just her little cousin. *Her little cousin*, that's what she called me. We were the same age but she always looked out for me, protected me.

"The girl turned the gun back to Anna, saying Anna was pretty. 'Too fucking pretty'—she kept saying it. I yelled at her to let us go. But she was having none of it. Anna wouldn't look at the girl, tears were running down her face and her lips were all jumpy. I grabbed her hand. It was so cold. The girls in the front seat were screaming. I told Butterfly Girl to just take off, but she didn't. Then all of sudden the black girl stops talking and pulls the trigger."

Libby bent over, held the blanket to her mouth, and sobbed. I rubbed her back, listening as her wailing turned into soft whimpering and then sniffling. Why hadn't Rory driven off and saved them? Strange how she hadn't mentioned at the Senator's fundraiser that she'd been with Anna when she died. The quiet of the apartment gave it a lonely, ghostly feel. I kept expecting Anna to come out of the bedroom. Finally, Libby sat up, puffy eyed, her face resolute.

"I gotta show you something."

CHAPTER FORTY-FIVE

August 21, 2008

OLYMPICS COMMITTEE TO VISIT CHICAGO

SOUTH SIDE PARK CLEANED FOR PROPOSED INSPECTION

Chicago Monthly

Libby brushed her hair into pigtails and pulled on clothes I recognized as Anna's—a midriff-revealing T-shirt with the word *Sucker!* emblazoned across her breasts, tight white shorts, and a pair of leather thong sandals. I supposed wearing Anna's clothes was Libby's way of feeling closer to her cousin.

She said little as we walked a block. Then she turned abruptly and skittered up the front steps of the neighborhood library. The building, on the register of historic places, had giant columns out front and a large vestibule with a curved ceiling engraved with Latin. I tried to read the inscription, but Libby pulled me through the ugly metal turnstiles. At the back of a large open reading room stood a bank of computers. Libby sat down and logged on as Anna.

"How do you know her logon and password?"

"We were cousins, stupid." She was making up for her weepy vulnerability earlier. "We shared everything. Well...almost everything." She sighed, and her shoulders drooped. "Ok, fine. I watched her when she didn't know I was looking."

Libby clicked on a browser where Anna had bookmarked her sites, tapping one called CTG. It linked to Chicago Thrill Girls, a website featuring pictures of girls snow skiing, swimming, and running. It looked like a site that would sell gear for outdoor sports, but it didn't sell anything, as far as I could tell.

"Are you sure this is where Anna spent her time?"

She rolled her eyes, then clicked a logon tab. A screen popped up, warning that only registered users could use the private portal. We looked at each other and grinned.

Libby typed in Anna's logon: ThrillGirl15 and her birth date, 9/9/92. Libby hovered the mouse over the OK button. Suddenly, Laila's and Harper's notations about the "T site" and Bethany's ThrillGirl29 email address made sense. They had all used this website.

I wondered if Anna's account had been dismantled since her death.

Libby clicked her mouse. The screen turned black, and a colorful swirling disk appeared. My heart sank. But then an image of a roller derby woman popped up. She was wearing a green hat turned backwards with a small Chicago flag sticking out of the brim. She had on shorts, a blue jersey, elbow and kneepads, and was crouched with one arm in a tackle stance. Then her lips opened and she said in an eerie, tough girl voice, "You want to dare me?"

I jumped back from the screen. "Fuck! That's freaking scary."

People glared at us, and a librarian shushed us.

Libby beamed. "Kind of cool, huh?"

"Yeah, but what is it?"

She moved the mouse around the girl's body, until the flag changed into a darker color, then she clicked and a page appeared with choices: Do. Dare. Vote. Compete. Libby moved her face next to the screen whispering the words out loud; I wondered whether she needed glasses. Then she looked at me for instruction.

"Go ahead. See what happens."

She clicked on "Do" and a list of Anna's completed dares appeared with photos she'd taken to prove her feats. Her adventures were listed chronologically. Libby moved the cursor over the first dare, "Meet strangers in the park," then looked at me for permission.

I nodded, fearing what we were about to see.

There was a picture of Libby and Anna with Lester and his boys. Libby stared at the screen as if she were seeing the image for the first time.

"Are you saying you knew nothing about this?"

Libby shook her head. "I swear."

She clicked the second dare, "Take pictures with a cop at a crime scene."

The photo was taken outside the Chinatown house the day they found Laila, Emily, and Harper. The dare listed the address where Anna was to go. I remembered her leaning into one of the crime scene officers as Libby shot the picture. So, she hadn't just happened to walk by on her way to get her tooth fixed after all.

The first dares seemed tame and innocuous. But the next dare was, "Do drugs with a stranger." She'd posted a photo of her and Lester standing in the woods, holding the crumpled tinfoil they'd used to cook brown sugar. She gave a detailed account of what had happened, including that "a woman reporter watched." She'd gotten dinged for not posting a photo of her smoking heroin.

It was as if everything Anna had done was based on dares. Had Anna befriended me in order to compete in this secret game? I thought back to all the times I'd been with Anna and counted only four instances in which she'd invited me—to the park, to the club, to their apartment before the drug dealer appeared, and lastly, to take her to the apartment building where she shot up. Scrolling through the list on the screen, I could see that all of those occasions involved specific dares and drugs. I remembered how I'd confronted her that night at the beach and demanded to know if she was playing me. She claimed she'd stopped, and I'd believed her. Now I felt stupid and used: a fifteen-year-old girl had manipulated me in a drug game.

"Was it all a lie—Anna wanting me to be around, to adopt her?"

Libby gave me an anguished look—corners of her eyes cinched, mouth soured into a half moon. It was the same grim expression she had worn since Anna's death.

"It wasn't like that," she whispered. "She liked you. She was always talking about you. Made me mad. She said you were *sisters*. Like *twin sisters*. But I was her *cousin*. I was the one who was *related*."

I tapped Libby's forearm. "*You* were her sister. She knew that. Believe me."

We stared at the bluish computer screen, not knowing what to say.

Libby moved the mouse over a recent dare, "Inject at a heroin house." I shook my head. We didn't need to be reminded of that horrific scene.

I told Libby to click on the "Compete" page. There, with gold stars beside her thumbnail picture, were all of Anna's dares and her ratings compared with other girls. All the girls had the same name, ThrillGirl, but were distinguished by a number beside their own tiny portraits. I looked for ThrillGirl29's list of complete dares. She had fewer than Anna, but she had higher ratings and more people voting for her. She was the Governor's daughter, after all. On each girl's "Compete" page, a line of colored badges reflected their levels of achievement. While some dares involved sex, most were drug-related. The site used the letters D.A.R.E., a parody of the government's anti-drug campaign.

Libby and I spent several hours sifting through the maze of links and challenges. Girls could dare other girls, rate other girls' dares, or post their own "adventures" on which girls could vote. Some of the comments on Anna's page were vociferous, criticizing her for being "a pussy" and "a scaredy bitch."

The girls were constantly prodding her to do more, to be more gutsy, to take more risks. Some called her a half-breed and made ugly comments about her mother being a gold-digger. It was hideous and animal-like how they clawed at each other. I had to look away, my head pounding under the sickly fluorescent light. I couldn't tell what felt worse—that Anna had hidden this ugly world from me or that she'd used me to compete in it.

"Are you okay?" Libby asked.

I closed my eyes. "Lib, why didn't you tell me?"

"I didn't know. I swear." Her voice cracked; she was close to tears. "She just said there were girls from her old neighborhood who had this website—a *secret website*. She made a big deal about that. She said it was a game and all the girls were doing it, and she had to do it. That's all I knew. She let me see the logon a few times because she thought the derby girl was cool." She swiped at her eyes with her shirt. "But I didn't know the website was about drugs. She didn't really talk about this stuff." She waved her hand toward the screen. "She was probably afraid I'd tell Daddy. She made me go read." She pointed to a nearby kids' corner with colorful beanbag chairs. "I just finished *Twilight*." She beamed.

I believed her. Unlike her cousin, Libby had no poker face.

Libby continued to click through the website. On one page, vices were ranked in the order of seriousness with corresponding monikers that signified levels of achievement. Cigarettes were at the lowest level. Girls who attained this level were called Nickies. The next level was marijuana and the girls were called Mary Janes. Then there were mushrooms (Shroomies), LSD (Hallies—for hallucinogens), butane (Flames), nitrous oxide (Hyenas). Prescription drugs were somewhere in the middle with various nicknames, then meth (Freaks), crack (Rockers), cocaine (Chalkers), heroin (Jesus Freaks).

At the top was fentanyl-laced heroin, or Poison. Girls who attained this level were called Poison Girls. And there were several. The only photos I immediately recognized were of Olivia, Madison, MacKenzie, Rory, and—Cate. Though she'd complained about her cousin doing Poison and criticized Olivia and the others, Cate eventually had joined them, too. That last dare, though, had claimed her life.

I felt a choking gloom. The computer light gave Libby's skin an unhealthy hue. She took her hand off the mouse and cupped it awkwardly over mine.

"We can stop."

I shook my head. "We have to keep going."

Anna had one outstanding dare to attain Poison Girl status. Several girls offered tips on how to obtain the drug. Most suggested going to a rave and telling the man with the blond dreads, "make me a vampire." For a hundred bucks, he'd take the girls to the South Side where a gangbanger would sell them a bag of Poison. "Dreads will show you how to do it," the post read.

What interest did Lester and Rapper X have in targeting white girls, and *these* particular white girls, whose parents had political ties? The only link I could think of was Mohammed X, who was not a fan of either the Hyde Park Senator's bid for the White House or the city's South Side land grab for the Olympics, which Olivia, Rory, and the Morrisey twins' fathers were leading. But I couldn't see Mohammed endorsing the murder of young girls, no matter what the cause. Someone else was directing these Poison hits.

I sorted through other girls' pages. There were several who were swiftly making their way to the top. A few girls were being taunted to do more. Among those who were lacking completed dares was a face I recognized from the fundraiser: Regina, the Senator's daughter.

• • •

Libby and I raced back to my apartment where we accessed the site from my laptop and printed copies of pages. I suppose I could have collected screen shots, but I was a print girl. I wanted to feel in my hands what I was now thinking of as "evidence." We spent the rest of the day methodically sifting through the website, noting the girls who were targets and those who were nearing their completion as Poison Girls. We made stacks in the living room, kitchen, and even piled them in the bathtub.

By late afternoon, Libby wanted to keep working, so I phoned Danny and asked if she could spend the night. At about three in the morning we called it a day. I covered the couch with sheets and gave Libby a T-shirt to sleep in. She cuddled with Deadline, petting her gently. I sat on the couch next to her.

"Why didn't you ever look up the Thrill Girl website on your own, especially after Anna died?" I tried not to sound accusative, but Libby's passive involvement didn't make sense, especially in light of her current determination.

She hung her head and hooded her eyes. "I was too afraid."

"But, Lib, Anna's killers are in jail."

"Not Anna's friends." Her eyes were wide with fear. "They're mean. I didn't want them coming after me."

"Why are you risking that now?"

She sat erect and pulled in her chin as if she were surprised by the question. "Because I'm with you. Daddy always said you were the bravest woman he knew. Anna said you weren't afraid of nothing. That's why she liked you."

"How am *I* brave? I got beat up by Lester and his boys. Your father had to save me. There's nothing heroic in that."

"But you came back. You went looking for Lester. You weren't afraid of *him*."

I leaned over and kissed her forehead, my chest swelling with happiness. The street light fell sharply across her face, highlighting her pug nose. I stroked the wispy baby hairs at her crown.

"Goodnight, Lib. Try to get some sleep."

"I don't want to sleep." She spoke in a faraway voice. "I just keep dreaming about that night, what happened. I can't get it out of my head." She stared at the ceiling as if recalling the events in her mind.

"There was so much blood. It sprayed in my eyes and my mouth. I could taste it. Blood was all over the backseat. I was sitting in it. My pants were soaked. I…" Her voice cracked.

"My God, Libby." I pressed my cheek to her face.

"I held her, you know. At the end. Until the firemen came. She was shaking for a while. I rolled her so I could see her other eye—the one that was still there. And I talked to her. I didn't know if she could hear me or if she was…gone. But then…I saw a tear running down her cheek. And I thought that, somehow, she was still alive. I wanted to believe she'd be okay, that she'd live. Then I looked down and realized, it was me. I was the one crying. Those were my tears falling on her face."

CHAPTER FORTY-SIX

August 22, 2008

POISON DEATHS INCREASE CRIME STATISTICS
HOMICIDE RATE HIGHEST IN NATION
Chicago Sentinel

I woke to the sound of clacking. When I crept into the living room, Libby was already at the computer.

"We're out of paper," she grumbled. "And ink."

"First coffee, then supplies." It was barely seven o'clock.

She tilted her head in disagreement, but let it go.

That morning we created flow charts to show how the girls had played their games. The pursuit energized us; we were building a trail of the leaders as well as the girls who were responsible for prodding Anna and others to their deaths.

I was impressed with Libby's tenacity. She was smart and analytically gifted, too. The matrix of the Thrill Girl website had intrigued her on a different level than it had me.

Libby's elaborate spreadsheets showed who was most active on the website and who was the most prolific in daring girls. The winner, hands down, was Olivia. Her entourage wasn't far behind, with Madison and MacKenzie bullying girls they thought weren't progressing through the levels fast enough. Cate never dared anyone, yet dutifully noted her "achievements," probably to get Olivia and the others off her back. Rory relentlessly taunted girls, pushing them to compete like their namesake. She seemed to view doing dangerous drugs as some sort of rite of passage.

By noon, Libby and I were starving. Libby borrowed an old pair of gym shorts that hung on her like culottes and a shirt that fell loosely around her waist. At a neighborhood diner, we ate heaping plates of pancakes and sausage. Libby looked happier than I'd seen her in weeks. We stopped at a thrift shop where she picked out a few pairs of jeans and several shirts. Maybe she'd stop wearing Anna's clothes. Then there was this other, secret thought, that maybe Danny wouldn't ask for her back, and I could just keep Libby. It was a silly fantasy, but one that made me giddy with happiness. When we got back to my apartment, I realized we hadn't mentioned Anna all day. It felt like such a relief.

Hours later, I had to pull Libby away from the computer. I'd promised her father she'd be home for dinner. We were in my car when my cell phone beeped, notifying me of a voicemail message.

"Miss Delaney." The man's voice sounded high-pitched and raspy on my phone speaker. "This is Joseph Spier. I'm the attorney for Kent Reid, Anna's father. Mr. Reid would like to meet with you to discuss his daughter. He knows this is unorthodox, but depending on the outcome of the meeting, he would consider dropping his lawsuit. Mr. Reid is on his way to Chicago. Please call me as soon as possible." He left the number of his downtown law firm.

"Do you know your uncle very well? Anna's father, I mean?"

Libby shook her head.

"I thought he was in prison."

Libby bit her lip. "That's what Anna said."

By the time we reached Libby's apartment, I felt sick. Libby made me lie on the couch, and dabbed my forehead with a cold cloth. She sat next to me rubbing my hand and humming a song under her breath. Her fingers on my face, the couch beneath me, her whispery singing tingling the hairs on my head—it all felt oddly familiar to the day her father had nursed me.

I must have dozed off. I woke sometime later in a cold sweat, unsure where I was. The light in the apartment had changed.

Outside, it was twilight, the sky a somber gray-brown. I looked around but didn't see Libby. Then I heard *him*, singing on the stairs.

He fumbled with his keys, then finally opened the door.

"Libby! Li-bee. Dad-dee is home." He was crouched low, walking slowly but unsteadily, weaving from side to side.

Libby came running from her bedroom and grabbed one arm. I grabbed the other and we pulled him to a kitchen chair.

"Had a little, Danny?"

"Oh, just a couple." He held his forefinger and thumb apart about an inch. Then his face erupted into a big grin, and he threw his arms around me. "Good to see you, Natalie."

I pulled back, the smell of whiskey overwhelming.

"I need to talk to you about Kent Reid." I sat at the table opposite him.

"Who?" he yelled.

"Your ex-brother-in-law? Did you know he's out of prison?"

"Did he go through the front gate or over the back fence?"

"He wants to meet with me." I stared at him hard, trying to will him sober.

"He's no good, Natalie. No good at all." He got up and stumbled around the kitchen, muttering to himself. "You can't trust no goddamn thing he says."

"You think he would hurt me?"

"He carried a gun. But he never did shoot anyone, not that I can say. He never beat Pam. And she'd tell me. He was just a lot of hot air. You know, talk, talk, talk." He mimed puppets with his hands. "He was always threatening, bragging, like some big gangster."

He stopped suddenly, and wiped his eyes. "He had a soft spot for Anna." His voice became whispery. "Loved that girl. Kind of spoiled her. Let her do anything she wanted. Probably why she turned out like she did. No, I just don't see any reason you'd want to meet up with that monster."

• • •

That night, I knocked on Sean's door.

"I've been contacted by the attorney for Anna's father. He says Kent Reid may be willing to drop the lawsuit if I meet with him." I handed Sean a scrap of a paper with the attorney's name and number.

Sean looked down at my spidery scrawl. "You'd be foolish to go near him."

CHAPTER FORTY-SEVEN

August 23 & 24, 2008

CHICAGO TIMES ANNOUNCES MORE LAYOFFS
CITY'S MAIN PAPER SUFFERING IN RECESSION
Chicago Sentinel

The next day Sean called and told me Anna's father, Kent Reid, had been released from prison into a federal witness protection program and had taken on a new identity. Reid's attorney refused to divulge what name Kent was going by and where he was living, but he said his client wanted to meet with me because he thought I could tell him about his daughter's final days. There was a peculiar twist to Reid's request: he wanted to meet at Anna's grave. U.S. Marshals would be nearby. Sean insisted it was a trap.

• • •

To say that Graceland is a cemetery is like saying the Sears Tower is just a Chicago skyscraper; Graceland is Chicago's most famous and storied burialground. Established in the mid-1800s and protected by miles of stone walls, Graceland is the final depository of politicians, governors, and entrepreneurs—Chicago's rich and famous. The fact that Anna's family had secured her a plot—space was limited—probably meant the Governor was involved.

The meeting was set for eight o'clock, just before the cemetery

closed, when there were fewer people. Sean argued about my agreeing to meet with Kent. He said I had nothing to gain by it. He'd
given the prosecuting attorney the polygraph results, which Sean
thought would get the charges dropped. After that, Kent Reid's
civil lawsuit was much less likely to be successful.

I insisted I had nothing to lose. Anna's father was suing me for
millions I didn't have. Besides, I thought Anna would have wanted
me to meet her father. Meeting at the grave was a bit macabre, but
apparently Kent was short on time and the U.S. Marshals felt the
cemetery would be easier to monitor.

When I arrived at the cemetery, Sean and Kent Reid's attorney, Joseph Spier, met me at the entrance and handed me a map
with an "x" marking Anna's grave.

"They'll drive you to the site," Spier said, pointing to an SUV
with tinted windows. "Kent will meet you there. When you're
done, the Marshals will bring you back here."

Sean stuffed what looked like a garage door opener in my
palm. "This is a panic button. If something doesn't feel right, press
it, and the U.S. Marshals will respond. I'll wait here."

Sean looked tense. I leaned over and whispered, "It's going to
be okay." But the strain in his face didn't relent.

A black Suburban pulled up, and the driver, a husky man with
a severe crew cut, barked out an open window, "Get in, and don't
look at the agents in the backseat, or I'll put a hood on your head."

I gave Sean a weak smile and jumped in the front seat. The
SUV lumbered along, passing rows of ornate grave markers. After
we'd rounded several bends, the driver pulled over.

"You know where you're going?"

"I'm fine." I stepped out of the truck and followed a trail
that the map showed would lead to Anna's grave. With my right
hand I felt in my pocket for the panic button. In my other hand,
I clutched a small bouquet of flowers, suddenly feeling silly for
bringing them. The path meandered through a wooded area that
opened to a small clearing dotted with headstones.

Grave marker 813 was at the end of a row, near a stand of

trees. No gravestone had been laid yet. Shoots of grass had sprouted in the fresh soil; an urn held withered flowers. I glanced around expectantly. Was Anna's spirit watching, hovering amid the trees? I couldn't shake the feeling that she was there somehow. I replaced the withered flowers with the fresh ones I'd brought. Bending over the urn, I heard a twig snap behind me.

"Nice ass," a gravelly voice said. He laughed, a cigarette smoker's rasp. "Get off your knees. You can stop praying for her. She's dead."

I turned and faced a stooped, potbellied man leaning on a cane. Though probably in his mid-forties, he looked much older. His iron-rust hair tinged with gray was sparse on top and knotted in a ponytail. He wore an army jacket that seemed much too large.

"I'm Natalie Delaney." I stood and held out my hand.

He ignored the gesture. "I know who you are or you wouldn't be here."

"So now that I'm here, what do you want?" I urged myself to be polite.

Kent plopped down on a marble headstone and rested his forearms on his cane. His puffy face was tanned, unshaven. A jagged scar descended from under his right eye to the right corner of his mouth.

"I wanted to meet the woman responsible for my daughter's death."

I took a step back. "Look, I don't blame you for being angry. But I didn't kill Anna. I hadn't seen her for several days when she died. I tried to get her to stop doing drugs."

"That's not what I hear." Kent grunted. "I understand you wanted to make a name for yourself by getting my daughter addicted."

"You've been listening to the wrong people, Mr. Reid."

"Why didn't you stop her? Why didn't you take away the heroin?" He talked as if he were speaking from a memorized script, his voice monotone, his inflections in the wrong places.

"Your daughter had her own ideas. She insisted on trying everything—even drugs that she knew might kill her."

Kent scratched his head and lowered his eyes. "How well did you know my Anna?" The edge in his voice faded.

"As well as anyone can know a teenage addict. I'm sorry she's dead. Even now I don't know what I could have done that would have made her quit."

"Why did you give her drugs?"

"Is that what the cops told you?" I scowled at him. He'd dragged me out to her grave so he could chastise me? "You're an ex-con. You should know what it's like to have the cops set you up for something you didn't do."

His scarred face softened. He looked at Anna's grave then fell to his knees. "I just want my baby back." He slammed his fist into the soft dirt. "I never got to see her before they put her in the ground."

I moved toward his crumpled form. "Please believe me. I tried to stop her."

Our knees touched in the dirt. His lower lip trembled and his eyes were tearing. I leaned into his chest and hugged him. Something poked me in the breast.

"What's this?" I touched his shirt and felt a nubby device.

Kent pulled back. "It's nothing." He turned his back and whispered into his chest.

"Are you wearing a wire?" I grabbed the sleeve of his jacket and swung him around. He was surprisingly fragile.

"They made me do it! They made me do it!" He shrieked and slapped his hands at me. "They said you were responsible!"

I slowly backed away from him, fishing in my pocket for the panic button.

"They lied. They know I had nothing to do with poisoned heroin. They're trying to frame me. And you're helping them."

I took off running, the plastic box in my hand. If I pressed it, who would respond? The U.S. Marshals or the Chicago police? Had the Chicago cops orchestrated this meeting?

The trees were thick in that part of the cemetery, and I tripped over a branch and fell, inadvertently setting off the panic button, its light glowing red. Car doors slammed. I got up and started running again, unsure of which direction I was moving. I headed toward the lights of the city, through a clearing and down another path. I could hear the swish of legs moving through grass behind me, then a man's heavy breathing.

"Stop! Natalie!" The voice sounded familiar.

I pushed harder, but he grew closer. His hands grabbed my shoulders and slammed me to the ground. We fell on a soft patch of grass, his body on top of mine. He pinned me facedown and twisted my arms behind my back as if he were going to handcuff me.

"What the fuck are you doing? Get off me!"

I flicked my shoulders. He let me roll onto my back. That's when I saw those familiar blue eyes and that boiling corona of hair. I lay there staring up in disbelief at Mo.

"Are you going to arrest me?"

"I can't let you leave. I have my orders." He was trying to catch his breath.

"Your orders, huh? Do you frame innocent people because your boss told you to do it? What happened to your honor, Mo?"

He shook his head. "I've got to do what *they* tell me."

I punched him in the leg. "You don't *gotta* do nothing."

Even in the dark I could read the shame on his face.

"What happened to your conscience, Mo? Did they take that, too? Did you forget that you're to 'serve and protect,' not 'frame and collect'? You're a fucking dirty cop now, Mo."

A car raced toward us and skidded to a stop, gravel flying. Sean jumped out. "Are you all right, Natalie? Did he hurt you?"

Sean kneeled and inspected my skinned face and torn jacket.

"I had to keep her from leaving," Mo said in his cop voice.

"Under what authority? She came here on her own volition, asshole. She's not under arrest. This wasn't part of the deal," Sean screamed.

Mo held up his hand. "I'm sorry, Natalie. I really am." Then he turned to Sean. "I'll let you sort it out with the state's attorney."

"I'll do that." Sean guided me toward the car.

Against my protests, Sean drove me to the emergency room. "This isn't so much about wiping your boo-boos. This is about documenting what he did to you, mounting a defense."

"I should have listened to you."

"You're goddamn right, you should have."

By the time the nurse cleaned my superficial cuts and bruises, it was nearly midnight. We rode home in silence. When the elevator stopped at our floor, he grabbed my arm.

"If you want to get out of this mess, you're going to have to start trusting your advisors—people who have your best interests at heart." He was still angry, his pride wounded.

"I don't want to live in fear. I can't let this change who I am."

"But, Natalie, it already has." He closed his door, leaving me alone in the hallway.

I unlocked my door only to be startled by Libby, quietly standing, like a statue, under the foyer's beam of yellow light, a look of shock and disbelief frozen on her face. I forgot I'd given her a key. The blackness in her eyes broadcast something dire.

"What's wrong, Libby?" I felt my heart pounding.

"They took down the site. It's not there anymore."

CHAPTER FORTY-EIGHT

August 24 & 25, 2008

INTERNATIONAL OLYMPICS
COMMITTEE VISITS CHICAGO

HEROIN EPIDEMIC HURTS CITY'S BID

Chicago Times

Libby fell asleep in my bed that night, snuggling up to me, smelling of strawberry shampoo. I wrapped my arms around her bony shoulders and held her like my mother used to hold me when I'd had a bad dream. I felt guilty for pulling Libby into what now seemed like a doomed pursuit. Why did I believe we could together solve a crime that had stumped dozens of police detectives?

We got up late the next morning, sluggishly moving around the apartment, picking up the piles of printouts and putting them in a box. We felt defeated. It was like the past forty-eight hours didn't exist, those days filled with a single-eyed pursuit, feeling we were avenging Anna's death. This time our despair felt heavier than ever.

That afternoon, before Sean came over to discuss my case, I gave Libby my iPod and sent her to my bedroom. I didn't want to worry her with the details of my legal situation.

"I'm afraid I have some bad news." He looked drained, his face pale and his eyes strained. "We wanted the state's attorney's office to make a decision in this case, and they have. They don't care that you passed a polygraph contesting the witness statements." Sean frowned, pinching the bridge of his nose. "Natalie, they're building a case for felony solicitation of a criminal enterprise."

I looked at him blankly.

"If convicted, it carries a twelve-year minimum sentence."

I shook my head in disbelief.

"It's an obscure law that normally is used to go after people who get kids to commit crimes. It's an orchestrated campaign to generate media coverage to smear you. They're trying to intimidate you to plead to a lesser, but still damaging, charge that would avoid a long and difficult trial."

"This is so overkill."

"That's not all—Kent Reid refuses to drop his lawsuit. He says you lied to him."

"I lied to *him*? He's the one who was wearing a fucking wire!"

My rant drew Libby out of the bedroom. "What's wrong?" Her eyes were wide with concern.

"It's nothing Libby, go back inside. I'm fine. I just got some upsetting news."

She slowly closed the door.

Sean whispered, "Who is that?"

"She's Anna's cousin. I'm just taking care of her for a few days."

"Are you out of your mind? The cops are saying you've had inappropriate influences over kids, and you've got a teenager staying at your house? Where does she sleep?"

I shook my head. "I'm not answering that."

"Well, you'll have to answer on the stand and the prosecuting attorney will make it look sullied. All he has to say is that you, a grown woman, were sharing a bed with a teenage girl—the cousin of the girl whose death you are accused of contributing to."

I felt numb. The thought of Libby leaving was unbearable. For once I didn't feel alone.

I briefly considered telling Sean about the Thrill Girl website. But he'd already chastised me about meeting with Kent and doing things my own way. I knew what would happen as soon as I showed him the printouts; he'd order me to stop poking around, then he'd hand everything to his own investigator to finish where I'd left off. No law firm investigator was more motivated than Libby and I to find the answers. Call it pride or a character defect, but reporters don't share information until they have a story wrapped up, an answer for every needling question an editor might ask. There were still too many unknowns: Who was pulling the strings on the website? What was their motive? And how were Mohammad X and Lester connected?

I admit I was prideful, but I wasn't stupid. I needed help—not from a law firm investigator who would take a week just to catch up to speed—but a real skilled digger, someone who could work quickly. It was time to call Julian. He had a lot more resources at his disposal—newspaper databases, access to state corporation records—as well as the guise of a journalist calling to inquire about a potential story.

• • •

Danny was carrying a box down the rickety back stairs when I pulled into the back lot at their apartment. His pickup truck was stuffed with used grocery store boxes and that ugly leopard-print chair. He smiled when he saw Libby in the front seat of my car, wearing an old pair of my sunglasses, her hair pulled back in a French braid I'd knotted that morning.

"Looks like you're moving."

"Yep, this is the last load. I was hoping to get it all done and then call you over to the new place."

Libby's smile faded. "You packed my stuff?"

"It's at our new apartment, hon." He threw an arm around her neck and pecked her on the cheek. "Wanted to surprise you."

Libby ducked under her father's arm and ran up the stairs.

"Thanks for taking her." He seemed embarrassed that he hadn't let me in on his secret. "I thought it would be easier if she wasn't around. Pam came over and boxed up Anna's stuff, too."

"Probably a good idea Lib wasn't here to see that. At least she

has some new outfits we bought for school. I was a little weirded
out when she wore Anna's clothes."

"That's not going to stop. Pam dropped off Anna's school uniforms. They're a little big, but she'll grow into them."

"School uniforms?"

He lowered his gaze. "Pam started a scholarship in Anna's
name at Queen of Angels." He'd been keeping more than the move
from me. "There wasn't enough time to—you know, put it in the
papers and stuff—so she gave the first one to Lib. It's only right to
give it to her cousin. Libby was Anna's best friend."

A nauseating dread ricocheted through me at the mention
of Queen of Angels. It seemed morbid that Libby would follow
in Anna's footsteps, attending the same school, even wearing her
clothes, as if she were a replacement child. A part of me feared
she'd fall in with the same clique as Anna had, or worse, the same
girls would go after Libby.

"Where's the new place? When can I come see it?"

He wiped his forehead with the back of a callused hand. "You
want to come now? It's in Rogers Park. I want Libby to walk to school."

"Sweet." I wondered if they would be neighbors with
Mrs. Wozniak.

"Listen, I'm sorry about the way you saw me the other day."
His voice turned soft. "I swear I don't do that a lot. You know,
Anna's death has been rough on all of us. I know all this legal shit
has got to be hard on you too. How are you holding up?"

"Libby's been a great help. You were right about your former
brother-in-law."

He snorted a laugh. "A real asshole, that one."

"Yeah, he's not giving up the lawsuit. I'm sure he'll subpoena
you to testify."

"I'm not saying shit for that guy. Even Pam wants no part of
his lawsuit."

"I thought she hated me?"

"She didn't like that you printed everything that Anna did.
That hurt *her reputation*. But she knows Anna's doing drugs was
not your fault."

"Good to know."

"I'm just glad Libby's taken a liking to you."

He grabbed my hand. The nerve endings in my fingers flashed, like an electrical shock.

"You and me, we're different. You don't judge me like most city gals do. I just…it's good that Libby has a girl in her life. I… mean a woman. Her mother pretty much won't have anything to do with her. But you, well, *we* like you. I don't want you to stop coming around Lib because we didn't work out."

Libby came thumping down the stairs. Danny and I stepped back from each other. "Everything's gone," she whined.

"I know, hon." Danny ruffled her hair. "It's at the new place. You'll like it. Now, get in." He pointed to the truck. "So we can go *home*."

Pouting, Libby got in the truck and shut the door without even saying goodbye. I tilted my head at Danny as if to say "oh well" and waved. I started my car and was about to back out when Libby came running toward me.

"I want you to have this." She stuck her arm through the open window, handing me a silver necklace. "I think you need it more than I do."

I looked at the tiny Confirmation cross in my palm.

"I had it on when Anna got shot. It protected me. Now it'll protect you."

"No, Lib…" When I tried to give it back, she stepped away.

"I heard what that man said—your lawyer." Her voice was resolute. "You're gonna go to prison for twelve years." She stared at me insolently, the sides of her sandals digging in the gravel, her arms folded against her chest. "I don't want you to go away. I'm gonna make those girls confess what they did to Anna."

Libby's blood-deep allegiance had shifted from Anna to me. Before I could object further, she ran back to the truck. I sat there, moved by her determination and affection. Now I wish I'd paid more attention. When a fifteen-year-old gives you her Confirmation cross and says she's going after a clique of mean girls, alarm bells should go off in your head.

CHAPTER FORTY-NINE

August 27, 2008

PRESIDENTIAL DEBATES FOCUS
ON CITY'S POISON DEATHS

HYDE PARK SENATOR RUFFLED BY ATTACKS

Chicago Times

Two days later, I was mindlessly rubbing the Confirmation cross between my fingers as I walked through my apartment building's dark-paneled lobby. Something fluttered in the shadows, startling me. When my eyes adjusted to the dark, I saw Julian, seated in a chair thumbing through the newspaper. I'd forgotten he'd said he might stop by. He must have discovered something substantial.

My apartment was stuffy, so we moved to the balcony, sipping beer while we watched the horizon glow orange, then pink as the afternoon merged into evening. Though we were no longer colleagues, Julian entertained me with newsroom gossip—details of Amy's latest debacle, who was sleeping with whom, and who had been let go in another round of layoffs. The newsroom was like a strange, eccentric family I'd been adopted into, and without it I felt like an orphan. Julian could see the misery in my face.

"It's not as exciting as you remember." The energy in his voice dropped. "Not too many gutsy reporters like you left." He cleared his throat and his face turned serious. "I looked into that company—Extreme Sports. It's real, all right, a division of Byrne Pharmaceuticals."

"Oliver Byrne, one of the richest men in Chicago—the man leading the city's Olympic bid—is behind the Thrill Girl website?"

"Oliver doesn't run the company anymore," he said, in that know-it-all tone that had hindered his standing in the newsroom. "Hasn't in years. His children run the company. The Extreme Sports division is a relatively new venture that deals with vitamins and health supplements. This new generation wants to move away from the expensive business of developing and marketing prescription medical drugs to selling more natural products that don't draw government oversight. The website you referred to was a beta site that his granddaughter had been testing for a few months, an experiment with social media to see how she could generate buzz about products."

"I spent hours on that website. There were no 'products.' It was a front for bullying girls to do drugs. How could it be part of a legitimate company?" I'd given Julian only basic details. "What's their explanation for suddenly taking the site down?"

"The spokeswoman said the granddaughter decided she'd gathered enough data. The site was intended to be exclusive, kind of like Facebook was early on. Girls had to be invited to join. Only three hundred were included. The spokeswoman emphasized that it was a private website, a place where girls could chat."

I retrieved the box of printouts and handed a few pages to Julian. "Does this look like innocent *chatting*?"

He squinted at the text in his hand, reading and turning pages with his mouth open, shaking his head. "This is pretty inflammatory stuff. They were provoking her."

"She's not the only one. There are others." I hesitated revealing that they'd even targeted the Senator's daughter. "How many of their members are dead?"

"Good question. I asked for the list of invitees. The company wouldn't give it to me, citing privacy and proprietary reasons." He leafed through the stack of printouts I'd handed him. "So what are you going to do?"

I squirmed in my chair. I still wasn't convinced Julian wasn't informing on me to the paper. My hesitation must have belied my suspicion.

He gave me a wilted look. "You still don't trust me, do you?" He handed me the printouts and his notes about the website's company. "I've got to get home."

I walked him to the door. We stood awkwardly. I was unsure what to say. I needed an ally, but I was beginning to question my own judge of character.

"By the way, I'm throwing a Labor Day party. Nothing fancy, just neighbors and a few friendly faces from the newsroom. You should come." The invite sounded like an afterthought, but we both knew it was payback for the time he'd invested. An invite to a work party was more burden than pleasure, and I owed him. "Besides," he said, "you need to get out of your…lair of paranoia."

CHAPTER FIFTY

Labor Day, September 1, 2008

POLICE ARREST MORE HEROIN DEALERS

ADDITIONAL INDICTMENTS PENDING

Chicago Times

Julian's house in Oak Park was easy to find: a blue and white Victorian with Santana blasting from the backyard. The front door stood open, and people came and went without knocking. I passed clumps of people camped out in the living room. Several young faces belonged to Julian's business reporting staff, which regarded him as a rockstar. Trailing the sound of his deep voice, I found him in the kitchen talking with neighbors.

"Hey there." I handed him a liter of expensive German beer.

He plopped the glass bottle into a cooler, not even reading the label, and dug out a couple of cans from the ice. "This okay?" He held out an MGD.

I politely sipped while listening to Julian's middle-aged neighbors discuss their house-maintenance issues. A high-pitched screeching from outside interrupted the conversation.

"What's that noise?"

"Oh…that." Julian blinked, then laughed knowingly from the side of his mouth. "Amy…"

"Amy is here?" I felt my chest tighten. She was the last person I wanted to see. "I thought you only invited a few reporters?"

"She lives a few blocks away. She just showed up. It was pretty hard to keep her out." He stared at his scuffed-up sneakers.

I started to walk out. He grabbed my arm. "Don't go. Please? She's drunk, and she's in the hot tub. I guess she wanted to show off her *Playboy* body." He winked.

I had to smile. I'd forgotten I'd told him about that scene in Amy's office. Our secret.

I followed her shrill laughter out to the patio. People were sprawled around the deck that encircled the tub. Several were dangling their feet in the bubbling water. Amy was in the middle of the hot tub, her bikini barely covering her breasts. A bald man with a pregnant gut groped at her. There was nothing I could say to her that would have made me feel better than seeing her in her pathetic drunkenness. For a moment I even pitied her.

Rising above the din was a familiar, lush voice. I stepped off the patio and onto the grass where people had crowded around a bonfire. Sparks flew up in the darkness lighting their faces. His was red from the fire and the wine he drank from a bulbous glass. I threw my arms around his neck before he had a chance to recognize me.

"Ben, Ben, oh my God, Ben. So good to see you. How are you?"

He pulled back and stared into my face as if he were searching for some new distinguishing feature. "Well, my Lord, aren't you a sight for sore eyes. Look at you, just as lovely as ever." He held up my hands by the ends of my fingers, as if we were about to sashay at some formal dance. "I can't say I'm surprised to see you. I was hoping that Mr. Ethnic Pants would finally find the nerve to ask you out."

I swatted the air between us. "We're *just friends*, Ben."

"Friends, my hairy little ass. That man looked at you in the newsroom with *intentions*."

"So, how's *Bon Appetit*?" Julian had told me that Ben had become the magazine's Midwest correspondent. "Guess you're not eating tuna from a can and watching soap operas after all?"

"I see what you're doing." He pointed at me with a gnarly

forefinger. "I don't get to work with anyone quite as exquisite as you, but yes, it's *lovely*. Besides, I get to travel the flat states eating in the best restaurants and interviewing the most *divine* chefs. What could be better than that?" He winked, and I knew by the exaggerated tone of his voice that he missed the newsroom as much as I did. "The question, dear, is how are *you*?"

I shrugged. "Trying to deal with this ridiculous police investigation and lawsuit."

He leaned into my ear. "From what I hear, dear, they may not be the only people coming after you. You're making some people in high places very uncomfortable."

"What? What are you talking about?" Anxiety rippled through my body.

"Oh, damn. I shouldn't drink so much." He looked unhinged, rubbing his hand over his bare head. He caressed my arm. "Dear, forgive me. It's a party. Let's not talk business." He pantomimed a phone to his ear. "Give me a ring and let's have lunch, a *real lunch*, my treat." He forced a smile but a shadow hung over his face. He knew something.

I moved through the yard, careening, my ears hot, my stomach queasy. Terror spread through me. I was searching for a bush, some kind of tall greenery behind which I could vomit, when I felt a reassuring hand on my arm.

"We're filling up the dance floor. You want to join?" Julian's voice was enthusiastic.

"Nah. Think I'll stay out here for a while."

"You have to put on your happy face, Natalie," he whispered. "It's a party."

"I shouldn't have come."

He held out his hand. "No one's unhappy while they're dancing."

I was stunned Julian was touching me, clasping his warm fingers into my own. We entered the back door and climbed down a narrow flight of stairs and into a low-ceilinged basement. The air smelled like burnt leaves; someone was smoking a joint. Julian pulled me past the shadowed faces. A blue light gave the room a dreamy underwater mood. In a back room, under a cerulean glow, people gyrated to disco music.

I stopped. "I can't dance to that."

"Yes, you can." Julian pulled me to the center of the room.

People were kicking up their feet, elbows flying, heads wobbling, mouths slack, hands waving in the air. The vibrations pounded my eardrums, disorienting me amid the heat and the darkness. Julian seemed different in his jeans and crew neck T-shirt, less pensive. He moved his hips and slung his head back. I closed my eyes and let my body bend to his. It was like the gravity of life had finally released its pull.

When a slow song came on, we all stopped and looked around with shocked faces, as if we'd just awakened. I started to walk away. Julian tugged at my shirt.

"After this song?" He pulled me close and wrapped his arms around me. We moved slowly. I buried my face into the hollow of his neck. He was drenched with sweat, yet he smelled sweet, musky, like…a man after sex.

Julian caressed my back, then mumbled: "Oh, baby. I want to hold you all night long."

I giggled and pulled back. "What did you say?"

He shook his head and smiled sheepishly. "Nothing."

We danced several more songs, then went outside to cool off. Sitting on a concrete bench in his backyard, feeling the cool, soon-to-be autumn air, the music still vibrating in our bodies, I felt an excitement stir within me, an aching attraction to this man next to me. I hadn't even noticed Julian as a *man*—until that night. He'd always been an *editor*, an androgynous being, in my mind. But there was no denying how my body tingled beside him. Was he thinking of me, too?

"You want to go again?" He slapped my thigh.

"I'm beat." I knew if we kept dancing, people would notice—if they hadn't already.

"You're probably right. I should get back to my other guests." He gazed at me for a moment too long. "I'll walk you to your car."

We walked in silence under the sway of old oak trees; the moon shined through silver branches. Julian's profile was sharp in the streetlights. Over his shoulders I could see partygoers spilling onto his front lawn.

"I had a great time tonight." I pulled out my car keys and opened my trunk. I handed him a box of printouts and other materials for safekeeping. "I want you have this, just in case…"

He laughed, a self-conscious titter. "Does this mean you trust me now?"

"It means whatever you want it to." What he didn't know was that I'd spent the day making several sets, including one for Sean, who was out of town on a case.

He looked around with a vague, unfocused urgency, shifting his weight, running his fingers through his hair. Then he bent down and whispered in my ear.

"I'd really like to see you again."

It might have been what I wanted to hear, but since my encounter with Ben, I couldn't shake this gloomy feeling. I was facing prison, and the last thing I needed was a man with two kids trying to woo me.

I forced a smile. "Maybe."

CHAPTER FIFTY-ONE

September 1–3, 2008

POLICE BRACING FOR HEROIN DEATHS OVER HOLIDAY WEEKEND

MORE PATROLS ADDED FOR FIRST DAY OF SCHOOL

Chicago Sentinel

I was heading back to my apartment, turning over in my mind what Ben had said, when my cell phone buzzed.

It was Danny, his voice strained and weepy—reminiscent of the day he'd called to tell me Anna was dead. "It's Libby. She's gone."

"Gone? Gone, where?" I could barely get the words out. It didn't make sense.

"She left a note saying she was going to track down the Poison Girls. Do you know what she's talking about?"

"Oh, shit."

• • •

Danny and I spent the night driving around in his truck, at one point staking out the Byrne estate in Wilmette. I couldn't shake the feeling something horrible had happened to Libby. Danny seemed to be in shock too: his eyes glassy, his muscular fingers clutching one cigarette after another. I bragged about Libby, how together we'd discovered Anna's secret world online where girls were taunting her. I thought he'd be mad at me for involving Libby, but he just stared out the windshield with a dazed, disoriented expression. When he finally spoke, his voice sounded watery as if he were swallowing his tears.

"I shouldn't've moved her so soon." He had pouches under his eyes. "I shouldn't've let Pam come take Anna's things. We should've stayed put. She hates her new school. She hates me."

I clapped my hand on his shoulder. "She's a teenager. It's her role in life to complain."

It was still dark when he pulled up at my condo building early the next morning. I didn't move to get out. We sat quietly for a long time, watching the skyline of the city, the horizon getting lighter.

"I didn't realize how serious she was when she said she was going to find the girls who taunted Anna. I should have told you."

Danny put his hand over mine. "Don't go beating yourself up. You ain't her mother."

"No, I *ain't*." The hurt was evident in my voice.

"Jesus, I didn't mean it like *that*."

"Well, just how the hell did you mean it?"

"She's not your *responsibility*. That's what I mean."

"Maybe I wish she were my responsibility. Then again, it's a damn good thing she's not. I just keep fucking it up." I slammed my fist against the dashboard.

"Whoa…" Danny grabbed my hand. I sobbed into his neck.

• • •

For the next two days, I huddled in my apartment near my landline and cell phone. I was afraid to leave, thinking Libby might turn up at any time rather than going home to her dad. Libby was now officially a missing teenager, her face plastered all over television, in the newspapers and on digital billboards next to the city's expressways. I was in agony, blaming myself for again recklessly endangering another child. When the phone rang late one afternoon, I had hoped it was Libby, but it was Sean, who I hadn't heard from in days.

"I just heard back from the state's attorney."

"And?"

"It's complicated. I'm at the courthouse. I'll be over in a few minutes."

I hated it when he wouldn't tell me what he knew. I opened a bottle of wine and poured a glass and then another while I waited.

An hour later, Sean showed up. "Any word from Libby?"

I shook my head grimly.

"Okay. It's like this: The cops are pushing for an arrest. They're now saying they have evidence to link you to other deaths besides Anna's—heroin deaths. The state's attorney is up against a wall. I mean, these are his star detectives—homicide cops. And they want you charged. They are pulling in all chits."

"They've already charged Lester and the Mickeys for the fentanyl murders. How can they charge me?"

"Lester's made a deal. He's going to testify that you were the one who got Anna addicted and the one who provided heroin to the other girls."

I stood up, woozy from the wine, and began circling the living room. "Those homicide guys don't believe Lester for a minute. They just want to pressure me until I cop a plea. Why is the state's attorney going along with this?"

Sean shook his head. "He doesn't have much choice. He says they have strong evidence—not just the flimsy witness statements—that he's presenting to the grand jury."

"But what 'evidence' could they possibly have?"

He shrugged. "He's given me a heads-up that unless we can come up with something—and he's not even sure what that something is—the jury is likely to return an indictment. Don't worry. We're not doing the 'cuff and stuff' routine. We'll arrange for you to turn yourself in. He's promised me that much."

I couldn't feel my hands or legs. My life as I had imagined it had just suffered its final blow. I grabbed the wine bottle and began chugging. Crimson liquid ran down my chin, seeped into my shirt, and spread across my chest like a Rorschach test.

Sean took the bottle. "Natalie, we're going to get through this. You can't fall apart now. We have to find something to counter what they are saying."

If the polygraph didn't matter to the state's attorney, why would printouts of a website that didn't exist anymore? Still, it was the only thing I had to offer. I pulled the box from under my desk and handed him the corporation documents Julian had given me.

"How's this for *something?*"

He slowly read one printout after another. "What is this?"

"Proof that the girls were being goaded to their deaths."

"Wow." He grinned. "This could be our Hail Mary."

I don't remember Sean leaving, but at some point I looked up, and the apartment was empty. I sat in the dark, listening to the lonely sounds of the city. I couldn't shake this sense of doom. I felt dead, as dead as Anna. And then I thought of what I'd been avoiding all day: Libby might be dead, too.

CHAPTER FIFTY-TWO

September 4, 2008

COUSIN OF DEAD GIRL GOES MISSING

LEAVES NOTE THAT SHE'S LOOKING FOR POISON KILLER

Chicago Sentinel

It had been four days since Libby vanished. I had hardly slept. I kept wondering which girl Libby would track down first. I guessed Rory, since she was the one who had driven the car the night Anna was shot.

Rory's father lived in Kenilworth, one of the most exclusive gated communities in the United States, just north of Chicago along Lake Michigan. Established by Joseph Sears as a restricted, non-Jewish community, the suburb held the distinction as one of the whitest places in the country. The average home cost over a million dollars. And with only 2,500 residents, practically everyone who lived there was someone of note—celebrities, tycoons, and politicians—including the Kennans.

I wasn't sure how I was going to get in. Kenilworth was a fortress. When I arrived at the security gate, I handed the guard Rory's address I'd gotten from online property records. He disappeared into his station, presumably to call Rory, and a few minutes later, to my surprise, the gate went up. I drove the wide parkway that ran parallel to the lake, intersecting wide sweeping lawns and monstrous homes, half-expecting Jay Gatsby to step out on a stone balcony and wave.

Rory's house looked like the White House. The person who answered the front door said that Rory was in the coach house. It was a steamy September afternoon. A wavy haze of heat outlined everything. On the other side of an azure blue pool stood a two-story white coach house, a miniature version of the main.

I ascended the round portico, but before I could knock, Rory opened the door.

"You lost? Or just curious to see how the one percent live?"

Her eyes gave me a quick appraisal. I hadn't showered, and my hair was pulled back in a ponytail, puckered in places. My face felt puffy from the bottle of wine I had drunk the night before. Rory was wearing gym shorts and a white, sleeveless T-shirt without a bra. Her dark nipples poked at her shirt. Her face was devoid of makeup. Her tongue worried at a lip ring curled on the corner of her mouth. Still, she had that smell of wealth—expensive lotions and soaps and the hint of a day-old spritz of perfume.

"Nice place. Impressive actually."

"I'll be sure to tell the architect. Oh, right. It was Daniel Burnham. He's dead." She was referring to the legendary architect who'd designed much of Chicago.

"There seem to be a lot of dead people surrounding you these days."

"Is that an accusation?" She leaned against the doorjamb.

"Why don't you show me some of your blue-blood hospitality and invite me inside?"

She swung her arm wide like Vanna White on the *Wheel of Fortune.*

The expansive front room had high ceilings and elaborate wainscoting. The walls were decorated with collectable Americana—images of bonneted women and men in long, tailored coats and top hats. Even without her smeared eyeliner, Rory looked incongruous amid the relics.

She sat down on a narrow loveseat and leaned toward a coffee table that had several white lines of what looked like heroin.

I took an adjacent chair. "Am I interrupting something?"

"Depends. What's the house call for?"

"Anna's cousin Libby is missing." I tried not to choke on the words. "She left a note saying she was going to find the Poison Girls."

Rory pulled out a cigarette from a pack on the table and lit it. "And this is supposed to mean something to me?"

"You don't need to pretend anymore. I know what you, Olivia, and the twins have been doing on your little website—taunting girls. You acted like the little vampires disgusted you, but all along you were part of them. Why?"

She studied me in that pensive way Mo did when he was debating what to tell me.

"It was all a game," she said, as if that explained everything. "Something to distract us from the boredom."

"A game? Just a game?" My tone was mocking, cynical. "Sixty-some girls died because of *your game*. How do you begin to justify that?"

She looked at me blankly. "Politics is a blood sport. These girls have grown up knowing the risks."

"And just how did you come up with *this game*?" I tried to hide my shock that Rory was admitting anything.

Rory looked out the window. The air felt tense, charged, as if a late summer thunderstorm were about to explode.

"One night," she began in a faraway voice, "at a fundraiser, we were bored out of our minds. Olivia and I started throwing ideas around about a game we could all play. We called it the Ultimate Vampire Contest. We invited the people we knew, people who wouldn't talk, *ever*, who wouldn't go to the police, whose families wouldn't want the world to know their precious daughters were doing drugs or shoplifting or fucking their friends' fathers. Yeah, I know you're judging me now. I can see it on your face. That's because you just don't get it. You don't get *us*."

"What's to get? You are fucking pathological."

She shrugged. "And maybe it's just a Darwinian sport. The

people who should survive, do. The others who are too stupid, well, you know what they say—survival of the fittest."

"Your friend Cate, she *deserved* to die?" There was a bitter taste on my tongue.

"Collateral damage," she said with a cool disregard. "It happens, even to the best warriors. Yeah, I was sad. But she knew the risks."

I blinked. "Wow. I don't even know what to say. Why are you telling me all this?"

She laughed sharply. "You still haven't figured it out, have you? You were just as much a part of the game as anyone else. You just didn't know it. And *that* made the game *so much better*. Even now, just talking to you is such a *rush*." She closed her eyes and fluttered her lashes.

A cold panic hit me. "I thought I creeped you out."

She crowed. "Is that what Anna told you? She was always trying to protect you, keep you away from us—the same as that half-wit cousin of hers. From the moment we read on her dare page how you'd watched her smoke heroin in the park, we wanted to make you part of the game. We told Anna to involve you, and she did, until she figured out *why* we really wanted you. You thought Anna was your friend, that she was telling you what you wanted to know because you were such a great reporter?" She grunted. "Did it ever occur to you to ask her *why* she was letting you hang around?"

"I don't get it. How was I involved?"

She stared at me, her eyes teeming with a vast secrecy.

"You don't cook much, do you?" Her hushed voice sounded creepy.

"Why are you asking?"

"Why didn't you ever report that break-in at your apartment?"

"How do you know about that?"

She smiled. "I was betting that no matter what, you—or the police—wouldn't look in your oven. A woman like you—a professional, with no kids and no husband and no boyfriend that I can see—probably didn't cook at all. Am I right?"

"What's that got to do with anything?" I squeezed my eyes shut, suddenly exhausted.

"Well, let's just say *hypothetically*, that someone could have broken into your place and stashed a brick of Poison in your oven. You never would have noticed, being such a feminist and all. I'll bet you've never even turned your oven on."

I felt a sharp pain in my side; the heaviness of what she said tugged at me.

"It was you? You set me up? All this time I thought it was the cops."

"The cops? You mean those idiots who've been chasing anonymous tips, taking witness statements saying that you provided heroin to girls?" She made a horrific sound. "It's amazing how little money it takes for someone to lie, how easy it is to destroy someone's reputation."

"So Lester and Rapper X? How were they involved?"

"They didn't choose us, *we* chose *them*. They're drug dealers. They wanted to make money. Rapper said he could get us any drug we wanted."

"So Mohammed X wasn't targeting the girls because of their parents' political contributions?"

Rory squinted at me. "Who the hell is Mohammed X? You act like we were the only ones buying heroin. There were lots of people dying of Poison that had nothing to do with us. We were just the only ones whose deaths got any attention. You should know, you're the one who focused on the white girls and ignored everyone else."

Her last point felt like a shot in my gut. She was right. The only deaths the paper cared about were the white girls', which were a fraction of those who'd died of Poison.

"So, what's the point of taking *me* down?" I could hear the despair in my voice.

She frowned, disappointed I wasn't keeping up. "The game wasn't only about getting girls to do drugs, but to have someone to take the fall. You think the cops are going to look at the daughters of political donors when they have gangbangers—and now a reporter they hate?" She shook her head. "Not likely."

"I admit it wasn't all skill," she continued. "We lucked out, in so many ways. I thought we'd have to expose you immediately after you discovered that Bethany had survived. What you didn't figure out—which disappointed me, *by the way*—was that Olivia pushed Bethany to do Poison so she could get her out of the way. She wanted Rex, and Bethany wouldn't give him up. Then we thought you were going to out Rex as the Heroin Superhero… and we couldn't let you ruin Rex's reputation. But you were fired, and we thought that was the end. Then someone started crawling around our website as if they were the ghosts of Anna and Harper. We assumed it was you and knew we really had to get rid of you then. You showing up here is completely off script, but has made things so much easier." She tapped her cell phone and held up the screen to show me a photo of cops outside a building. "Take a closer look. The picture was taken five minutes ago." Her cheeks were flushed with excitement.

I stared at the screen, then swallowed hard, realizing they were outside my apartment building.

"But the Thrill Girl website? It was all there."

"Washed." Her tone was spiteful. "No one will ever find a trail. And why would they believe *you*? You're a drug dealer, according to all those kids."

I felt cornered, sick with the thought that the police now had hard evidence that would link me to the Poison deaths. Something inside me snapped. I lunged at her, squeezing her neck, the blue wings of her butterfly tattoo squishing in my fingers.

"What did you do with Libby?"

"Haven't…touched…her," she squeaked, grinning with a feverish pleasure.

I tightened my hands. I wanted to choke her to death. I could taste the anger in my mouth, burning my tongue. She kneed me in the stomach. I fell backwards on the coffee table, scattering her white lines.

"I swear, if Libby is hurt in any way…"

She rubbed at her neck, her butterfly now red with my finger-prints. "Don't make threats you can't keep. You don't have what it takes to kill me."

I glared at her, knowing what she said was true. "I still don't get it. Why'd you tell me?"

She snorted. "It's no fun beating someone if they don't know they lost. Besides, I wanted to see your face when you realized your precious Anna was playing you all along. You're cooked, sister. Doesn't matter what I tell you. Doesn't matter what you know. You can't prove it. You're going to prison for a long, long time. I wanted to make sure you thought of me every day."

CHAPTER FIFTYTHREE

September 5, 2008

COUSIN OF MURDER VICTIM STILL MISSING

FAMILY FEARS FOUL PLAY

Chicago Times

I'm not sure what made me convinced Mo wouldn't turn me in, but I wanted to believe I hadn't completely misjudged his character. We agreed to meet in the parking lot of Belmont Harbor, where he was on a stakeout. He told me to look for a black, vintage Mustang with tinted windows and white racing stripes. The car was parked under a tree near the harbor. I rapped on the passenger window. He unlocked the door.

"Nice undercover car." I slid into a bucket seat.

The inside reeked of alcohol, Mo's aftershave, and his blunt cigars. He looked thinner. There were creases under his eyes and around his mouth.

"How the hell, girl, did we wind up here?"

I shrugged.

He was sipping from a thermos cup that smelled of bourbon. "Nightcap?" He held out a Styrofoam cup.

I shook my head. I was queasy enough from my conversation with Rory. I needed to be sober to figure out what to do next. I couldn't go home; cops had surrounded my building. I was hoping Mo would help me find a way out.

We looked out at the white sailboats rocking in their slips only a few yards away. The sky was clear and dark enough to show off a few stars.

"So why'd you agree to meet me?" I asked.

"I figured I owed it to you after Graceland." He leaned over and inspected my cheek. "Looks like your face healed up pretty good."

"Jesus, that was a weird scene. Never expected you to try to arrest me."

"Live long enough, and you'll see a lot of stuff you never expected."

"You mean like the cops finding Poison in my oven?"

He forced a laugh. "So you know about that?"

"Yeah, your anonymous tipster put it there when she broke into my apartment."

"*She*, huh?"

"Mo, I'm being set up. I thought it was Nickles and his guys dishing out payback for the snitch articles. Now I know you guys have been following what looks like legitimate leads planted by someone else."

Mo wasn't interested in talking about my predicament just yet. "Where did you get off calling *me* a 'dirty cop' at Graceland?" He jabbed his finger at me. "Who the hell are *you* to be judging *me*? That was low, that was real low, Nat. It was your expense account that fucked me, by the way. Now I owe my job and my soul to Nickles. I'm just hanging in long enough to retire in two years with a twenty-year service pension."

We let out frustrated sighs. This was going to be harder than I thought. We were both still angry.

"Look." I shifted in the leather seat. "I tried to warn you about the expenses. I paged you. You never called back."

He leaned toward me so forcefully I thought he was going to punch me. I jerked back.

"Jesus, Nat, since when did you become so twitchy?"

"Since men—including you—keep beating me up."

"I said I'm sorry about that. What can I do to make it up to you?" He put his hand gently on my shoulder, like we were on a date, and I realized we'd never been in a car together. We'd always met in dark bars, sitting across from each other, smoking and drinking, kvetching about our jobs. But here, we were like two teenagers having a spat at a drive-in movie.

"I'm in a lot of trouble, Mo."

"Trouble ain't the word for it, girl. You're in a world of hurt. And there's nothing I can do. I want you to know that I'm not part of it. At all."

A boat horn blared. We watched as it sailed through the marina gates, then disappeared into the blackness.

"How can I get out of this?"

A shadow cut across his face as he leaned back. The leather beneath him rubbed against his jeans, a noise that reminded me of making out in parked cars with Jake. For a desperate moment, the thought of Jake made me feel less alone. But I shivered with the realization that I was more alone than I'd ever been. I couldn't even go home to my cat.

Mo pulled out a pack of cigars, cracked his window, and offered me one. I wrinkled my nose.

"It's hard to say." He exhaled smoke and pulled a piece of tobacco from his lower lip.

"Do you believe me?"

He cocked his head. "Do I think you gave poisoned heroin to white girls to make a name for yourself? No. But then again, I know you. Nickles doesn't. And what he does know about you, he doesn't like."

Mo held his hand to his chest as if he could feel my pain. "Natalie, it's in their interest to not question the evidence. To tell you the truth, I think Nickles believes it. He blames you for that girl's death. Besides, you sure did make us look like a bunch of asses."

"You guys did that all on your own when you fucked up the case. You shouldn't have arrested the Mickey Cobras and then ignored every piece of evidence that pointed to someone else as the Poison killer." I was unsure what Mo and I could ever agree on.

"There's a lot you don't know, Natalie. I've saved *your ass*. A lot over the years. This time I couldn't. I tried to warn you. I told you this involved the Mayor, the Governor, the FBI. Ever since the Dead Angels, we've known that someone was targeting kids of political donors. We warned wealthy Democrats, but that didn't stop the deaths. And just so you know, Lester was a puppet. We can only connect him to the Angels' deaths. And that's all he'll cop to."

"Who was running Lester?"

Mo pulled a pair of binoculars from beneath his seat. A large sailboat turned into the canal and was slowly making its way through the no-wake zone. Mo turned up the volume on a hand-held radio on the console, and it began to crackle.

"I want to see if this is my guy."

We listened to men talk on the radio in what sounded like code. After a few minutes Mo seemed convinced the men were genuine sailors and sat back, looking even more tired.

"Who was controlling Lester?" I pressed again.

He smoothed his mustache, considering what he was willing to share. "The Mickey Cobras manufactured the first batches of Poison that killed several addicts, mostly old niggas. No one seemed to notice. In fact, it drove up business because you know those H-heads love a good trip, and pretty soon everyone wanted to buy Poison. By the time the Mickeys were arrested, other dealers had already cut into their business. In fact, we think one of the competing dealers snitched on the Mickeys."

"Lester?"

"No. A white guy. Calls himself Rapper X. Claims he's half black, but his daddy is just as white as you—"

"I met him." So, it was just as the Mickeys had told me. Rapper X was the mystery buyer.

He bunched up his bottom lips, impressed. "He's part of Mohammed X's inner circle. We think Mohammed X and the Gangster Disciples were trying to take over the Mickey Cobras' drug territory. Rapper X started buying Poison from the Mickeys and selling it, knowing it would kill a bunch of folks, and their deaths would be traced back to the Mickeys. Pretty clever, if you ask me. Better than using guns to kill each other like they normally do."

"Why did Rapper X need Lester?"

"Lester was a street dealer. Rapper worked the clubs. Those white girls were paying for the *experience* of buying drugs from a black gangbanger. It was about slumming on the South Side, doing this risky business of buying heroin that might be laced with fentanyl and shooting up in some ratty, shithole.

"Lester claims he didn't know the heroin he was selling was Poison," he continued. "He says he only figured out what was going on when the Angels died. And he passed a lie detector."

"Those things can be fooled."

"Yeah, I understand you passed one too." We both broke out laughing.

"Jesus, you are such a fucking cop."

He put his arm around my neck. "Oh, girl, I wish things were different. I'm afraid for you, what will happen to you."

"I can't go to prison. God as my witness, I tried to save Anna. You have to believe me."

"Doesn't matter what I believe."

"What do I do?"

"You asking me to save your ass again, Ms. Delaney?"

"You claim that's what you're good at."

He laughed, briefly choking and coughing. "You gotta play the game, and you have to have something to wager. You gotta barter what you know. If someone's framing you, you're going to have prove it, give up what you've been holding close to the vest."

"What makes you think I'm keeping something?"

"Hmm. Because it's in your nature. You always had something extra special in that notebook. You better start horse trading with the state's attorney, or you're going to prison."

The glow of the harbor lights cast a yellowish hue on Mo's

face. I wondered whether I should trust him. Then again, he hadn't turned me in, which would have boosted his standing with Nickles.

"Off the record?"

"Hell, there's a warrant out for your arrest. I'm not telling anyone about this conversation." He held out his fist, and I bumped my knuckles against his.

"What if Mohammed and his crew weren't targeting the girls? What if it was the *girls* who sought out Rapper X and Lester for Poison?"

Mo chewed on the inside of his cheek. "That's an interesting theory. Got any proof?"

"What if all these dead girls belonged to a secret club where they were dared to do Poison? And what if the leaders in this club set up Lester and Rapper to take the fall for the girls' deaths at the same time Lester, Rapper, and Mohammed were framing the Mickeys?"

"Let me get this straight." Mo held up a finger. "You're saying a bunch of suburban white girls framed Lester and Rapper while those guys were part of Mohammed's scheme to frame the Mickeys? What would that be? A frame of the framers? Or the framers get framed? Oh, and now someone is *framing* you?" Mo laughed, then his tone turned sour. "Natalie, coming up with some cockamamie conspiracy theory isn't going to save you."

I had always enjoyed hashing theories with Mo, even the most outrageous ideas, but now he seemed defensive. The Chicago police had one of the highest records of wrongful convictions in the nation, costing the city millions in court settlements every year. I could tell Mo didn't like the idea that he and his colleagues might have been wrong about the Mickeys and Mohammed.

"Besides," he said. "Lester's already admitted that Mohammed X was behind it all, that Mohammed wanted to target girls whose parents had donated to the Olympics. There was no way Mohammed was going to let a bunch of rich white guys take over his part of the city."

"Lester would tell you whatever he thinks will get him out of going to prison for the rest of his life."

"You defending Lester now? You know the guy is pointing a finger at you, saying you got those girls hooked on heroin, right?" Mo cracked a smile and slapped me on my back. "Girl, you sure got an imagination."

I was staring out at the sailboats, debating whether I should give Mo a copy of the website printouts in the trunk of my car, when he leaned over and pressed his lips against mine.

I pushed him away. "What was *that*?"

He shrugged. "Thought it was my last chance to kiss you."

CHAPTER FIFTY-FOUR

September 5 & 6, 2008

SECRET GRAND JURY INDICTMENTS IMMINENT
DOZENS TO BE ARRESTED, SOURCES SAY
Chicago Sentinel

I got out of the car in a huff, slamming the door even as Mo was profusely apologizing. It was easier to forgive him for tackling me in the cemetery than for coming onto me. There was no way I was giving him the website pages. Once in my car, though, I panicked: I had to find somewhere to hide quickly. If I called Sean, he'd tell me to turn myself in. But I wasn't ready. Not yet. I drove down the Eisenhower—Heroin Highway—trying to ignore what was gnawing at me: Mo's kiss felt so final, so *fait accompli*, so much like the kiss of death.

It was after midnight. I didn't know if Julian's kids were at their mother's. I rang his doorbell while batting away moths circling the outside light. Julian quickly appeared, his face garish in the harsh light.

"Oh my God, Natalie. What happened?"

"They're going to arrest me."

He took my hand and pulled me inside. "I'm so sorry."

We were standing in his dark foyer. There was a tense stillness. "What about the printouts?"

"No match for the brick of Poison they found in my oven."

"Jesus, I can't believe this is happening."

He wrapped his arms around me, holding me longer than a colleague should. I closed my eyes and nuzzled my face against the soft cotton of his bathrobe, breathing in the remains of his cologne. I felt safe, as if I'd taken refuge in a friendly embassy. He stepped back, his face hovering above mine. We stood there in an awkward slow dance, unsure how to act. Then I felt his lips move slowly over mine. They felt soft, velvety.

"Stay here tonight."

He led me up the stairs to Alex's bedroom.

"I don't want to be alone tonight," I protested.

Julian didn't say anything, just put his hand gently on my back, and guided me to his own bedroom. He kept the light off, and I slipped underneath the covers in my clothes. He drew me close. I put my head on his chest and listened to his heartbeat. The sound lulled me to sleep.

I woke early the next morning. We lay next to each other for a long while, dozing in and out, until the sunlight in the window turned bright. He looked so beautiful, his skin radiating warmth, his black eyes piqued with mystery. Sometimes I think back to that moment and try to remember that fleeting bliss.

Minutes later we heard pounding at the front door. It was almost a relief, ending the dread that had been bobbing in my throat. I knew they'd found my car parked on the street. I hadn't bothered to hide it.

We looked at each other. Julian forced a smile.

"So this is it, huh?" His voice stretched thin.

I nodded, stifling tears, afraid to speak.

We silently got out of bed. Julian trudged down the stairs to answer the door. By the time I emerged from the bedroom, Nickles was waiting at the bottom of the stairs.

"Good morning, Ms. Delaney." He smiled poisonously as I descended.

"Good morning, Detective Nickles."

"Place your hands behind your head, and turn around."

I did as he said, woozy with apprehension. He grabbed my

wrists, pulled them behind my back, and handcuffed me. Then he slid his palms down my sides, a perfunctory check for weapons.

"Ms. Delaney, you are under arrest for felony conspiracy of a criminal enterprise and class one felony possession of a controlled substance with intent to deliver or manufacture."

Nickles guided me down the front steps. Fighting back tears, I looked back at Julian, the shock of disbelief on his face.

"Be strong, Natalie. We'll get you out!"

Nickles held his hand over my head as he directed me into the back of his car. I'd never been in the backseat of a police cruiser, always the front, riding along with cops when they made their arrests, when they wanted to publicize their drug stings or their gangbanger roundups. Nickles drove an unmarked detective car, so there were no iron bars between us. It was like riding in a jitney cab.

"So why are *you* arresting me?" I glared at Nickles's face in the rearview mirror. "The state's attorney promised I would be allowed to turn myself in."

He grinned and wrinkled his eyebrows. "Guess I didn't get that memo."

With my hands bound behind my back, I had to lean forward and steady myself with my feet, especially when Nickles took a corner too fast.

He cleared his throat. "My boys are busy arresting other folks, people with X's in their names. Weird thing to call yourself, if you ask me, unless you're one of the X-Men. Turns out these men were selling fentanyl-laced heroin. But I guess you already know that since you bought Poison from them." He stared at me in the rearview mirror, waiting for a response.

I turned my gaze out the window at the bikers and the roller bladers slicing through the breeze on the Lake Shore trail, wishing I were one of them. I touched Libby's crucifix, wishing it could protect me.

"I saved you for myself," he tried again. "Wanted to see that look on your face, that disbelief that this couldn't be happening to a prize-winning reporter like Natalie Delaney. Guess your pal,

Mo, didn't tell you this was coming, eh?" His lip curled up with perverse pleasure. "Mr. Mobley doesn't know everything that goes on in my department. But *I've* known for some time about y'all's little arrangement. The best part is—it's Saturday. The banks are closed. With high felony charges like this, you won't get bonded out. You'll have to sit in the Cook County Jail with all the other hoi polloi." He tilted his head and bellowed viciously. I'd never seen him open his mouth so wide. He had squat yellow teeth, like rows of rotting corn.

"I hope you like women, because there are a lot of dykes in prison. I'm sure you'll be *very popular.*"

I closed my eyes. There was no way I would give Nickles the satisfaction of seeing me blubbering in his backseat.

"You should be *really careful* in jail," he continued. "So many prisoners get shanked. You just never know what can happen."

Nickles hit a pothole, sending me careening. "Don't worry, pretty soon you'll be bending over and spreading your ass so some guard can stick her gloved hand up your privates."

The car stopped abruptly. A deputy opened the back door, pulled me out, and led me inside a brown brick building I knew well. The Cook County Jail is the largest in the United States. People went there on minor charges, but with the criminal court's backlog in cases, didn't get out for years.

I was patted down and ordered to turn this way and that while I was fingerprinted and photographed. Then a deputy pushed me into a gated bullpen with a dozen other women, all waiting for bond court. I guessed most were my age or younger, but they looked older and haggard, their hair peroxided and oily, their arms and necks discolored with tattoos. I tried to imagine their offenses: kiting and passing bad checks, smoking crack, cooking meth, stealing cars. Their poor choice in men had left scars, deep purple bruises and misaligned features, as if bones had been broken and healed incorrectly. A few younger women were coming off whatever drugs they'd been on, and they were either lying on the floor, moaning and sweating, or wide-eyed and pacing. One was rolled up in a fetal position, crying. The room smelled of menstrual blood and cheap perfume. I sat on the edge of a bench wondering what trauma would hit me next.

CHAPTER FIFTY-FIVE

September 6–8, 2008

MOHAMMED X ARRESTED IN POISON DEATHS
SEVERAL CAUGHT IN SWEEP,
INCLUDING FORMER *TIMES* REPORTER
Chicago Sentinel

Two guards shackled the dozen of us together with a long chain, as if we were dogs they were taking for a walk. We shuffled down a dark underground passageway, then silently packed into a freight elevator, and finally were unloaded into a metal cage that looked out into a chaotic courtroom. I searched amid the faces beneath the courtroom's yellow florescent lights for Sean. Instead, a young lawyer wearing a much too expensive suit caught my eye and darted to the metal cage, bug-eyed and breathing hard. Great. A newbie.

"Where's Sean?"

He shook his head. "He's taking a deposition out of town." He spit out his words like gunfire. "Look, you're probably not getting out today. The state's attorney is going to be a real ass about this, since they arrested you in hiding—"

"Hiding? My car was parked—"

"Facts matter little in a political case." He sounded as if he were quoting from a TV script. "Just hang on. I'll do my best."

The judge banged his gavel, and my attorney, whose name I didn't get, scampered back to his seat. A few minutes later, I heard my name called; a bailiff pulled me from the cage and placed me next to my attorney, who was sweating profusely. Standing there under the pallid lights in that windowless room—the judge speaking in a bored, monotone voice, not even looking up from his legal papers—felt like an out-of-body experience, as if they were talking about someone else. The state's attorney laid out the alleged crimes with perverse detail; I sounded like a monster. My attorney asserted a half-hearted argument in the manner of a freshman debate contender, his voice thin and metallic, his hands moving in jerky gestures in between mopping the beaded gloss on his forehead. I knew I was doomed. Calling me a flight risk, the judge set no bail.

If court seemed surreal, jail proved to be all too real. A female guard wearing gray waders and thick rubber gloves up to her biceps greeted us once we returned from court. She ordered us to strip, then hosed us down with icy water. I stood shivering and clinging to the metal pipes on the wall, until it was my turn to be scrubbed with delousing shampoo, the guard using what looked like a toilet brush. Then she made me bend over, and with her fat gloved hands, poked and prodded.

After that humiliation, I was given a blue uniform that looked like medical scrubs.

Another stout guard shoved a rolled-up mattress at me, then piled a sheet and a wool blanket on top. Prisoners weren't allowed to have pillows, she said. I struggled to carry the bedroll as she escorted me to a "tier"—a two-story, glassed day room with cells lining the walls. Each tier, the size of a large townhouse, held forty-eight women. The building once housed serial murderers John Wayne Gacy and Richard Speck, she noted proudly. Gacy had raped and killed dozens of boys and buried their bodies under his house; Speck raped and tortured eight young nurses.

When we reached my assigned tier, another female guard, encased in a booth at the front, buzzed open the door. She was the only guard for the entire tier. Sealed off in her glass box, she tracked an array of video monitors. Prisoners, wearing the same dull blue cotton shirts and pants, were either seated at metal tables or dangled their feet from second-floor catwalks. A reality television program blasted from a flat screen mounted high on a wall.

When I entered, the women turned and stared. They looked gray, like the gray floor, the gray institutional tile, and the gray light of the dim fluorescent lights. Most prisoners were African-American, but there were a few Caucasian women, mostly wrinkled addicts with ugly, green tattoos running up their forearms. Was I supposed to hang with this segregated group? The guard pushed me past the vacant eyes, toward cells at the back of the room. Her thick keys clanked as she unlocked a heavy steel door, then opened it to reveal a four-by-ten foot cell with two metal slabs attached to the wall that served as bunk beds and a reflective metal sink and toilet. A dark-haired, pale woman in her thirties was sitting on the bottom bunk.

"Name's Mary," she said, opening her thin lips to reveal hardened gums where her front teeth should have been.

"Natalie." I unrolled my mattress, laid down a sheet, and opened the toiletry sack I'd been issued: a toothbrush, toothpaste, and two maxi pads. I held up the pads like foreign objects.

"Them's worth something in here if you wanna trade," Mary informed me, making hissing sounds across her gums.

I smiled and stretched out on the thin sheet. A guard had laughed when I'd asked for dental floss.

"Yous better get what you need," Mary said, handing me a wrinkled paper sack. "They kick us outta here in a few minutes. This be nap time, and it'd be about over."

People talk about brutal attacks—rapes in the shower, getting shanked in a dark corner—as the most visceral part of being incarcerated. Nothing prepared me for the more prevalent assaults: noise and toxic smells. Lying on the top bunk, I couldn't imagine trying to sleep through the racket that ricocheted around our cell. The clatter of voices, yelling and raucous bursts of laughter bounced off the tiled walls, encircling us and pressing out every shred of silence in our brains. My ears buzzed with the babble. The hot air smelled like soiled underwear. My mattress reeked of urine.

And I dreaded having to use the toilet, with Mary's head resting next to the commode.

I stared up at the pin-holed ceiling, wondering which level of purgatory I'd fallen into. A few minutes later, a guard announced over the scratchy intercom that the cell doors would be opening; we had to get out.

I climbed down from my bunk and followed Mary into the big room. White underwear and bras hung drying from a railing. A short Asian woman paced the back wall. A young girl sat on the floor beneath the stairs, looking goo-goo-eyed and talking to herself in a baby voice. The only windows were narrow slivers near the ceiling, the light filtering down on us as if we were in the bottom of a giant pit. The low-wattage fluorescent lights with their sickly glow made me feel nauseated. I sat at one of the big tables where women with plain, unvarnished faces were playing cards. I tried not to look directly at anyone. They reeked of chemical odors—hair straighteners and dyes, homemade concoctions they "cooked" from fruit and bread.

Overwhelmed, I laid my head on the table. Somehow, in the midst of that cacophony, I fell asleep, waking only when I felt a hand stroking my back. I looked up at an unfamiliar face layered with wrinkles. "It's time for bed, Rusty," she said in a gravelly, cancerous voice. Behind her, women filed into their cells.

That night I lay on my hard bunk, smothered by an aroma of fecal and female odors. I sorted through my memories of Anna, trying to parse what was real and what the Poison Girls had orchestrated. At first, Anna had to be cajoled to let me hang around. And it seemed she'd never talk to me again after I'd questioned Lester's motives. But the next day, she'd acted as if our spat had never happened, even inviting me to the downtown rave and introducing me to Rory, Olivia, and the others. She had nothing obvious to gain by that. I was convinced that's when it had started, when the Poison Girls had insisted she include me in her dares. At some point, though, Anna must have realized they were manipulating me through her. Perhaps that's why she picked a fight with me and insisted I never come back. She must have been trying to get me away from them. All that seemed evident after Rory's admission that I'd been part of the game.

But there was one detail that troubled me. That night at the beach, Anna told me she didn't believe Bethany and the others had died accidentally. She thought they'd been goaded into doing Poison by a rival who had spiked the heroin. Later, Rory admitted Olivia had used Poison to try to get rid of Bethany. If that were the case, could Rory have used the same play and made Anna's death look like a random shooting when really it was payback for her refusal to involve me? That would mean the tripped-up black girl who shot Anna was following a script Rory had orchestrated. It would explain why Rory didn't drive off when the girl started waving the gun and why the senseless shooting occurred.

• • •

The next day guards raided cells and collected contraband, including Mary's homemade dildo. She proudly detailed how she'd crafted the device by wrapping maxi pads around a pen, even painting it flesh color by using roll-on deodorant and ink from a magazine. All down the corridor, there were screams and jolts and piercing cries, women weeping over the loss of the few possessions they'd harbored. My mind shut down, the conscious part of me cowering in the back of my brain. At lunch, I offered up my tray of gray food to hands that quickly snapped it up and went to sit under the stairs, toilet paper stuffed in my ears.

I was sitting there several hours later, still in my dazed state, when someone tapped me on my shoulder. I bolted upright and ducked my head, expecting a fist in my face. But when I turned around, it was a guard, a big-boned woman with a fat, round face and tiny, sunken eyes.

"Your attorney's here." She waved for me to follow. We trudged along the corridor, the guard smacking gum in rhythm with her boots. "Saw your picture on the news last night. You're a real star in general population. Just watch your back. It's always the celebrities who end up getting hurt, and it ain't always by the other prisoners."

She unlocked and opened the door to an interview room, then grabbed my arm. "Remember what I said."

Sean was standing in the corner, combing his fingers through his hair. He gave me a tired smile. Two middle-aged men with square black hair, dark suits, and sensible shoes were seated at the table.

Sean walked over and put his hand on my back, not bothering to introduce the strangers.

"How are you holding up? I'm so sorry they arrested you. This wasn't the way this was supposed to go down."

"Did you give the state's attorney the printouts? When am I getting out of here?"

There was an uncomfortable silence. His eyes twitched and he sucked in his lips. He was holding back something, but I couldn't tell if it was good news or bad.

"The state's attorney is not interested in going after the daughters and granddaughters of the city's biggest donors." He sounded irritated. "Oliver Byrne and John Pretz—or does he go by Joana now?—whatever—and Richard Morrisey are also the Senator's largest donors. You understand what that means, right?"

"So Olivia, Rory, and Madison and MacKenzie are just going to get off?"

"There's a lot of supposition and circumstantial evidence here." His voice trailed off as he walked to the barred window in the corner. "There were many people daring and prodding girls on that site. And they could always deny it was them and claim someone used their logons. Those sites have faulty security. Even *you* were able to log on using the accounts of dead girls."

I felt heartsick and broken. "So this is it? Chicago justice?"

He laughed cynically. "Not exactly. I insisted the cops dust the brick of Poison they pulled from your oven. Your fingerprints weren't there—in fact, your fingerprints weren't *anywhere* on the oven…In this case, it might be a good thing that you never cooked. Then there's the break-in. You had two witnesses, including your own attorney, who can testify when that occurred. So that puts a big question mark on that evidence.

"The so-called witness statements have started falling apart. It seems they already spent the money Rory gave them, and now they're looking for a better deal. So those statements will get thrown out.

"And then," he said, more quietly. "I was combing through those printouts, and I saw what you saw—that there were more targets, including the Senator's daughter."

Our eyes met.

"Yeah, I recognized her," he said.

"So you used your direct number to the Senator?"

"No. Not exactly. I mean, that's what I'd planned to do."

"So what happened?"

He turned around and his face broke into a huge grin. "The most unexpected thing. Like you couldn't make this up."

The men sat at the table quietly watching us, their faces devoid of emotion, their fingers fanned out in front of them, waiting.

"What? Just tell me, please."

"It was Libby. Can you believe it? She took a series of buses trying to catch up to the Senator's campaign stops. Finally, she arrived before one of his appearances in Iowa and made sure to tell his handlers that she had come all alone from Chicago to give the Senator a message about why girls were dying of poisoned heroin in Chicago. The handlers looked up her name and realized that not only did she have a cousin who died trying to buy heroin, but Libby was a missing kid."

He started pacing, talking fast as he recounted the past twenty-four hours. "They knew they had a great photo op—a missing kid who was so convinced the Senator could do something about drugs in Chicago that she took a bus across two states to talk to him personally. Yeah, that would pretty much drown out the other presidential candidate's press coverage for several days."

He stopped, looked down at the floor, and shook his head again. "So with the national press corps's cameras clicking away and the video microphones on, the Senator's handlers sent Libby up on the stage to meet with the candidate. But in all their excitement, they forgot to ask Libby just exactly what her message was. When Libby got to the Senator, she handed him a printout from the Thrill Girl website in which girls were daring his own daughter to do drugs."

Sean looked at me then and we simultaneously erupted in crazy, goofy laughter.

"Damn, that kid has guts," I said, amazed.

"She sure does. So while the press is recording this exchange, Libby is telling him that the reporter who discovered all this has been arrested and is in jail."

"Wait. How did she know I was in jail?"

"It's…kinda been on the news," he said sheepishly. "The cops held a press conference announcing your arrest along with that of Mohammed X and Rapper X."

"My tier only watches reality TV."

"Well, it made the national news. Libby told the Senator that the same girls who were bullying his daughter were framing you and that the cops had fallen for it all."

"Oh, Jesus. She didn't."

"She did. And the press corps ate it up. Your picture and details about the website and how the girls had dared other girls to do Poison are all the over the news, every channel, every news website. You're the woman of the weekend."

So that's what the guard was talking about.

"As soon as the Senator got off the stage, he called the U.S. Justice Department. That's where these two gentlemen come in. They'd like to hear your story."

CHAPTER FIFTY-SIX

September 10, 2008–June 13, 2009

STATE'S ATTORNEY TO RE-OPEN POISON HEROIN CASE
VICTIMS' FAMILIES FILE LAWSUIT
Chicago Inquirer Online

They didn't let me out right away. It took two days from the visit of the U.S. Justice Department lawyers until the state's attorney announced it was opening a new investigation into the Poison deaths. It wasn't long before the Justice Department announced it was investigating the Chicago police for the way they had handled the case.

Julian threw me a party, calling it the "Free Delaney Affair." Guests were required to come dressed in their favorite jailhouse wardrobe. Julian's kids wore black-and-white-striped outfits and ran around hyped up on Coke and chocolate, like it was Halloween. It was a raucous celebration. At one point, a police officer showed up at Julian's door with a warrant for my arrest. When I started hyperventilating, he stripped off his uniform, gyrated in a tight Speedo, and serenaded me to Johnny Cash's "Folsom Prison Blues."

A week later, the Mickey Cobras all pleaded down from murder to possession of heroin and manufacturing with intent to sell. Their sentences varied from six to sixteen years. None were charged in connection with the Poison deaths, and no one was expected to serve more than ten years. All charges against Mohammed X were dropped for lack of evidence. Randy—aka Rapper X—got off on a technicality. I'd heard that the evidence against him was conveniently "misplaced." Lester's attorney negotiated a plea deal: eighteen years. That's how only one person was convicted of more than 250 Poison deaths.

The controversy surrounding the fentanyl-laced heroin—including the stories of Olivia, Rory, the Morrisey twins, and their famous fathers' business dealings—derailed Chicago's bid for the Olympics. The International Olympics Committee awarded the 2016 Summer Olympics to Brazil.

The Senator managed to successfully distance himself from Oliver Byrne—even though the two men owned property together—and won the presidential election. Rex Kennan quickly broke up with Olivia, and at age 22, became the youngest person to be elected to the Chicago City Council. He's now my alderman, representing the Lakeview neighborhood. Political analysts predict he will have a long and successful career, following in the footsteps of his political uncles.

The families of the dead girls filed a slew of lawsuits against Byrne Pharmaceuticals for negligence and wrongful deaths for hosting the website. Others filed a class-action lawsuit seeking hundreds of millions against Olivia, Rory, the Morrisey twins, and their wealthy families, which threatened to bankrupt the girls' families and their companies.

A judge threw out Kent Reid's lawsuit against me and the *Times*—something to do with the requirements of his federal witness protection, which compelled him to keep a low profile and maintain his cover. But everyone knew that the story about the Poison Girls goading Anna to do drugs had undermined Kent's claims. Without a pending lawsuit, the paper was sold to a private equity group. The new editors immediately killed the paper's print editions. Now the *Times* is an online news website, with an even smaller staff. Julian managed to stay on and was appointed managing editor. He's now Amy's boss. Yeah, she's still there. Her type never voluntarily leaves.

After months of investigation, a grand jury declined to charge

Olivia, Rory, or the Morrisey twins. The state's attorney said he found it impossible to determine the girls' intent when they dared other girls to do drugs. And just as Sean predicted, the Poison Girls insisted that their computers had been hacked and someone had stolen their online identities. The Justice Department's investigation is still ongoing. I suspect it will continue until the Senator is no longer president, and then it will quietly be closed.

The seventeen-year-old girl who shot Anna insisted the gun went off accidentally. She received a ten-year sentence. I keep tabs on her through my prison sources. I'm certain she will tire of her circumstances and start talking about how Rory set her up. I'm hoping it's the break needed to convict Rory and the others. Despite all her tough talk, Rory isn't likely to go down by herself. She'll rat out her friends if she thinks it will save her.

My situation is a bit more complicated. I agreed not to file a false arrest and imprisonment lawsuit, and in exchange the state's attorney quietly forced Nickles to retire. Mo got to keep his job. I made sure of that. He and I are trying to make amends. He owes me big time, and I plan on collecting now that I'm a reporter for a startup called the *Chicago Inquirer Online*. We're a small, scrappy group—mostly folks laid off from the *Times*, the *Sentinel*, and other local publications. For the most part, the editors let me do the stories I want to do, and no one says shit about me being a woman, or cautions me about hanging out in certain neighborhoods.

The biggest change in my life is that Libby now lives with me. She tried living with her mother, but after each fight, she ended up at my apartment and eventually moved in for good. Danny didn't put up much resistance. Libby attends a magnet science high school near my apartment and says she wants to become a crime analyst—or an FBI agent. She can't decide. One weekend a month, she takes the South Shore train to be with her father in Indiana. After all that happened, Danny decided to return to farming.

Julian and I get together occasionally, often with our dependents in tow. He's just as prying about the stories I'm reporting, and I'm just as guarded since we work for competing online papers.

We're trying to figure out our in-between geography, an unnamed place of more-than-friends and not-quite-lovers.

I still haven't come to terms with my role in Anna's death. I think of her often, especially at Libby's major milestones. Anna would have been proud to see Libby inducted into the honor society, to watch her blossom into a confident girl able to stand up for herself. If I were completely honest, I'd say some of my affection and attention for Libby is borne out of my regret about Anna as well as my guilt about Jake.

Occasionally, Libby and I go to Graceland, where Anna's grave now has a large statue crafted in her image, a likeness I find disturbing. I often find myself sorting through the various images of Anna in my head, wondering which one was real. I'll run across something of hers—the scarf Danny gave me, a piece of clothing that turns up in the wash from Libby—and the grief and pain and blame hit all over again.

Libby and I frequently turn up at our secret beach, as if all roads lead there. Libby never asks why we come. We sit at the deformed cement shoreline and silently gaze at the cobalt blue water. Sometimes I imagine Anna is the swimmer slicing through the waves toward the horizon. Other times I see her in the faces of girls jostling along the shore, their hair whipping in the wind. But mostly I see her, as I did that day, splashing in the water, giggling, her freckles catching the sun, her green eyes playful and mesmerizing—that fearless face so familiar to my own, so full of hope and adventure.

AUTHOR'S NOTE AND ACKNOWLEDGMENTS

Poison Girls is a work of fiction inspired by real events. As a crime reporter in the 1990s, I spent months reporting about young girls addicted to crack cocaine. One of the girls I'd gotten to know fairly well was tragically shot while she and her friends were trying to buy more drugs. Her death deeply affected me. A decade later, a fentanyl-laced heroin epidemic felled hundreds of Chicago-area teenagers and struck me as eerily similar. I started writing this book. That was in July 2005.

Since then, many people have provided invaluable help and assistance. I want to thank former *Chicago Sun-Times* colleagues Steve Patterson and Eric Herman who introduced me to key people at the Cook County Jail and Cook County Court House. Cook County Judge Anna Helen Demacopoulos graciously fielded many questions and opened the door to court drug counselors, as well as Dan Bigg from the Chicago Recovery Alliance, and Judge Lawrence Fox, who ran a special Chicago drug court. Many thanks to Fire Capt. Kent Wardecke, an old source of mine from Dayton, Ohio, who offered his professional knowledge as a first responder to many heroin overdose victims.

As the manuscript began to take shape, authors Stuart Dybek and Janet Burroway and editor John Paine read draft chapters and offered literary advice. I'm indebted to my friend Cara Birch for her suggestions. Thanks to my son, Nick Stricharchuk, who offered commentary on language and pop culture. My students at the Westville, Indiana Correction Center volunteered details about gangs and drugs that I might not have gotten elsewhere. I'm appreciative of my colleagues and teachers at Northwestern University's Creative Writing program, especially Sandi Wisenberg, J-L Deher-Lesaint, Ankur Thakkar, and Jeremy Wilson. Also thanks to writers Melody Jeter, Dilek Aykul Bishku, and Patrick Somerville.

I am greatly indebted to my first reader and biggest advocate, my husband, Greg Stricharchuk, who read the manuscript countless times, offering edits and critical feedback that only a seasoned editor and best friend can provide.

I am grateful to my literary agent Wendy Sherman for her support, determination, and diligence in finding the book a home and to publisher/editor Jaime Levine for providing that home at Diversion Books. Jaime is that rare kind of editor who really tries to preserve the writer's vision for the book. Thanks also to all the folks at Diversion Books, especially Sarah Masterson Hally, Samantha Moyer, and Erin Mitchell.

There are others whose names I haven't mentioned here—either because they preferred to remain anonymous or because of my faulty memory. Please accept my apologies and gratitude.

Finally, I'd like to thank those who shared intimate details about their loved ones' fatal struggle with drugs. Their honesty and candor allowed me to further understand the heartache of loving someone seduced by drugs.

CHERYL L. REED is a veteran journalist. She is the author of *Unveiled: The Hidden Lives of Nuns*, which chronicles her four years living off and on with nuns across the country. A former editor and reporter at the *Chicago Sun-Times* and other newspapers, Cheryl has won many awards for her investigative reporting, including Harvard's Goldsmith Prize. She earned her MFA in Creative Writing-Fiction from Northwestern University and recently was a U.S. Fulbright Scholar teaching investigative reporting in Ukraine where freedom of the press is still in its infancy. She is currently an assistant professor at Syracuse University's Newhouse School of Communication. Cheryl's reportage of deadly drug use among girls is the inspiration for this novel. *Poison Girls* is her fiction debut.

CPSIA information can be obtained
at www.ICGtesting.com
Printed in the USA
BVOW03s1633020917
493859BV00001B/1/P